Vassall Morton
A Novel

by
Francis Parkman

Vassall Morton
A Novel
by Francis Parkman

Copyright © 2024

All Rights reserved.

No part of this publication may be reproduced, stored in a retrieval system, or transmitted in any form or by any means, electronic, mechanical, photocopying or Otherwise, without the written permission of the publisher.
The author/editor asserts the moral right to be identified as the author/editor of this work.

ISBN: 978-93-68095-47-7

Published by

DOUBLE 9 BOOKS

2/13-B, Ansari Road
Daryaganj, New Delhi – 110002
info@double9books.com
www.double9books.com
Tel. 011-40042856

This book is under public domain

ABOUT THE AUTHOR

Francis Parkman (1823–1893) was an American historian and author, best known for his vivid accounts of early American history. He is particularly renowned for The Oregon Trail: Sketches of Prairie and Rocky-Mountain Life, which vividly describes his travels along the trail, and for his monumental seven-volume work France and England in North America, which examines the colonial history of North America from a unique perspective. These works are still valued both as important historical sources and as literary achievements due to Parkman's engaging writing style and deep insights into early American history.

Born on September 16, 1823, in Boston, Massachusetts, Parkman was educated at Harvard University, where he also studied law. Despite his academic training, he became deeply interested in history, especially the early exploration and settlement of North America. Parkman faced significant health challenges throughout his life, which did not prevent him from producing a large body of work. He was the son of Francis Parkman and Caroline Parkman and had a daughter, Katherine Scollay Coolidge. Parkman died on November 8, 1893, in Massachusetts, leaving behind a legacy that continues to influence both historians and literary scholars.

CONTENTS

CHAPTER I 9
CHAPTER II 12
CHAPTER III 13
CHAPTER IV 18
CHAPTER V 22
CHAPTER VI 30
CHAPTER VII 33
CHAPTER VIII 36
CHAPTER IX 39
CHAPTER X 41
CHAPTER XI 42
CHAPTER XII 46
CHAPTER XIII 55
CHAPTER XIV 60
CHAPTER XV 68
CHAPTER XVI 71
CHAPTER XVII 75
CHAPTER XVIII 79
CHAPTER XIX 84

CHAPTER XX	90
CHAPTER XXI	94
CHAPTER XXII	96
CHAPTER XXIII	101
CHAPTER XXIV	103
CHAPTER XXV	105
CHAPTER XXVI	107
CHAPTER XXVII	113
CHAPTER XXVIII	115
CHAPTER XXIX	118
CHAPTER XXX	121
CHAPTER XXXI	125
CHAPTER XXXII	127
CHAPTER XXXIII	130
CHAPTER XXXIV	132
CHAPTER XXXV	135
CHAPTER XXXVI	138
CHAPTER XXXVII	140
CHAPTER XXXVIII	145
CHAPTER XXXIX	147
CHAPTER XL	150
CHAPTER XLI	152
CHAPTER XLII	154
CHAPTER XLIII	165
CHAPTER XLIV	170
CHAPTER XLV	172

CHAPTER XLVI	174
CHAPTER XLVII	182
CHAPTER XLVIII	184
CHAPTER XLIX	186
CHAPTER L	189
CHAPTER LI	197
CHAPTER LII	202
CHAPTER LIII	208
CHAPTER LIV	212
CHAPTER LV	220
CHAPTER LVI	225
CHAPTER LVII	228
CHAPTER LVIII	229
CHAPTER LIX	234
CHAPTER LX	239
CHAPTER LXI	241
CHAPTER LXII	243
CHAPTER LXIII	252
CHAPTER LXIV	254
CHAPTER LXV	257
CHAPTER LXVI	260
CHAPTER LXVII	262
CHAPTER LXVIII	264
CHAPTER LXIX	265
CHAPTER LXX	268
CHAPTER LXXI	270

CHAPTER LXXII 275
CHAPTER LXXIII 279
CHAPTER LXXIV 281

CHAPTER I

Remote from towns he ran his godly race.—*Goldsmith*.

"Macknight on the Epistles,—that's the name of the book?"

"Yes, sir, if you please. I am desirous of consulting it with a view—"

"Well, this way, Mr. Jacobs. Here's the librarian. Mr. Stillingfleet, let me introduce my friend, the Reverend Mr. Jacobs, of West Weathersfield."

"I am proud to make your acquaintance, sir," said Mr. Jacobs, taking the librarian's hand with an air of diffident veneration.

"Mr. Jacobs wishes to consult Mackwright on the Epistles."

"Macknight, if you please, Dr. Steele."

"O, Macknight. Will you be so kind as to let him have the use of it in my name?"

"If you will go with Mr. Rubens, sir," said the librarian, "he will show you the book."

"Thank you, sir," replied Mr. Jacobs, to whom the words were addressed; and he followed the assistant among the alcoves in a timid, tiptoe progress, for, to him, the very air he breathed seemed redolent of learning, and the dust beneath his feet consecrated to science.

Dr. Steele remained behind, conversing with the librarian.

"My friend has something of the ancient apostolic simplicity hanging about him still. He looks with as much awe at Harvard College library as I did myself forty-five years ago, when I came down from Steuben to join the freshman class."

"So you came from Steuben! Did not old John Morton come from the same place?"

"To be sure he did. He was the glory of the town. He pulled down the old clapboard meeting house that his father used to preach in, and built a new one for him: besides giving a start in business to half the young men of the village."

"Do you see that undergraduate at the end of the hall, standing by the last alcove, reading?"

"Yes; what about him? He seems a hardy, good-looking young fellow enough."

"He is John Morton's son."

"Is it possible? I remember him when he was a child, but have not seen him for these ten years. After his father's death, his mother took him to Europe, to be educated; but she never came back; she died in Paris."

"He is Mr. Morton's only child—is he not?"

"Yes; his first wife had no children; and after he had buried her,—which, by the way, I believe was the happiest hour of his life,—he married a very different sort of person, Margaret Vassall, this boy's mother."

"What, one of the old Vassall race?"

"Exactly; and, I suppose, the last survivor. I used to know her. She was a handsome woman, and, bating her family pride, altogether a very fine character. She managed her husband admirably."

"Why, what need had John Morton of being managed?"

"O, Morton was a noble old gentleman, a merchant of the old school, and generous as the day; but he had his faults. He made nothing of his three bottles of Madeira at dinner, and besides— Ah, Mr. Jacobs, so you have found Macknight."

"Yes, sir," said Mr. Jacobs, coming up, "I have the volumes."

"See that young man, yonder. That's the son of your old friend, Mr. Morton."

"Really! upon my word! Ah! Mr. Morton *was* a friend to me, sir—a very kind friend."

And, in the simplicity of his heart, Mr. Jacobs glided up to the student, and blandly accosted him.

"How do you do, young gentleman? I knew your worthy father. I knew him well. I have often sat at his hospitable board on anniversary week."

Thus addressed, Vassall Morton looked up from his book,—it was Froissart's Chronicle,—inclined his head in acknowledgment, and waited to hear more.

"Ahem!" coughed Mr. Jacobs, a little embarrassed: "your father was a most worthy and estimable gentleman: a true friend of the feeble and destitute. Ahem!—what class are you in, Mr. Morton?"

"The junior class," said the young man, a suppressed smile flickering at the corner of his mouth.

"Ahem! I hope, sir, that, like your father, you will long live to be an honor to your native town."

"Thank you, sir."

"I wish you good morning."

"Good morning, sir," said Morton, divided between an inclination to smile at the odd, humble little figure before him, and an unwillingness to wound the other's feelings.

"Are you ready to go, Mr. Jacobs?" said Dr. Steele.

"If you please, sir, we will now take our departure;"—gathering the four volumes of Macknight on the Epistles under his arm;—"Good morning, Mr. Stillingfleet; good morning, Mr. Rubens. I am indebted to your kindness, gentlemen—ahem!"

"This is the way out, Mr. Jacobs," said Steele to his diffident friend from West Weathersfield, who, in his embarrassment, was going out at the wrong door.

"I beg your pardon, sir—ahem!" replied Mr. Jacobs, with a bashful smile. And Dr. Steele, pointing to the true exit, ushered his rustic and reverend protégé from the sacred precinct of learning.

CHAPTER II

Richt hardie baith in ernist and play.—*Sir David Lyndsay.*

"Morton, what was the little old fogy in the white cravat saying to you just now in the library?"

"Telling me that my father was a worthy man, and that he hoped I should make just such another."

"Ah, that was kind of him."

"What a pile of books you are lugging! Here, let me take half a dozen of them for you. You look as if you were training to be a hotel porter."

"I am laying in for vacation."

"What sense is there in that? Let alone your Latin, Greek, and mathematics; what the deuse is vacation made for? Take to the woods, as I do, breathe the fresh air, and see the world at large."

"Do you call it seeing the world at large, to go off into some barbarous, uninhabitable place, among mosquitoes, snakes, wolves, bears, and catamounts? What sense is there in that? What can you do when you get there?"

"Shoot muskrats, and fish for mudpouts. Will you go with me?"

"Thank you, no. There's no one in the class featherwitted enough to go with you, except Meredith, and he ought to know better."

"Stay at home, then, and improve your mind. I shall be off to-morrow."

"Alone?"

"Yes."

Mr. Horace Vinal shrugged his shoulders, a movement which caused Sophocles and Seneca to escape from under his arm. Morton gathered them out of the mud, and thrusting them back again into their place, left his burdened fellow-student to make the best of his way towards his den in Stoughton Hall.

CHAPTER III

O, love, in such a wilderness as this!—*Gertrude of Wyoming*.

Morton, *en route* for the barbarous districts of which Vinal had expressed his disapproval, stopped by the way at a spot which, though wild enough at that time, had ceased to be a wilderness. This was the Notch of the White Mountains, perverted, since, into a resort of *quasi* fashion. Here, arriving late at the lonely hostelry of one Tom Crawford, he learned from that worthy person, to whom his face was well known, that other guests, from Boston, like himself, were seated at the tea table. Accordingly, descending thither, he saw four persons. The first was a quiet-looking man, with the air of a gentleman, and something in his appearance which seemed to indicate military habits and training. Morton remembered to have seen him before. At his side, and under his tutelary care, sat two personages, who, from their dimensions, must have been boys of some seven years old, but from the solemnity of their countenances, might have passed for a brace of ancient philosophers. They looked so much alike that Morton thought he saw double. Each was seated on a volume of Clark's Commentaries, to raise his chin to the needful height above the table cloth. Both were encased in tunics, strapped about them with shining morocco belts. Their small persons were terminated at one end by morocco shoes of somewhat infantile pattern, and at the other by enormous heads, with chalky complexions, pale, dilated eyes, wrinkled foreheads, and mouths pursed up with an expression of anxious care, abstruse meditation, and the most experienced wisdom.

In amazement at these phenomena, Morton turned next towards the fourth member of the party; and here he encountered a new emotion, of a kind quite different. Hitherto, in his college seclusion, he had not very often met, except in imagination, with that union of beauty, breeding, and refinement which belongs to the best life of cities, and which he now saw in the person of a young lady, a year or two his junior. He longed for a pretext to address her, but found none; when her father—for such he seemed—broke silence, and accosted him.

"I beg your pardon; is it possible that you are the son of John Morton?"

"Yes."

"He was my father's old friend. I thought I could scarcely mistake your likeness to your mother."

"I believe I have the pleasure of speaking to Colonel Leslie."

Leslie inclined his head.

"My title clings to me, I find, though I have no right to it now."

He had left the army long before, exchanging the rough frontier service for pursuits more to his taste.

"Upon my word," pursued Leslie, after conversing for some time with the new comer on the scenery and game of the mountains, "you seem to be *au fait* at this sort of thing."

"At least I ought to be; I have spent half my college vacations here."

"It is unlucky for us that we must set out for home in the morning. You might have given us good advice in our sightseeing."

"Crawford will tell you that I am tolerably well qualified to be a guide."

"You do not look like a collegian. They are generally thin and pale with studying."

"Oftener with laziness and cigar smoke."

"Very likely. You seem too hardy and active for a student."

Morton's weak point was touched.

"I can do well enough, I believe, in that way. Crawford was boasting, last year, that he could outwrestle any man in New England. I challenged him, and threw him on his back."

"You! Crawford is twice as heavy and strong as you are."

"I am stronger than I seem," replied Morton, with great complacency.

And Leslie, observing him with an eye not unused to measure the thews and sinews of men, saw that, though his frame was light, and his shoulders not broad, yet his compact proportions, deep chest, and muscular limbs, showed the highest degree of bodily vigor.

"You are quite right. I would enlist you without asking the surgeon's advice."

Here the nurse, attendant on the two philosophers, appeared at the door; and they, obedient to the mute summons, scrambled gravely from their seats, and, with solemn steps, withdrew. Miss Leslie presently followed, and Morton and her father were left alone.

"You are from Harvard—are you not?"

"Yes."

"Do you know Horace Vinal?"

"Very well; he is my classmate."

"Is he not thought a very promising young man?"

"He is our first scholar."

"I hear him spoken of as a young man of fine abilities."

"And he knows how to make the best of them."

"Not at all dissipated."

"Not at all."

"And a great student."

"Digs day and night."

"A little ambitious, I suppose."

"A little."

"But very prudent."

"Uncommonly so."

"An excellent young man," exclaimed Leslie; "I think very highly of Horace Vinal."

Morton cast a sidelong glance at him, and there was a covert smile in his eye. He began to see a weak spot in his companion.

"He will certainly make his way in the world," pursued Leslie.

"No doubt of it."

"He is not so fond of out-door exercises as you seem to be."

"He is good at one kind of exercise."

"What's that?"

"He can draw the long bow."

Leslie did not see Morton's meaning, and took the words literally, as the latter intended he should.

"What, have you an archery club at college?"

"No; but there are one or two among us who use the long bow, now and then, and Vinal beats them by all odds. But he is very modest on the subject, and never alludes to it. In fact, there are very few who know his skill in that way."

"It is all the better for his health to have some amusement of the kind."

"Yes, it would be a pity if his health should suffer."

"I have often thought that his mind was too active for his constitution."

Morton cast another sidelong look at Leslie. Though he admired the daughter, he refrained with difficulty from quizzing the father.

"You seem to know Vinal very well."

"Yes, thoroughly; I have known him from childhood; he is the son of my wife's sister, and I am his guardian. I watch his progress with great interest."

"You will see him, I dare say, reach the top of the ladder. At least, it will be no fault of his if he does not."

"I am very glad to hear my good opinion of him confirmed by one who has seen so much of him."

And, rising, he left the room.

"A very good young man, this seems to be," he thought to himself, as he did so.

"Amiable, good natured, and all that; but very soft, for a man who has seen hard service," thought Morton, on his part.

The party reassembled in the inn parlor. Masters William and Marlborough, having gained a reprieve from their banishment, busied themselves at the table, the one in poring over Brewster on Natural Magic, the other in solving a problem of Euclid. Leslie viewed these infant diversions by no means with an eye of favor, and soon banished the students to a retirement more suited to their tender years. The sentence overcame all their philosophy, and they were carried off howling.

Morton, meanwhile, was breathing a charmed air; and though diffident in the presence of ladies, and not liberally endowed by nature with the gift of tongues, his zeal to commend himself to the good opinion of Miss Edith Leslie availed somewhat to supply the defect. He had never mixed with the world, conventionally so called, and knew as much of ladies as of mermaids. But having an ardent temperament and a Quixotic imagination; being addicted, moreover, to Froissart and kindred writers; and, indeed, visited with a glimmering of that antique light which modern folly despises, he would have been ready, with the eye of a handsome woman upon him, for any rash and ridiculous exploit. This extravagance did him no manner of harm. On the contrary, it went far to keep him out of mischief; for in the breast of this youngster a chivalresque instinct battled against the urgency of vigorous blood, and taught his nervous energies to seek escape rather in ceaseless bodily exercises, rowing, riding, and the like, than in any less commendable recreations.

The close of the evening found him with an imagination much excited. In short, decisive symptoms declared themselves of that wide-spread malady, of which he had read much and pondered not a little, but which had not, as yet, numbered him among its victims. Among the various emotions, novel, strange, and pleasurable, which began to possess him, came, however, the dismal consciousness that, with the morning sun, the enchantress of his fancy was to vanish like a dream of the night.

CHAPTER IV

What pleasure, sir, find we in life, to lock it
From action and adventure? — Cymbeline.

Morning came, and the Leslies departed. Morton watched the lumbering carriage till it disappeared down the rugged gorge of the Notch, then drew a deep breath, and ruefully betook himself to his day's sport. He explored, rod in hand, the black pools and plunging cascades of the Saco; but for once that he thought of the trout, he thought ten times of Edith Leslie.

Towards night, however, he returned with a basket reasonably well filled; and, as he drew near the inn, he saw a young man, of his own age, or thereabouts, sitting under the porch. He had a cast of features which, in a feudal country, would have been taken as the sign of noble birth; and though he wore a slouched felt hat and a rough tweed frock, though his attitude was careless, though he held between his teeth a common clay pipe, at which he puffed with much relish, and though he was conversing on easy terms with two attenuated old Vermont farmers, with faces like a pair of baked apples, — yet none but the most unpractised eye would have taken him for other than a gentleman.

As soon as Morton saw him, he shouted a joyful greeting, to which Mr. Edward Meredith, rising and going to meet his friend, replied with no less emphasis.

"I thought," said Morton, "that you meant to do the dutiful this time, and stay with your father and family at the sea shore."

"Couldn't stand the sea shore," said Meredith, seating himself again; "so I came up to the mountains to see what you were doing."

"You couldn't have done better; but come this way, out of earshot."

"Colonel," said Meredith, in a tone of melancholy remonstrance, "this seat is a good seat, an easy seat, a pleasant seat. Why do you want to root me up?"

"Come on, man," replied Morton.

"Show the way, then, Jack-a-lantern. But where do you want to lead me? I won't sit on the rail fence, and I won't sit on the grass."

"There's a bench here for you."

"Has it a back?"

"Yes, it has a back. There it is."

Meredith carefully removed a few twigs and shavings which lay upon the bench, seated himself, rested his arm along the back, and began puffing at his pipe again. But scarcely had he thus composed himself when the tea bell rang from the house.

"Do you hear that, now? Another move to make! Didn't I tell you so?"

"Not that I remember."

"Please to explain, colonel, what you expect to gain by always bobbing about as you do, like a drop of quicksilver."

"To hear you, one would take you for the laziest fellow in the universe."

"There's reason in all things. I keep my vital energies against the time of need, instead of wasting them in unnecessary gyrations. Ladies at the table! New Yorkers in full feather, or I'll be shot! Now, what the deuse have lace and ribbons to do in a place like this?"

During the meal, the presence of the strangers was a check upon their conversation.

"Crawford," said Meredith, when it was over, "have you had that sofa taken into my room?"

"Yes, sir."

"And the arm chair?"

"Yes, sir."

"And the candles?"

"Yes, sir."

"All right. Now, then, colonel, *allons.*"

The name of *colonel* was Morton's college sobriquet. Meredith led the way into a room which adjoined his bed chamber, and which, under his direction, had assumed an air of great comfort. Morton took possession of the sofa; his friend of the arm chair.

"What's the word with you?" began the latter; "are you bound for the Adirondacks, the Margalloway, or the Penobscot?"

"To the Margalloway, I think. You mean to go with me, I hope."

"To the Margalloway, or the antipodes, or any place this side of the North Pole."

"Then, if you say so, we'll set off to-morrow."

"Gently, colonel. One day's fishing here. We have six weeks before us. What sort of thing is that that you are smoking?"

"Try, and judge for yourself," said Morton, handing his cigar case. Meredith took a sample of its contents between his fingers, and examined it with attention.

"I always thought you were a kind of heathen, and now I know it. Where did you pick up that cigar?"

"Do you find it so very bad?"

"It would not poison a man, and perhaps might pass for a little better than none at all. But nobody except a pagan would touch it when any thing better could be had."

"I forgot to bring any from town, and had to supply myself on the way."

"That goes to redeem your character. Fling those away, or give them to the landlord; I have plenty of better ones. But a pipe is the best thing at a place like this, and especially at camp, in the woods."

"So I have often heard you say."

"Mine, though, made a sensation, not long ago."

"How was that?"

"The whole brood of the Stubbs, bag and baggage, passed here this afternoon."

"Thank Heaven they did not stop."

"They came in their private carriage. I nodded to Ben, and touched my hat to Mrs. S. You should have seen their faces. They thought there must be something out of joint in the mechanism of the universe, when a person of their acquaintance could be seen smoking a pipe at a tavern door, like a bog-trotting Irishman."

"You should have asked Ben to go with us."

"It would be the worst martyrdom the poor devil ever had to pass through. Ben seemed displeased with the scenery. He says that the White Mountains are nothing to any one who, like himself, has seen the Alps."

"Pray when did Stubb see the Alps?"

"O, the whole family have seen the Alps,—the Alps, Italy, the Rhine, the nobility and gentry, and every thing else that Europe affords. They all swear by Europe, and hold the soil of America dirt cheap. You can see with half an eye what they are—an uncommonly bad imitation of an indifferent model."

"Let them pass for what they are worth. Have you come armed and equipped—rifle, blanket, hatchet, and so forth?"

"Yes, and I have brought an oil cloth tent."

"So much the better; it is more convenient than a birch bark shanty."

"I give you notice that I mean to take my ease in that tent."

"I hope you will."

"One can be comfortable in the woods, as well as elsewhere. Remember, colonel, that we are out for amusement, and not after scalps. Last summer, you drove ahead, rain or shine, through thickets, and swamps, and ponds, as if you were on some errand of life and death. For this once, have mercy on frail humanity, and moderate your ardor."

Morton gave the pledge required. They passed the evening in arranging the details of their journey, set forth and spent three or four weeks in the forest between the settled districts of Canada and Maine, poling their canoe up lonely streams, meeting no human face, but smoking their pipes in great contentment by their evening camp fire. They chased a bear, and lost him in a *windfall;* killed two moose, six deer, and trout without number; and underwent, with exemplary patience, a martyrdom of midges, black flies, and mosquitoes. And when, at last, they turned their faces homeward, they wiled the way with plans of longer journeyings,—more bear, more moose, more deer, more trout, more midges, black flies, and mosquitoes.

CHAPTER V

Youth on the prow, and Pleasure at the helm;
Regardless of the sweeping whirlwind's sway,
That, hushed in grim repose, expects his evening prey. — Gray.

It was a week before "class day," — that eventful day which was virtually to close the college career of Morton and his contemporaries. The little janitor, commonly called Paddy O'Flinn, was ringing the evening prayer bell from the cupola of Harvard Hall, — its tone was dull and muffled, some graceless sophomore having lately painted it white, inside and out, — and the students were mustering at the summons. The sedate and the gay, the tender freshman and the venerable senior, the prosperous city beau and the awkward country bumpkin, one and all were filing from their respective quarters towards the chapel in University Hall. The bell ceased; the loiterers quickened their steps; the last belated freshman, with the dread of the proctor before his eyes, bounded frantically up the steps; and for a brief space all was silence and solitude. Then there was a murmuring, rushing sound, as of a coming tempest, and University Hall disgorged its contents, casting forth the freshmen and juniors at one door, and the sophomores and seniors at the other.

Of these last was Morton, who, with three or four of his class, walked across the college yard, towards the great gateway. By his side was a young man named Rosny, carelessly dressed, but with a lively, dare-devil face, and the look of a good-natured game cock.

"I shall be sorry to leave this place," said Morton; "I like it. I like the elms, and the gravel walks, and the scurvy old brick and mortar buildings."

"Then I am not of your mind," said Rosny; "gravel or mud, brickbats or paving stones, they are the same to me, the world over. Halloo, Wren," to a mustachioed youth who just then joined them; "we are bound to your room."

"That's as it should be. But where are the rest?"

"Coming — all in good time; here's one of them."

A dapper little person approached, with a shining beaver, yellow kid gloves, a switch cane, and a very stiff but somewhat dashing cravat, surmounted by a round and rubicund face.

"Ah, Chester!" exclaimed Wren; "the very man we were looking for. Come and take a glass of punch at my room."

"Punch, indeed!" replied Chester, whose face had changed from a prim expression to one of great hilarity the moment he saw his friends—"no, no, gentlemen, I renounce punch and all its works. The pure unmixed, the pure juice of the grape for me."

"But, Chester," urged Wren, "won't the pure mountain dew be a sufficient inducement?"

"The good company will be a sufficient inducement," said Chester, waving his hand,—"the good company, gentlemen,—and the good liquor. But what have we here? Meredith and Vinal walking side by side. Good Heavens, what a conjunction!"

The objects of Chester's astonishment, on a flattering invitation from Wren, joined the party, which, however, was weakened by the temporary secession of Rosny, who, pleading an errand in the village, left them with a promise to rejoin them soon. His place was in a few moments more than supplied by a new party of recruits, among whom was Stubb. Arrived at Wren's room, the desk and other appliances of study were banished from the table; bottles and glasses usurped their place, and the company composed themselves for conversation, most of them permitting their chairs to stand quietly on all fours, though one or two, like heathen Yankees from the backwoods, forced them to rear rampant on the hind legs, the occupant's feet resting on the ledge over the fireplace.

A few minutes passed, when a quick, firm step came up the stairs, and Rosny entered.

"How are you again, Dick?" said Meredith.

"Good evening, Mr. Rosny," echoed Stubb, who sat alone on the window seat.

"Eh? what's that?" demanded Rosny, turning sharp round upon the last speaker, with a face divided between indignation and laughter.

"I said, 'Good evening,'" replied Stubb, much disconcerted.

"And why didn't you say, 'Good morning,' yesterday, eh?—when I met you in Boston, eh? He gave me the cut direct," turning to the company. "Mr. Benjamin Stubb, here, gave me the cut direct! It was the pepper-and-salt coat and the thunder-and-lightning breeches that Stubb couldn't think of bowing to when he was walking in —— Street, with a lady. Look here, Stubb," —again facing the victim, —"what do you take me for? and what the devil do you take yourself for? I know your dirty family history. Your grandfather was a bricklayer, and the Lord knows who your great grandfather was. The best Huguenot blood of France runs in *my* veins! My ancestors were fighting at Ivry and Jarnac, while yours were peddling coal and potatoes about London streets, or digging mud in a ditch, for any thing you or I know to the contrary." Stubb gasped. "Your father has a crest painted on his carriage; but where did he get it? Why, Cribb, the engraver, stole it for him out of the British peerage."

Stubb, who was weak and timorous, here rose in great confusion, muttered something about conduct unbecoming to a gentleman, and meaning to require an explanation, and abruptly left the room.

"That job is finished," said Rosny, composedly seating himself. "*His* bill is settled for him."

"But, Dick," said Morton, who had been laughing in his sleeve during the scene, "do you want to be considered as a Frenchman or an American?"

"I'm an American," answered Rosny—"an American and a democrat, every inch."

Rosny had adopted democratic principles and habits partly out of spite against the class to which Stubb belonged, and which he was pleased to designate as the "codfish aristocracy," and partly because he thought that he could thus most effectually gain the ends of his impatient, hankering ambition. His ancestor, the head of an eminent Huguenot race, had been driven to America by the persecutions which followed the revocation of the edict of Nantes. The family had lived ever since in poverty and obscurity; yet this fiery young democrat nourished an inordinate pride of birth, and never forgot that he was descended from a line of warlike nobles.

"No, no," said Rosny, as Morton pushed a glass towards him, "drinking is against my rule— Well, as it's about the last time," —filling the glass, — "here's to you all."

"The last time!" said Morton; "that's a dismal word. If my next four years are as pleasant as these last have been, I will never complain of them."

"I tell you, boys," said Meredith, who was tranquilly puffing at his cigar, "the cream of our lives is skimmed already. Rough and tumble, hurry and worry—that will be the story with most of us, more or less, to the end of our days."

"Rough and tumble!" exclaimed Rosny; "so much the better. 'Scots play best at the roughest game'—that's just my case. Who wants to be always paddling about on smooth water? Close reefed topsails, a gale astern, and breakers all round—that's the game."

"Every one to his taste," said Chester, shrugging his shoulders. "I suppose a salamander loves the fire, but I don't. 'The race of ambition'— 'the unconquerable will'—pshaw! *Cui bono?* One chases after his object, and when he has got it, he turns from it, and chases another. I profess the philosophy of Horace—enjoy the hour as it flies. Ah! he was a model man, a man after my own heart, a gentleman and a man of the world. He could drink his Falernian, and thank the gods for their gifts."

Rosny whispered in Morton's ear, "Chester ought to have been born a century ago, among the John Bulls, up in the cockloft of Brazen Nose College, or some such antediluvian hole."

In spite of these derogatory remarks, Chester, besides being one of the best scholars in the class, was noted for a social, jovial disposition, which, though, like Fluellen's valor, a little out of fashion, made him a general favorite.

"Speaking of the next four years," said Wren, "I wonder what plans each of us has made for that time. For my part, I have no plan at all, and should be glad to profit by the suggestions of the rest. Come, Chester, what do you mean to do?"

"Expatiate," said Chester, expanding his hands, and thereby revealing an odd little antique ring which he wore; "take mine ease, roaming, like the bee, from blossom to blossom. I will leave the earnest men—bah!—the men with a mission—to grub on in their vocation. I will renounce this land of cotton mills and universal suffrage. First for Paris, to walk the Boulevards, and go to the masked balls and the opera;—*vive la bagatelle!*—then for Rome, to saunter through the Vatican and the picture galleries,—but not to moralize with a long face over fallen grandeur, and the mutability of human affairs. No, no, gentlemen, I belong to another school of philosophy. I will sit among the ruins of the Forum, and laugh, like Democritus, at the image of Death. Then I will recreate myself at Capri, like the Cæsars before me; then enjoy the *dolce far niente* at Florence, and read the Tuscan poets in the shades of Vallombrosa."

"But, Chester," interposed Wren, "don't you ever mean to marry and settle down?"

"I object to that phrase, 'settle down.' It calls up disagreeable images. It reminds one of the backwoods, log cabins, men in shirt sleeves, and piles of pine boards and lumber. Yes, certainly, I mean to marry. What man of taste would leave matrimony out of his scheme of life? One likes to gather his treasures round him, his pictures, his vases, and statues; and how can he adorn his rooms with an ornament more exquisite—where can he find a piece of furniture more charmingly moulded—than a beautiful woman?"

This flourish, between jest and earnest, he pronounced with a graceful wave of his hand.

"If, when you have married your beautiful woman," said Morton, "you find you have caught a Tartar, it will serve you right."

"Hear him," said Chester; "hear the barbarian. He will always be conjuring up some image of disquiet. 'Rest, rest, perturbed spirit.'"

"He could not rest, if he tried," said Horace Vinal.

"No, he is one of those unfortunates who lie under a sentence of endless activity. It is a disease, with which men are afflicted for the sins of their ancestors; and for the sins of mine I was born among a whole nation of such. Perpetual motion, bustle and whirl,—I grow dizzy to think of it. They cannot rest themselves, and will not let any one else rest. Always pursuing, always doing, never enjoying. A true American cannot enjoy. He would build a steam saw mill in Arcadia, and dam up the four rivers of Paradise for cotton factories."

"But, Chester," said Wren, "that is not at all like Morton; you know he hates utilitarianism."

"Yes, but still he cannot rest. He would not build saw mills and dams; but he would be sure to fire his rifle at some of Adam's live stock, and set all Eden by the ears. Come, Morton, I have told the company my plans. Let us hear what yours are."

"My guardian wishes me to enter the law school."

"You are twenty-one now," said Vinal, "and can do as you please."

Vinal was a very tall and slender young man, with a strongly marked face, though thin and pale; a grave, thoughtful eye, and compressed lips, expressing a kind of nervous self-control. His dress was very elaborate and scrupulous, though without the smallest trace of foppery. He was less popular in the class than Morton, but had the reputation of greater talents. This he owed, perhaps, to his habitual reserve; for every one thought that he understood Morton thoroughly, while few pretended to fathom the silent and self-contained Vinal.

"I should like well enough to study law," was Morton's non-committal answer.

"I thought, Morton, that you were more of a philosopher. Here you are, a young fellow, full of blood, and worth half a million, and yet you speak of buckling down to the law. That is all well enough for poor dogs like me, who go into the mill from necessity. We drudge on for twenty years or more, till we have scraped together a competency, or something better, perhaps, and then we find that we have forgotten how to enjoy it. We have grown so used to harness that we are good for nothing out of it, and sacrifice body and soul to our profession. You have reached already the point that we are straining for. The world is all before you, man; launch out and enjoy yourself."

"Didn't you just say," asked Rosny, "that Morton couldn't rest, if he tried?"

"I said he could not rest, but I did not say he could not enjoy himself. Look at him: his cheek is ruddier and browner than any of us. Nobody would believe that a fellow like that was not made to enjoy life. I know Morton. He could roam from blossom to blossom, as Chester says, with as good a will as any body. He has an eye for the fair sex, correct as he is at present. He knows a pretty face from a plain one. The devil will catch him yet with a black eye and a rosy cheek."

"Then," said Morton, "he will show his good opinion of my taste."

Rosny, who had his own reasons for disliking Vinal, here broke in without ceremony,—

"Be gad, Vinal, he will bait his hook differently when he fishes for you."

"How will that be, Dick?" said Meredith.

"With a five dollar bank note, and a lying puff in a newspaper; and Vinal will jump at it like a mackerel at a red rag."

Vinal laughed, but with a bad grace.

"Riches and fame!" said Chester, anxious to smooth away all traces of irritation—"riches and fame! I call those legitimate objects of pursuit; and the black eye is positively praiseworthy. Come, Morton, let us hear your plan. You have not told it yet."

"I defer to Rosny—he is my senior. Dick, some ten or twelve years from this, I suppose I shall vote against you for the presidency."

"Thank you. By that time you will have no whig party left to vote with. The democrats will have it all their own way."

"I have often wondered what could have induced a driving man of the world like you to come to college at all. You have been here more than a year; and in the same time, with your previous knowledge, you might have learned as much any where else at half the cost. You are not the fellow to regard a degree of A. M. with superstitious veneration."

"You are right there, colonel. I am of no kith nor kin to some of your New England old fogies, who would give their souls for a D. D. or an LL. D.—and get it, too, though they know no more Greek or Hebrew than I know of Choctaw, and can barely manage to stumble along through the Latin Testament. What's a piece of sheep's skin to me? Humbug is the current coin all the world over, and just as much in this free and enlightened country as any where else. I have schemes on foot,—not political,—no matter what they are,—out in the western country; and I happen to know that a degree from Harvard University is the medicine that suits my case; with that for my credentials, I shall carry it over all competitors. Yes, boys, gammon is the word; and the man who would rise in the world must use the stepping stones."

"You're a victim of the national disease, Rosny," said Chester. "Rising in the world!—that's the idea that ruins us. It's that that makes us lean, starveling, nervous, restless, dyspeptic, hypochondriac,—the most prosperous and most uncomfortable people on earth. Sit down, man, and take your ease. What garden will thrive if every plant in it must be dug up every day, and set out in a better place?"

"Ah, that's good doctrine for you. You have got nothing to gain, and a good deal to lose. Stand up for the *status quo*, old boy; I would, in your place. Look at me, though. I was cut adrift at fourteen,—parents dead,—not a cent in my pocket,—and since then I have tumbled along through the world as I could. You can't kill me. I have more lives than a cat. I have been thrown on my back a dozen times; but the harder I was flung down, the higher I bounced up again. Why, I have known the time when I was glad to earn a shilling by shovelling snow off a sidewalk. I have tried my hand at every thing,—printer's work, lecturing, politics, editing, keeping school,—and do you suppose I shall be content to rest in the mud all my days? Not a bit of it. I know my cue better. The time will come when you'll see me shooting up like a rocket."

Here a broad glare against the window interrupted him, and, looking out, his auditors saw a bonfire blazing with peculiar splendor under the windows of the chamber where the Faculty were at that moment in solemn session. Three proctors and a tutor were hastening towards the scene of outrage, when a stentorian voice from the adjacent darkness roared forth a warning that there was a canister of gunpowder in the fire expected every moment to explode. The prudent officers therefore kept their distance, busying themselves with noting down the names of several innocent spectators, while the bonfire subsided to a natural death, the gunpowder hoax having perfectly succeeded.

Mr. Wren's guests resumed their seats, mingling with graver matters the usual badinage of a college gathering; and when at length they separated, only a lonely light or two glimmered from among the many windows of the academic barracks which overlook the college green.

CHAPTER VI

As if with Heaven a bargain they had made
To practise goodness—and to be well paid,
They, too, devoutly as their fathers did,
Sin, sack, and sugar, equally forbid;
Holding each hour unpardonably spent
That on the leger leaves no monument.—Parsons.

Mr. Erastus Flintlock sat at his counting room, in his old leather-bottomed arm chair. Vassall Morton, his newly emancipated ward, just twenty-one, stood before him, the undisputed master of his father's ample wealth.

"What, no profession, Mr. Morton? None whatever, sir?"

"No, sir, none whatever."

The old man's leathery countenance expressed mingled wrath and concern.

Flintlock was a stanch old New Englander, boasting himself a true descendant of the Puritans, whose religious tenets he inherited, along with most of their faults, and not a few of their virtues. He was narrow as a vinegar cruet, and just in all his dealings. There were three subjects on which he could converse with more or less intelligence—politics, theology, and business. Beyond these, he knew nothing; and except American history and practical science, he had an indistinct idea that any thing more came of evil. He distrusted a foreigner, and abhorred a Roman Catholic. All poetry, but Milton and the hymn book, was an abomination in his eyes; and he looked upon fiction as an emanation of the devil. To the list of the cardinal virtues he added another, namely, attention to business. In his early days, he had come from his native Connecticut with letters to Morton's father, who, seeing his value, took him as a clerk, placed unbounded trust in him, and at last made him his partner. He was a youth of slow parts, solid judgment, solemn countenance, steady habits, and a most unpliable conscience. He had no follies, allowed himself no indulgences, and could enjoy no other pleasures than business and church-going. He attended service morning, afternoon, and evening, and never smiled on Sundays. His old age was as upright and stiff-necked as might have been augured from such a youth. He thought the rising generation were in a very bad way, and once gave his son a scorching lecture on vanity and arrogance, because the latter, who had been two years at college, very modestly begged to be excused from carrying a roll of sample cotton, a yard and a half long, from his father's store at one end of the town, to the shop of a retail dealer at the other.

"What, no profession, Mr. Morton?"

"None whatever, sir."

Morton was prepared for the consequence of these fatal words, and sought to arm himself with the needful patience. It would be folly, he knew, to debate the point with his guardian, who was tough and unmanageable as a hickory stump; who would never see any side of a question but his own, and on whose impervious brain reasons fell like rain drops on a tarpauline. Flintlock, therefore, opened fire unanswered, and discoursed for a full hour on duty, propriety, and a due respect for what he called the general sense of the community, which, as he assured his auditor, demands that every one should have some fixed and stated calling, by which he may be recognized as a worthy and useful member of society. Sometimes he grew angry, and scolded his ward with great vehemence; then subsided into a pathetic strain, and exhorted him, for the sake of his excellent father, not to grow old in idleness and frivolity. Morton, respectful, but obdurate, heard him to an end, assured him that, though renouncing commerce and the professions, his life would by no means be an idle one, thanked him for his care of his property, and took his leave; while the old merchant sank back into his chair, and groaned dismally, because the son of his respected patron was on the road to perdition.

A moment's retrogression will explain the young man's recusancy.

On a May evening, some two months before the close of his college career, Morton sat in lonely meditation on a wooden bench, by the classic border of Fresh Pond. By every canon of polite fiction, his meditation ought to have been engrossed by some object of romantic devotion; but in truth they were of a nature wholly mundane and sublunary.

He had been much exercised of late upon the choice of a career for his future life. He liked none of the professions for itself, and had no need to embrace it for support. He loved action, and loved study; was ambitious and fond of applause. He had, moreover, enough of the American in his composition never to be happy except when in pursuit of something; together with a disposition not very rare among young men in New England, though seldom there, or elsewhere, joined to his abounding health and youthful spirits—a tendency to live for the future, and look at acts and things with an eye to their final issues.

Thierry's Norman Conquest had fallen into his hands soon after he entered college. The whole delighted him; but he read and re-read the opening chapters, which exhibit the movements of the various races in their occupancy of the west of Europe. This first gave him an impulse towards ethnological inquiries. He soon began to find an absorbing interest in tracing the distinctions, moral, intellectual, and physical, of different races, as shown in their history, their mythologies, their languages, their legends, their primitive art, literature, and way of life. The idea grew upon him of devoting his life to such studies.

Seated on the wooden bench at the edge of Fresh Pond, he revolved, for the hundredth time, his proposed scheme, and summed up what he regarded as its manifold advantages. It would enable him to indulge his passion for travel, lead him over rocks, deserts, and mountains, conduct him to Tartar tents and Cossack hovels, make him intimate with the most savage and disgusting of barbarians; in short, give full swing to his favorite propensities, and call into life all his energies of body and mind. In view of this prospect, he clinched his long-cherished purpose, devoting himself to ethnology for the rest of his days.

He had a youthful way of thinking that any resolution deliberately adopted by him must needs be final and conclusive, and was fully convinced that his present determination was a species of destiny, involving one of three results—that he should meet an early death, which he thought very likely; that he should be wholly disabled by illness, which he thought scarcely possible; or that, in the fulness of time, say twenty or twenty-five years, his labors would have issue in some prodigious work, redounding to his own honor and the unspeakable profit of science.

CHAPTER VII

'Tis a dull thing to travel like a mill horse,
Still in the place he was born in, round and blinded.
Beaumont and Fletcher.

A novel-maker may claim a privilege which his betters must forego. So, in the teeth of dramatic unities, let the story leap a chasm of some two years.

Not that the void was a void to Morton. His nature spurred him into perpetual action; but his wanderings were over at length; and he and Meredith sat under the porch of Morton's house, a few miles from town. The features of the latter were swarthy from exposures, while those of his friend were somewhat pale, and had the expression of one insufferably bored.

"Colonel, you are the luckiest fellow I know. Here you have been following the backbone of the continent from Darien to the head of the Missouri, mixing yourself up with Spaniards and Aztecs, poking sticks into the crater of Popocatapetl, and living hand and glove with Blackfeet and Assinnaboins, while I have been doing penance among bonds and mortgages, and title deeds and leases. My father has thrown up responsibility and gone to Europe—and so has every body else—and left all on my shoulders."

"Your time will come."

"I hope so."

"But what news is there?"

"Nothing."

"What, nothing since I went away?"

"The old story. You know it as well as I. Now and then, a new engagement came out. Mrs. A. approved it, and Mrs. B. didn't; and then characters were discussed on both sides. Something has been said of the balls, the opera, and what not; with the usual talk about the wickedness of the democrats and the fanaticism of the abolitionists."

"You appear to have led a gay life."

"Very!—we need a war, an invasion,—something of the sort. It would put life into us, and rid us of a great deal of nonsense. You were born with a stimulus in yourself, and can stand this stagnant sort of existence; but I need something more lively."

"Then go with me on my next journey."

"Are you thinking of another already? Rest in peace, and thank Heaven that you have come home in a whole skin."

"I have done the North American continent; but there are four more left, not to mention the islands."

"And you mean to see them all?"

"Certainly."

"Your science is a convenient hobby. It carries you wherever you fancy to go."

"You could not do better than go with me."

"I know it; but, if wishes were horses— — I am training Dick to take my place. I am a model elder brother to that youngster in the way of cultivating his mind and morals; and when I have him up to the mark, I shall gain a year's furlough for my pains. But when is your next journey to begin—next week?"

"No, I mean to pin myself down here, and dig like a mole, for the next ten months, at least."

"If I had not had ocular proof of what a determined dig you can be, I should set down your studies as mere humbug."

"But I wish to hear the news."

"I would tell it willingly, if I knew any."

"Have the Primroses come home from Europe yet?"

"Yes."

"And the Everills?"

"I believe not."

"Nor the Leslies, I suppose."

"For a reasonably sensible and straightforward fellow, you have a queer way of making inquiries. You question like a lady's letter, with the pith in the postscript. You ask after the Primroses and the Everills, a stupid, priggish set, for whom you care nothing, as earnestly as if you were in love with them, and then grow indifferent when you come to the Leslies, whom you like."

"Did I?" said Morton, in some discomposure; "I ask their pardon. Have they come home?"

"Not yet, but I believe they mean to come as soon as they have staid their year out."

"And that will be very soon—early in the spring, or sooner."

"Now I think of it, I made the acquaintance, a few evenings ago, of a person who, I believe, is a relation or connection of yours—Miss Fanny Euston."

"O, yes, she is my third, fourth, or fifth cousin, or something of that sort; but I have not seen her since she was ten years old. She was a great romp, then, and very plain."

"That last failing is cured. She has grown very handsome."

"The first failing ought to be cured, too, by this time."

"I am not so clear on that point. She is a girl with an abundance of education, and a good deal of a certain kind of accomplishment—music, and so on—but no breeding at all. If she had had the training of good society, she would have been one of a thousand. As it is she cares for nobody, and does and says whatever comes into her mind, without the least regard to consequences or appearances."

"Does she affect naturalness, independence, and all that?"

"No, she affects nothing. The material is admirable. It only needs to be refined, polished, and toned down. It's unlucky, colonel, but in this world every thing worth having is broken in pieces and mixed with something that one doesn't want. It's an even balance, good and bad; there's no use in going off into raptures about any thing. One thing is certain, though; this cousin of yours has character enough to supply material for a dozen Miss Primroses, without any visible diminution."

"I should like to see her. I'll go to-morrow."

"You'd better. But now tell me something more about your journey."

And, in reply to his friend's questions, Morton proceeded to relate such incidents as had befallen him.

CHAPTER VIII

> Beauty is a witch
> Against whose charms faith melteth into blood.
> D. Pedro.—If thou wilt hold longer argument,
> Do it in notes.
> Benedick.—Now, divine air, now is his soul ravished.
> *Much Ado about Nothing.*

Morton visited his cousin, Miss Fanny Euston, a guest, for a few days, at a friend's house in town. By good fortune, as he thought it, he found her alone; and, as he conversed with her, he employed himself—after a practice usual with him—in studying her character, and making internal comments upon it. These insidious reflections, condensed into a paragraph, would have been somewhat as follows:—

"A fine figure, and a very handsome face; but there is a lurking devil in her eye, and about the corners of her mouth." Here some ten minutes of animated dialogue ensued before his observations had shaped themselves into further results. "She is exceedingly clever; she knows how to think and act for herself. I should not like to cross her will. There is fire enough in her to make a hundred women interesting. She is none of our frosty New England beauties. She could love a man to the death, and hate him as well. She could be a heroine or a tigress. Every thing about her is wild and chaotic, the unformed elements of a superb woman."

Here, the conversation having lasted a half hour or more, his imagination began to disturb the deductions of his philosophy, and he was no longer in a mood of just psychological analysis, when, to his vexation, his cousin's hostess, Miss Jones, entering, brought his *tête-à-tête* to a close. She displayed a marvellous fluency of discourse, and was eloquent upon books, parties, paintings, and the opera.

"I need not ask you, Mr. Morton, if you have seen Tennyson's new poem."

"Yes—at the bookseller's."

"But surely you have read it."

"No, I am behind the age."

"Then thank Heaven for it," exclaimed his unceremonious cousin; "for of all insipidity, and affectation, and fine-spun, wire-drawn trash, Tennyson carries away the palm. Every body reads him because he is the fashion, and every body admires him because he is the fashion. But he is a bubble, a film, a gossamer; there's nothing in him."

This explosion called forth a protest from the poet's admirer.

"May I ask," said Morton to his cousin, "who are your literary favorites?"

"Not the latter-day poets—the Tennysonian school; their puling mannerism is an insult to the Saxon tongue."

"But," urged Miss Jones, "you are not quite reasonable."

"Of course I am not. It's not a woman's province to be reasonable."

"Do you subscribe to these poetical heresies, Mr. Morton?"

"On the contrary, I think that Tennyson has often great beauties."

"If he sometimes wrote like an angel," pursued Fanny Euston, "I should find no patience to see it in a man who could put upon paper such parrot rhymes as these:—

>'Not a whit of thy tuwhoo,
>Thee to woo to thy tuwhit,
>Thee to woo to thy tuwhit,
>With a lengthened loud halloo,
>Tuwhoo, tuwhit, tuwhit, tuwhoo-o-o!'

Bah! it puts one in a passion to hear such twaddle."

"I see," said her friend, "that nothing less than your own music will calm your indignation. Pray let us hear the ballad which you set to music this morning."

"I will sing, if you wish it; but not that ballad."

And she seated herself before the open piano.

"What do you choose, Mr. Morton?"

"The Marseillaise. That, I think, is in your vein."

"Ah! you can choose well!"

And, running her fingers over the keys, she launched at once into the warlike strains of the hymn of revolution. Her voice and execution were admirable; and though by no means unconscious that she was producing an effect, she sang with a fire, energy, and seeming recklessness that thrilled like lightning through her auditor's veins. He rose involuntarily from his seat. For that evening his study of character was ended, and philosophy dislodged from her last stronghold.

Half an hour later he was riding homeward in a mood quite novel to his experience. He pushed his horse to a keen trot, as if by fierceness of motion to keep pace with the fiery influence that was kindling all his nerves.

"I have had my fancies before this," he thought,—"in fact I have almost been in love; but that feeling was no more like this than a draught from a clear spring is like a draught of spiced wine."

That night he fully expected to be haunted by a vision of Fanny Euston; but his slumbers were unromantically dreamless.

Three days later, he ventured another visit; but his cousin had returned to her home in the country. By this time he was conscious of a great abatement of ardor; and his equanimity was little moved by the disappointment. In a week he had learned to look back on his transient emotion as an effervescence of the moment, and to regard his relative with no slight interest, indeed, yet by no means in a light which could blind him to her glaring faults. He summoned up all that he could recall of herself and her family, and chiefly of her father, whom he remembered in his boyhood as a rough, athletic man, whose black and bushy eyebrows were usually contracted into something which seemed like a frown. These boyish recollections were far from doing Euston justice. He was a man of masculine and determined character. His will was strong, his passions violent; he was full of prejudices, and when thwarted or contradicted, his rage was formidable. His honor was unquestioned; he was most bluntly and unmanageably honest. Yet through the rock and iron of his character, there ran, known to but few, a delicate vein of poetic feeling. The music of his daughter, or the verses of his favorite Burns, could often bring tears to his stern gray eyes. For his wife, whom he had married in a fit of pique and disappointment, when little more than a boy, he cared nothing; but his fondness for his daughter was unbounded. He alone could control her; for she loved him ardently, and he was the only living thing of which she stood in awe.

CHAPTER IX

Elle ne manque jamais de saisir promptement
L'apparente lueur du moindre attachement,
D'en semer la nouvelle avec beaucoup de joie, — *Le Tartufe.*

Among Morton's acquaintance was a certain Miss Blanche Blondel. They had been schoolmates when children; and as, at a later date, Miss Blanche had been fond of making long visits to a friend in Cambridge, during term time, Morton, in common with many others, had a college acquaintance with her, so that they were now on a footing of easy intercourse. Not that he liked her. On the contrary, she had inspired him with a very emphatic aversion; but being rather a skirmisher on the outposts of society, than enrolled in the main battalion, she was anxious to make the most of the acquaintance she had. She had the eyes of an Argus, and was as sly, smooth, watchful, and *rusée* as a tortoise shell cat; wonderfully dexterous at finding or making gossip, and unwearied in sowing it, broadcast, to the right and left.

One evening Morton was at a ball, crowded to the verge of suffocation. At length he found himself in a corner from which there was no retreat, while the stately proportions of Mrs. Frederic Goldenberg barred his onward progress. But when that distinguished lady chanced to move aside, she revealed the countenance of Miss Blondel, beaming on him like the moon after an eclipse. She nodded and smiled. There was no escape. Morton smiled hypocritically, and said, "Good evening." Blanche, as usual, was eager for conversation, and, after a few commonplaces, she said, turning up her eyes at him with an arch expression,—

"I have a piece of news to tell you, Mr. Morton."

"Ah!" replied Morton, expecting something disagreeable.

"A piece of news that you will be charmed to hear."

"Indeed."

"Why, how cold you are! And I know that, in your heart, you are burning to hear it."

"If you think so, you are determined to give my patience a hard schooling."

"Well, I will not tantalize you any more. Miss Edith Leslie sailed from Liverpool for home last Wednesday."

"Ah!"

"How cold you are again! Are you not glad to hear it?"

"Certainly—all her friends will be glad to hear it."

"Upon my word, Mr. Morton, you are worse and worse. When a gentleman dances twice with a young lady on class day, and twice at Mrs. Fanfaron's ball, and joins her in the street besides, has she not a right to feel hurt when he hears with such profound indifference of her coming home after a year's absence?"

Morton could hardly restrain the extremity of his distaste and impatience.

"Miss Leslie, I imagine, would spend very little thought upon the matter." And he hastened, first to change the conversation, and then to close it altogether.

Having escaped from his fair informant, he remained divided between pleasure at the tidings, and annoyance at the manner in which they had been told.

In a few days Miss Leslie arrived. Her beauty had matured during her absence. She was conspicuously and brilliantly handsome, and was admired accordingly,—a fact which, though she could not but be conscious of it, seemed to affect her very little. Morton found her but slightly changed, with the same polished and quiet frankness, the same lively conversation, not without a tinge of sarcasm, and the same enthusiasm of character, betraying itself by an earnestness of manner, and never by any extravagance of expression. He had many opportunities of seeing her, Miss Blanche Blondel being but rarely present, and, in his growing admiration of her, the charms of his unbridled cousin faded more and more from his memory.

CHAPTER X

> For three whole days you thus may rest
> From office business, news, and strife.—*Pope*.

When the summer heats set in, Meredith, one evening, drove to Morton's house, and, arrayed in linen and grass-cloth, smoked his cigar under his friend's veranda with as much contentment as the thermometer at ninety would permit. The window at his side was that of the room which Morton used as his study, and the table was covered with books.

"Colonel," said Meredith, "what a painstaking fellow you are! Ever since you left college—except when you were off on that journey, which was one of the most rational things you ever did in your life—you have been digging here among your books, as if you were some half-starved law student, with a prospect of matrimony."

"I've done digging for the present. It's against my principles to work much in July and August."

"What do you mean to do?"

"Set out on a journey."

"I suppose so. You are a lucky fellow."

"Give yourself a vacation, and come with me."

"No, I'm in for it for the next two months; but I will have my revenge before long."

"Three days from your office will never ruin you or your family. Come with me to New Baden, if you can't do better."

"I think I can manage that,—and I will."

Accordingly, on Monday morning, they took the train thitherward.

CHAPTER XI

> The company is 'mixed,' (the phrase I quote is
> As much as saying, they're below your notice.) — *Byron*.

On reaching New Baden, towards night, they learned that there was to be a dance that evening, in the hall.

"The deuse!" ejaculated Meredith, as they entered; "have we come all this distance to find old faces again at New Baden? Look at that corner."

Morton looked, and beheld a solemn group taking no part in the amusements, but scrutinizing the scene with the air of superior beings. He recognized the familiar countenance of Mrs. Primrose, with her daughter, Miss Constance Primrose, and her daughter's friend, Miss Wallflower. There, too, was Mr. Benjamin Stubb, Morton's classmate, and Miss Primrose's reputed admirer, with several other kindred spirits. Stubb was a tall and very slender young man, with a grave and pallid visage, and an uncompromising rigidity of cravat. Though his brain was unfurnished, his morals were reasonably good, and he went regularly to church, believing that there was, he could not tell how, an inseparable connection between good society and the ritual of the English church. He prided himself on his gentlemanly deportment, and regarded a lady as a being who is under no circumstances to be approached, except through the medium of certain prescribed forms and ceremonies. He seldom noticed those whom he thought his inferiors, and was very formal and exact towards the select few whom he acknowledged as his equals. As to superiors, he confessed none, except in the highest ranks of the English aristocracy, upon whom he looked with great reverence. He thought that there was no really good society in America, except the society of Boston, of which he regarded himself and his connections as the *crême, de la crême*. He cherished a just hereditary scorn of upstarts and parvenus; for already nearly half a century had expired since the Stubbs began to rise on golden wings from their native mud. Nor was this their only claim to ancestral eminence; since a judicious investment of a little surplus income at the College of Heralds had revealed the gratifying truth that the Stubbs of Boston were lineal descendants of King Arthur.

Mrs. Primrose was a very benevolent and estimable person, who knew nothing of the world beyond her own circle, and looked with dire reprehension on any deviation from the standard of morals and manners which she had been accustomed to regard as the correct and proper one. Miss Constance Primrose realized Stubb's most exalted ideal of a young lady. She was very pretty, but with a face cold and unchanging as marble. She carried an unquestionable air of good, not to say of high breeding; having in this point an advantage over her mother, whose style savored a little of the simplicity of her early surroundings. The material, indeed, was very slender; but it had received a creditable polish; and though she had nothing to say, she said it with an undeniable grace.

Morton and Meredith paid their compliments to the group, the former hastening to mingle with the crowd again, while Meredith remained to exchange a few words with the pretty, modest, and too-much-neglected Miss Wallflower.

"Upon my word, Mr. Meredith," said Mrs. Primrose, "Mr. Morton has found a singular pair of acquaintances."

"O, yes," said Meredith; "those are particular friends of his."

"Very singular!" murmured Mrs. Primrose.

Morton was walking slowly up the hall, conversing with an odd-looking couple—a heavy, thick set man, in the fantastic finery of a Broadway swell, and a woman of five feet ten, thin and gaunt, with a yellow complexion, and a pair of fierce, glittering eyes, like an Indian squaw in ill humor. She was gorgeous in silk, brocade, and diamonds, and her huge, gloveless, bony fingers sparkled with jewelry. Her husband, on his part, displayed a mighty breastpin, in the shape of a war horse rampant, in diamond frostwork.

"Mr. Meredith," murmured the horrified Mrs. Primrose, "pray who are those persons?"

"Aborigines from Red River. Mr. and Mrs. Major Orson, of Natchitoches. He is a speculator, I believe, of more wealth than reputation."

"And *are* they friends of Mr. Morton?"

"O, Morton is a student of humanity. He met them at the tea table, and thinks them remarkable specimens of natural history."

Mrs. Primrose did not hear this explanation. The trio had now approached within a few yards; and her whole attention was absorbed in listening to the high, penetrating voice of the female ogre.

"There's one great and glorious thing about Natchitoches," remarked Mrs. Orson.

"What's that?" asked Morton.

"You can get every thing there to eat that heart can wish."

"That's a fact," said the major; "there ain't no discount on that."

"Game, and fish, and fruit, and vegetables," pursued the lady; "any thing and every thing. The north can't compete with it, I tell *you*. There's the pompano! O, my! Did you ever eat a pompano?"

"Never."

"Then you *have* got something to look forward to. That's a fish that *is* a fish. Why, sir, you can begin at the tail, and eat him clean away to the head, and the bones is just like marrow! It makes my mouth water to think of it!"

"O, hush!" cried the major, with sympathetic emotion.

"And then the fruit! Think of the peaches! They beat your nasty little northern peaches all holler!"

"Yes," added the major, and to have your own boys to shin up the tree and throw 'em down to you; and to sit under the shade all the afternoon eating 'em;—that's the way to live!"

"It's all the little niggers is good for, just to pick fruit."

"Troublesome animals, I should think," observed Morton.

"Well, they be; and the growed-up niggers ain't much better. To think of that girl, Cynthy, major. My! wasn't she one of 'em! The major is, out of all account, too tender to his niggers, and if it warn't for me, they wouldn't get a speck of justice done. Why, what are all those folks moving for? My! supper's ready. I'll go in with this gentleman, major, and you may foller with any pretty gal that you can get to come with you. I ain't a jealous woman"—turning to Morton—"I let the major do pretty much what he pleases."

Mrs. Primrose drew a deep breath. "There must be"—thus she communed with herself—"something essentially vulgar in the mind of that young man, if he can neglect a cultivated and refined young lady like Constance, and at the same time find pleasure in the conversation of a person like that." And she considered within herself whether it would not be best to warn Constance not to encourage any advances which he might in future make. On second thoughts, reflecting that his position was unquestionable, his wealth great, and that she had never heard any thing against his morals, she determined to suspend all action for the present, keeping a close watch, meanwhile, on his behavior.

While Morton was thus brought to the bar in the matronly breast of Mrs. Primrose, while the jury were bringing in a verdict of guilty, joined to a recommendation to mercy, the unconscious young man was leading his companion to the supper room; where, furnishing her with a huge plate of oysters, he left her in perfect contentment.

Not long after, he encountered Meredith.

"How do you like your friend in the diamonds?"

"She's a superb specimen; about as civilized, with all her jewelry, as a Pawnee squaw. She has a vein of womanhood, though. I saw her, in the tea room, fondle a kitten whose foot had been trodden upon, as tenderly as if it had been a child."

"If you had not been so busy with her, you would have met a person much better worth your time."

"Who's that?"

"Miss Fanny Euston."

"Do you mean that she is here?"

"She *was* here,—in that room adjoining. But she has gone; you'll see nothing of her to-night."

"Will not her being here induce you to stay?"

The question, as he spoke it, had a sound of frankness; but the shameful truth must be confessed, that, in spite of his friendship for Meredith, and his admiration of Miss Leslie, he was a little jealous of his friend.

"No," replied Meredith, "it's out of the question. I must be off the day after to-morrow. By the way, you never told me how you liked Miss Euston."

"A rough diamond, needing nothing but to be cut, polished, and set!"

"It's too late, I think, for that. The polishing should have begun before eighteen. She is quite unformed, and quite unconscious of being so. I'll leave you here to fall in love with her, if you like; but if you do, colonel, you'll be a good deal younger than I take you for."

There was something in his friend's tone which led Morton half to suspect the truth. Meredith had himself a *penchant* for Miss Fanny Euston, held in abeyance by a very lively perception of her faults.

CHAPTER XII

Will you woo this wildcat? — *Katharine and Petruchio.*

Meredith went away, as he had proposed, leaving Morton at New Baden. The latter soon came to the opinion that he had never yet found so interesting a subject of psychological observation as that afforded him in the person of his relative, Miss Euston. She seemed to him the most wayward of mortals; yet in the midst of this lawlessness, generous instincts were constantly betraying themselves, and a certain native grace, a charm of womanhood, followed her wildest caprices. She often gave great offence by her brusqueries; yet those who best knew her were commonly her ardent friends.

Mrs. Primrose looked upon her with her most profound and unqualified disapprobation. Her daughter copied her sentiments; while Stubb thought her an outside barbarian of the most alarming character. Fanny Euston's perceptions were very acute. She saw the effect she had produced, and seemed to take peculiar delight in aggravating it, and shocking the prejudices of her critics still more.

One afternoon, Miss Primrose, Mr. Stubb, Fanny Euston, Morton, and several others, set out on a horseback excursion, matronized by Mrs. Primrose. At a few miles from New Baden, Morton found himself riding at his cousin's side, a little behind the rest.

"Do you know, I came this morning, to ask you to join us on our walk to Elk Ridge."

"Ah, I am sorry I was not there."

"You were there; but you seemed so deep in Ivanhoe, or some other of your favorites, that I had no heart to interrupt you."

"But that was quite absurd. I should like to have gone."

"I am curious to know what book you were so busy with. Something of Scott's — was it not?"

"Not precisely."

"Nor one of the new novels," pursued Morton—"those are not after your taste."

"Not at all; they are all full of some grand reform or philanthropic scheme, or the sorrows of some destitute, uninteresting little wretch, with whom you are required to sympathize."

"You are not moulded after the philanthropic model. But may I ask, what book was entertaining you so much?"

"Napier's Life of Montrose."

"And do you like it?"

"Indeed I do."

"And you like Montrose?"

"Certainly I like him."

"I could have sworn it. Do you remember his verses to the lady of his heart?"

"That I do," said Fanny Euston,—

> "'Like Alexander I will reign,
>   And I will reign alone;
> My heart shall evermore disdain
>   A rival on my throne.
> He either fears his fate too much,
>   Or his deserts are small,
> Who puts it not unto the touch,
>   To win or lose it all.
>
> "'But if thou wilt be constant then,
>   And faithful of thy word,
> I'll make thee famous by my pen,
>   And glorious by my sword;
> I'll serve thee in such noble ways
>   Was never heard before;
> I'll dress and crown thee all with bays,
>   And love thee evermore.'"

"Admirable! I thought I had a good memory, but you beat me hollow. You repeat the lines as if you liked them."

"Who would not like them?"

"And yet his fashion of wooing would be a little peremptory for the nineteenth century."

"There are no Montroses in the nineteenth century."

"They are out of date, like many a good thing besides. Not long ago, I saw some verses in a magazine—a kind of ballad on Montrose's execution."

"Can you repeat it?"

"I cannot compete with you; but I think I can give you a stanza or two:—

> "'The morning dawned full darkly,
>   The rain came flashing down,
> And the jagged streak of the levin bolt
>   Lit up the gloomy town:
> The thunder crashed across the heaven,
>   The fatal hour was come;
> And ay broke in, with muffled beat,
>   The 'larum of the drum.
> There was madness on the earth below,
>   And anger in the sky,
> And young and old, and rich and poor,
>   Came forth to see him die.
>
> "'But when he came, though pale and wan,
>   He looked so great and high,
> So noble was his manly front,
>   So calm his steadfast eye,—
> The rabble rout forbore to shout,
>   And each man held his breath,
> For well they knew the hero's soul
>   Was face to face with death.'"

Fanny Euston's eye kindled, as if at a strain of warlike music.

"Go on."

"I have forgotten the rest."

"Then pray find the verses and send them to me. Why is it that, as you say, such men are out of date?"

"What place, or what career, could they find in a commercial country?"

"Then why were we born in a commercial country?"

"You seem to make an ideal hero of Montrose."

"Not I. I am not the school girl you take me for. I have no ideal hero. I do not believe in ideal heroes. Montrose was a man, with the faults of a man; full of faults, and yet not a bad man either."

"Very far from it."

"He had great faults, but grand qualities to match them,—worth a thousand of the small, tame, correct virtues that one sees hereabouts."

"Dangerous ideas, those, Mrs. Primrose would tell you."

"Deliver me from Mrs. Primrose!" ejaculated Fanny.

They rode in silence for a few minutes, Morton's companion murmuring to herself fragments of the lines which he had just repeated.

"Look!" she cried, suddenly. "How slowly our horses have been walking! The rest are almost out of sight. We had better join them. Will you race with me?"

"Any thing you please."

"Come on, then."

She touched her horse with the whip, and they set forward at full speed. Fanny, who was by far the better mounted, soon gained the day.

"Rein up," cried Morton, as they came near the party, "or your horse will startle the others."

Fanny drew the curb, but not quite successfully; and her rapid arrival produced some commotion. Stubb's horse, in particular, began to prance and curvet in a manner which greatly disturbed his rider's equanimity.

"Whoa! Whoa, boy!" said Stubb. "Steady, now! steady, sir! Whoa!"

Fanny's eyes twinkled with malicious delight. She had a great contempt for Stubb, who, on his part, was mortally afraid of her.

"That's a good horse of yours," pushing close to his side.

"Yes, a very fine horse, indeed. Steady, boy! Steady, now!"

"A capital horse; but he needs a spirited hand like yours to manage him."

"Whoa! Quiet, now!—poor fellow!"

This last endearing address was checked by a sudden jolt, produced by a spasmodic movement of the horse, which shook the cavalier to his very centre.

"Punish him well with your spurs, Mr. Stubb, and let him run; that's the way to cure him of his tricks. Suppose we try a race together."

"Thank you, Miss Euston, but the fact is— Whoa, boy! whoa!— I mean, the stableman told me that he is rather short of breath."

"O, never mind the stableman. Come, let's go."

"Thank you, Miss Euston, I believe not to-day."

"You astonish me. I will lay any bet you like—you shall name the wager—any thing you please."

"Really, this is a little too bad!" soliloquized the horrified Mrs. Primrose. "Miss Euston, I entreat of you—I beg—that we may have no more racing. It is very dangerous, besides being——"

"What is it besides being dangerous, Mrs. Primrose?"

"*Very* indecorous."

"I am very sorry, for I have set my heart on a race with Mr. Stubb."

"Mr. Morton," said the distressed lady, aside to that young gentleman, "you are a prudent and sober-minded person; pray use your influence."

She was interrupted by a most uncanonical ejaculation from the author of her embarrassments, which, though couched in a foreign language, petrified her into silence. A sharp gust of wind had blown away Fanny's veil, and she was on the point of dashing off in pursuit of it.

"Stop!" cried Morton, "you'll break your neck. Let me get it for you."

The veil sailed away before the wind, and Morton spurred in pursuit, delighted to display his horsemanship before ladies, though it had no other merit than a tenacious seat and a kind of recklessness, the result of an excitable temperament. The ground was rough and broken, and studded with rocks and savin bushes, and as he galloped at a breakneck speed down the side of the hill, in a vain attempt to catch the veil flying, even Fanny held her breath. He secured his prize, as it caught against a bush, and returned to the road.

"Now, Miss Euston," said Mrs. Primrose, looking folios at the offender, "I trust we shall be allowed to go on in peace."

There was an interval of repose. Stubb regained his peace of mind. Miss Primrose, with whom he fancied himself in love, smiled upon him, and his self-conceit, before shaken in its stronghold, was returning in full force, when Fanny, who nourished a peculiar spite against this harmless blockhead, and whom that afternoon a very Satan of mischief seemed to possess, again rode to his side, and renewed her solicitations for a race.

"Miss Euston," said Mrs. Primrose, "I am certain you would do nothing so unladylike as to force Mr. Stubb to race against his will. Consider the example you would set to Georgiana Gosling, who always imitates what she sees you do."

The words were mild and motherly; but the countenance of the outraged matron had an uncompromising look of reprehension, which exasperated Fanny's wayward humor beyond measure. She began, it is true, a lively conversation on general topics with the intelligent Stubb, but, meantime, by alternately checking and exciting her horse, and urging him to play a variety of antics, she contrived to infect her companion's steed with the like contagion. He pranced, plunged, and chafed, till his rider was brought to the verge of despair.

The road had become quite narrow, running through a thick forest, frequented chiefly by woodcutters in the winter, and hunters of the picturesque in summer. Fanny's imitator, the adventurous Miss Gosling, a little girl of fourteen, had ridden a few rods in advance of the rest, when suddenly they saw her returning, astonished and disconsolate.

"We can't go any farther; there's a great tree fallen across the road."

A severe thundergust of the night before had overthrown a hemlock, the trunk of which, partly sustained by the roots and branches, formed a barrier about four feet from the ground. It was impossible to pass through the woods on either side, as they were very dense, and choked with a tangled growth of laurel bushes.

"How very annoying!" said Miss Primrose.

"What shall we do?" inquired Miss Gosling.

"Why, jump over it, to be sure," said Fanny. "Mr. Stubb and I will show you the way."

"You are surely not in earnest!" cried Mrs. Primrose.

"Of course I am. I have taken higher leaps at the riding school, twenty times."

"You had better not," said Morton, who had alighted by the roadside to draw his saddle girth.

"It is too dangerous to be thought of for a single moment," added Mrs. Primrose.

"Our horses," pursued the indiscreet Stubb, "are not used to leaping, and some of the ladies would certainly be hurt."

"The fool!" thought Morton. "He has done it now."

Fanny threw a laughing, caustic glance at her victim.

"*Mine* will leap, I know; and you are not a lady. Come, Mr. Stubb."

"Miss Euston," interposed the excited Mrs. Primrose, "this must not be. I am here in your mother's place, and she will hold me responsible for your safety. I forbid you to go, Miss Euston."

Fanny looked for a moment in her face. Morton caught the expression. It was one of unqualified, though not ill-natured, defiance.

"Come," cried Fanny again, and ran her horse towards the tree. She leaped gallantly, and cleared the barrier; but it was evident that she had lost control of the spirited animal, who galloped at a furious rate down the road.

Morton was still on foot, busied with his saddle girth.

"The crazy child!" exclaimed Mrs. Primrose; "her horse is running away. Go after her—pray!—Mr. Stubb—somebody."

"O, quick! quick!—do," cried little Miss Gosling, who idolized Fanny, and was in an agony of fright for her.

Thus exhorted, the desperate Stubb cried, "Get up," and galloped for the tree; but his horse balked, and, leaping aside, tumbled him into the mud. The ladies screamed. Morton would have laughed, if he had not been too anxious for Fanny.

"Get out of the way, Stubb," he cried, mounting with all despatch.

Miss Primrose's admirer gathered himself up, regained his hat, which had taken refuge in a puddle, and looked with horror at a ghastly white rent across his knee. Morton spurred his hack against the barrier, which the beast cleared with difficulty, striking his hind hoofs as he went over. After riding a short distance, he discovered Fanny, and saw, to his great relief, that she was regaining control over her horse. Half a mile farther on, the road divided. The larger branch led to the right, Morton did not know whither; the smaller turned to the left, and after circling through the woods for two or three miles, issued upon the high road. Fanny, who was ignorant of the way, took the right hand branch. In a few minutes after, she had brought her horse to a trot, and Morton rode up to her side.

"You are wiser than I am, if you know where we are going."

"I thought you knew the way. You were to have been our guide."

"We are on the wrong road. You should have turned to the left."

"But have you no idea where this will lead us?"

"Into a cedar swamp, for what I know. Had we not better turn back?"

"O, don't speak of turning back. I am in no mood for turning back. Let us keep on. I am sure this will bring us out somewhere."

"As you please," said Morton, knowing himself to be in the position of an angler, whose only chance of managing his salmon is to give it line.

"Where are all the rest?"

"Holding a convention behind the tree, I suppose. At least, I left them here."

"And did not Mr. Stubb dare the fatal leap?"

"He tried, and was thrown into a mud puddle."

"No bodily harm, I hope."

"No; beaver and broadcloth were the principal sufferers. But his conceit is shaken out of him for twenty-four hours, at least."

"Then I have wrought a miracle, and can claim to be canonized on the strength of it."

"I hope you may be; but I never expected to see your name in the calendar of saints."

"As you will not allow me to be a saint, I suppose you consider me as mad. Sanctity and madness, they say, are of kin."

"A hair's breadth, or so, on this side madness."

"Then I am entitled to great credit for keeping my wits at all. What reasonable girl would not be driven mad with Mrs. Primrose to watch her, and disapprove of her, and correct her? Strange—is it not?—that some people—if Mrs. Primrose will allow me to use so inelegant an expression— are always rubbing one against the grain."

"To give you your due, I think you have paid off handsomely any grudge you may owe in that quarter."

"There is consolation in that. Tell me—you are of the out-spoken sort— are you not of my opinion? Let me know your mind. Mr. Stubb is— —"

"A puppy."

"And the Primroses are— —"

"Uninteresting."

"For uninteresting, say insufferable. If Lucifer wishes to gain me over to his side, let Mrs. Primrose be made my guardian angel, and his work is done."

"Your horse has cast a shoe," said Morton, abruptly,—"yes; and he is lame besides."

"It is this broken, stony road. I wish we were at the end of it."

"So do I. If the clouds would break for a moment, and show us the sun, I could form some idea of the direction we are following."

"Why," said Fanny, in alarm, looking at her watch, "the sun must be very near setting."

Morton began to be very anxious, for his companion's sake, when, a moment after, they came upon a broader track, which intersected the other, and seemed a main thoroughfare of the woodcutters.

"This looks more promising," said Morton; and turning to the left, they pushed their horses to their best pace. Twilight came on, and it was quite dark when they emerged at length upon the broad and dusty highway. In a few minutes they saw a countryman, with his hands in his pockets, and a long nine between his lips, lounging by the roadside.

"How far is it to New Baden?"

"Wal," replied the man, after studying his querist in silence for about half a minute, "it's fifteen mile strong."

Morton looked at Fanny, whose horse was very lame, and who, in spite of her spirit, began to show unmistakable signs of fatigue.

"Is there a public house any where near?"

"Yas; it ain't far ahead to Mashum's."

"How far?"

"Rather better nor a mile."

On coming to the inn, Morton commended Fanny to the care of the landlady, an honest New Hampshire woman, remounted without delay, and urged his tired horse to such speed that he reached the hotel before half past nine. His arrival relieved the anxieties, or silenced the tattle of the inmates; and in the morning Fanny's uncle drove to the inn, and brought back the adventurous damsel to New Baden.

CHAPTER XIII

> Men will woo the tempest,
> And wed it, to their cost.—*Passion Flowers.*
>
> Then fly betimes, for only they
> Conquer love that run away.—*Carew.*

Morton had been for some time of opinion that he had better leave New Baden; yet still the philosophic youth staid on,—a week longer,—a fortnight longer,—and still he lingered. It would be too much to say that he was in love with his handsome, dare-devil cousin; but his mind was greatly troubled in regard to her—shaken and tossed with a variety of conflicting emotions. The multiplied and constantly changing phases of her character, its strong but utterly ungoverned resources, its frankness, enthusiasm, detestation of all deceit or pretension, and, in spite of her wildness, a deep vein of womanly tenderness which now and then betrayed itself, all conspired to keep his interest somewhat painfully excited.

One evening he left the crowded piazza of the hotel, and, intending to flirt with solitude and a cigar, walked towards a rustic arbor, overgrown with a wild grape vine, and standing among a cluster of young elms at the foot of the garden. As he drew near, he saw the gleam of ladies' dresses, and found the seats already occupied by Miss Fanny Euston and two companions. Morton knew them well, and joined the party. As neither the affected graces of the one companion nor the voluble emptiness of the other had much interest in his eyes, he directed his conversation chiefly to Fanny. In a few minutes the two girls exchanged glances, rose, and alleging some pretended engagement, returned to the hotel, bent on making this casual interview assume the air of a flirtation.

Morton and his companion sat for a moment in silence.

"We are cousins—are we not?" said the former, at length.

"At least they would call us so in the Highlands."

"Then give me a cousin's privilege, and allow me to be personal. Are you not out of spirits to-night?"

"Why do you think me so?"

"From your look and manner."

"Are you not tired to death of New Baden?"

"Not yet."

"I am. What is it all worth?—weary, and vapid, and flat, and stale, and unprofitable! I have had enough of it."

"Then why not change it?"

"To find the same thing in a new shape!"

"Pardon me if I call that a freak of the moment. You are the gayest of the gay."

"No, I am not."

"You are a belle here; a centre light. The moths flutter about you, though you do, now and then, singe their wings. You frighten them, and they repay you with fine speeches."

"I am weary of them. For Heaven's sake, abuse me a little. I know you have it often in your heart."

"Abuse is sometimes nothing but flattery in disguise."

"Why do you smile? That smile was at my expense."

"Why should you imagine so?"

"I insist on your telling me its meaning."

"I was only thinking that when tribute in an old shape has become wearisome, one may like to have it paid in a new one."

"That certainly is not flattery. Do you know I am beginning to be afraid of you?"

"I could not have thought you afraid of any one."

"Yes, I am afraid of you."

"Why?"

"Because you are always observing me. Because you penetrate my thoughts and understand me thoroughly."

"I am less deep than you suppose."

"At least you know all my faults. You are always, in a quiet way, making gibes and sarcasms at my expense, and touching upon my weakest points."

"Does it make you angry?"

"No; I rather like it; but I wish to repay you. I wish to find your weaknesses, but cannot. Have you any?"

"Yes, an abundance."

"And will you tell me what they are?"

"What, that you may use them against me! The moment you know them, you will attack me without mercy; and if you see me wince, it is all over with me."

"What do you mean?"

"I mean that you cease to like one as soon as you find that you can gain the least advantage over him. If I could really make you a little afraid of me, you would like me all the better for it. No, I will show you none of my weaknesses; and perhaps, if I did, you would not find them of a kind that you could use against me. I can strike at you, but you cannot hurt me. I am armed in proof. I defy you."

In saying this, at least, Morton showed some knowledge of his companion's character. To defy her successfully was a great step towards gaining her good graces; for with all her wildness she was very sensitive to the good or ill opinion of those who could compel her to respect them. She became very anxious to know what Morton thought of her.

"You say that you do not understand me thoroughly. What is there in me that you do not understand?"

"You may say that I do not understand you at all."

"That is mere evasion."

"Who can understand the language of Babel?"

"Do you mean that I speak the language of Babel?"

"Who can understand chaos?"

"And am I chaos? You are beginning your peculiar style of compliment again."

"Do not be displeased at it. All the power and beauty of the universe rose out of chaos."

"Now you are flattering in earnest."

"You are difficult to satisfy. What may I call you? A wild Arab racer without a rider?"

"That will answer better."

"Or a rocket without a stick?"

"I have seen rockets; but I do not know what the stick is. What is it? What is it for?"

"To give balance and aim to the rocket—make it, as the transcendentalists say, mount skyward, and end in stars and 'golden rain.'"

"Very fine! And how if it has no stick?"

"Then it sparkles, and blazes, and hisses on the ground; flies up and down, this way and that, plays the deuce with every thing and every body, and at last blows itself up to no purpose."

"Ah, I see that the stick is very necessary. I will try to get one."

"You speak in a bantering tone," said Morton, "but you are in earnest."

"I am in earnest!" exclaimed Fanny Euston, with a sudden change of voice and manner. "Every word that you have spoken is true. I am driven hither and thither by feelings and impulses,—some bad, some good,—chasing every new fancy like so many butterflies or will-o'-the-wisps,—without thinking of results—restless—dissatisfied—finding no life but in the excitement of the moment. Sometimes I have hints of better things. Glimpses of light break in upon me; but they come, and they go again. I have no rule of life, no guiding star."

Morton looked at his companion not without a certain sense of victory. He saw that he had gained, for the moment at least, an influence over her, and roused her to the expression of feelings to which, perhaps, she had never given utterance before. Yet his own mind was any thing but tranquil. Something more than admiration was stirring within him. He felt impelled to explore farther the proud spirit which had already yielded up to him some of its secrets. But he felt that, with her eyes upon him, he could not speak without committing himself farther than he was prepared to do. In this dilemma he determined to retreat—a resolution for which he was entitled to no little credit, if its merit is to be measured by the effort it cost him. He rose from his seat.

"Find your star, Fanny, and you may challenge the world. But I see people coming down the garden towards us. We shall be invaded if we stay here. Let us walk back towards the house."

When he found himself alone again, he paced his room in no very enviable frame of mind.

"What devil impelled me to speak as I did? It was no part of mine to be telling her of her faults. Am I turning philanthropist and busybody? If I wished to gain her heart, I suspect I have been taking the right course. What with any other lady would have been intolerable presumption and arrogance, is the most effectual way to win her esteem. And why should I not wish to gain her heart? There is good there in abundance, if one could but depend on it. No; I am not blinded yet. This last outburst was a momentary impulse, like all the rest; and to-morrow she will be reckless as ever. She delights in lawlessness, and rejoices in the zest of breaking established bounds. Her wayward will is like a cataract, and may carry her, God knows whither. No; I will not walk in this path; I will not try to marry her. Her heart is untouched—that is clear as the day. I wish she could say as much of mine. I will leave this place to-morrow, cost what it will."

A letter from Boston gave him a pretext; and bidding farewell to his cousin and her mother, he took the early train homewards. The newsboy brought him a paper, and his eyes rested on the columns; but his thoughts centred on Fanny Euston and his last evening's conversation with her at the foot of the garden.

CHAPTER XIV

> * * * *One fire burns out another's burning,*
> *One pain is lessened by another's anguish;*
> *Turn giddy, and be holp by backward turning;*
> *One desperate grief cures with another's languish.*
> *Take thou some new infection to thine eye,*
> *And the rank poison of the old will die.* —Romeo and Juliet.

All day the train whirled along, and Morton's troubled thoughts found no rest.

"Matherton!" cried the conductor, opening the door of the car, as the engine stopped in a large station house, at five o'clock in the afternoon. Several passengers got out; two or three came in; the bell rang, and with puffing and clanking, the train was on its way again. A newsboy passed down the car with a bundle of newspapers and twopenny novels. Morton bought one of the latter as an anodyne; but even "Orlando Melville, or the Victim of the Press Gang," failed to produce the desired soporific effect, and his thoughts soon recurred to their former channel. Suddenly a violent concussion, a crashing, thumping, and grating sound, the outcries of a hundred passengers,—the women screaming, and some of the men not silent,—with a furious rocking and tossing of the car, ejected every thought but one of his personal safety. All sprang to their feet, he among the rest. The first distinct impression which his mind received was that of the man in front of him making a flying leap out of the open window of the car, carrying the sash with him—a dexterous piece of gymnastics, only to be accounted for by the fact that the performer was a distinguished artist of the Grand National Olympic Circus. His boots twinkled at the window, and he was gone, alighting on his feet like a cat, but Morton was too much frightened to laugh. In a few moments the car came to a rest, without being overturned, though the front was partly broken in, and the whole swung off the rails to an angle of forty-five degrees. On looking out at the window, the first object that met Morton's eye was the baggage car, thrown on its side, with the door uppermost. As he looked, the door opened, and a head emerged—like a triton from the deep, or Banquo's ghost from a trap door— white with wrath and fright, and swearing with wonderful volubility. Then appeared another, rising by the side of the first, equally pallid, but much less profane. The heads belonged to two men, who had been seated in the compartment of the baggage car allotted to the mails, and when it was flung off the track, had been rattled together like dice in a box, suffering various bruises, but no serious harm. The breaking of the defective cast iron axle of the tender had caused the whole disaster, which would doubtless have produced fatal consequences had not the train been moving at a very slow rate. As it happened, a few contusions were its worst results, and one of the morning papers,

"for profound
And solid lying much renowned,"

solemnly averred that none but Providence was responsible for it.

There was abundant noise and vociferation. The passengers left the train, some lending their bungling aid to repair the mischief, while others withdrew to an inn which chanced to be in the neighborhood. After looking for a time at the downfallen tender and the uprooted rails, Morton, from some idle impulse, entered the car which he had lately left. It was empty; and, passing through it, he looked into that immediately behind, which had remained safely upon the rails. This also was empty, with the exception of a single person, a young female figure, seated at one of the windows. She was closely veiled, yet there was in her air that indefinable something which told Morton at a glance that she was a lady. He stepped to the ground, conjecturing whether or no she had a companion.

Five minutes after, glancing at the window, he saw the solitary traveller seated in the same position as before, and became convinced that she was unattended. The women in the train had left it at the outset. The busy and clamorous throng of men alone remained; and Morton easily conceived that her situation must be an embarrassing one. He therefore reëntered the car and approached her.

"I am afraid we shall be detained here for two or three hours, and perhaps till late at night. There is a public house a little way off, to which the ladies in the train have gone. If you will allow me, I will show you the way."

So he spoke; or, rather, so he would have spoken; but he had scarcely begun when the veiled head was joyfully raised, and the veil was thrown aside, disclosing to his astonished eyes the features of Edith Leslie. She explained that she was on her way from her father's country seat at Matherton; and that he was to meet her at the station on the arrival of the train. When the accident took place, she had been led to suppose, from the conversation of two men near her, that the train would not be very long detained, and had preferred remaining in the car to mingling with the tumultuous throng outside.

"It is too fine an afternoon," said Morton, as they left the spot, "to be mured in that tavern. This lane has an inviting look. Have you a mind to explore it?"

They walked accordingly in the direction he proposed; and, as they did so, Morton cast many a stolen glance at the face of his companion. The mind of the young philosopher was that day in a peculiarly susceptible state. It seemed as if Fanny Euston had kindled within him a flame which could not fix itself upon her, yet must needs find fuel somewhere; and as his eye met that of Edith Leslie, he began to feel that she held a deeper place in his thoughts than he had ever before suspected.

By the side of the lane stood an ancient abode, whose rotten shingles supported a rich crop of green mosses; and in the yard an old man, who looked like a relic of Bunker Hill fight, was diligently chopping firewood.

"What does this lane lead to?" asked Morton, looking over the fence.

The woodchopper leaned on his axe, wiped his brows with the tatters of a red handkerchief, and seemed revolving the expediency of communicating the desired information.

"Well," he returned, after mature reflection, "if you go fur enough, it'll take you down to the Diamond Pool."

"The Diamond Pool," said Miss Leslie; "that has a promising sound."

The lane soon began to lead them down the side of a rugged hill, between barberry bushes and stunted savins, with neglected stone walls, where the striped ground squirrels chirruped as they dodged into the crevices. In a few moments they had a glimpse of the water, shining between the branches of the trees below.

"Upon my word," said Morton, as they stood on the margin, "the Diamond Pool is not to be despised. We have chosen our walk well, and found a tempting place of rest at the end of it."

"A grassy bank,—a clear spring, with cardinal flowers along the edge—a cluster of maple trees——"

"And a flat rock at the foot of one of them, for you to rest upon. We are well provided for."

"Except that a seat for you seems to have been forgotten."

"No, if I wish to rest, this mound of grass will serve my turn. I am used to bivouacs."

The sun had just vanished behind the rocky hill on the farther side of the water; a sea of liquid fire, clouds blazoned in gold and crimson, betokened his recent presence. The lake lay like a great mirror framed in green. Another sunset glowed in its depths; rocks, hills, and trees grew downward; and the kingfisher, as he flitted over it, made a dash at the surface, as if to peck at the adversary bird, which seemed shooting upward to meet him.

"One might imagine," said Miss Leslie, "that we were a hundred miles away from railroads, factories, and all abominations of the kind."

"They will follow soon," said Morton; "they are not far off. There is no sanctuary from American enterprise."

"I know it is omnipotent at spoiling a landscape; but I hope that this one may escape,—at least if there is no mill privilege in the neighborhood."

"There is—an excellent one—at the outlet of the pond, beyond the three elms yonder. I prophesy that in five years there will be a brick factory on that meadow, with a row of one story houses for the operatives."

"It will be a scandal and a profanation. It is too beautiful for such base uses. But at least that old cedar tree, rooted in a cleft of the precipice, has found a safe sanctuary. There it was growing in King Philip's time; in its younger days it saw Indian wigwams standing on this bank; and there its offspring will grow after it, safe from Yankee axes."

"One cannot be sure of that. A time will come yet, when those rocks will be blasted to build a town hall, or open another railroad track."

"But they cannot build railroads and factories in the clouds. Our New England sunsets will still remain to remind one that there is an ideal side of life—something in it besides locomotives and cotton gins."

"There it is that you are wiser than we are. You are mistresses of a domain of which men, for the most part, know little or nothing."

"Pray what domain may that be?"

"One that is all mystery to me—a world of thoughts and sentiments which to most men is a cloudland, an undiscovered country, of which they may possibly recognize the existence, but of whose geography they know nothing."

"Why should they be more ignorant of it than women?"

"Because they are commonly given over to practicalities, mixed hopelessly with rivalries and ambitions. Even in their highest pursuits, they propose to themselves some definite point to be gained, some object to be achieved; but women are left to the world of their own minds—there they can expatiate at will."

"That is a dangerous privilege."

"They have leisure to muse on the joys and troubles of life, and explore depths which we bridge over."

"Either your mind has very much changed, or I have very much mistaken it. Pardon me, but I fancied that you were like Iago, 'nothing if not critical;' or at least that you sympathized with his slanderous opinions of womankind."

"Heaven forbid! What treasonable thought did you suppose me to harbor against the better part of humanity?"

"At all events, I never supposed you to believe that the better part of humanity passed their leisure time in metaphysical reveries and abstruse meditations."

"You were speaking, just now, of ideals. May not I have mine?"

"So your ideal woman is a transcendental philosopher, seated in the midst of your undiscovered cloudland."

"Deliver me from such a one! My ideal is full of thought and of feeling; but no one yet ever dreamed of branding her as a philosopher. But why did you think me so very critical? I am hardly old enough yet to make an Iago or a Rochefoucault."

"And yet you used always to have some saying of Rochefoucault at your tongue's end."

"I detest him, nevertheless, for a French Mephistopheles,—and all his tribe with him."

"When I said as much, you always told me that his sayings had a great deal of truth in them."

"And have they not a great deal of truth?"

"I cannot pretend to know mankind well enough to answer; but I sincerely hope, not much. Life would be worse than a blank if men and women were what he represents them to be."

"I think not; for if one cannot learn to be enthusiastic in regard to the actualities of human nature, he can console himself by a boundless faith in its possibilities. And now and then, thank God,—Rochefoucault to the contrary notwithstanding,—one finds the possibility realized."

His companion made no reply; and Morton stood for a moment with his eyes bent upon her face, which, to his enamoured fancy, seemed to reflect the calm beauty of the landscape on which she was gazing. He thought of Fanny Euston; he recalled his last evening's conversation with her, and felt blindly impelled to give some form of expression to the feeling which began to master him.

"Miss Leslie, were you ever in a storm at sea?"

"Yes, in a slight one; but the ship was strong; there was very little danger."

"Then you were never flung about, as I have been, in an indifferent egg shell of a craft, out of sight of land, at the mercy of winds and waves."

"I did not know that you had been at sea. Ah, yes, you were at school in France, when you were a boy—were you not?"

"Yes; but this happened since I have become a man, and not long ago. I think I shall never forget it. The sun was bright at one moment, and all was black as a hurricane the next. The wind came from every point of the compass—always shifting, never resting. I had not an instant's peace. It was all watching—all anxiety—and yet there was a kind of pleasure in it. If I had had wings, I doubt if I should have found heart to use them. It was a strange gale. It blew hot and cold by fits; I thought I should lose my reckoning altogether, and be blown away, body and soul."

"Really, I cannot imagine where your tempest is going to carry you."

"Nor could I; when, of a sudden, I found myself safe on shore. My good star led me to a place beautiful as the May sunshine could make it; a scene where art and nature were blended so harmoniously, that they seemed to have grown together from the same birth; full of repose, and tranquil, graceful power; such a scene, in short, as made me wish that Nature would embody herself in a visible form, that I might swear homage to her forever."

Had an interpreter been needed, Morton's look and voice must have betrayed, at least, some part of his meaning. The color deepened slightly on his companion's cheek, but she replied, without any further sign of consciousness,—

"I never knew that you were quite so ardent a votary of nature. You had better put your emotions into verse, and sell them to the magazines, after the true poetic custom. In a little time, I don't doubt, Dr. Griswold would find a place for you in his constellation of poets."

"Ah," said Morton, "it is cruel of you to fling cold water on my rhapsodies. But my flight is over. And now I will try my best to gain the esteem in your eyes of a man of sense and a sound mind."

"And now those night-hawks over head are beginning to tell us that we had better go back to the railroad. I suppose you will place it among the other frailties of women; but I cannot help being a little afraid that if we stay longer, that crippled train will run away and leave us behind."

"Then good night to the Diamond Pool," said Morton, as they left the place. "I shall not forget it; I owe it double thanks. It has shown me a pretty landscape, and made me a wiser man."

"I can hardly see how that may be."

"It has taught me not to speak too earnestly with my friend, lest she should banter me; and by no means to be drawn into any absurdity, lest she should laugh at me outright."

"Do you mean that you thought that I laughed at you?"

"Did you not?"

"If I gave you cause to think that I did, I can only say, frankly and heartily, that I am very sorry for it."

"Now I am emboldened to be absurd again, and speak more parables. I have found a locked-up treasure — a sealed fountain. I long to open it, but cannot."

"Your figures are too deep for me. I can make nothing of them."

"Then I will sink to plain prose. I have a friend whose heart is full of warm feeling and earnest thought; but, out of reserve, or Heaven knows what, she will express it to nobody but one or two intimate companions. She tantalizes the rest with a bantering word; and sometimes, when she is most in earnest, she seems to be most in jest. But why do you smile?"

"Ask your friend Mr. Sharpe. He is your friend — is he not?"

"I suppose so, though he is old enough to be my father. But why should I ask him?"

"Because he once described to me a person very much like the one you have just described."

"Who was the person?"

"Mr. Sharpe said that, though he was in general quite frank and undisguised, yet, if he were particularly in earnest on any subject, he was apt to speak lightly of it, or perhaps ridicule it, to hide his real feeling."

"Pray, who was this person? What was his name?"

"Mr. Vassall Morton."

"Did Sharpe say that of me? It is not a month since I was walking with him,—his evening constitutional,—and he said the very same thing of you. Now, as I hope to live an honest man, I was never half so much flattered in my life, as by being slandered in such company."

Here he was interrupted abruptly, for, turning a corner, they came full upon the inn, or hotel, as its sign proclaimed it to be. Discontented male passengers were lounging about the bar room; disconsolate female passengers sat, in bonnets and shawls, in the parlor; and an unspeakable air of uneasiness and discomfort pervaded the whole place.

"Our walk is over," sighed Morton; "I wish it had a more propitious ending. And now let me be your courier, or do your commands in any other capacity in which I can serve you."

At eleven o'clock that night the train rolled into the station house at Boston, some four hours behind its time.

"My father will certainly be here," said Miss Leslie; but her father was nowhere to be seen. Morton conducted her to a carriage. Her trunks and his own had already been placed upon it, when, by the lantern of one of the porters, Morton descried the agitated colonel threading the crowd in anxious search of his daughter. He had been waiting nervously since seven o'clock, and, when the train came in, had looked for her in every place but the right one. Morton hastened to relieve his fears.

"What do you mean to do with yourself to-night?" Leslie asked, as the carriage drove towards his house.

"Drive to my house in the country."

"Your people will not expect you, and will be in bed before you can get there. You had much better come home with me."

Morton was but too glad to accept the invitation.

Having bade good night to his host and his host's daughter, he passed some hours in dreamy cogitation; then tried to sleep; but sleep long kept aloof, the consciousness of being under the same roof with Edith Leslie brought with it so strange a sensation. But as delicate health, that grand auxiliary of sentiment, was quite unknown to him, nature prevailed in the end, and at seven the next morning, a servant's knock wakened him from a deep sleep, a vision of Mount Katahdin, and an imaginary moose hunt.

CHAPTER XV

Yet even these joys dire jealousy molests,
And blackens each fair image in our breasts.—*Lyttleton.*

Descending to the breakfast room, he found Leslie, as usual, quiet, cordial, and gentlemanly, beguiling the moments of expectancy with a newspaper, while his daughter presided at the coffee urn. Leslie happened to be in a garrulous mood, and talked incessantly about his former military frontier life, of which, though he had detested it in the experience, he was very fond in the retrospect. Morton, who had some acquaintance with such matters, was a tempting auditor, though he would gladly have exchanged the profuse anecdotes of white-wolf running and deer shooting for a few moments' conversation with Miss Edith Leslie. This her father's busy tongue put out of the question; but Morton consoled himself with the thought that to bask in her presence was, in itself, no mean privilege.

His cup of nectar, such as it was, was in a few minutes dashed with gall; for the street door opened without a summons from the bell, a man's step sounded in the hall, and Horace Vinal came in, with a bundle of papers in his hand.

Vinal had become of late all-important to his former guardian. He was his chief business agent, and Leslie was never tired of expatiating on his talents, energy, application, and elevated character. In short, he was fast becoming dependent on him, and felt towards him the affection which a weak and kindly man may feel towards one of far greater force and capacity, whom he believes sincerely attached to him and devoted to his interests.

Vinal, as he entered, had the air of a man versed in affairs, and acquainted both with that vast and various theatre which men call the world, and with those conventional circles which ladies call the world. He had been absent for a few days on a mission of business, from which he had returned the evening before. Leslie received him with a most warm greeting, and his daughter with a smile of easy friendship, which was wormwood to the troubled spirit of Morton. The two rivals—for such, by a common instinct, each felt the other to be—regarded each other with faces of courtesy and hearts of wrath.

"How came this fellow here?" thought Vinal, as he smilingly grasped his classmate's hand.

"The devil take him!" thought Morton, as he returned the greeting, but with a much worse grace.

They seated themselves on opposite sides of the table, while the Helen who had kindled this covert warfare in their breasts dispensed a cup of coffee to each in turn.

There was a singular contrast between the adversaries. On the one side, the self-dependent Vinal, with little health and no other wealth than his busy and able brain; with thin features, wan cheek, and pale, firm lip; with piercing observation and rapid judgment; self-contained, self-controlled, self-confiding. But for his measuring five feet ten, he might have stood for Dryden's Achitophel:—

"A fiery soul, which, working out its way,
Fretted the pygmy body to decay,
And o'er informed the tenement of clay."

On the other side sat the pet of fortune, fondled, if he could have endured such blandishment, in the very lap of affluence; with a cheek brown with wind and weather, and an eye which, as he often boasted, could look the sun in the face. His nature was so happily tempered, that to the degree of nervous stimulus which engenders, or is engendered by, an energetic character, he joined an indefinite capacity both of endurance and enjoyment; and yet the possessor of all these gifts was just now in a mood of extreme dissatisfaction and discomfort.

Leslie began to speak with Vinal upon business. Morton snatched the opportunity to converse with the person most interesting to him. Vinal glanced at him askance. Each began to hate the other, after his own fashion. Morton would gladly have come to open rupture, and flung defiance at his rival; but Vinal was far remote from any wish of the kind.

Morton remained at the house as long as he in decency could, and then bade them good morning, execrating Vinal as he went down the steps.

That very afternoon, as he was walking near his cottage in the country, ruminating on Edith Leslie and Horace Vinal, he raised his head and saw a lady and gentleman, on horseback, emerging into view from a wooded bend of the road. A thrill ran through him from head to foot. They were the two persons of whom he was thinking. He bowed to Miss Leslie. She replied with a frank bow and smile; and Vinal, as he passed, made an easy nonchalant gesture of recognition. The jealous pedestrian turned and looked after them. They had ridden a few rods when Vinal also turned his head, but, catching Morton's eye, instantly averted it again. Morton fairly ground his teeth with anger and vexation. To be jealous was bad enough; but that Vinal should be conscious of his jealousy, and perhaps triumph in it, goaded him beyond endurance. He went home, saddled and bridled a horse with his own hands, mounted, and ranged the country for an hour or two, to get rid of the vulture that was preying on him. At length he grew more rational, and was able to reflect that Vinal's riding with Miss Leslie did not necessarily imply that he stood, in any special sense, within her favor, since he was the near relative of her mother-in-law, and had formerly been for years an inmate of her father's house.

On the next day, at a time when he thought that Vinal must be safe in his office, Morton took heart of grace, and called on Miss Leslie. An old woman, an ancient dependant of the family, raised, as she would have phrased it, in the backwoods of Matherton, opened the door.

"Is Miss Leslie at home?"

"No; she was took sick yesterday, very sudden."

"Miss Leslie!" ejaculated the visitor.

"Yes; the doctor says she's goin' to die, sartin; right away, may be."

"What?" gasped Morton.

"It wasn't only this morning we heered on it," said the old Yankee housekeeper, "and Miss Edith's gone up to Matherton, to tend on her."

"O, you mean Mrs. Leslie."

"Yes; Miss Leslie, Miss Edith's mother-in-law; she never was a well woman, ever since I've knowed her."

And the old woman closed the door; while Morton walked away, without knowing in what direction he was moving.

CHAPTER XVI

Sganarelle. O, la grande fatigue quo d'avoir une femme, et qu'Aristote a bien raison quand il dit qu'une femme est pire qu'un démon! —*Le Médecin Malgré Lui.*

Thus day by day and month by month we past;
It pleased the Lord to take my spouse at last—*Pope.*

It was nine years since, in an evil hour, Leslie had first seen Miss Cynthia Everille, playing on a harp, and accompanying herself in a thin, sweet voice, with words of her own composing. His weak heart succumbed: he fell in love off hand; and within a year after the death of his first wife, Edith's mother, her picture was taken from the wall, and a second Mrs. Leslie reigned in her stead.

"Sweet," —"charming," —"fascinating," —were the least of the adjectives lavished on the interesting bride. Some of his lady acquaintance felicitated him that he had espoused an angel, an embodied beatitude not more than half pertaining to this world. In fact, there was a certain aerial grace in her movements, a certain translucency in her small alabaster features, which might countenance such a notion. The winning smile, too, with which she met her visitors on her reception Thursdays, savored wholly of the angelic. She breathed courtesies around her as the beneficent royalty of Naples scatters sugar plums among his loving subjects at the carnival, and, on the next day, sends them to prison by the cart load.

The tyranny of the strong is bad enough; but the tyranny of the weak is intolerable; and this latter visitation came upon Leslie in its most rueful form—that, namely, whose weapons are sobs, sighs, vapors, and the dire coercion of hysteric fits. He was a soft-hearted fool, and a fair subject for such oppression. Not that his newly-installed mistress—his mistress, since she made him her slave—was naturally of an ill temper. On the contrary, she was somewhat amiable, or, at least, much given to tears and tenderness; but in process of time, this profuse sensibility had all centred on herself. In short, she was profoundly selfish, though nothing could have astonished her more than to tell her so; for, in her own eyes, she seemed a miracle of sensibility, as indeed she was, though her sensibility had learned to give little response to any woes but her own. What these woes might be would be hard to say: she had a wonderful talent for finding and inventing grievances. She was submerged and drowned in a sentimental melancholy, which wore in turn ten thousand different aspects, each worse than the other. She was a sea-anemone, covered with a myriad of filaments, all more shrinking and sensitive than a snail's horns.

One reads of famished wretches who have tried to nourish life from the current of their own veins. So, in a figurative sense, did she. She was always anatomizing her own ridiculous heart; groping among the depths of her own sickly fancies, and making them her daily food. She was a busy gatherer of tokens, souvenirs, and mementoes, and was beset with blighted hopes, vain longings, sad remembrances, and all the spectral ills engendered between a frail mind and a depraved stomach. She was a great reader, and floated rudderless through a sea of books, fishing out of it all that was tender, morbid, and despairing, and stowing it up in albums.

It may be thought that some disconsolate memory, some affection nipped in the bud, or the like catastrophe, had brought her to this pass. Far from it. She mourned that her fate had been too flat and sterile; that the rapturous emotions of her heart had never been awakened; that no sentimental passion, in short, had ever stirred her soul from its depths. This was the grievance which rankled most in her reveries. To give her her due, she never told it to her husband; but she brooded upon it in secret; and the result was, a multitude of affecting verses, which she treasured in her album as anonymous.

Leslie, though none of the wisest of men, was one of the most amiable; and, under his wife's discipline, he learned to be one of the most discreet. It behooved him to be watchful and circumspect. His married life was a voyage through shoals and shallows, and needed sagacious pilotage; for no common eye could see where the danger lay. There was an endless variety of subjects tabooed to him; matters to all appearance quite indifferent, but to which he must never allude, because, Heaven knows how, they touched some trembling susceptibility, or wakened some grievous memory from its blessed sleep. The penalty, if the case were mild, would be a deep-drawn sigh; if more aggravated, a flood of tears; if extreme, an hysteric fit. And if, in his efforts to console her, he ventured to add any thing in the form of remonstrance, or let fall any word which might intimate that her conduct was not quite reasonable, the outraged sufferer would cease weeping, cast up her eyes reproachfully, and murmuring, "O William, is it come to this?" relapse again instantly into the depths of sobbing affliction. It was only by the most abject submission, coupled with all the resources of conjugal eloquence, that Leslie could succeed at length in purchasing a look of resignation and a faint smile of forgiveness.

Use, it is said, will blunt the sharpest of troubles. In time, he became acclimated to his fate; yet, on one or two occasions, his equanimity was quite overset. He thought that his wife was losing her wits; for, as he came into her room, she fixed on him a melting gaze, sank on his shoulder, and flooded him with such a freshet of tears, that he might have complained with De Bracy, that a water fiend possessed her. The truth was, she had just been musing on her own dissolution, and imagining, in a luxury of woe, her own funeral, with all the circumstance of that sad event. As she looked around and bethought her how desolate that chamber would be when she was gone, and how each trifle that had once been hers would be treasured by those she left behind, her sensitive heart had dissolved in tenderness, and produced the hydraulic demonstration just mentioned.

This libel on womankind became the mother of a pair of twins—the same infant prodigies whom Morton had seen at the White Mountains. Both perished at the age of seven, their precocious brains having by that time usurped all the vitality of their miserable little bodies. She was inconsolable at their death, though, while they lived, her delicate nerves could seldom abide their presence for five minutes at a time.

There was once an idiot, who, being of a conciliating temper, thought to appease a fire and persuade it to go out by feeding it with fuel till it should be satisfied, and crave no more. On the same principle Leslie tried to satisfy the exacting spirit of his wife by a most watchful and anxious devotion to all her whims; but the greater his devotion, the more exacting she grew. She felt her power, and used it without mercy. She was, withal, intolerably jealous, not so much of any living rival, as of the memory of a dead one, Leslie's former wife. Here, indeed, she had some show of reason; for the poles are not wider asunder than were the characters of herself and her predecessor.

Those who had known the latter in her maidenhood—she married young, or perhaps she would never have married Leslie—knew her as the dominant belle of the season, conspicuous for her beauty, her position, and for a degree of culture rare in America at that time; devoted and ardent towards a few close friends, haughty and distant towards the many; greatly loved by her few intimates, and either greatly admired or greatly disliked by most others around her. Those who knew her in the last years of her life knew her as one who had passed through a fiery ordeal. Of her many children, only one was left. They had fallen around her in a sudden and sharp succession, till it seemed to her that a destroying doom had gone forth against her race, and that the world of her affections was turned to a field of carnage. Leslie felt the shock acutely, not to say intensely, for a while; but the storm passed, and left on him very little trace. It sank into the deeper nature of his wife with such a penetrating sense of the vanity of life and the rottenness of mortal hope, as, in the olden time, drew saints and anchorites to renounce the world and give themselves to penance and seclusion. It made no anchorite of her. She rose from her baptism of fire saddened, but not broken nor unstrung; with a rooted faith and an absolute resignation; a nice perception of all human suffering; sympathies broad and embracing as the air; a benevolence pervading as the sunshine; and a spirit so calm in its elevation that no wind of calamity had power to ruffle it.

Edith Leslie was a child when her mother died, yet old enough to feel the loss profoundly, and to be greatly shocked and cast down at the alacrity with which her father contrived to forget it. Having reduced Leslie to obedience, his bride essayed the same experiment on his daughter, but failed notably. There was something in the nature of the latter which revolted so impatiently against the selfish caprices and morbid fooleries which were played off hourly before her,—she was so indignant, moreover, at seeing her father sunk inch by inch in the slough of matrimonial thraldom,—that the issue might easily have been a protracted household feud. None but herself could know with how costly an effort she schooled herself to patience. With a caustic wit, and a fervent fancy which haunted her with images of an ideal life brighter than the work-day world around her, a nature with impulses which, less curbed and tempered, might have carried her through all the mazes of morbid rebellion, she still bent herself to accept her lot as she found it, in the full faith that flowers may be taught to grow on the flintiest soil. And now that the imagined maladies of a lifetime were turned at last into a mortal reality, and her step-mother lay on her death bed, Edith Leslie watched by her side with as much care as if this wretched piece of perverted sensibility had deserved her affection and esteem.

CHAPTER XVII

> Beshrew me, but I love her heartily,
> For she is wise, if I can judge of her;
> And fair she is, if that mine eyes be true;
> And true she is, as she hath proved herself;
> And therefore, like herself, wise, fair, and true,
> Shall she be placed in my constant soul.—*Merchant of Venice.*

A week after he had heard the tidings from the old housekeeper, Morton saw Dr. Steele coming out of a patient's door and getting into his chaise.

"Good morning, Dr. Steele."

"Sir, your servant," said the old-fashioned doctor.

"I'm sorry to hear that Mrs. Leslie is so ill."

"It's very sad," said the doctor. "Now, what the deuse is this young fellow stopping me for?"—this was his internal comment.

"I hope you don't despair of her."

"Well, sir, she will hold out to-morrow, and the next day, too."

"I beg your pardon. Your check rein is loose. Let me make it right."

"Thank you, Mr. Morton," said the doctor, somewhat mollified.

"Ahem!—Colonel Leslie is well, I hope."

"Apparently so, sir."

"And—ahem!—his family, too."

"I wasn't aware he had a family."

"I mean—that is to say—his daughter—Miss Leslie."

The shrewd doctor turned his gray eyes sideways on the querist.

"Ah, his daughter. What did you wish to know of her, sir?"

"Merely to inquire——" said Morton, stammering and blushing visibly. "I mean only to ask if she is well."

"I know nothing to the contrary. She seemed very well when I brought her down from Matherton last evening. I dare say, though, she can tell you herself a great deal better than I can. Good morning, Mr. Morton."

And with a slight twinkle in his eye, Dr. Steele drove off.

Morton looked after the chaise, as it lumbered down the street.

"May I be hanged and quartered if I ever question you again; you are too sharp, by half."

The doctor's information was very welcome, however; and, armed with an anxious inquiry after her mother's health, Morton proceeded to call upon Miss Leslie. She had come to the city, as he had already judged, on some mission connected with the wants of the invalid, and was to go back to Matherton, with Dr. Steele, in the afternoon.

Thenceforward, for a week or upwards, he saw her no more; but, during the interval, he contrived, by various expedients, to keep himself advised of the condition and movements of the family at Matherton. Among other incidents, he became aware of two visits made them by Vinal, and was tormented, in consequence, with an unutterable jealousy. One morning he met the purblind old housekeeper, mousing along in spectacles through the crowded street, and, stopping her, to her great alarm and perplexity, he made his usual inquiry concerning Mrs. Leslie's health. This investigation led to the discovery that Miss Edith was coming from Matherton that very afternoon.

Morton, upon this, grew so restless, that he could not refrain from going to the railroad station, a little before the train was to come in. And here his worst fear was realized; for he beheld, slowly pacing along the platform, the hated form of Horace Vinal. Morton retreated unseen, went into a neighboring hotel, and seated himself, a little withdrawn from a window, where he could see all that passed. The train arrived; and soon after Vinal appeared, conducting Miss Leslie to a carriage, with an air, as Morton thought, of the most anxious devotion. He grasped his walking stick, and burned with a feverish longing to break it across his rival's back.

He saw Miss Leslie on the next day, and thus added fuel to a flame which already burned high enough. In short, he found himself in that most profoundly serious and profoundly ridiculous of all conditions, the condition of being over head and ears in love, — and his zeal for science was merged utterly in a more engrossing devotion. By one means or another, he contrived to keep pace with the course of things at Matherton, and learned from day to day that Mrs. Leslie was worse, — that she seemed to revive a little, — that she was on the point of death, — that she was dead. By the time this sad climax was reached, he had been starving a fortnight from the sight of his mistress, having the consolation to know that meantime his rival had made at least four visits to Matherton.

One morning Morton was pacing the street in an abstracted mood, his looks bent on the bricks, when, chancing to look up, he saw those very eyes which his fancy had been that moment picturing, employed in guiding their owner's steps over a crossing towards him. As Edith Leslie stepped upon the sidewalk, she saw him for the first time. He bowed, joined her, spoke a few bungling words of condolence, and walked on at her side. After the fashion of those who are peculiarly anxious to appear at their best advantage, he appeared at his worst. And when his companion bade him good morning on the steps of her father's house, she left him in a most unenviable mood, muttering maledictions against himself and his fate, and brought, indeed, to the borders of despair. This depression, however, was not long in producing its reaction, under the influence of which, adopting his usual panacea against mental ailments, he mounted his horse, and spurred into the country.

Here, about sunset, he beheld a horseman, slowly pacing along the road in front. On this, he drew rein, and began to look about him for the means of escape; for in the person of the rider he recognized his classmate Wren, to whose society he was far from partial. Neither lane nor by-road was to be seen.

"At the worst," he thought, "it is but a mile or two;" and, setting forward at a trot again, he was in a moment at his classmate's side.

"How are you, Wren?"

"Ah, Morton, good evening," exclaimed Wren, with a graceful wave of his hand. "I'm delighted to see you. A charming evening—isn't it?"

"Charming."

"That's a fine horse you have."

"Tolerably good."

"Did you ever observe this fellow that I'm riding? Do you see how long and straight he is in the back? Well, that's the Arab blood that's in him. His grandfather was a superb Arab, that the Pacha of Egypt gave my uncle when he was travelling there;" and he proceeded to dilate at large on the merits and pedigree of his horse, the truth being that he and his ancestry before him had been born and bred in the State of Vermont. Morton listened with civil incredulity, and wished his companion at the antipodes.

"Ah, there's my cousin's house," exclaimed Wren, pointing to a very pretty cottage and grounds which they were approaching—"Mary Holyoke, you know—Mary Everard that was some three months ago. What a delightful retreat for the honeymoon!"

"Very," said Morton.

"Stop there with me, will you? I'm going in for a few minutes, to wish them a pleasant journey. They are going to Niagara to-morrow."

"Thank you, I believe I won't stop."

"As you please, my dear fellow. I think they are quite right to travel now; it's a better season than the spring; and a honeymoon journey, after all, isn't *all* romance, you know. Besides, they are going to have a charming companion—Miss Leslie."

"I thought that she had just lost her mother-in-law."

"That's the very thing. She's almost ill with watching night after night; so Mary,—they used to be friends at school,—has been very anxious that she should make the journey with them, for a change of scene, you know,—and Colonel Leslie has persuaded her to go."

"When will they leave town?"

"To-morrow. They mean to spend a few days at Trenton, and then go to the Falls. But here we are; won't you change your mind, and come in?"

"No, thank you. Good night."

"Good evening, then;" and waving his hand again, Wren trotted up the avenue.

"Virtue never goes unrewarded," thought Morton; "if I hadn't joined the fellow, I might not have known about this journey."

On the next day he discovered that they had actually gone, and that, as Wren had said, Niagara was to be the ultimatum of their tour. On the following morning, he himself took the western train, and made all speed for the Falls.

CHAPTER XVIII

If folly grows romantic, I must paint it.—*Pope*.

On the American side of the Niagara, a few miles below the Falls, is a deep chasm, bearing the inauspicious christening of the Devil's Hole. Near it there is—or perhaps was, for things have changed thereabouts—a path winding far down among rocks and forests, till it leads to the brink of the river. Here, darkened by the beetling cliffs and sombre forests, the Niagara surges on its way, like a compressed ocean, raging to break free. At the verge of this watery convulsion stood Holyoke and his wife, Miss Leslie, and Morton, whom they had chanced to meet that morning.

"It is very fine, no doubt," said the good-natured, though very shallow Mrs. Holyoke, "but I have no mind to take cold in these dark woods. If we stay much longer, I believe I shall go mad, looking at that rushing, foaming water, and throw myself in. Come, Harry, let us go back to daylight again."

"Just as you please," said the model husband, offering his arm.

"Come, Edith;—why, she really seems to like it;—Edith!—she don't hear me; no wonder, in all this noise;—Edith, we are going back to the upper world. You can stay here, if you please, with Mr. Morton."

But Miss Leslie chose to follow her friend; while Morton aided her up the rough path.

"I have observed," he said, as they came to smoother ground, "in our excursions yesterday and to-day, that Mrs. Holyoke has not much of your liking for rocks, trees, and water. I mean, that she has no great taste for nature."

"At all events, she has an eye for what is picturesque in it. She is an artist, you know, and paints in water colors extremely well."

"Yes, and whenever she sees a landscape, she thinks only how it would look on paper or canvas, and judges it accordingly. That is not a genuine love of nature. One does not value a friend for good looks, or dress, or air; and so, in the same way, is not a true fondness for nature independent, to some extent at least, of effects of form, or color, or grouping?"

"It does not imply, I think, any artistic talent, or even a good eye for artistic effect. And yet I cannot conceive of a great landscape artist being without it, any more than a great poet."

"If he were, he would be no better than a refined scene painter. We are in a commercial country; so pardon me if I use commercial language. This liking for nature is a capital investment. She is always a kind mistress, a good friend, always ready with a tranquillizing word, never inconstant, never out of humor, never sad."

"And yet sometimes she can speak sadly, too."

Edith Leslie said no more; but there came before her the remembrance of her long watchings in the room of the dying Mrs. Leslie, when, seated by the window, open in the hot summer nights, she had listened, hour after hour, mournfully, drearily, almost with superstitious awe, to the chirping of the crickets, the plaintive cry of the whippoorwill, and now and then the hooting of a distant owl.

"Here in America," continued Morton, "we ought to make the most of this feeling for nature; for we have very little else."

"And yet there is less of it here than in some other countries; in England, for instance."

"We are too busy for such vanities. Besides, we are just now in an unlucky position. A wilderness is one thing; savageness and solitude have a character of their own; and so has a polished landscape with associations of art, poetry, legend, and history."

"And we have destroyed the one, and have not yet found the other."

"And so, between two stools we fall to the ground."

"If you have a liking for a wilderness and primitive scenery, I don't think that you have much reason to complain; for you, at least, have contrived to see something of them."

"And you of the other sort; art and history wedded to nature; at Tivoli, for example,—at the Lake of Albano; where else shall I say?"

"Say, at Giardini, in Sicily."

"Why at Giardini? I never heard of it before."

"Not that the view there is finer than in some other places, though towards evening it is very beautiful. You see the ocean on one side, and the mountains on the other, covered to the top with orange, lemon, and olive trees, and Mount Etna rising above them all, with a spire of white smoke curling out of its crater, tinted with red, yellow, and purple, where the sunset strikes it. On the mountain above you there is an ancient theatre, where a Greek audience once sat on the stone benches, and after them, in their turn, a Roman. On the peak of the mountain over it is a Saracen castle, and, not far off, a Norman tower."

"So that the whole is an embodiment of poetry and history from the days of the Odyssey downwards."

"Nobody, I think, who has seen that eastern shore of Sicily can have escaped without some strong impression from it. The Fourrierites, you know, pretend to believe that the earth is a living being, with a soul, only a larger one, like ours that creep on the outside of it. One is sometimes tempted to adopt their idea, and fancy that the changing face of nature is the expression of the earth's thoughts, and its way of communicating with us."

"A landscape will sometimes have a life and a language,—that is, when one happens to be in the mood to hear it,—and yet, after all, association is commonly the main source of its power. The Hudson, I imagine, can match the Rhine in point of mere beauty; but a few ruined castles, with the memories about them, turn the tables dead against us."

"You have always—have you not?—had a penchant for the barbarism of the middle ages."

"Not for their barbarism, but for the germs of civilization that lay in the midst of it. Religion towards God, devotion towards women—these were the vital ideas of the middle ages."

"But how were those ideas acted on? Their religion was not much better than a mass of superstitions."

"Not more gross and vulgar than the spirit rapping superstition, the last freak into which this age of reason has stumbled. And, for the other idea, the fundamental idea of chivalry, we are beginning to replace it with woman's rights, Heaven deliver us!"

"Pardon me if I doubt whether ladies in the middle ages were better treated than they are now. The theory was admirable, no doubt, but the practice, if there were any, seems at this distance a little ridiculous."

"Chivalry was like Don Quixote, who stands for it—fantastic and absurd enough on the outside, but noble at the core."

"But you would not imply seriously that you would prefer the age of chivalry to this nineteenth century."

"No, the reign of shopkeepers is better than the reign of cutthroats. But the nineteenth century has no right to abuse the middle ages. The best feature of its civilization is handed down from them. That feeling which found a place in the rough hearts of our northern ancestry, half savages as they were, and gave to their favorite goddess attributes more high and delicate than any with which the Greeks and Romans, at the summit of their refinement, ever invested their Venus; the feeling which afterwards grew into the sentiment of chivalry, and, hand in hand with Christianity, has made our modern civilization what it is,—that is the heritage we owe to the middle ages, and for which we are bound to be grateful to them. It was a flower all the fairer for springing in the midst of darkness and barbarism; and now that we have it in a kinder soil, we can only hope that it is not fast losing its fragrance and brightness."

"Of that, I imagine, a woman is a very poor judge; but if it has lost its antique freshness, at all events we can enjoy it in peace and tranquillity, and be spared the risk of life and limb in gathering it. Those sweetbrier blossoms that grow yonder, down the side of the precipice, are very pretty, but it would require nothing less than a paladin, or a knight errant, made crazy with the hope of a smile, to get them and bring them up."

"Now it is you that asperse the present, and I that will defend it." And the words were hardly spoken before the young fool was over the edge of the cliff, scarcely hearing his companion's startled cry of remonstrance.

The rock sloped steeply to a few feet below the spot where the brier grew, and then sank in a sheer precipice of a hundred feet or more, so that if hand or foot had failed him, his career would have ended somewhat abruptly. To the spectatress above the danger seemed appalling; but, with the climber's practised eye and well-strung sinews, it was in fact very slight. Once, indeed, a fragment of stone loosened under his foot, and fell with a splintering crash upon the rocks below, followed by a shower of pebbles and gravel, rattling among the trees. But he soon reached his prize, secured it in his hatband, and grasping the friendly root of a spruce tree, drew himself up to the level top of the cliff.

Here he saw the fruit of his Quixotism. Edith Leslie, pale as death, seemed on the very verge of fainting. He sprang in great consternation to her aid, supported her to a rock near at hand, on which she could rest; and as her momentary dizziness passed away, she began to distinguish his eager words of apology and self-reproach.

"You will think that I have grown backward into a child again. Think what you will; I deserve your worst thought; only do not believe that I could fancy such paltry exploits and paltry risks could be a tribute worthy of you; or that you are to be served with such boy's service as that. Here are the flowers: throw them away, or keep them as a memento of my absurdity;

but let them remind you, at the same time, that wherever your wish points, there I would go, if it were into the jaws of fate."

Here, looking up, he saw the expediency of curtailing his eloquence; for not far off appeared their two companions, returning to look for them. Both Miss Leslie and he had much ado to explain, the one why her face was so pale, the other why his dress was so dusty and disordered. The carriage was waiting for them on the road near by; and their morning's excursion being finished, they proceeded towards it, Morton leading the way in silence.

His first feeling had been one of compunction and indignation at himself; but close upon it followed another, very different—a sense of mixed suspense and delight. What augury might he not draw from the pale cheek and fainting form of his companion?

CHAPTER XIX

For, in the days of yore, the birds of parts
Were bred to speak, and sing, and learn the liberal arts.
                                      The Cock and the Fox.

Thine is the adventure, thine the victory;
Well has thy fortune turned the dice for thee.
                                      Palamon and Arcite.

During the rest of the journey, Morton, on Mrs. Holyoke's invitation, was one of the party. Again and again he was impelled to learn his fate; but recoiled from casting the die, dreading that his hour was not come. Still, though every day more helplessly spell-bound, his mood was not despondent.

They came to the town of — —, a half day from home.

"My household gods are not far off," said Morton. "My father was born at Steuben, a few miles below, where my grandfather used to preach against King George, and stir up his parish to rebellion. I have relations there still, and have a mind to spend to-morrow with them."

This announcement proceeded much less from family affection than from another motive. Mrs. Holyoke saw it in an instant.

"Excellent! Then Miss Leslie can accept her friend's invitation to make a day's visit at this place; and you will meet her and escort her to Boston."

And Morton, much rejoiced at this successful issue of his diplomacy, repaired to his relatives at Steuben; Holyoke and his wife proceeded homeward; while Miss Leslie remained to accomplish the visit with her country friend.

Morton spent a quiet day in the primitive New England village, a place of which boyish association made him fond. On the next morning, Miss Leslie was to come to Steuben, with her hostess; but as there was an abundance of time before the train would appear, he strolled along a quiet road leading back into the country. He soon came to an old inn, over whose tottering porch King George's head might once have swung. Nothing human was astir. The ancient lilacs flaunted before the door; the tall sunflowers peered over the garden fence; the primeval well-sweep slanted aloft, far above the mossy shingles of the roof. The rural quiet of the place tempted him. He sat under the porch, and watched the swallows sailing in and out of the great barn whose doors stood wide open, on the opposite side of the road.

A voice broke the silence—a voice from the barn yard. It was the voice of a hen mother, the announcement that an egg was born into the world. Not the proud, exulting cackle which ordinarily proclaims that auspicious event, but a repining, discontented cry, now rising in vehement remonstrance with destiny, now sinking into a low cluck of disgust. Morton, skilled in the language of birds, construed these melancholy cacklings as follows:—

"Whither does all this tend? Why is my happiness blighted, my aspirations repressed? Why am I forever penned up within these narrow precincts, amid low domestic cares, and sordid, uncongenial, unsympathizing associates? And thou, my white and spotless offspring, what shall be thy fate? To be steeped in hot water, and eaten with a spoon? Or art thou to be the germ of an existence wretched as my own, doomed to a ceaseless round of daily parturition? O, weariness! O, misery! O, despair!"

And throwing her ruffled feelings into one indignant cackle, the hen was silent.

The advent of a human biped here enlivened the scene. This was a young gentleman on horseback, a collegian to all appearance, admirably mounted, but bestriding his horse with the look of one who has just passed his first course under the riding master, and rides by the book, as Touchstone quarrelled. This important personage, with an air oddly compounded of assumption and timidity, proceeded to call the hostler, and order oats for his horse, after which he strutted into the house, switching his leg with his whip.

As ample time remained, Morton continued his walk along the road, his mood in harmony with the brightness of the morning. He was in a humor to please himself with trifles. A ground squirrel chirruped at him from a crevice of the wall. He stood watching the small, shy visage, as it looked out at him. Then a red squirrel, a much livelier companion, uttered its trilling cry from a clump of hazel bushes. Morton seated himself on a stone very near it. The squirrel resented the intrusion, ran out on a fence rail towards the offender, chattered, scolded, swelled himself like a miniature muff, made his tail and his whole body vibrate with his wrath; then suddenly dodged down behind the rail and peered over it at the trespasser, his nose and one eye alone being visible; then bolted into full sight again, and scolded as before, jerking himself from side to side in the extremity of his petulance; till at last, without the smallest apparent cause, he suddenly wheeled about and fled, bounding like the wind along the top of the stone wall.

This interview over, Morton looked at his watch, saw that it was time to go back towards the village, and began to retrace his steps accordingly. He had gone but a few paces, when he saw a countryman, a simple-looking fellow, running at top speed, and in great excitement, up a byway, which led to the railroad, the latter crossing it by a high bridge, at some distance from the station.

"What's the matter?" demanded Morton.

"The railroad cars!" gasped the countryman.

"What of them?"

"They'll all go to smash, and no mistake."

"What!" cried Morton, aghast.

"Fact, mister. Some born devil has been and sawed the bridge timbers most through in the middle."

"What!" cried Morton again.

"Sure as I stand here! I seen the heaps of sawdust on the road. That's the way I come to take notice. The minute the locomotive gets on the bridge, down she'll go, and no two ways about it."

Morton had no doubt that the man was right. The newspapers, within the last few weeks, had contained various accounts of impediments, great and small, maliciously placed on railroads. It was a species of villany which was just then having its run, as incendiarism will sometimes have; and a like case of a bridge partly sawed through had lately occurred in a neighboring state.

"You fool!" exclaimed Morton, in anguish and despair; "why didn't you get on the track, and stop the train?"

"I'd like to see you stop the train!" retorted the man.

Morton turned to run for the road, bent on stopping the engine, or letting it pass over him. But as he turned, a new arrival caught his eye. This was the cavalier who had baited his horse at the inn, and who, seeing the excited looks of the two men, had checked his pace, and was looking at them with much curiosity.

Crazed with agitation, and hardly knowing what he did, Morton leaped towards him, seized his horse, a powerful and high-mettled animal, by the head, and, with a few broken words of explanation, called on him to dismount. The astonished collegian did not comply. Morton bore back fiercely on the bit; the horse plunged and snorted; the rider clutched the pommel; Morton took him by the arm, drew him to the ground, mounted at a bound after him, and, as he touched the saddle, struck his whalebone walking stick with all his force over the horse's flank. The horse leaped forward frantically, and rushed headlong down the road. His discarded rider saw his hoofs twinkling for an instant out of the cloud of dust, and thought he had had a Heaven-directed escape from a madman.

The small village above Steuben, at which Miss Leslie and her friend were to take the train, was three miles off. The road ran almost directly towards it for more than three fourths of the way, when it made a bend to the right. Morton, with his furious riding, very soon reached this point. He could see the station house before him, on the left, and not more than a third of a mile distant. The space between, though uneven, had no visible impediments but a few low fences and scattered clumps of bushes. Morton pushed through the barberry growth that fringed the road, galloped over the hard pasture, leaped one fence, passed a gap in another, and half way to his goal, found himself and his horse in a quagmire. At this moment, straining his eyes towards the cluster of houses, he saw, with agony at his heart, a white puff of vapor rising above the trees beyond. Then the dark outline of the train came into view, checking its way, and stopping, half hidden behind the buildings.

Morton knew that it would stop only for a moment, and plied his horse with merciless blows. The horse plunged through the mire,—the mud and water spouting high above his rider's head,—gained the firm ground, and bounded forward wild with fright and fury. It was too late. The bell rang, and with quicker and quicker pants, the engine began to move. Morton shouted,—gesticulated,—still it did not stop, though the passengers seemed to take alarm, for a head was thrust from every window, while the occupants of an open carriage drawn up on the road were bending eagerly towards him.

Morton wheeled to the left, and urged his horse up the embankment in front of the train. With a violent effort, he reached the top. The engineer was running against time, and cared for nothing but winning his match. He blew the steam whistle; and as Morton dragged on the curb with desperate strength, the horse reared upright, pawing the air. But, as he rose, Morton disengaged his feet, slid over the crupper to the ground, and let go the rein. The horse leaped down the bank, and scoured over the meadow, mad with terror. Morton took his stand in the middle of the track, and facing the advancing train, stood immovable as a post. The engineer reversed the engine, brought it to a stand within a few yards of him, and, with a profusion of oaths, demanded what he wanted.

Before the breathless Morton could well explain himself, the passengers began to leap out of the cars, and running forward, gathered about him. He soon found words to make the case known. But one object alone engrossed him. He pushed on among the throng of questioning, eager men, mounted the foremost car, and made his way through it, the crowd pushing behind and around him, and plying him with questions, to which, in the confusion and abstraction of his faculties, he gave wild and random answers. He looked at every face. Edith Leslie was not there. He crossed the platform into the next car, passed through it, and still could not find her. It was the last in the train. And now a strange feeling came over him, a bitterness, a sense of disappointment, as if his efforts and his pangs had been uncalled for and profitless; for so intensely had his thoughts been concentred on one object, that he forgot for the moment the hundred men and women whom he had saved from deadly jeopardy.

The train rolled back to the station, the distance being only a few rods. Morton got out and leaned against the wall of the house. Men thronged about him with questions, exclamations, thanks, praises. The reaction of his violent emotion produced in him a frame of mind almost childish. He was restless to free himself from the crowd.

"It's nothing; it's nothing," he answered, as fresh praises were showered on him. "I saw the train going to the devil, and did what I could to save it. Any of you, I dare say, would have done as much. Be good enough to let me have a little air."

The crowd gave way, and he walked forward past the corner of the building. Here, standing on the road, close at hand, he suddenly saw an open carriage, and in it, pale as death, sat Miss Leslie, with her friend, and a boy of twelve, her friend's brother. He sprang towards it with an irrepressible impulse.

"My God! Miss Leslie, I thought you were in the train."

"And so we should have been," said the boy, "but the cars came in three minutes before their time."

Edith Leslie did not utter a word.

Some of the passengers were soon about him again. He repeated to them what he knew of the danger, and told them how he had learned it. In a few minutes, several men were seen at a distance on the railroad, running forward with a handkerchief tied to a stick to warn off the train. A few minutes later, a Connecticut pedler, one of the passengers, came up to Morton.

"Mister, they're going to do the handsome thing by you. They're getting up a subscription to give you a piece of silver plate."

"The deuse they are!" was Morton's ungrateful response.

Going into the room where the passengers were met, he found that the pedler had told the truth; on which, for the first and last time in his life, he addressed an assemblage of his fellow-citizens. He told them that he thanked them for their kind intention; but that if he had done them a service, he wished for no other recompense than the knowledge of it, and urged them, if they did any thing in the matter, to devote their efforts to gaining the arrest and punishment of the scoundrel who had attempted the mischief. His oratory was much applauded; many, who had thought themselves in for the subscription, joyfully buttoned their pockets, and, instead of the plate, he received a series of complimentary resolutions, to be published in the newspapers.

Meanwhile, having made his speech, he had lost no time in making his escape also. Going back to the carriage, Miss Leslie's friend asked him to accompany them home, whence they could return to take the afternoon train, when the bridge would, no doubt, be repaired. Morton, however, declined the invitation, and, having sent two men to catch the horse, with instructions to refer the distressed owner to him, he drove in a farmer's wagon to Steuben. In a few hours, he rejoined Miss Leslie and her friend; and having escorted both safely to town, took leave of the former, that evening, at the door of her father's house.

Several of the newspapers next morning contained the resolutions passed by the passengers, trumpeting Morton's humanity, presence of mind, &c. He himself very well knew that the praise was undeserved, since he had neither thought nor cared for the objects of his supposed humanity, and, far from acting with presence of mind, had scarcely known what he was about.

The bridge had been cut by an Irish mechanic in the employ of the road, who, for some misdemeanor, had been reprimanded and turned out, and who had passed half the night in preparing his demoniac revenge. It afterwards appeared that he had been a state's prison convict in a neighboring state, and that he would have been still in confinement, had not the officious zeal of certain benevolent persons availed to set him loose before his time.

CHAPTER XX

> For true it is, as *in principio, Mulier est hominis confusio;* Madam, the meaning of this Latin is, That woman is to man his sovereign bliss.
>
> A woman's counsel brought us first to woe, And made her man his paradise forego.— These are the words of Chanticleer, not mine; I honor dames, and think their sex divine. —*Dryden.*

On the day after their return, Morton visited Miss Leslie to learn if she had suffered from the fatigues and alarms of yesterday; and, in truth, she had the pale face of one whose rest has been short and broken.

"It has been my fate to terrify you," said the anxious Morton.

During his visit, the door bell was most obtrusively busy. Messages, parcels, notes, cards, visitors came in, and expelled all hope of a *tête à tête.*

Soon after he left the room, Leslie entered.

"Who gave you those flowers, Edith?"

"Mr. Morton, sir."

"Humph!" ejaculated Leslie, with a look by no means of gratification.

Meanwhile, Morton, walking the street in an abstracted mood, overtook unawares his bachelor friend Mr. Benedick Sharpe, jurist, philosopher, and man of letters—a personage whose ordinary discourse was a singular imbroglio of irony and earnest.

"Why, Morton, what problem of ethnology are you at now? the unity of the human race, and the descent from Adam—science versus orthodoxy—is that it?"

"Nothing so deep."

"What, nothing ethnological?"

"Nothing at all."

"Ah, then I begin to tremble for you. There's but one thing else could lose you in such a maze. The flame of a candle is very pretty; but the moth that flies into it scorches his wings, poor devil."

"I am too dull to see through your metaphors."

"There's another blind divinity besides Justice. Beware the shoal of matrimony! Many a good fellow has been wrecked there."

"Harping on your old string! You are a professed woman hater."

"Who, I? Now that is a scandalous libel. I admire them,—of course."

"And yet there's not a lady of your acquaintance whom I have not heard you analyze, criticise, cavil at, and disparage."

"My dear fellow!"

"You have no conscience to deny it."

"I protest I have the greatest—ahem!—admiration for the ladies of our acquaintance. We have an excellent assortment,—we have witty women; brilliant women; women of taste and genius; exact and fastidious women,—a full supply,—accomplished women; finished and elegant women,—not too many, but still we have them; learned women; gentle, amiable, tender women; sharp and caustic women; sensible and practical women; domestic women,—all unimpeachable,—all good in their kind."

"Then why is matrimony so dangerous?"

"No, no, not dangerous, exactly,—thanks to discreet nurture and northern winters; not dangerous hereabouts as it was in the days of the old satirists. A wise man may be safe enough here from any climax of matrimonial evil; but there are minor mischiefs, daily *désagrémens*."

"What, in spite of that catalogue of feminine virtues which you delivered just now?"

"Vanity of vanities! Admirable in the abstract; excellent at a safe distance; but to be tied to for life, bed and board, day light and candle light,—that's another thing."

"Even the tender and amiable,—is there risk even there?"

"One cloys on perpetual sweetmeats."

"And the domestic women?"

"Who incarcerate themselves in their nurseries, and have no brains but for their babies; who are frantic if the infant coughs, and are buried and lost among cradles, porringers, go-carts, pills, and prescriptions."

"The brilliant woman, then?"

"Brilliant at dinner tables and *soirées;* but, on the next day, your Corinne is disconsolate with a headache. Her wit is for the world,—her moods and mopings, caprices and lamentations,—those she keeps for her husband."

"You are a cynic. The woman of taste and genius; where do you place her?"

"What are the rude heart and brain of a man to such exalted susceptibilities? What homage is too much for him to render? Be a bond slave to the sweet enthusiast. Bow yourself before the delicate shrine. Do your devoirs; she will not bate you a jot."

"But there are in the world women governed by reason."

"My dear Morton, are you demented? A woman always rational, always sensible, always consistent; a logical woman; one who can distinguish the relations of cause and effect, one who marches straight to her purpose like a man,—who ever found such a woman; or, finding her, who could endure such a one?"

"You fly into extremes; but women may be rational, as well as men."

"I like to see the organ of faith well developed,—yours is a miracle. Granted, a rational woman; and with a liberal rendering of the word, such, I admit, are now and then seen,—women always even, always cheerful, never morbid, always industrious, always practical; busy with good works,—charity, for example, or making puddings,—pious daughters, model wives, pattern mothers——"

"At last you have found a creditable character."

"Very creditable; but far from interesting. The truth is, Morton, the very uncertainty, the flitting gleams and shadows, the opalescent light, the chameleon coloring of a woman's mind are what make her fascination,—the fascination and the danger,—there lies the dilemma. Shun the danger, and you lose the charm as well. A woman's human nature is not our human nature; the tissue is more cunningly woven; the string more responsive; the essence lighter and subtler,—forgive the poetic style,—appropriate to the theme, you know. In their virtues and their faults they shoot away into paths where we do not track them. They can sink in a more abject abasement; and sometimes, again, while we tread the earth, they are aeronauts of the pure ether. Stable, stubborn, impassive man holds the steadfast tenor of his walk, little moved by influences which, on the one hand, bury his helpmate in ruin, or, on the other, wing her on a flight to the zenith. They out-sin us, and they out-saint us; weak as a reed, and strong as an oak; measureless in folly, profound in wisdom; for the deepest of all wisdom springs, not out of a questioning brain, but out of a confiding heart; and all human knowledge must find its root at last in a blind belief. There, I have given you a sublime touch of eloquence; and, for the moral to it,—shun matrimony. It is Satan's slyest mantrap. No, not so, at all; it is a blessed institution for perfecting mankind in patience, charity, and meekness, and booking their names in the catalogue of saints. So be wise, in time. Good by. Look before you leap!"

And, with an ironical twinkle in his eye, Sharpe vanished.

CHAPTER XXI

Quelle diable de fantaisie t'es tu allé mettre dans la cervelle?
Tu le veux, amour; il faut être fou comme beaucoup
d'autres. — *Le Malade Imaginaire*.

Matherton, renowned through both hemispheres for the manufacture of glass ware, stands, unless this history errs, on the line of the Northern Central Railroad, the distance from its post office to the post office at Boston being just thirty-three miles. Four miles from the village is the tract of land which Leslie's forefather, far back in New England antiquity, bought of the Indians. The original purchase covered several square miles, since dwindled to some two hundred acres. Here, in a sequestered and very beautiful spot, stands the mansion which Leslie's grandfather built some eighty-five years ago. In its day it was reputed of matchless elegance, and, with Leslie's repairs and improvements, it might still pass as a very handsome old country residence. Sagamore Pond, or Lake Sagamore, as the last Mrs. Leslie, who had lived in England, insisted on calling it, washes the foot of the garden; and along the northern verge of the estate, Battle Brook steals down to the pond, under the thick shade of the hemlock trees. Here King Philip's warriors once lay in ambush, through a hot summer's day; here many pious Puritans were butchered, and many carried off into doleful captivity.

At the house at Battle Brook, Leslie, during spring, summer, and autumn, had always spent every leisure moment that he could snatch from his affairs. Since his connection with Vinal, these intervals had become both long and frequent. And, since grief has a privilege, and since, moreover, a somewhat alarming cough had lately begun to trouble him, he now committed all to Vinal's hands, and, on the day after his daughter's return, repaired with her to his favorite homestead, there to remain till the autumn frosts should warn them back to town. Forthwith Matherton became the focus to which all the thoughts of Morton concentred.

Thither, pretext or no pretext, he resolved to go. He went, accordingly, and made his quarters at the grand hotel of Matherton. Fortunately, Battle Brook was then the best trout stream in Massachusetts; and this would give, he flattered himself, some faint color to his proceeding. He arrived in the afternoon, and, mounting a horse, rode to the inn at the edge of Sagamore Pond, a mile or more from Leslie's house.

He had scarcely reached it, when a brief sharp thunder shower came up, and passed away as quickly. As the sun was setting, he rowed out in a small boat upon the pond. Here, skirting the brink of a sequestered cove, which the beech and tupelo trees overhung, and where every thing was still but the evening singing of a robin, and the mysterious whisper of the raindrops, falling from innumerable leaves, with countless tiny circles on the breathless water,—here, where his boat glided as if buoyed on a liquid air, while, over the pebbly bottom, the perch and dace fled away from under the shadowing prow,—he lingered dreamily for a while, and then, bending to his oars, bore out into the middle of the pond. The west was gorgeous with the sunset, while, far in front, glimmering among the trees, he could see the shrine of his idolatry, the roof that sheltered Edith Leslie.

A light breeze crisped the water, the ripples murmured with a lulling sound under his boat, and, lying at ease, he gave himself up to his reveries.

His passion-kindled fancies ranged earth, sea, and sky; wandered into the past, lost themselves in the future; evoked the shadows of dead history; mixed in one phantom conclave the hairy war gods of the north, the bright shapes of Grecian fable, the enormities of Egyptian mythology; and, looking into the burning depths above him, he mused of human hopes, human aspirations, human destiny. That oddly compounded malady which had fastened on him had brought with it the intense yet tranquil awakening of every faculty with which it will sometimes visit those of the ruder sex whom it attacks with virulence.

The magic of earth and sky; the black pines rearing their shaggy tops against the blazing west; the shores mingling in many-tinted shadow; the fiery sky, where three little clouds hovered like flaming spirits; the fiery water, where he and his boat floated as in a crimson sea; the whole glowing scene, glowing deeper yet in the fervid light of passion,—penetrated him like an enchantment. He scarcely knew himself; and in his supreme of intoxication, the familiar world around him was sublimed into a vision of Eden.

CHAPTER XXII

If it were now to die,
'Twere now to be most happy; for I fear,
My soul hath her content so absolute,
That not another comfort like to this
Succeeds in unknown fate.—Othello.

It was a day of cloudless sunshine when Morton set forth for the house at Battle Brook; but his mind was far from sharing the brightness of the world without. The hope that flowed so full and calmly the night before had ebbed and left him dry. He was shaken with doubts, misgivings, perturbations. He walked his horse up the avenue, till he came within view of the house, a large, square mansion, with a veranda on three sides, a quiet-looking place enough, but in Morton's eyes priceless as Aladdin's palace, and sacred as Our Lady's house at Loretto. A monthly honeysuckle twined about one of the columns of the porch; the hall door stood open, and the air played freely through from front to rear.

He gave his horse to the charge of an old Scotchman who was mowing the lawn, rang at the door, asked for Miss Leslie, and was shown into the vacant parlor. With its straw carpeting and light summer furniture, it was bright and cheerful as every thing else about it. Engravings from Turner and Landseer, framed in black walnut, hung against the walls; and on a small table in a corner stood a bird cage, with the door left purposely open. The inmate was hopping about the room, without attempting to escape, though the windows also were open.

"No wonder it will not leave her," thought the visitor.

He seated himself by the window, and looked out on the fields and the groves beyond. Far down in the meadow, the yellow-tufted rye was undulating in the warm summer wind, wave chasing wave in graceful succession. The birds would not sing,—the afternoon was too hot,—but the buzz, and hum, and chirrup of a myriad of insects rose from their lurking-places in the grass, while now and then the cicala raised its piercing voice from a neighboring apple tree.

Suddenly Morton's heart began to beat; a light step on the staircase reached his ear, and the rustling of a dress. Miss Leslie came in with her usual natural and quiet ease of manner, while he rose to receive her with his heart in his throat. And now, when he needed them most, his wits seemed to fail him. He tried to converse, and produced nothing but barren commonplace. Again and again the conversation flagged; and the hum and chirrup of the insect world without filled the pauses between.

He glanced at his companion.

"Be a man, you idiot," he apostrophized himself.

He looked at her again, as she bent over the embroidery with which her fingers were employed.

"I must speak out, or die," he thought.

He rested his arm on the table. He leaned towards her. Heaven knows what nonsense was on his lips, when the sound of a man's footstep in the hall made him subside into his chair, and do his best to look nonchalant. Leslie entered, cast an uneasy glance at the visitor, and greeted him with somewhat cool courtesy.

"I have just met Miss Weston and her sister," said Leslie to his daughter; "I think they will be here in a few minutes."

Morton looked at a Landseer on the wall, and gnawed his lip with vexation.

Leslie took a turn or two about the room, looked out at the window, remarked that it was a hot afternoon, said that the hay crop had been the heaviest ever known, in consequence, he opined, of the joint effects of heat, moisture, and guano; and was descanting on the ravages committed by the borers on a certain peach tree, when Miss Weston and her sister appeared.

"It's all up with me. She does not care for me a straw," thought Morton, as he saw the easy cordiality with which Miss Leslie received her guests. He was introduced. Miss Weston complimented him on the affair of the railroad. His reply was cold and constrained. Leslie soon left the room. Morton felt himself *de trop*, yet could not muster strength of mind to go. Conversation flagged. Every body became constrained. Miss Weston suspected the truth, and glanced at her sister that they should take their leave, when, at this juncture, a servant came to announce tea.

The ebbs and flows of the human mind are beyond the reach of astronomy. As they went into the next room, Morton became conscious of a faint and indefinite something in the face of his mistress, which, he could not tell why, cast a gleam of light into his darkness, and lifted him out of the slough of despond in which he had been floundering for the last half hour. A flush of hope dawned on him. His constraint passed away, and Miss Weston's opinion of him was wonderfully revolutionized. At length, much to his delight, one of the visitors remarked to the other, that they had better go home before it grew too dark. But here a new alarm seized him. Might he not be expected to offer them his escort? Terrified at this idea, and oblivious of all gallantry, he made his escape into the garden, impelled—so he left them to infer—by a delicate wish to free them from the restraint of his presence. Here he walked to and fro behind the hedge, in no small agitation, but with all his faculties on the alert.

In a quarter of an hour, he heard voices at the hall door; and approaching behind a cluster of high laurels, saw Edith Leslie accompanying her two friends down the avenue. After walking with them a few rods, she bade them good evening, and turned back towards the house. Morton went forward to meet her.

"There is a beautiful sunset over the water, beyond the garden. Will you walk that way?"

They turned down one of the garden paths.

"What did you think of me this afternoon?" asked Morton—"did you think me ill, or bewitched, or turned idiot?"

"Neither. I thought you a little taciturn, at first."

"I am fortunate if that was your worst opinion. I believe I was under a spell. Did you never dream—all people, I believe, have something in common in their dreams—of being in some great peril, without power to move hand or foot to escape?—of being under some desperate necessity of speaking, without power to open your lips?—or of seeing before you some splendid prize, without power to make even an effort to grasp it? Something like that was my case." Here he came to an abrupt stop, walked on a pace or two, then turned to his companion with a vehemence which startled her—"Miss Leslie, you heard your friend praise me for humanity—courage—what not? It was all a mistake—all a delusion. I thought you were in the train. I was wild with agony; and when the people were crowding after me, I thought that all had been for nothing, because I had not saved you. I can hardly tell what I did; it was mere blind instinct. I could have ridden into the fire, and perhaps not have felt the burning. There *is* a spell upon me. I am changed—life is changed—every thing is changed. I scarcely know myself. It mans me, and it makes me a child again. The world puts on a new face; just as this sunset lights the earth with purple and vermilion, and turns it to a fairy land. Forgive me; I don't know what I am saying. I am in fear that all this brightness will change of a sudden into winter and night, and cold, rocky commonplace. You know what I would say. I have no words fit to say it. You are my judge, to lift me up, or cast me down."

Here he stopped again abruptly, and looked at his companion in much greater agitation than he would have felt if he had just thrown the dice for life or death. She stood for a moment with her eyes fixed on the earth, as if waiting for him to go on, then slowly raised them to his face.

"You risked your life to save mine. You need not believe that I could ever forget it."

Morton's heart sprang to his lips. Nature had not been liberal to him in the gift of tongues, but the energy of his emotion supplied the defect. Nor were his words thrown away; for with all its outward calm, the nature that responded to them was earnest and ardent as his own.

It was an hour or more since the whippoorwills had begun their evening cries, when they returned to the house. Candles were lighted, and Leslie was sitting with two persons from the neighborhood, an agent of the Matherton factories and a lawyer, conversing upon railroad stocks. He looked very uneasily at his daughter and Morton, but said nothing. The latter was engrossed with one idea; but he forced himself to join in the conversation, and favored the company with his views—not very lucid on this occasion—upon the topic under discussion. He soon, however, contrived to whisper to Miss Leslie, "I shall go in five minutes—will you meet me in the hall?" She left the room in a few moments; and Morton, after a short interval, took his leave, in much alarm lest his intended father-in-law should strain courtesy so far as to follow him. Leslie, however, remained quiet; and he found his mistress waiting for him at the hall door. Their interview was short, but Morton never forgot it. After bidding her good night some eight or ten times, he compelled himself to leave the house, mounted his horse, waved his hand to Edith Leslie, whom he saw watching him from a side window, wheeled, rode down the avenue, turned as he reached the entrance of the trees, and waved his hand again towards the window. His heart was full to overflowing, and tears, not of sorrow, ran down his cheeks. "Good Heaven!" laughed Morton, as he brushed them away, "this has not happened to me before these twelve years." He waved a farewell once more, and spurring his horse, rode down the avenue into the high road.

It was a soft, warm, starlight evening, and, as he passed along, he heard the voices of the whippoorwills from far and near, while the meadows, the orchards, and the borders of the woods sparkled with fireflies. With loosened rein, he suffered his horse to canter lightly forward, and gave himself up to the enchantment of his dreams. A thousand times in his after life did he recall the visions of that evening's ride.

About a mile before reaching the town, the road passed, for a few rods, through a belt of thick woods. While riding through the darkest of the shadow, a strange cry startled him—a shriek so wild and awful that the blood curdled in his veins, and his horse leaped aside with fright. There was a rustling among the branches over his head, a flapping and fanning of broad pinions, and the dusky form of some great bird sailed away into the innermost darkness of the woods. Morton knew the sound. It was the voice of the great horned owl, rarely found in that part of the country, though he had once or twice before heard its midnight yells in the lonely forests of Maine.

The cry long rang in his ears. It seemed fraught with startling portent, clouded his spirits, and umbered the rose-tint of his reveries. He turned his face to the stars, and breathed a prayer for the welfare of his mistress.

CHAPTER XXIII

L'ambition, l'amour, l'avarice, la haine,
Tiennent comme un forçat son esprit à la chaîne. — Boileau.

Nobody knew Vinal but Vinal himself. *Know thyself* was his favorite maxim. He practised upon it, as he flattered himself, with a rigorous and unsparing logic, applying the dissecting knife and microscope to the secrets of his mind, probing, testing, studying, pitilessly ripping up all that would fain hide itself. The aim of all this scrutiny was, thoroughly to comprehend the machine, in order to direct and perfect it to its highest efficiency.

Vinal, as men go, knew himself very well; and yet there were points of his character which escaped him, or which, rather, he misnamed. He knew perfectly that he was ambitious, selfish, unscrupulous: this he confessed in his own ear, pluming himself much on his philosophic candor. But he never would see that he was envious. In his mental map of himself, envy was laid down as pride and emulation. The wrestlings of human nature are not all of the sort figured in the Pilgrim's Progress and set forth in the Catechism. Vinal had an ideal; he had cherished it from boyhood, and battled ever since to realize it. He would fain make himself the finished man of the world, the unflinching, all-knowing, all-potential man of affairs, like a blade of steel, smooth and polished, but keen, searching, resistless. This was his aim; but nature was always balking him. He was the victim of a constitutional timidity, his scourge from childhood. He had been known to swoon outright, on being run away with in a chaise, and he never could muster nerve enough to fire a gun. Against this defect his pride rose in revolt. It thwarted him at every turn, and conflicted with all his aspirations. In short, he could not endure its presence, and fought against it with an iron energy of will. Thus his life was a secret, unremitting struggle, whose mark was written on his pale, nervous, resolute features. It's an ill wind that blows no good. This painful warfare achieved a singular vigor and concentration of character, and would have led to still better issues, had the assailing force been marshalled under a better banner. A lofty purpose may turn timidity to heroism; but a purpose like Vinal's is by no means so efficacious, and the man remains, if not quite a coward, yet something very like one.

It would have been well for Vinal if, like Morton, he had been born to a fortune. In that case—for he had no aptitude for pleasure hunting—his restless energies would probably have spurred him into some creditable field of effort, natural science, mathematics, or philology, to all of which he inclined. But Fate had not been so propitious; and to achieve the task which she had forgotten was the zenith of his aspirations.

There was one person who had always been an eyesore to him, and a stumbling block in his way. This was Vassall Morton. Morton, at twenty-three, was, in feeling, still a boy; Vinal, at twenty-three, was a well-ripened man. But the man hated the boy; and the boy retorted with a dislike which was largely dashed with scorn. Vinal felt the scorn, and it cut him to the quick, the more so, that he could not hide from himself that he stood in awe of Morton. He hated him, too, because he had that which he, Vinal, lacked—fortune, good health, steady nerve. He hated him, because he thought that Morton understood him; because the frankness of the latter's nature rebuked the secrecy of his own; and, above all, because he saw in him his most formidable rival in the affections of Edith Leslie.

Vinal's nature, self-drilled as it was, could not be called a cold one. It had in it spots and veins of sensitiveness. When a child, this sensitiveness had often been morbidly awake, and had caused him much suffering; but as he grew towards manhood, it had been overlaid and hidden by very different qualities, not often found in connection with it. Of late, however, he had been in love,—with Edith Leslie, as well as with her money,—and the dormant susceptibilities of his childhood had been in some sort reawakened.

His mind, inharmonious and unhappy as nature and himself had jointly made it, had never yet felt a pang so sharp as when, arriving at Matherton, he learned privately from Colonel Leslie the engagement which had passed between Morton and his daughter. Miss Leslie's twice rejected suitor compressed his thin lips in silence; it was his usual sign of strong emotion. Leslie pressed his favorite's hand,—he would fain have called him son-in-law,—and, turning away abruptly, Vinal left the house.

The man whom he envied and hated had triumphed; robbed him of fortune, and robbed him of happiness; happiness of which Morton had had already his full share, and a fortune which would but swell the ample bulk of his possessions. Vinal was frenzied with grief, rage, and jealousy.

CHAPTER XXIV

Clo. That she should love this fellow and refuse me!
If it be sin to make a true election, she is damned.—*Cymbeline*.

Morton sat in the reading room of the National, the grand hotel of Matherton. It was by no means an elegant apartment. In the middle was a table covered with newspapers; at the sides were desks, likewise covered with newspapers, padlocked together in files. The walls and the ceiling glared a drear monotony of white, broken, however, by sundry ornaments, worthy the attention of the curious. Here, framed in birdseye maple, was the engraved likeness of "Old Hickory," with hat and cane in hand, a cloak to hide the gauntness of his figure, and hair bristling in electrified disorder. Here, too, was a colored print of the favorite steamboat "Queen of the Lake;" Niagara Falls, by a license of art, forming a blue curtain in the background. At its side was a lithograph of the Empire Hotel, New York, the sidewalk in front being embellished with groups of pedestrians, dressed with matchless elegance, after the fashion plates; and, over against this, an advertisement of Jessup's steel, encircled with a lithographed halo, composed of chisels, axes, hammers, saws, and ploughshares.

The apartment, thus furnished and thus adorned, had, besides Morton, but two occupants; the one a factory agent, who stood at a desk, absorbed in the New Orleans Picayune; the other a country tailor, who displayed the sign of the "Full-dressed Man" at the neighboring village of Mudfield, and was now seated at a window, busied in polishing a huge garnet ring, which he wore, with a red silk handkerchief.

In a window recess, aloof from the tailor's, sat Morton, scarcely conscious of any presence but that of his own thoughts. He had found a philosopher's stone; and through the rest of his life, this comfortless reading room of the Matherton Hotel, this sanctuary of dry and weary Yankeedom, was linked in his memory with dreams of golden brightness.

A firm, quick step crossed the threshold, and paced the sanded floor. Till this moment, Morton had remained absorbed, shut in from the outer world; but now an influence, which believers may call magnetism, made him look up and bend forward from the recess to see who the sudden stranger might be. The stranger turned also, and showed the pale, fixed face of Horace Vinal.

Morton was disposed to be on good terms with all the world, and more especially with his defeated rival.

"Good morning, Vinal," he said, holding out his hand, which Vinal took, his cold, thin fingers trembling in the warm grasp of Morton. He had had no thought of finding him there; the encounter was unlooked for as it was unwelcome; and, as he muttered a few passing words of commonplace, his features grew haggard with the violence of struggling emotion. He turned away, went to a desk, pretended to read a newspaper for a few moments, and then left the room.

Morton looked after him. He had no doubt that Vinal had heard of his misfortune; and the first sense of pain which, since the evening before last, the successful lover had felt, now crossed his mind.

"It's devilish hard for him, poor fellow," he thought, as, measuring Vinal's passion by his own, a vivid image of the latter's suffering rose upon him.

Vinal strode along a corridor of the hotel. There was no one to see him. His forehead was knit, his nostrils distended, his jaws clinched. A man, whom he knew, came from a side passage. Instantly Vinal's face was calm again, and as the other passed he greeted him with a smile. He went out into the main street of the town, along which he walked for a few rods with his usual air of alert composure; then turned down a narrow and unfrequented by-way. Here his whole bearing changed. He trod the gravelled sidewalk with a fierce, nervous motion; and with hands clinched and eyes fixed on the ground, muttered through his set teeth,—

"Fair or foul, by G—, I'll be even with him."

CHAPTER XXV

> O, quha is this has done this deed,
> This ill deed done to me?
> To send me out this time o' the zeir,
> To sail upon the sea.—*Percy Reliques.*

> A slave whose gall coins slanders like a mint.—*Troilus and Cressida.*

"Your proposal flatters me, Mr. Morton; and, in many points of view, the connection you offer would be a desirable one,—a very desirable one. But I must say to you plainly, that if my wishes alone were consulted, my daughter would bestow her hand elsewhere. Perhaps I need not tell you that Horace Vinal, who was my ward, and my late wife's relation, and who has been my partner in business for a year or more, is a young man whom I have looked upon as my son, and whom it was my very earnest hope to have seen such in reality. You who have had an opportunity of knowing him can hardly be surprised that, after so long an intimacy, I should prefer this connection to any other. I have seen him in all the relations of life, and the more I have seen the more I have learned to esteem him."

"You speak with a good deal of emphasis of his character. May I ask if any part of your objection to me rests on that score."

"In a matter like this, I am bound to be frank with you. In many quarters, I hear you very highly spoken of,—so highly, in fact, that I am disposed to take with every qualification what I have heard to your disadvantage."

"Pray, what is that?"

"I was a soldier once, and don't incline to inquire too closely into the way young men may see fit to amuse themselves. But on a point where my daughter's happiness might be involved——"

"Upon my word, sir, I don't understand you."

"Well, Mr. Morton, I hear—that is, I have learned—that, like other young men of leisure, you have had your *bonnes fortunes*, and winged other game than partridges and woodcock."

Morton looked at him in surprise. The truth was, that, some time before, the discreet and far-sighted Vinal had contrived to inoculate his patron with this calumny, which he thought the species most likely to take readily. And such had been his tact, that Leslie, though well imbued with the idea, would have been puzzled to say whence he had received it. A man of shallow-brained uprightness like his, if he yields too easy a belief to falsehood, has the advantage of yielding also an easy belief to truth. A few words from Morton sufficed to carry conviction to the frank-hearted auditor, who, feeling that, at least as regarded its worst features, his charge must be groundless, hastened to make the *amende*.

"Your word is enough, Mr. Morton, and I owe you an apology for imagining that you could be false or heartless in any connection whatever. I think, however, that you can see how, without disparagement to you, I should still regret that Horace Vinal, who is personally so near to me, so devoted to my interests, and so strongly attached to my daughter, should be disappointed. I advised him, yesterday, to go to Europe, to recruit his health. I am told that you had yourself some plan of the kind."

"A very indefinite one, sir; in fact, amounting to none at all."

"Go this autumn; be absent a year,—that is not too long for seeing Europe,—and if at the end of that time you and my daughter should remain as earnest in this matter as you are now, why, I am not the man to persist in opposing her inclination."

The sentence was hard; but there was no appeal. Leslie had told Vinal the day before that he would despatch Morton on his travels, intimating a hope that a long separation might bring about a change in his daughter's feelings. Morton saw nothing for it but acquiescence; to which, indeed, Miss Leslie urged him, confiding in the strength of his attachment, and happy to reconcile adverse duties and inclinations at any price.

Meanwhile, he had not the smallest suspicion of the subtle trick which his rival had played him. "This is a charitable world!" he thought; "one must keep the beaten track, look demure, and talk virtue, or, in one shape or another, it will be the worse for him."

CHAPTER XXVI

Then loathed he in his native land to dwell.—*Childe Harold*.

Slend. A gentleman born, Master Parson, who writes himself *Armigero;* in any bill, warrant, quittance, or obligation, *Armigero!*

Shal. Ay, that I do; and have done any time these three hundred years.—*Merry Wives of Windsor*.

The engagement of Miss Leslie and Morton was to be kept secret till the latter's return. None knew it but Leslie and Vinal. Vinal, within a few weeks, sailed for Europe, meaning, however, to be absent only three or four months. Other motives apart, he felt, and Leslie saw, that his health, always shivering in the wind, demanded the change.

Meanwhile, Morton made the best of a six weeks' reprieve; and hampered as he was by the injunction of secrecy, and the precautions which it demanded, he crowded the short interval with half a lifetime of mixed pleasure and pain, expectation and anxiety.

It was past but too quickly; in three days more he must set sail. Walking the street in a rueful mood, he met his classmate, Chester, who, having made the tour of Europe, had lost his obsolete ways, and grown backward into a man of the present world.

"Good morning, Morton. Making calls?—I see it by your face."

"Yes; it's a thing that must be done sometimes."

"*Pour prendre congé*, I suppose. I hear you are off very soon."

"The day after to-morrow."

"You couldn't do a wiser thing. When a man finds himself in a scrape, he had better get out of it as soon as possible; therefore, if he finds himself born in America, he had better forswear his country."

"Patriotic sentiments those."

"I can't answer for the patriotism; but they are the sentiments of a true son of the Pilgrim Fathers, who renounced their country because they couldn't stand it, and came over here. I mean to follow their example, and go back again. They fled—so the story goes—from persecution. I mean to fly from persecution too,—the persecution of a social atmosphere that I find hostile to my constitution, and a climate not fit for a reasonable being to live in."

"I don't know why you should be so fierce against the climate. By your look, you seem to thrive in it."

"The bodily man thrives passably well. It's the immortal part that suffers. Fierce! why, the climate makes me fierce. Who can be a philosopher in such a climate?—or a poet?—or an artist?—any thing but a steam engine? It is a perpetual spur, an unremitting goad. Nobody is happy in it except the men who ride on locomotives and conduct express trains,—always on the move. O, so you go in here, do you?"

"Yes, to see Mrs. Primrose. Will you come too?"

"No, thank you," replied Chester, walking away, with a comical look.

Morton rang the door bell, and found Mrs. Primrose at home.

There was a book on the table. He took it up. It was a novel, lately published.

Morton praised it.

Mrs. Primrose dissented, with great emphasis.

"You are severe upon the book."

"Not more so than it deserves," replied Mrs. Primrose; "it is too coarse to be permitted for a moment."

"And yet the moral tone seems good enough."

"I do not blame the morality so much as the bad taste. It is full of slang dialogue, and was certainly written by a very unrefined person."

"It makes its characters speak as such people speak in real life."

"It is not merely that," said Mrs. Primrose, slightly pursing her mouth; "it contains, besides, expressions absolutely reprehensible."

"One does not admire its good taste; but a little blunt Saxon never did much harm."

"No daughter of mine shall read it," said Mrs. Primrose, with gravity.

"I imagine that if literature is to reflect human life truly, it can hardly be limited to the language of the drawing room."

"Then it should be banished from the drawing room," said Mrs. Primrose, with severity.

Here several visitors appeared, and Morton presently took leave.

He was but a few rods from the door, when a quick step came behind him.

"Hallo, colonel, where are you going at such a rate?"

Morton turned, and saw his classmate, Rosny.

"Why, Dick, I'm glad to see you."

"They tell me you're bound for Europe."

"Yes."

"Well, it's a good move. If a man has money, he had better enjoy it."

"I shall be driving out of town in an hour. Come and dine with me."

"Sorry, colonel, but it can't be done. I'm out on the stump in the cause of democracy. Shall be off westward in two hours, and shake the dust from my shoes against this nest of whiggery and old fogyism."

"Democracy is under the weather just now, Dick."

"Just now, I grant you. What with log cabins and hard cider, and coons, the enlightened people are pretty well gammoned. But there's a good time coming. Before you know it, democracy will be upon you again like a load of bricks. Why, what can you expect of a party that will take a coon for its emblem? I saw one chained up this morning in the yard of Taft's tavern, a dirty, mean-looking beast, about half way between a jackal and an owl. He looked uncommonly well in health, and could puff out his fur as round as a muff. But, when you looked close, there was nothing of him but skin and bone; exactly like the whig party. He put up his nose, and smiled at me. I suppose—damn his impudence—he took me for a whig. That coon is going into a decline. It won't be long before he is taken by the tail and tossed over Charles River bridge; and there he'll lie on the mud at low tide, for a genuine emblem of the defunct whig party, and a solemn warning to all coon worshippers."

"Let the whigs alone, Dick; and if you won't dine with me, come in here and drink a glass of claret."

"That I'll do." And they went into the hotel accordingly.

As Rosny took up his glass, Morton observed a large old seal ring on his finger.

"Do you call yourself a democrat, and yet always wear that ring of yours?"

"Why, what's the matter with the ring?"

"Nothing, except that it is a badge of feudalism, aristocracy, and every thing else abominable to your party."

"Pshaw, man. Look here: do you see that crest, cut in the stone? That crest followed King Francis to Pavia, and when Henri Quatre charged at Ivry, it wasn't far behind him. It is mine by right. It comes down to me, straight as a bee line, through twenty generations. And do you think I'm going to renounce my birthright? No, be gad!"

"I wouldn't. But what becomes of your democracy?"

"Democracy is tall enough to take care of itself. I wear that ring; but it don't follow that I stand on my ancestry. You needn't laugh: the case is just this. If the blood in my veins makes me stand to my colors where another man would flinch, or hold my head up where another would be sprawling on his back; if it gives me a better pluck, grit, go-ahead; why, *that's* what I stand on,—*that's* my patent of nobility. What the deuse are you laughing at?—the personal quality,—don't you see?—and not the ancestry."

"If you stand on personal merit, you'll be sure to go under before long. The democracy are growing as jealous of that as of ancestry, or of wealth either."

"Why, what do you know about politics? You never had any thing to do with them. You are no more fit for a politician than for a fiddler."

"I'm glad you think so. If I must serve the country in any public capacity, I pray Heaven it may be as a scavenger sooner than as a politician. Who can touch pitch and be clean? I'll pay back your compliment, Dick. You are a great deal too downright to succeed in public life."

"I'll find a way or make one. But I tell you, colonel,"—and a shade of something like disappointment passed over his face,—"if a man wants the people's votes, it's fifty to one that he's got to sink himself lower than the gutter before he gets them."

"Yes, and when the people have turned out of office every man of virtue, honor, manliness, independence, and ability, then they will fling up their caps and brag that their day is come, and their triumph finished over the damned aristocracy."

"You are an unbeliever. You haven't half faith enough in the people. Now I put it to your common sense. Isn't there a thousand times more patriotism in the laboring classes in this country—yes, and about as much intelligence—as in the rabble of sham fashionables at Saratoga, or any other muster of our moneyed snobs and flunkeys?"

"Exceptions excepted, yes."

"War to the knife with the codfish aristocracy! They are a kind of mongrel beast, expressly devised and concocted for me to kick. I don't mean the gentlemen with money; nor the good fellows with money. I know what a gentleman is; yes, and a lady, too, though I do make stump speeches, and shake hands all round with the sovereign people. That sort are welcome to their money. No, sir, it's the moneyed snobs, the gilded toadstools, that it's my mission to pitch into."

"Excuse me a moment, Dick," said Morton, suddenly leaping from his seat, as a lady passed the window.

"A lady, eh! Then I'll be off."

"No, no, stay where you are. I'll be back again in three minutes."

He ran out of the hotel, and walked at his best pace in pursuit of Fanny Euston, who, on her part, was walking with an earnest air, like one whose thoughts were engaged with some engrossing subject. He reached her side, and made a movement to accost her; but she seemed unconscious of his presence.

"Miss Fanny Euston, will you pardon me for breaking in upon your reveries?"

She turned and recognized him, but her smile of recognition was a very mournful one.

"I have stopped you to take my leave,—a good deal more in short hand than I meant it should have been. I shall sail for Europe the day after to-morrow."

"Yes? Is not that a little sudden?"

"More sudden than I wish it were. I am not at all in a travelling humor. I have been too much pressed for time to ride out, as I meant to do, to your father's house."

"We are all in town now. My father came from New Orleans yesterday, very ill."

"I did not hear of it. I trust not dangerously ill."

"He is dying. He cannot live a week."

Morton well knew the strength and depth of her attachment to her father. He pressed her hand in silent sympathy.

"It grieves me, Fanny," he said, after a moment, "to part from you under such a cloud."

"Good by," she replied, returning the friendly pressure. "I wish you with all my heart a pleasant and prosperous journey."

Morton turned back, wondering at the sudden dignity of manner which grief had given to the wild and lawless Fanny Euston.

CHAPTER XXVII

Ham. Thou wouldst not think how ill's all here about my heart, but it is no matter.

Hor. Nay, good my lord — —

Ham. It is but foolery; but it is such a kind of gain-giving as would perhaps trouble a woman.

Hor. If your mind dislike any thing, obey it.

Ham. Not a whit. We defy augury.

Morton's day of departure came. It was a comfortless, savage, gusty morning, an east wind blowing in from the bay. The hour to set sail was near; he should have been on board; but still he lingered with Edith Leslie. The secrecy on which her father insisted made it impossible for her to go with him to the ship.

Morton forced himself away; his hand was on the door, but his heart failed him, and he turned back again. On the mind of each there was something more than the pain of a year's separation. A dark foreboding, a cloud of dull and sullen portent, hung over them both. The smooth and bright crusting with which habit and training had iced over the warm nature of Edith Leslie was broken and swept away; and as Morton seized her hands, she disengaged herself, and, throwing herself on his neck, sobbed convulsively. Morton pressed her to his heart, and buried his face in her clustering tresses; then, breaking from her, ran blindly from the house. He repaired to the house of Meredith, who met him at the door.

"You've no time to lose. Here's the carriage. Your trunks are all right. Come on."

They drove towards the wharf.

"I'd give my head to change places with you," said Meredith.

"I wish you could."

There was so much pain and dejection in his look, that his friend could not fail to observe it.

"You don't want to go, then? I have noticed all along that you seemed devilish cool about it."

"Ned," said Morton, "I never used to think myself superstitious; but I begin now to change my mind. Heaven knows why, but I have strange notions running in my brain. My dog howled all last night; and not long ago, an owl yelled over my head, and that, too, at a time—— But you'll think I have lost my wits."

Meredith, in truth, was greatly amazed at this betrayal of a weakness of which, long and closely as he had known his companion, he had never suspected him.

"Why, colonel, I have seen you set out on a journey as long and fifty times as hazardous as this, as carelessly as if you were going to a dinner party."

"I know it; but times are changed with me. I am not quite the child, though, that you may suppose."

"If you have such a feeling about going, I would give it up. It's not too late."

"No, I haven't sunk yet to that pass." And, as he spoke, the carriage stopped at the pier.

CHAPTER XXVIII

> I can't but say it is an awkward sight
> To see one's native land receding through
> The growing waters.—*Byron.*

The day brightened as the steamer bore out to sea, and the sun streamed along the fast-receding shore. Morton stood at the ship's stern, gazing back longingly towards his native rocks. Though far from inclining to echo those set terms of praise which the progeny of the Puritans are fond of lavishing on themselves, he felt himself bound with enduring cords to the woods and hills of New England, the scene of his boyish aspirations, of his pure ambition, and his devoted love; and while the crags of Gloucester faded from his sight, his eyes were dimmed as he turned them towards those rugged shores.

"Well, young man, seems to me you look a leetle kind o' streak-ed at the idee of quitting home," said a husky voice at his elbow.

Morton turned, and saw a small man, with a meagre, hatchet face, and a huge pair of black whiskers hedging round a countenance so dead and pallid that one could see at a glance that he was in a consumption. He had an eye hard as a flint, one that might have faced a Gorgon without risk. Morton regarded him with an expression which told him, as plainly as words, to go about his business; but he might as well have tried to look an image of brass out of countenance.

"Now *I*," pursued the small man, "have some reason to feel bad. It's an even bet if ever I see Boston lighthouse again—about six of one and half a dozen of the other. I consider myself a gone sucker. I've ben going, going, for about two years, and pretty soon I expect I shall be going, going, gone."

These words, uttered in a sort of bravado, were interrupted by a violent fit of coughing.

"Ever crossed the pond before?" asked the small man, as soon as he could gain breath.

"Yes."

"Business?"

"No."

"I thought not. You don't look like a business man. I know a business man, a mile off, by the cut of his jib. I'm a business man myself, and a hard used one at that."

Here a fresh fit of coughing began.

"Bad health; bad health, and damned hard luck, that's what has finished up this child. If it worn't for them, I should be worth my hundred thousand dollars this very minute."

Another fit of coughing.

"So you've ben across before. Well, so've I. That was three years ago, by the doctors' advice. It's great advice they give a man. It's good for their pockets, and there's deused little else it's good for. I spent that year over three thousand dollars; and if I'd staid to home, and stuck to my business, *I* should have ben jest about as well, and cleared,—well, yes, I should have cleared double the money, at the smallest figger."

More coughing.

"I expect you travel for pleasure."

Morton replied by an inarticulate sound, which the other might interpret as he pleased. He chose to interpret it in the affirmative.

"Well, that's all very well for a young man like you. You are young enough to like to look at the curiosities, and take an interest in what's going on; but I'm too old a bird for that. One night I was down to Palermo, there was an eruption of Mount Etna going on. We were on the piazzy at the back of Marston the consul's house, and there it was blazing away to kill, way off on the further side of the island. Well, the ladies was all O-ing and Ah-ing like fits. 'Nonsense!' says I; 'it ain't a circumstance to the fire that burnt down my splendid new freestone-front store on Broadway. Now that was something worth saying O at.'"

More coughing.

"There was a young man there from Boston, and we went round to look at the churches. He was all for staring at the pictures, and the marble images, and the Lord knows what all, while I went and paced off the length of the church from the door up to the altar, and then again crosswise. There wasn't a church in Palermo worth shaking a stick at that I didn't know the size of, and have it all set down on paper."

"And what good did that do you?"

"What good did that do me? Why, I had something to show for my pains, something that would keep. They wanted me to ride up on the back of a jackass to the top of a mountain to see a cavern where some she saint or other used to live,—St. Rosa Lee, or some such nigger-minstrel name."

"St. Rosalie, I suppose you mean."

"St. Rosaly or St. Rosa Lee, it comes to pretty much the same. She was fool enough to leave a comfortable home—inside of a palace, too, be gad—and go and live all alone by herself in that cavern. Well, they wanted me to ride up on the jackass and see it. 'No,' says I, 'you don't ketch me,' says I; 'if I did, I might as well change places with the jackass right away,' says I."

A fresh fit of coughing.

"Yes, sir, bad health and hard luck, that's ben the finishing of me, or else this minute I could show you my solid hundred thousand. The fire was what begun it all. A splendid freestone-front store, that hadn't its beat in all New York, chock full of goods, that worn't more than half covered by the insurance, burnt clean down to the sidewalk! Then come the great failure you've heard of—Bragg, Dash, and Bustup. I tell you, I was sucked in there to a handsome figger. Top of all that, my health caved in,—uh,—uh,—uh." Here the coughing grew violent. "Well, I'm a gone sucker, and it's no use crying over spilt milk. But if it worn't for bad health and damned hard luck, I should have been worth a hun—uh—uh—uh—a hundred thousand dol—uh—uh—dollars,—uh—uh—uh—uh—uh."

"This wind is too sharp for you," observed Morton.

"Fact," said the invalid; "I can't stand it no how."

He went down to the cabin, Morton's eye following him in pity and disgust.

CHAPTER XXIX

The useful science of the world to know,
Which books can never teach, nor pedants show. —*Lyttleton.*

The steamer, in due time, reached Liverpool; but Morton remained only a few days in England, crossing to Boulogne, and thence to Paris. Here he arrived late one afternoon; and taking his seat at the *table d'hôte* of Meurice's Hotel, he presently discovered among the guests the familiar profile of Vinal, who was just returned from a flying tour through the provinces. Vinal seemed not to see him; but at the close of the dinner, Morton came behind his chair and spoke to him. At his side sat a young man, whose face Morton remembered to have seen before. Vinal introduced him as Mr. Richards. When a boy, he had been a schoolmate of them both, and now called himself a medical student, living on the other side of the Seine. Having been in Paris for two years or more, he had, as he prided himself, a thorough knowledge of it; that is to say, he knew its sights of all kinds, and places of amusement of high and low degree. The sagacious Vinal thought himself happy in so able and zealous a guide.

"Mr. Vinal and I are going on an excursion about town to-night," said Richards; "won't you go with us?"

"Thank you," replied Morton, "I have letters to write, and do not mean to go out this evening."

Vinal and Richards accordingly set forth without him, the latter acquitting himself wholly to his companion's satisfaction and his own. Vinal, who inclined very little to youthful amusements, contemplated all he saw with the eye of a philosopher rather than of a sybarite, looking upon it as a curious study of human nature, in the knowledge of which he was always eager to perfect himself. In the course of their excursion, they entered a large and handsome building on the Boulevard des Italiens. Here they passed through a succession of rooms filled with men engaged in various games of hazard, more or less deep, and came at length to two small apartments, which seemed to form the penetralia of the temple.

In the farther of these was a table, about which sat some eight or ten well-dressed men, and at the head, a sedate, collected, vigilant-looking person, with a little wooden rake in his hand.

"*Messieurs, tout est fait. Rien ne va plus,*" he said, drawing towards him a plentiful heap of gold coin, almost at the instant that Vinal and Richards came in. The game was that moment finished.

As he spoke, a strong, thick-set man rose abruptly from the table, muttering a savage oath through his black moustache, and brushing fiercely past the two visitors, went out at the door. Richards pressed Vinal's arm, as a hint that he should observe him. As the game was not immediately resumed, they soon left the room; and after staking and losing a few small pieces at another table, returned to the street.

"Did you observe that man who passed us?" asked Richards.

"Yes. He seemed out of humor with his luck."

"He was clean emptied out; I would swear to it. I was afraid he would see me as he went by, but he didn't."

"Why, do you know him?"

"O, yes; and you ought to know him too, if you want to understand how things are managed hereabouts. He's a patriot,—agitator,—democrat,—red republican,—conspirator,—you can call him whichever you like, according to taste. He's mixed up with all the secret clubs, secret committees, and what not, from one end of the continent to the other. He's a sort of political sapper and miner,—not exactly like our patriots of '76, but all's fair that aims a kick at the House of Hapsburg."

"Has he any special spite in that quarter?"

"He has been intriguing so long in Austria and Lombardy, that now he could not show his face there a moment without being arrested. So he is living here, where he keeps very quiet at present, for fear of consequences."

"What is his name?"

"Speyer,—Henry Speyer."

"A German?"

"No; he's of no nation at all. He belongs to a sort of mongrel breed, from the Rock of Gibraltar,—a cross of half the nations in Europe. They go by the name of Rock Scorpions. Speyer is a compound of German, Spanish, English, French, Genoese, and Moorish, and the result is the greatest rascal that ever went unhung. Still you ought to know him; he is a curiosity,— one of the men of the times. If you want to know the secret springs of the revolution that all the newspapers will be full of not many years from this, why, Speyer is one of them."

"But is there not some risk in being in communication with such a man?"

"Yes, if one isn't cautious. But, as I'll manage it, it will be perfectly safe."

Vinal, though morbidly timorous as respected peril to life or limb, was not wholly deficient in the courage of the intriguer—a quality quite distinct from the courage of the soldier. Any thing which promised to show him human nature under a new aspect, or disclose to him a hidden spring of human action, had a resistless attraction in his eyes. He therefore assented to Richards's proposal, and promised that, at some more auspicious time, he would go with him to the patriot's lodging.

CHAPTER XXX

> Those travelled youths whom tender mothers wean
> And send abroad to see and to be seen,
> Have made all Europe's vices so well known,
> They seem almost as natural as our own.—*Churchill.*

On the next morning, Vinal, Morton, and two other young Americans were seated together in the coffee room at Meurice's. They were discussing plans of travel.

"Then you don't intend to stay long in Paris," said one of the strangers to Morton.

"Not at present. I shall set out in a few days for Vienna, and then go down the Danube."

"That's an original idea. What will you find there worth seeing?"

"It's a fancy of mine. There is no place in Europe where one can see such a conglomerate of nations and races as in the provinces along the Danube. I like to see the human animal in all his varieties,—that's my specialty."

"But what facilities will you find there for travelling?"

"O, I shall be content with any that offer; the vehicles of the country, whatever they are. I don't believe in travelling *en grand seigneur*. By mixing with the people, and doing at Rome as the Romans do, one learns in a month more than he could learn in ten years by the other way."

"You'll take your servant with you, I suppose."

"No. I shall discharge him when I leave Paris."

After conversing for some time longer, Morton and the two young men left the room, while Vinal still remained faithful to the attractions of his omelet. He was interrupted by the advent of the small man who had accosted Morton in the steamer, and had since favored him with his company from Liverpool to Paris.

"Well, here's a pretty business, damned if there isn't," said the new arrival, seating himself indignantly.

"What's the matter?" asked Vinal.

"What's the matter! Why, there's a good deal the matter. There was a young man in Philadelphy named Wilkins,—John Wilkins,—I've known him ever sence he was knee high to a toad, and a likelier young feller there isn't in the States. He was goin' on to make a right smart, active, business man, too. Well, he was clerk in one of the biggest drug concerns south of New York city,—Gooch and Scammony,—I tell you, they do a tall business out west, and no mistake. No, *sir*, Gooch and Scammony ain't hardly got their beat in the drug business nowhere."

"But what about the clerk?"

"What about him? Why, that's just what I was going on to tell you. Well, John, he had a little money laid up; so he thought he'd just come out and see a bit of the world. Well, there was a German there at Philadelphy who had to cut stick from the old country on account of some political muss or other. John and he worn't on good terms;—it was about a gal, John says. However, jest about the time John talked of coming out to Europe, the German comes and makes it up, and pretends to be friends again. 'John,' says he, 'I've got relations out to Vienny, where I come from; first-rate, genteel folks; now,' says he, 'perhaps you might like me to make you acquainted with 'em. They'd do the handsome thing by you, and no mistake.' 'Well,' says John, 'I don't mind if you do.' So the German gives him some letters; and, sure enough, they treated him very civil; but the very next morning, before he was out of bed, up comes the police, and carries him off to jail; and that, I guess, would have been about the last we'd ever have seen of John Wilkins, if, by the slimmest ghost of a chance, he hadn't got word to our minister, and the minister blowed out so hard about it, that they just let John go, and said they was very sorry, and it was all a mistake, but he'd better make tracks out of Austria in double quick time, because if he didn't, they didn't know as there was any body there would undertake to be responsible for what might happen."

Here the orator's breath quite failed, and he coughed till his hatchet face turned blue. Vinal reflected in silence.

"Wasn't he an Amerikin?" pursued the small man, "and didn't he have an Amerikin passport in his pocket? I expect to go where I please, and keep what company I please,—uh,—uh,—uh. I'm an Amerikin,—uh,—and that's enough; and a considerable wide margin to spare,—uh,—uh,—uh."

"But what evidence is there that the German had any thing to do with the affair?"

"That's the deused part of the business. There ain't no evidence to fix it on him."

"Were the letters he gave your friend sealed?"

"Not a bit of it. They was open, and read jest as fair as need be."

"Probably he was imprudent, and said something which compromised him. Stone walls, you know, have ears in Austria."

"Well, I don't know."

"It is very easy for an American to get into trouble with the Austrian government. There is a natural antipathy between them."

"Damn such a government."

"Exactly; you're quite right there."

"Why, if you or me was to go down to Austria, and happen to rip out what we thought of 'em, where's the guarantee that they wouldn't stick us down in some of their prisons, and nobody be any wiser for it?"

"There is no guarantee at all."

"I've heerd said that such things has happened."

"No doubt of it. About this German,—I should advise your friend to be cautious how he accuses him of any intention of having him arrested. If the letters had been sealed, there might have been some ground for suspicion; but as the case stands, I do not see how there can be any. And it is a little hard upon a man, when he meant to do a kindness, to charge him with playing such a trick as that."

"Well, it may be as you think. It looks like enough, any way."

The small man addressed himself to his breakfast. Vinal sat playing with his spoon, his brain filled with busy and feverish thoughts.

In a few minutes, a messenger from an American banking house came in, looking about the room as if in search of some person. Observing Vinal, whom he had seen before, he asked if he knew where Mr. Morton was.

"Letters there for me?" demanded Vinal, taking several which the messenger held in his hand, and glancing over the directions.

"No, sir, they are all Mr. Morton's."

At that instant Vinal discovered the well-remembered handwriting of Edith Leslie. His pale face grew a shade paler.

"O, Mr. Morton's! I don't know where you will find him," and he gave back the letters to the messenger, who presently left the room.

Vinal sat for a few minutes more, brooding in silence; then slowly rose, and walked away. In going towards the room of the hotel which he occupied, he passed along a corridor, opposite the end of which opened a parlor occupied by Morton. The door was open, and Vinal, as he advanced, could plainly see his rival within. Morton had been on the point of going out. His hat and gloves lay on the table at his side; near them were three or four sealed letters; another—Vinal well knew from whom—was open in his hands; and as he stood bending over it, there was a sunlight in the eye of the successful lover which shot deadly envy into the breast of Vinal. Hate and jealousy gnawed and rankled at his heart.

CHAPTER XXXI

Though I do hate him as I do hell pains,
I must throw out a flag and sign of love.—*Othello.*

That day Vinal drove to the Quartier Latin, called upon his friend Richards, and asked him to dine at the Trois Frères Provençaux. Mr. Richards was never known to decline such an invitation.

To the Trois Frères accordingly they repaired. Richards, whose social position at home was much inferior to that of his entertainer, thought the latter a capital fellow; especially when Vinal flattered him by deferring to his better taste and experience in the ordering of the dinner. But when, after nightfall, they issued forth again upon the open area of the Palais Royal, the delicate Vinal shivered with the cold. A chill wind and a dreary rain had set in, and Vinal, always cautious in such matters, said that before proceeding on their evening's amusements, he would go to Meurice's and get an overcoat.

The overcoat being found, Vinal, buttoned to the chin, came down the stairway, and rejoined Richards.

Morton had just before sent a servant for a carriage, to drive to the opera, and was waiting wrapped in his cloak, on the steps outside the door.

"What shall our first move be?" asked Richards of Vinal, as they passed out.

"Whatever you like."

"You had better give the word."

"Then suppose we go and see your friend, the professor."

"Who the deuse is Richards's friend, the professor?" thought Morton, as the others passed without observing him.

"The professor" was a cant term for Mr. Henry Speyer.

Speyer lived in an obscure part of the Latin quarter; and Richards, who was vain of his intimacy with this scoundrel, as indicating how deeply he was versed in Paris life, approached his lodging with much circumspection, by dim and devious routes.

"My name is Wilton, and I hail from New Orleans," said Vinal, as they reached the patriot's threshold.

As Mr. Wilton, of New Orleans, then, Vinal became known to Mr. Henry Speyer. The latter's quarters were any thing but commodious or attractive; and Richards invited him to a *petit souper* at his own lodgings, which were not very remote. Leaving Speyer to make his own way thither, he proceeded to summon two additional guests, in the persons of two friends of his own, his favorite partners at the Chaumière. With the aid of wine and cigars, the party became, in time, very animated. Vinal, who had a quick and pungent wit, drew upon himself much applause, and Speyer regarded him with especial commendation. But while he played his part thus successfully, he was studying his companions, as a scholar studies a book; studiously keeping himself cool; sipping a few drops of his wine, and slyly spilling the rest under the table, while he did his best to stimulate the others, and especially Speyer, to drink. Speyer drank, indeed, but the wine seemed to produce no more effect on him than water. He remained as cool as Vinal himself. The latter, young as he was, was a close and penetrating judge of men; and when, at two o'clock in the morning, he returned to his hotel, he carried with him the conviction that, in his present beggared condition, a few hundred francs would bribe the patriot to commit any moderately safe villany.

The evening, however, had had one result which Vinal regretted. Mr. Richards, being obfuscated with champagne, had repeatedly called him by his true name; so that Speyer was fully aware that his new acquaintance was not Mr. Wilton, of New Orleans, but Mr. Horace Vinal, of Boston.

CHAPTER XXXII

And, far the blackest there, the traitor friend.—*Dryden*.

Several days had passed, during which Vinal contrived to have more than one private interview with his new acquaintance, Speyer. He had sounded him with much astuteness; found that he could serve him; and was confirmed in his assurance that he would.

Morton, he knew, was to leave Paris on the next morning. The time to act was now, or never.

At about three in the afternoon, he discovered his rival sauntering along an avenue in the garden of the Tuileries; and walking up behind, he joined him.

"There are some of us," said Vinal, after a few moments' conversation, "going to Versailles to-morrow. Will you go?"

"I mean to leave Paris to-morrow."

"To-morrow! That's very sudden."

"I shall come back again in a few months."

"Your first move is to Italy, I think you said."

"No, to Austria and the Danube."

"O, I remember; it is West who is going to Italy. I think he has chosen the better route of the two."

"Yes, as far as history and works of art are concerned. But the Austrian provinces are the best field for me. I am mounted on a hobby, you know, and my time is so short that I must make the most of what I have."

"You wish to see the people—the different races—is that it?"

"Yes."

"You ought to be well booked up before you go, or you'll lose time. By the way, I made an acquaintance a little while ago in the diligence from Strasburg—a very agreeable man, a professor at Berlin— —"

"O, the professor whom you and Richards were going to see, the other night."

A thrill shot through Vinal's nerves; but the unsuspecting Morton almost instantly relieved his terror.

"I was standing on the steps as you went out, and heard you say that you were going to visit him. From the way in which you spoke, I imagined him to be some professor of the noble art of self-defence."

"Ha, ha!" laughed Vinal, not quite recovered from his surprise; "no, not precisely that; Speyer is a philologist—that's his department."

"And Richards knows him, too?"

"Yes, through my introduction."

"From your calling him 'his friend, the professor,' I imagined that the acquaintance began the other way."

"Yes, his friend, with a vengeance. Confound the fellow, as I was walking with him the other day, we met Speyer, and I, thinking no harm, introduced them; but it wasn't twenty-four hours before Richards was at him to borrow money, which Speyer let him have. I dare say Richards has bled you as well."

"No."

"No? Then you are luckier than I am. I advise you to keep out of his way, or he'll pin you before you know it."

"I should judge as much."

"I spoke of Professor Speyer because he was born in some outlandish corner of the Austrian empire,—Croatia, I think he told me,—and had his head full of political soap bubbles founded on the distribution of races in that part of the world. He put me to sleep half a dozen times with talking about Pansclavism and the manifest destinies of the Sclavic peoples. He is the very man for you; and I am sorry I didn't think of it before."

"Well," said Morton, "I must blunder through as I can."

"Are you at leisure? I'll go with you this afternoon, if you like, and call on him."

"I dare say my visit would bore him."

"Get him upon the races in the Austrian empire, and he will be more apt to bore you. Are you free at four o'clock?" pursued Vinal, looking at his watch.

"Yes, quite so."

"Very well. I'm going now to my tailor's. Every genuine American, you know, must have a new fit-out in Paris. I'll meet you at Meurice's at four, and we'll go from there to Speyer's."

Vinal had three quarters of an hour to spare. He spent a part of them in forging the next link of his chain. At four he rejoined Morton, and they walked out together.

"I think you'll like Professor Speyer," said Vinal. "I have become quite intimate with him, on the strength of a fortnight's acquaintance. He urges me to go to Hungary and Transylvania, and offered me introductions to his friends there. It would not be a bad plan for you to ask him for letters. They would not make you acquainted with the Austrian *haut ton*, but they would bring you into contact with men of his own stamp,—people of knowledge and intelligence, who could be of great service to you, and with whom you needn't be on terms of much ceremony.—Here's the place;—he lives here."

It was a lodging house on the Rue Rivoli. Vinal rang the bell. The porter appeared.

"Is Professor Speyer at home?"

"*Non, monsieur; il est sorti.*"

Vinal had just bribed the man to give this answer.

"That's unlucky," he said. "Well, if you like, we can come again this evening."

"I am engaged to dine this evening at Madame ——'s."

Vinal had known of this engagement.

"I don't see, then, but that you will lose your chance with Speyer. Well, *fortune de guerre*. I should like to have had you see him, though."

And they walked towards the Boulevards, conversing on indifferent matters.

CHAPTER XXXIII

> Whose nature is so far from doing evil
> That he suspects none; on whose foolish honesty
> My practices ride easy. — *King Lear*.

Early the next morning, Morton was writing in his room, when Vinal came in.

"Are you still bent on going off to-day?"

"Yes, within an hour."

"I was passing last evening by Professor Speyer's lodgings, and, seeing a light at his window, went in. I told him that I had come to find him in the afternoon with an old acquaintance of mine, who was going to the Austrian provinces, and that I had advised you to ask introductions from him to his friends there. He was a good deal interested, as I knew he would be, in what I told him about the objects of your journey. 'I'm very sorry,' he said, 'that I did not see your friend, for I could have given him letters which I don't doubt would have been of great use to him. But wait a few minutes,' said he, 'and I'll write a few lines now.' Here they are," continued Vinal, giving to Morton four or five notes of introduction. "You can put them in your pocket, and use them or not, as you may find convenient."

"I'm very much obliged to you," said Morton. "Tell Professor Speyer that I am greatly indebted to his kindness, and shall be happy to avail myself of it. You are looking very pale; are you ill?"

"No, not at all," stammered Vinal, "but, what is nearly as bad, I have been kept awake all night with a raging toothache."

He had been awake all night, but not with toothache.

"There is one consolation for that trouble; cold steel will cure it."

"Yes, but the remedy is none of the pleasantest. I won't interrupt you any longer. Good by. I wish you a pleasant journey."

He shook hands with Morton, and, pressing his haggard cheek, as if to stifle the pain, left the room.

With a new letter from Edith Leslie before him, Morton saw the world in rose tint. Happiness blinded him, and he was in no mood to doubt of human nature. He blamed himself for his harsh opinions of Vinal.

"It's very generous of him to interest himself at this time, in my affairs. ''Tis my nature's plague to spy into abuses.' I have misjudged him. He is a better fellow than I ever took him for."

The notes were written in a peculiarly neat, small hand, and bore the signature of Henry Speyer. They all spoke of Morton as interested in a common object with the person addressed; but, with this exception, there was nothing in them which drew his attention, especially as they were in German, a language with which he was not very familiar. As for the circumstance of their having been given at all to a person whom the writer had never seen, Morton accounted for it on the score of the good natured professor's desire to oblige his valued friend Vinal.

CHAPTER XXXIV

Things bad begun make strong themselves by ill. —*Macbeth.*

The requisites of a successful villain are manifold. The toughened conscience, the ready wit, the sage experience, the mind tutored, like Iago, in all qualities of human dealing,—all these, in some reasonable measure, Vinal had; but he miserably lacked the vulgar, but no less needful requisite of a sound bodily fibre to support the workings of his brain. His mind was a good lever with a feeble fulcrum; a gun mounted on a tottering rampart. When every breath of emotion that touches the fine-strung organism quivers along the electric chord to the brain, kindling there strange perturbations, then philosophy must lower her tone, and stoicism itself must soon confess that its only resource is to avoid the enemy with whom it cannot cope. Vinal was but ill fitted to act the part he had undertaken. The excitements of villany were too much for him. Peace of mind was as needful to him as food and drink. He had been battling all his life against what he imagined to be a defect of his mental forces, but which had, in the main, no deeper root than in the sensitiveness of his bodily constitution. In prudence and common sense, he was bound to seek asylum in that blissful serenity, that benignant calm, said to be the unfailing attendant on piety and good works. Never did Nature give a sharper hint than she gave to Vinal to eschew evil courses, and leaving rascality to tougher nerves, to tread the placid paths of virtue and discretion. Vinal saw fit to disregard the hint, and the consequences became somewhat grievous.

While his intrigue was in progress, his nerves had given him no great trouble. Hate and jealousy absorbed him. He was steadfast in his purpose to get rid of his rival. But now that the mine was laid, and the match lighted, a change began to come upon him. It was his maiden felony; his first *début* in the distinct character of a scoundrel; and, though his conscience was none of the liveliest, it sufficed to visit him with some qualms. Anxieties, doubts, fears, began to prey upon him; sleep failed him; his nerves were set more and more on edge; in short, body and mind, mutually acting on each other, were fast bringing him to a state quite adverse to the maxims of his philosophy.

When a sophomore in college, his favorite reading had been Foster's Essay on Decision of Character, and he had aspired to realize in his own person the type of character therein set forth; the man of steel, who, in his firm march towards his ends, knows neither doubts, nor waverings, nor relentings. Of this ideal he was now falling lamentably short; and as, at two o'clock in the morning, he rose from his restless bed, and paced his chamber to and fro, vainly upbraiding his weakness, and struggling to reason down the rebellious vibration of his nerves, he was any thing but the inexorable hero of his boyish fancy.

"The thing is done,"—so he communed with himself,—"it was deliberately done, and well done. That hound is chained and muzzled, or will be so soon. For a time, at least, he is out of my path. But is he? What if he should escape the trap? What if those men to whom I have sent him are less an abomination in the eyes of the government than there is reason to think them? No doubt he will be compromised; no doubt he will get into difficulty; but if he should get out again! if, within a year from this he should come home to charge me with trapanning him! Pshaw! he could prove nothing. He would be thought malicious if he accused me. But he may suspect!" and this idea sufficed to fill his excited mind with fresh agitation. For three nights he had been without sleep; and now his irritable system was wrought almost to the point of fever.

"Half measures are nothing! The nail must be driven home and clinched! I must make sure of him." And early in the morning he went to find Speyer.

Speyer was not to be found. In his eagerness, he went again and again to seek him, though he knew that there was risk in doing so. At length he succeeded; and in spite of his resolute and long-practised self-control, his confederate saw at a glance, in his shining eye, flushed cheek, and the nervous compression of his lips, that he was under a great, though a painfully repressed excitement.

"Well, monsieur, do you hear any thing from your friend?"

"No, it is not time to hear."

"You will have to wait a long while before the time comes."

"Your letters were very well so far as they go; but the thing should be done thoroughly. What I wish you to do is this. Write to him a letter, implicating him in your revolutionary plot. He will be under suspicion. Every letter sent to him will be stopped and opened by the police."

"If that is done, I will warrant you quit of him; at least for some years to come."

"They will imprison him," said Vinal, nervously, "but that will be the whole,—his life will be in no danger."

"His life!" returned Speyer, glancing sidelong at his visitor; "don't be troubled on that score. They won't kill him."

"Then write the letter," said Vinal, laying a rouleau of gold on the table, "and write it in such a way that it shall spring the trap on him, and keep him caged till doomsday."

The letter was written. Vinal read it, re-read it, sealed it, and with a quivering hand thrust it into the post office.

CHAPTER XXXV

> Thy hope is young, thy heart is strong, but yet a day may be,
> When thou shalt weep in dungeon deep, and none thy weeping see.
>
> *The Count of Saldana.*

Morton had left Vienna, and was journeying in the diligence on the confines of Styria. The cumbrous machine had been lumbering on all night. Awaking at daybreak from his comfortless sleep, and looking through the breath-bedimmed panes before him, he saw the postilion's shoulders wearily jolting up and down with the motion of the lazy horses. He had one fellow-traveller in the compartment which he occupied, a man of thirty-five or thereabouts, who had taken the diligence late the evening before, and who now, his shoulders supported by the leather straps which hung for the purpose from the roof, and his head tumbling forward on his chest, was dozing with a ludicrously grim expression of countenance. At length a sudden jolt awakened him; he started, shook himself, looked about him, inclined his head by way of salutation to his fellow-traveller, and opened a conversation with a remark on the chillness of the morning. After conversing for a time in French, the stranger said in excellent English, "I see there is no need of our speaking French, for by your accent I judge that you are English. I myself have a little of the English about me; that is to say, I was four years at Oxford, though I am German by birth."

"I am not English, though my ancestors were."

"You are American, then?" said the stranger, looking at him with some curiosity; and from this beginning, their acquaintance ripened fast. The German, regarding his companion as a young man of more intelligence than experience, conversed with an ease and frankness which fast gained upon Morton's confidence. He proved, indeed, a storehouse of information, discoursing of the people, the country, and even the government, with little reserve, and an admirable copiousness and minuteness of knowledge. At length he asked Morton if he had any acquaintance in Austria.

"None, excepting one or two persons at Vienna, to whom I had letters."

"Then you have probably made agreeable acquaintances. The society of Vienna is a very pleasant one."

"My letters were, or purported to be, to *savans* and literary men."

"There, too, you should have found persons well worth the meeting."

"I have no doubt of it."

"You do not speak," said the investigating stranger, with a smile, "like one who has been much pleased with his experience."

"I have had no opportunity to judge fairly of the Viennese *savans*."

"Your letters gave you no opportunity?"

"They were given me at Paris, in a rather singular way; and, to say the truth, the persons to whom they introduced me were so little to my taste, that after delivering one or two of them, I determined not to use the rest."

"You appear to have been very unfortunate. Will you allow me to ask to whom your letters were addressed?"

"They were written by a person whom I never saw, and were given to me by a friend,—an acquaintance,—of mine, as a means of gaining information about the country; such information as that for which I am indebted to you. I have been a good deal perplexed as to the character of the persons to whom they were written."

"Very probably I could aid you."

Morton mentioned the names of the men he had seen.

The German at first looked puzzled, then amazed, then distrustful.

"Your letters were got for you by a friend of yours?"

"Yes."

"And were written by——"

"A professor from Berlin, named Speyer,—Henry Speyer."

"Henry Speyer!" repeated the German, in astonishment.

"You were saying that you had lived for some years at Berlin. Perhaps you can tell me who and what he is."

"I know of no Professor Henry Speyer at Berlin."

"This man, I am told, is well known as a philologist."

"There is a Henry Speyer who is a philologist, so far as speaking every language in Europe can make him one; but he was never a professor in Berlin or any where else."

Morton looked perplexed. The German studied his face for a moment, and then said,—

"You say that a friend of yours gave you letters from Henry Speyer to the men you just named?"

"Yes."

"I beg your pardon! Have you ever quarrelled with your friend? Are you on terms with your friend's mistress? or do you stand between your friend and a fortune?"

A cold thrill passed through Morton's frame. There was an approach to truth in both the two last suppositions.

"Either you are very much deeper than I know how to comprehend you, or else you are the victim of a plot."

"What kind of plot?" demanded the startled Morton; "who is Speyer, and who are the other men?"

"I will tell you. Speyer is an intriguer, a revolutionist, a man in every way infamous. As for his being a professor, he is no more a professor than he is a prime minister, and you may ascribe what motives you please to your friend for giving him the name. He dares not set foot in Austria. If he did, it would go very hard with him. The other men are of the same kidney—his aiders, abetters, fellow conspirators; known or suspected to be plotting for the overthrow of the government."

"Then why are they at liberty?"

"Do you call it liberty to be day and night under the eye of the police—to be dogged and watched every hour of their lives? They serve as a sort of decoy. All who hold communication with them are noted down as dangerous; and my only wonder is, that you have not before this heard from the police."

"And what would you advise me to do?"

"Get out of Austria as soon and as quietly as you can. When you have passed the frontier you will be safe, and not before."

CHAPTER XXXVI

> Monsieur, j'ai deux mots à vous dire;
> Messieurs les maréchaux, dont j'ai commandement,
> Vous mandent de venir les trouver promptement,
> Monsieur.—*Le Misanthrope.*

That evening Morton arrived at the post house at — —. He was alone, his companion of the morning, whose route lay in another direction, having left him long before. At the head of the ancient staircase, the host welcomed him with a "good night," and ushered him into a large, low, wooden room, where some thirty men and women were smoking, eating, and lounging among the tables and benches. Old Germans talked over their beer pots, and puffed at their pipes; young ones laughed and bantered with the servant girls. A Frenchman, *en route* for Laibach, gulped down his bowlful of soup, sprang to the window when he heard the postilion's horn, bounded back to finish his tumbler of wine, then seized his cane, and dashed out in hot haste. A small, prim student strutted to the window to watch him, pipe in hand, and an amused grin on his face; then turned to roar for more beer, and joke with the girl who brought it.

Morton sat alone, incensed, disturbed, anxious. He had resolved to go no farther without taking measures to secure his own safety; and a day or two, he hoped, would place him out of the reach of danger. Meanwhile, what with his horror at the villany which had duped him, his anger with himself at being duped, and the consciousness that the hundred-handed despotism of Austria might at any moment close its gripe upon him, the condition of his mind was far from enviable.

As he surveyed the noisy groups around him, three men appeared at the door. Morton sipped his wine, and watched them uneasily out of the corner of his eye. One of them was a military officer; another was a tall man in a civil dress; the third was the conductor of the diligence in which Morton had travelled all day. The conductor looked towards him significantly; the tall man inclined his head, as a token that he understood the sign. Then approaching, hat in hand, he said very courteously, in French,—

"Pardon, monsieur; I regret that I must give you some little trouble. I have a carriage below; will you have the goodness to accept a seat in it?"

"To go whither?" demanded Morton, in alarm.

"To the office of police, monsieur."

The Austrian Briareus had clutched him at last.

CHAPTER XXXVII

Are you called forth, from out a world of men,
To slay the innocent? What is my offence?
Where is the evidence that doth accuse me?
What lawful quest have given their verdict up
Unto the frowning judge?—*Richard III.*

"You have trifled long enough," said the commissioner; "declare what you know, or you shall be dealt with summarily."

A long journey, manacled like a felon, and guarded by dragoons with loaded carbines; a rigorous imprisonment, already five months protracted; repeated examinations before a military tribunal; cross-questionings, threats, and insults, to extort his supposed secrets;—all these had formed a sharp transition from the halcyon days of Vassall Morton's prosperity.

"Declare what you know, or you shall be dealt with summarily."

"I know nothing, and therefore can declare nothing."

"You have held that tone long enough. Do you imagine that we are to be deceived by your inventions? Tell what you know, or in twenty minutes you will be led to the rampart and shot."

"I am in your power, and you can do what you will."

The commissioner spoke in German to the corporal of the guard, who took Morton into custody, and was leading him from the room.

"Stop," cried the official, from his seat.

Morton turned.

"You are destroying yourself, young man."

"It is false. You are murdering me."

"Do not answer me. I tell you, you are murdering yourself. Are you the fool to fling away your life in a fit of obstinacy?"

"Are you the villain to shoot innocent men in cold blood?"

The commissioner swore a savage oath, and with an angry gesture sent the corporal from the room.

The corporal led his prisoner along the corridor, which had grown ruefully familiar to Morton's eye; but instead of following the way which led to the latter's cell, he turned into a much wider and more commodious passage. Here, at his open door, stood Padre Luca, confessing priest of the castle.

Padre Luca had mistaken his calling, when he took it upon him to discharge such a function. He was too tender of heart, too soft of nature; ill seasoned, moreover, to his work, for he had been but a week in the fortress, and this was the first victim whom it behooved him to prepare for death. And when he saw the young prisoner, and learned the instant doom under which he stood, his nerves grew tremulous, and he found no words to usher in his ghostly counsels.

Corporal Max Kubitski, with a face unperturbed as a block, unfettered Morton's wrists, left him with the confessor, and withdrew, placing a soldier on guard at the door without. Morton sat silent and calm. The hand of Padre Luca quivered with agitation.

"My son," he began; and here his voice faltered.

"I trust," he said, finding his tongue again, "that you are a faithful child of our holy mother, the church, and that the heresies and infidelities of these times— —"

"Father," said Morton, willingly adopting the filial address to the kind-hearted priest, "I am a Protestant. I was born and bred among Protestants. I respect your ancient church for the good she has done in ages past, and for the good men who have held her faith; but I do not believe her doctrine, nor approve her practice."

The priest's face betrayed his discomposure.

"My son, my dear son, it is not too late; it is never too late. Listen to the truth; renounce your fatal errors. I will baptize you; and when you are gone, I will pray our great saint of Milan to intercede for you, and I will say masses for your soul."

Morton smiled faintly, and shook his head.

"I thank you; but it is too late for conversion. I must die in my heresy, as I have lived."

"So young!" exclaimed Padre Luca; "and so calm on the brink of eternity! Ah, it is hard to die, when so much is left to enjoy; but it is worse to plunge from present suffering into everlasting despair." And he proceeded to give a most graphic picture of post-mortal torments, drawn from the Spiritual

Exercises of Saint Ignatius, a work very familiar to his meditations. This dire imagery failed to convince the dying heretic.

"My mind is made up. I cannot believe your doctrine, but I can feel your kindness. You have spoken the first friendly words that I have heard for months."

"It is hard that you should die so unprepared, and so young. You have relatives? You have friends?"

"More than friends! More than friends!" groaned Morton. And as a flood of recollection swept over him, his heart for a moment was sick with anguish.

"Come with me," whispered Padre Luca. He led the way into the chapel of the castle, which adjoined his room. Here he bowed and crossed himself before an altar, over which was displayed a painting of the Virgin.

"Our Blessed Mother is full of love, full of mercy. See,—hang this round your neck"—placing in his hand a small medal on which her image was stamped. "Go and kneel before that altar, and repeat these words," pointing to the Ave Maria in a little book of devotion. "Call on her with a true heart, and she will have pity. She cannot see you perish, body and soul. She will appear, and teach you the truth."

There was so much of earnestness and sincerity in his words, that Morton felt nothing but gratitude as he answered,—

"It would be no better than a mockery, if I should do as you wish. I cannot— —"

Here a clear, deep voice from the adjacent room interrupted him.

"Mother of heaven!" cried Padre Luca, greatly agitated.

"I am ready," answered Morton, in a voice firm as that which summoned him.

He returned to the priest's apartment, and in the doorway stood the athletic corporal, like the statue of a modern Mars.

"*Mio figlio! Mio caro figlio!*" faltered Padre Luca, laying a tremulous hand on the young man's shoulder. The kindly accents of the melodious Italian fell on his ear like a strain of music.

"You must not die now; you are not prepared. I will go to the commissioner. He will grant time."

He was pushing past the corporal, when Morton gently checked him.

"I thank you, father, a thousand times; but if I must die, there is no mercy in a half hour's delay. Let me go. This sentence may be, after all, a kindness."

The corporal took him into custody; and, with three soldiers before and three behind, he moved towards his place of execution. He seemed to himself like one not fully awake; the stern reality would not come home to his thoughts, until, as he was mounting a flight of steps leading to the rampart, a vivid remembrance glowed upon him of that summer evening when, in her father's garden, Edith Leslie had accepted his love. It was with a desperate effort of pride and resolution that he quelled the emotion which rose choking to his throat, and murmuring a petition for her safety, walked forward with an unchanged face.

A light shone in upon the passage, and they stood in a moment upon the rampart, whence a panorama of sunny mountains opened on the view. It was a space of some extent, paved with flag-stones, and compassed with battlements and walls. On one side stood, leaning on their muskets, a file of Bohemian soldiers, in their close frogged uniforms and long mustaches. These, with their officer, Corporal Kubitski, with his six men, a sub-official acting for the commissioner, and Padre Luca, were the only persons present, besides the prisoner. The latter was placed before the Bohemians, at the distance of twelve or fourteen paces. The corporal and his men drew aside.

"Now," demanded the deputy, "will you confess what you know, or will you die?"

"I have told you, once and again, that I have nothing to confess."

"Then take the consequence of your obstinacy."

He motioned to the officer. A word of command was given. Each soldier loaded with ball, and the ramrods rattled as they sent home the charge. Another command, and the cocked muskets rose to the level, concentrating their aim against the prisoner's breast.

"If you will speak, speak now. You have a quarter of a minute to save yourself." And the deputy took out his watch.

Morton turned his head slowly, and looked at him for an instant in silence.

"Speak, speak," cried Padre Luca, pressing towards him; "tell him what you know."

The sharp voice of the officer warned him back.

Morton stood with compressed lips, and every nerve at its tension, in instant expectation of the volley; already, in fancy, he felt the bullets plunging through his breast; but not a muscle flinched, and he fronted the deadly muzzles with an unblenching eye. The deputy scrutinized his face, and turned away, muttering. At that moment a man, who through the whole scene had stood hidden in the entrance of a passage, ran out with a pretence of great haste and earnestness, and called to stop the execution, since the commissioner had granted a reprieve. In fact, the whole affair was a sham, played off upon the prisoner to terrify him into confession.

The Bohemians recovered their muskets, and the bewildered Morton was once more in custody of the corporal, who led him, guarded as before, back towards his cell. Padre Luca, who thought that an interposition of the Virgin had softened the commissioner's heart, hastened to his oratory to pray for the heretic's conversion. Faint and heartsick, Morton scarcely knew what was passing, till he was thrust in at his narrow door. The jailer was there, but the corporal entered also, to aid in taking the handcuffs from his wrists.

One might have looked in vain among ten thousand to find a nobler model of masculine proportion than this soldier. He stood more than six feet high, and Morton, who loved to look upon a man, had often, even in his distress, admired his martial bearing and the powerful symmetry of his frame. His face, too, was singularly fine in its way, and though the discipline of long habit usually banished from it any distinct expression, yet the cast of the features, and the manly curve of the lip, which the thick brown mustache could not wholly hide, seemed to augur a brave, generous, and loyal nature.

More stupefied than cheered at being snatched, as he supposed, from the jaws of death, Morton stood passive while his hands were released. The jailer left him for a moment, and crossed over to the opposite corner of the cell. His back was turned as he did so. The corporal's six soldiers were all in the passage without. At that instant, Morton felt a warm breath at his ear, and heard whispered in a barbarous accent,—

"*Courage, mon ami! Vive la liberté! Vive l'Amerique!*"

He turned; but the martial visage of the corporal was unmoved as bronze; and, in a moment more, the iron door clanged behind him as he disappeared.

CHAPTER XXXVIII

O Death, why now so slow art thou? why fearest thou to smite?
Lamentation of Don Roderick.

When all the blandishments of life are gone,
The coward sneaks to death, the brave live on.—*Sewell.*

The whispered words of the corporal kindled a spark of hope in Morton's breast; but it was destined to fade and die. Once he was sure that he heard the tones of his voice in the passage without his cell; but weeks passed, months passed, and he did not see him again.

And now let the curtain drop for a space of three years.

Morton was still a prisoner. Despair was at hand. He longed to die. His longing at length seemed near its accomplishment. A raging fever seized him, and for days he lay delirious, balanced on the brink of death. But his constitution endured the shock; and late one night he lay on his pallet, exhausted, worn to a skeleton, yet fully conscious of his situation.

The locks clashed, the hinges jarred, and a physician of the prison, a bulky German, stood at his side.

He felt his patient's pulse.

"Shall I die, or not?" demanded the sick man.

"Die!" echoed the German, a laugh gurgling within him, like the first symptom of an earthquake; "all men die, but this sickness will never kill you. It would have killed ninety-nine out of a hundred; but you are as tough as a rhinoceros."

Morton turned to the wall, and cursed the hour when he was born.

The German gave a prescription to his attendant; the locks clashed again behind him, and Morton was left alone with his misery.

The lamp in the passage without shone through the grated opening above the door, and shed a square of yellow light on the black, damp stones of the dungeon. They sweated and trickled with a clammy moisture; and the brick pavement was wet, as if the clouds had rained upon it. Morton lay motionless as a dead man. The crisis of his disorder was past; but its effects were heavy upon him, and his mind shared the deep exhaustion of his body. Perilous thoughts rose upon him, spectral and hollow-eyed.

"By what right am I doomed to this protracted misery? By what justice, when a refuge is at hand, am I forbidden to fly to it? I have only to drag myself from this bed, and rest for a few moments on those wet, cold bricks, and all the medicines in Austria could not keep me many days a prisoner. And who could blame me? Who could say that I destroyed myself? It is not suicide. It is but aiding kindly nature to do a deed of mercy."

He repelled the thought; but it returned. He repelled it again, but still it returned. The insidious demon was again and again at his ear, stealing back with a noiseless gliding, smoothly commending her poison to his lips, soothing his worn spirit as the vampire fans its slumbering victim with its wings. But his better nature, not without a higher appeal, fortified itself against her, and struggled to hold its ground.

When the French besieged Saragossa; when her walls crumbled before their batteries; when, day by day, through secret mine or open assault, foot by foot, they won their way inward towards her heart; when treason within aided force without, and famine and pestilence leagued against her,—still her undespairing children refused to yield. Sick men dragged themselves to the barricades, women and boys pointed the cannon, and her heroic banner still floated above the wreck.

Thus, spent with disease, gnawed with pertinacious miseries, assailed by black memories of the past, and blacker forebodings of the future, did Morton maintain his weary battle with despair.

CHAPTER XXXIX

Who would lose,
Though full of pain, this intellectual being,
These thoughts that wander through eternity?

To be weak is miserable,
Doing or suffering.—*Paradise Lost*.

Morton recovered slowly. The influences about him were any thing but favorable to a quick convalescence, and it was months before he was himself again. Even then, though his health seemed confirmed, a deeper cloud remained upon his spirits: his dungeon seemed more dark and gloomy, his prospects more desperate.

One day he paced his cell in a mood of more than usual depression.

"Fools and knaves are at large; robbery and murder have full scope; vanity and profligacy run their free career; then why is honest effort paralyzed, and buried here alive? There are those in these vaults,—men innocent of crime as I,—men who would have been an honor to their race,—who have passed a score of years in this living death. And canting fools would console them with saying that 'all is for the best.' I will sooner believe that the world is governed by devils, and that the prince of them all is bodied in Metternich. Why is there not in crushed hope, and stifled wrath, and swelling anguish, and frenzy, and despair, a force to burst these hellish sepulchres, and blow them to the moon!

"It is but a weak punishment to which Milton dooms his ruined angel. Action,—enterprise,—achievement,—a hell like that is heaven to the cells of Ehrenberg. He should have chained him to a rock, and left him alone to the torture of his own thoughts; the unutterable agonies of a mind preying on itself for want of other sustenance. Action!—mured in this dungeon, the starved soul gasps for it as the lungs for air. 'Action, action, action!—all in all! What is life without it? A marsh, a quagmire, a rotten, stagnant pool. It is its own reward. The chase is all; the prize nothing. The huntsmen chase the fox all day, and, when they have caught her, fling her to their hounds for a worthless vermin. Alexander wept that he had no more worlds to conquer. What did it profit him that a conquered world lay already at his feet? The errant knights who roamed the world with their mistress's glove on their helmet, achieving impossibilities in her name,—which of them could have endured to live in peace with her for a six-month? The crusader master of Jerusalem, Cortes with Mexico subdued, any hero when his work is done, falls back to the ranks of common men. His lamp is out, his fire quenched; and what avails the stale, lack-lustre remnant of his days?

"Action! the panacea of human ills; the sure resource of misery; the refuge of bad consciences; a maelstroom, in whose giddy vortex saints and villains may whirl alike. How like a madman some great criminal, some Macbeth, will plunge on through his slough of blood and treachery, frantic to dam out justice at every chink, and bulwark himself against fate; clinching crime with crime; giving conscience no time to stab; finding no rest; but still plunging on, desperate and blind! How like a madman some pious anchorite, fervent to win heaven, will pile torture on torture, fast, and vigil, and scourge, made wretched daily with some fresh scruple, delving to find some new depth of self-abasement, and still struggling on unsatisfied, insatiable of penance, till the grave devours him! Human activity!—to pursue a security which is never reached, a contentment which eludes the grasp, some golden consummation which proves but hollow mockery; to seize the prize, to taste it, to fling it away, and reach after another! This cell, where I thought myself buried and sealed up from knowledge, is, after all, a school of philosophy. It teaches a dreary wisdom of its own. Through these stone walls I can see the follies of the world more clearly than when I was in the midst of them. A dreary wisdom; and yet not wholly dreary. There is a power and a consolation in it. Misery is the mind-maker; the revealer of truth; the spring of nobleness; the test, the purger, the strengthener of the spirit. Our natures are like grapes in the wine press: they must be pressed to the uttermost before they will give forth all their virtue.

"Why do I delude myself? What good can be wrung out of a misery like mine? It is folly to cheat myself with hope. This hell-begotten Austria has me fast, and will not loosen her gripe. Abroad in the free world, fortitude will count for much. There, one can hold firm the clefts and cracks of his tottering fortunes with the cement of an unyielding mind; but here, it is but bare and blank endurance. Yet it is something that I can still find heart to face my doom; that there are still moments when I dare to meet this death-in-life, this slow-consuming horror, face to face, and look into all its hideousness without shrinking. To creep on to my end through years of slow decay, mind and soul famishing in solitude, sapped and worn, eaten and fretted away, by the droppings of lonely thought, till I find my rest at last under these cursed stones! God! could I but die the death of a man! De Foix,— Dundee,—Wolfe. I grudge them their bloody end. When the fierce blood boiled highest, when the keen life was tingling through their veins, and the shout of victory ringing in their ears, then to be launched at a breath forth into the wilderness of space, to sail through eternity, to explore the seas and continents of the vast unknown! But I,—I must lie here and rot. You fool! you are tied to the stake, and must bide the baiting as you can. Will you play the coward? What can you gain by that? You cannot run away. What wretch, when misery falls upon him, will not cry out, 'Take any shape but that?' In the familiar crowd, in the daily resort, how many an unregarded face masks a wretchedness worse than this! some shrunken, cankered soul, palsied and world-weary, more hopelessly dungeoned than you. Crush down your anguish, choke down your groan, and say, 'Heaven's will be done.'

"Muster what courage you may. Not those spasms of valor that make the hero of an emergency, and when the heart is on fire and the soul in arms, bear him on to great achievement. Mine must be an inward flame, that warms though it cannot shine; a fire, like the sacred Chaldean fire, that must never go out; a perpetual spring, flowing up without ceasing, to meet the unceasing need.

"And you, source of my deepest joy and my deepest sorrow,—do not fail me now. Come to me in this darkness; let your spirit haunt this tomb where I lie buried. In your presence, the evil of my heart shrank back, rebuked; its good sprang up and grew in life and freshness. You rose upon me like the sun, warming every noble germ into leaf and flower. You streamed into my soul, banishing its mists, and gladdening it to its depths with summer light. These are no girl's tears. Towards myself and my own woes, I have hardened my heart like the barren flint. I should be less than man if I did not weep when I think of you. You must pass the appointed lot; you must fade with time and sorrow; but to me you will be radiant still with youth and beauty. So will I bide my hour, anchored on that pure and lofty memory, waiting that last release when the winged spirit shall laugh at bolts and dungeon bars."

CHAPTER XL

> Lost liberty and love at once he bore;
> His prison pained him much, his
> passion more.— *Palemon and Arcite.*

Since his illness, Morton had had some of an invalid's privilege. He had been allowed to walk on the rampart for half an hour daily. In the distance, a great mountain range bounded the view, and, nearer, the Croatian forest stretched its dark and wild frontier. The scene recalled kindred scenes at home; and when he was led back to his cell, when the heavy door clashed and the bolts grated upon him, he leaned his forehead on his hand, and stood in fancy again among the mountains of New England, with all their associations of health, freedom, and golden hopes. The White Mountains seemed to rise around him like a living presence, rugged with their rocks and pines, scarred with avalanches, cinctured with morning mists; and, standing again on the bank of the Saco, he seemed to feel their breezes and hear the brawling of their waters. Then his roused fancy took a wider range; carried him across the Alleghanies and along the Ohio, up the Mississippi to its source, and downward to the sea, picturing the whole like the shifting scene of a panorama.

"Ah," he thought, "if my story could be blown abroad over those western waters! How long then should I lie here dying by inches? The farmers of Ohio, the planters of Tennessee, the backwoodsmen of Missouri, how would they endure such outrage to the meanest member of their haughty sovereignty! A hopeless dream! I have looked my last on America. My wrongs will find no voice. They and I are smothering together, safely walled up in sound and solid mason-work. Strange, the power of fancy! Heaven knows how or why, but at this moment I could believe myself seated on the edge of the lake at Matherton, under the beech trees, on a hot July noon. The leaves will not rustle; the birds will not sing; nothing seems awake but the small yellow butterflies, flickering over the clover tops, and the heat-loving cicala, raising his shrill voice from the dead pear tree. The breathless pines on the farther bank grow downward in the glassy mirror. The water lies at my feet, pellucid as the air; the dace, the bream, and the perch glide through it like spirits, their shadows following them over the quartz pebbles; and, in the cove hard by, the pirate pickerel lies asleep under the water lilies.

"On such a day, I came down the garden walk, and found Edith reading under the shade of the maple grove. On the evening of such a day, I heard from her lips the words which seemed to launch me upon a life of more than human happiness. Could I have looked into the future! Could I have lifted the glowing curtain which my fancy drew before it, the gay and gilded illusion which covered the hideous truth! Where is she now? Does she still walk in the garden, and read under the grove of maples? She thinks me dead: almost four years! She has good cause to think so; and perhaps at this moment some glib-tongued suitor, as earnest and eager as I was, is whispering persuasion into her ear, winning her to his hearth stone and his arms. Powers of hell, if you would rack man's soul with torments like your own, show him first a gleam of heaven; bathe him in celestial light; then thrust him down to a damnation like this."

And he groaned between his set teeth, in the extremity of mental torture.

CHAPTER XLI

The manly heart must sometimes cease to languish,
Ruled by the manly brain.—*Bayard Taylor.*

One day the jailer came in at his stated hour. He was, by birth, a German peasant, stupid and brutish enough; but, his calling considered, he might have been worse, and, in the lack of better company, Morton had diligently cultivated his acquaintance. On this occasion he was more than commonly dogged and impenetrable; and, on being taken to task for some neglect or malperformance of his functions, he made no manner of reply, by word, look, or gesture. Being again upbraided, he turned for a moment towards the prisoner a face as expressive as a block of pudding stone, and then sullenly continued his work as before. Morton laughed, partly in vexation, and resumed his walk, of just three paces, to and fro, the length of his cell. He followed the jailer with his eye, as the latter closed the door.

"'God made him, and therefore let him pass for a man.' Measure the distance from Shakspeare down to that fellow, and then from him again down to a baboon, and which measurement would be the longer? It would be a knotty problem to settle the question of kindred; and yet, after all, a soul to be saved, such as it is, and an indefinite power of expansion and refining, give Jacob strong odds against the baboon. He has human possibilities, like the rest of us; his unit goes to make up the sum of man; man, the riddle and marvel of the universe, the centre of interest, the centre of wonder. When I was a boy, I pleased myself with planning that I would study out the springs of human action, and trace human emotion up to its sources. It was a boy's idea,—to fathom the unfathomable, to line and map out the shifting clouds and the ever-moving winds. De Staël speaks the truth— 'Man may learn to rule man, but only God can comprehend him.' View him under one aspect only. Seek to analyze that pervading passion, that mighty mystic influence which, consciously or unconsciously, directly or indirectly, prevails in human action, and holds the sovereignty of the world. It is a vain attempt; the reason loses and confounds itself. What human faculty can follow the workings of a principle which at once exalts man to the stars, and fetters him to the earth; which can fire him with triumphant energies, or lull him into effeminate repose; kindle strange aspirations and eager longings after knowledge; spur the intellect to range time and space, or cramp it within narrow confines, among mean fancies and base associations? In its mysterious contradictions, its boundless possibilities of good and ill, it is a type of human nature itself. The soldier saint, Loyola, was right when he figured the conflicts of man's spirit by the collision of two armies, ranked under adverse banners; for what is the spirit of man but a field of war, with its marches and retreats, its ambuscades, stratagems, surprises, skirmishings, and weary life-long sieges; its shock of onset, and death-grapple, throat to throat? And whoever would be wise, or safe, must sentinel his thoughts, and rule his mind by martial law, like a city beleaguered.

"How to escape such strife! There is no escape. It has followed hermits to their deserts; and it follows me to my prison. It will find no end but in that decay and torpor, that callousness of faculty, which long imprisonment is said to bring, but which, as yet, I do not feel. Perhaps I may never feel it; for strive as I will to prepare for the worst, by inuring my mind to contemplate it, that spark of hope which never, it is said, dies wholly in a human heart, is still alive in mine. And sometimes, of late, it has kindled and glowed, as now, with a strange brightness. Is it a delusion, or the presage of some succor not far distant? Let that be as it may, I will still cling to the possibility of a better time. Whatever new disaster meets me, I will confront it with some new audacity of hope. I will nail my flag to the mast, and there it shall fly till all go down, or till flag, mast, and hulk rot together."

CHAPTER XLII

> But droop not; fortune at your time of life,
> Although a female moderately fickle,
> Will hardly leave you, as she's not your wife,
> For any length of days in such a pickle.—*Don Juan.*

Here his reflections were interrupted by the opening of the outer door of his cell, and a voice somewhat sternly pronouncing his name.

It was a regulation of the prison, that twice a day an official should visit each cell, to prevent the possibility of the tenant's attempting to escape, or hold communication with neighboring prisoners. This duty was commonly discharged by non-commissioned officers of certain corps in the garrison. Each cell had two doors. The outer one was of massive wood, guarded by iron plates and rivets. The inner door, though much less ponderous, was secured with equal care; but in the middle of it was an oblong aperture, much like that of a post office letter box, though shorter and wider. The visiting official opened the outer door, and without opening the inner, could see the prisoner by applying his eye to this aperture.

"What are you doing there?" demanded the voice, in the usual form of the visitor's challenge.

The voice was different from that to which Morton had been accustomed; and, as he gave the usual answer, he looked towards the opening. Here he saw a full, clear, blue eye, with a brown eyebrow, very well formed; altogether a different eye from that which had formerly presented itself,—a contracted, blackish, or mud-colored organ, furrowed round about with the wrinkles called "crow's feet;"—altogether a mean and vulgar-looking eye, belonging, indeed, to a rugged old soldier, whose skull might safely have been warranted sabre-proof.

Morton looked at the eye, and the eye looked at him, with great intentness, seemingly, for some twenty seconds. Then it disappeared, but returned, and resumed its scrutiny for some moments longer.

"A new broom sweeps clean," thought Morton; "that fellow means to do his duty."

The eye vanished at length, the door closed, and the step of the retiring visitor sounded along the flag-stones.

Morton thought little more of the matter, but busied himself with his usual masculine employment of stocking knitting, till seven in the evening, when the visitor came on his second round, and the same voice challenged him through the opening. He looked up, and saw the eye again; when to his astonishment, the low, hissing sound—"s—s—t"—used by Italians and some other Europeans when they wish to attract attention, sounded from the soldier's lips. At the next instant, however, something seemed to have alarmed him; for the eye disappeared, and the door closed abruptly.

Morton perplexed himself greatly with conjectures about this incident, and had half persuaded himself that the whole was a cheat of the fancy; when, on the next morning, as he was led back, under a guard, from his walk on the rampart, he saw, on entering a long gallery of the prison, a tall man approaching from the farther end. He recognized him at once. It was Max Kubitski, the corporal, who long before had guarded him to his sham execution, and whose friendly whisper in his cell had wakened in him a short gleam of hope. As the corporal passed, his eye met Morton's for an instant, with, as the latter thought, a glance of recognition.

In vain he tried to reason down the new hope that, in spite of himself, this meeting kindled. Of one thing he was sure; the corporal's eye was the eye that looked in upon him through the hole in the door; and he felt assured, moreover, that, from whatever cause, the corporal inclined to befriend him.

He waited, in great expectancy and some agitation, for the next visit; and at the stated hour, the outer door was opened, and the eye appeared.

Morton, as he replied to the challenge, made a gesture of friendly recognition.

"You remember me, eh?" whispered a voice, in broken French; "be always close to the door when I come. I shall have something to tell you."

The moustached lips whence the whisper issued were withdrawn from the opening, and Morton was left to his reflections.

To have a friend near him, however humble, was much, and the hope, slender as it seemed, that this friend might aid him, filled him with a feverish excitement. Why the corporal should interest himself in his behalf, he could not imagine; and he waited restlessly for his next coming.

In due time, the eye appeared.

"Look here," whispered Max, and thrust a paper through the opening, waiting only long enough to see Morton pick it up.

The chirography was worse, if possible, than the spelling; but Morton at last deciphered words to the following purport.

"You are brave. Don't despair. I shall help you, if I can. Long live America! Down with the emperor! Only be patient. Be sure to chew this paper, and swallow it."

The last injunction had its objections, and the prisoner compromised the matter by tearing the paper into small pieces, and stuffing them into the crevices of the floor.

At the next appearance of the eye, Morton, in a few rapid words, expressed his gratitude; adding that if the corporal would help him to escape, and go with him to America, he would make him rich for life.

The intimation probably had its effect; and yet in the case of Max it was not needed. Though his tastes and habits savored of the barrack, the corporal was one of the most simple-hearted and generous of men, with, besides, much of that kind of enthusiasm of character which is apt to be rather ornamental than useful to its owner. His birth and connections were not quite so low as might have been argued from his mean station in the service, in which his life had been spent from boyhood. He was a native of Gallicia. Several of his brothers, and others of his relatives, had been deeply compromised in the Polish rising of 1831, and had suffered heavy and humiliating penalties in consequence. His eldest brother, however, had escaped in time, and gone to America, where, being very different in character from Max, he had thriven wonderfully. After a long absence, he had reappeared, travelling with a United States passport, as an American, inveighing against European despotisms, and dilating on the glories of his adopted country. Max, the only auditor of these declamations, was greatly excited by them. He had long been tired of his thankless position in the Austrian service; and listening to his brother's persuasions, he agreed to desert, and go with him to America, the seat, as he began to imagine, of more than earthly beatitude. But before he could find opportunity, his cautious brother took alarm; and seeing some indications that his identity was suspected by the police, decamped with the promptness and alacrity which had always distinguished him in times of danger. Max, therefore, was left alone; his adviser, for fear of compromising him, not daring to attempt any communication.

It was soon after this, that, being on guard in the commissioner's inquest room at Ehrenberg, Max first saw Morton, brought in for examination, and learned from the questions and replies, that the prisoner was an American. His interest was greatly stirred; for he had never seen one of the favored race before; and, like the commissioner, he had no doubt that Morton had come on a revolutionary mission. His interest was inflamed to enthusiasm, when, being ordered to guard Morton to his execution, he saw the calmness with which the latter faced his expected fate. Indeed, his soldier heart was moved so deeply, that in the flush of the moment he conceived the idea of helping Morton to escape, and going with him to the land of promise. It was an idea more easily conceived than executed; and before he could find an opportunity, his corps was removed from the castle, and sent on duty elsewhere.

Max had always detested the life of a garrison, and especially of a prison garrison, and the change proved very agreeable to him. Though brave as the bravest, he had not much energy or forecast, and commonly let his affairs take care of themselves. He lived on from day to day, neither abandoning his plan of desertion, nor acting upon it; until, after more than two years, he was remanded to Ehrenberg, where his old disgust returned in greater force than ever. In this state of his mind, the duty of visitor was assigned to him, thus bringing him in contact with Morton, reviving his half-forgotten feeling, and, at the same time, promising him an opportunity to carry his former scheme into effect.

To this time, Morton had borne his troubles with as much philosophy as could reasonably have been expected; but now that something like a tangible hope began to open on him, the excitement became intense. He waited the daily visits of the soldier with a painful eagerness and suspense. At the stated hours, Max always came; and, at each return, some whispered word of friendship greeted the prisoner's ear.

Two days after the first paper, he thrust in another; and Morton read as follows:—

"We must wait; but our time will come; perhaps in ten days; perhaps in a week. I shall watch for a chance. Only be patient."

Five long and anxious days succeeded; when, on the forenoon of the sixth, Max thrust in a third paper; and Morton, with a beating heart, read,—

"When the jailer comes this afternoon, make him talk with you, and keep him with his back to the door. *I shall come.* Be cool and steady. I shall tell you what to do."

Illness and long confinement had wrought upon Morton's system in a manner which made it doubly difficult to preserve the coolness which the emergency demanded; but he summoned his utmost resolution to meet this crisis of his fate.

The jailer was nowise addicted to conversation; and how to engage him in it, was a problem of some difficulty. There was only one topic on which

Morton had ever seen him at all animated. This was the battle of Wagram, in which, in his youth, he had taken part, and where he had received a sabre cut, which had left a ghastly blue scar across his cheek. In dilating on this momentous passage of his life, the old German would sometimes be roused into a great excitement; and Morton had often amused himself with trying to comprehend the jargon which he poured out, in thick gobbling tones, about cannonading and charging, sabres and bombshells, pointing continually at his scar, and laboring to impress his hearer with the conviction, immovably fixed in his own mind, that he, Jacob, was one of the chief heroes of the day.

At his usual hour, about the middle of the afternoon, Jacob appeared. As he came in, he closed the outer door, which secured itself by a latch. This latch could be moved back from within or without, by a species of key in the jailer's keeping, Max also, as visitor, having a duplicate. The jailer alone had the key of the inner door; but this, during his stay in the cell, he never thought it necessary to close.

Jacob went through his ordinary routine, breathing deeply, meanwhile, and talking unconsciously to himself, after his usual manner.

"Do you know, Jacob," said Morton, seating himself on a stool in the farther corner, "I was dreaming the other night of you and the battle of Wagram."

"Eh!" grunted the jailer.

"What you have been telling me about it is a lie. You were never in that battle at all."

"Eh!"

"You were frightened, and ran off before the fighting began."

"Run! I run off!" growled Jacob, the idea slowly penetrating his brain.

Morton nodded assent.

The jailer turned and stared at him for a moment with open eyes and mouth. Then, as his wrath slowly mounted, he began to pour forth a flood of denial, mixed with invective against his assailant, appealing to his scar as proof positive of his valor.

"A sabre never made that scar," said Morton, as the other paused in his eloquence.

Jacob stared at him, speechless.

"You got it in a drunken row."

At this Jacob's rage seemed to choke his utterance; and Morton thought he would attack him bodily, as he stood before him, shaking his fists, and stamping on the pavement.

This pantomime was brought to a sudden close by a pair of strong hands clinched around Jacob's neck from behind, with the gripe of a vice.

"Shut the door," whispered Max.

On entering, he had left it ajar. Morton hastened to close it. The corporal meanwhile laid Jacob flat on the floor of the cell.

"Take my bayonet, and run it through him if he makes a sound."

Morton drew the bayonet from its sheath at the belt of Max, and kneeling on the jailer's breast, pressed the point of the weapon against his throat. Max then loosed his grasp, and gagged him effectually with a piece of wood and a cord which he had brought for the purpose. Jacob lay, during the whole, quite motionless, glaring upward with glassy, bloodshot eyes, stupefied with fright and astonishment.

"You must put on his clothes," said Max.

They accordingly took off the jailer's outer garments, which Morton substituted for his own, drawing the deep-visored cap over his eyes. Max, at the same time, bound the jailer, hand and foot, with strings of leather, which he took from his pocket.

"Look out into the gallery," he said, unclosing the door, "and see if there's any body in the way."

Morton, in his jailer's dress, went out, and, looking back, reported that the coast was clear. Max followed, and closed the door. The helpless Jacob remained a prisoner, till some other functionary of the castle should come to his relief.

They passed along the gallery, down one flight of steps, and up another, meeting no one but a soldier, to whom Max gave a careless nod of recognition. There were several private outlets to the castle, but each was guarded by a sentinel; and it was chiefly his preparation against this difficulty that had caused Max's delay.

Among his acquaintance was an old soldier, called Peter,—a Prussian by birth. He had learned to read and write, and being inordinately vain of his superior acquirements, looked upon himself as the most learned of men. When off duty, he was commonly to be found in a corner of the barrack, poring over a greasy little book, which he always carried in his pocket. As his temper was exceedingly sour and disagreeable, he was no favorite; indeed, he was the general butt of his brother soldiers, who delighted to exasperate his crusty mood. Max, however, with a view to the furtherance of his scheme, had of late courted his good graces, flattering him on his learning, often asking him to drink, and otherwise cajoling him. Finding that, on this day, Peter's turn had come to stand guard at a certain postern of the prison, he had contrived to drug him with a strong dose of opium, mixed with a dram of bitters. Max, who was a singular compound of simplicity and finesse, the former the result of nature, the latter of circumstance, plumed himself greatly on this exploit.

As they approached the narrow door in question, Max stooped and took off his shoes, motioning Morton to do the same. At a few paces farther on, they saw the sentinel, walking to and fro on his post, with no very military gait.

Max, who was wonderfully cool and composed, pressed Morton's arm.

"*Voilà, monsieur,*"—he was now and hereafter very respectful in his manner towards the man he was saving,—"*voilà;* look at the old booby; how he reels and staggers about—ah! do you see?"

Peter had stopped in his walk, and was leaning against the wall, nodding his head with a look indescribably sleepy and silly. Meanwhile his musket was slowly slipping down between his arm and his side, in spite of one or two efforts to clutch it. At last the butt struck on the pavement. The sound roused the sentinel from his torpor. He shook himself, and began his walk again; but in a few moments stopped, leaned his shoulder against the wall, on the farther side of the door, let his musket this time rest fairly on the floor, and began nodding and butting his head, in a most ludicrous manner, into an angle of the wall.

Max again pressed Morton's arm, and gliding on tiptoe past the drugged sentinel, they went out at the door without alarming him. They were now in an obscure and narrow precinct of the castle, flanked on one side by a high wall of ancient masonry, and on the other by the rear of various outbuildings. The place did no great credit to the neatness of the garrison, being littered with a variety of refuse; but no living thing was visible; none, that is, but a gray cat sneaking along under the wall of a shed, with a newly-killed rat dangling from her mouth.

They next passed into a wider area, overlooked on the left by the rear of the principal range of barracks.

"Hallo, Max, where are you going?" cried a voice.

Max looked up, and saw a brother corporal leaning out at one of the barrack windows, with a fatigue cap on one side of his head, and a German pipe between his moustached lips.

"To the village."

"Who gave you leave?"

"The lieutenant."

"It's good company you are in. What are you going to do below?"

"Get me a pipe. Mine is broke. What is a man fit for without his pipe?"

The other at the window replied by a joke, not very refined, levelled at Max and his companion. Max retorted only by a ludicrous gesture of derision, which drew a horse laugh from a soldier at another window, under cover of which they passed out of the area, and reached a pathway leading down the height.

A natural gully, or shallow ravine, twisted and zigzagged down the side of the rock. In wet weather, it became a little watercourse, conducting all the rain that fell on the western roofs of the castle down to the filthy and picturesque hamlet of Ehrenberg, with its dirty population of five hundred Wallack and Croat peasants, and a horde of dirtier gypsies, nested in the outskirts. In dry weather, the gully served as a pathway, which the soldiers often used in their descents to the village.

Max began to descend, and Morton followed at his heels. The fresh wind, the open view, the unwonted sense of treading mother earth, wrought on him strangely; not, as on the wrestler of old, to nerve him with renewed force. He grew faint, dizzy, and half blind; and as he staggered after his guide, he felt for the first time how the prison had sapped away his strength.

In ten minutes, they were at the bottom, and picking their way past the rear of the squalid cottages, among rickety outhouses, broken fences, heaps of litter, pigs, children, and other impediments. Most of the men were absent; a few women only stared at them as they passed. With one very pretty Wallack girl, Max, for the sake of appearances, exchanged a few words of bantering gallantry. She stood looking after him admiringly. Behind the next cottage, a yellow Hungarian shepherd dog, large as a wolf, jumped suddenly from a heap of rotten straw, on which he had been dozing, and made a fierce dash at Max's leg; but the latter gave him a kick in the teeth, which sent him off yelping, followed by a brickbat, and a curse from the Wallack damsel.

Beyond the village, the ground was without trees or shrubs for a full half mile; yet it was uneven,—not to say broken; and Max, who had made a careful reconnaissance, knew that if they could but reach unnoticed a hollow some twenty rods from the skirts of the hamlet, no eye from the ramparts could see them. Towards this, therefore, he walked, with an air of great nonchalance, Morton following, his heart in his throat. Their movements were either unseen, or failed to excite suspicion; and taking a beaten track into the hollow, they came upon a spring at the foot of a rock, where three women were pounding clothes on a stone with clubs, by way of washing them; while a lazy boor, in a broad felt hat, lay on the ground listlessly watching the process.

In five minutes more, the hollow ceased to conceal them; and, to Morton's great dismay, they stood again within eyeshot of the castle. Max, however, with the skill of an old deer stalker, soon managed to place, first, a large rock, then the rugged shoulder of a hill, between themselves and the detested battlements. Next they gained the partial shelter of the scattered scrub oaks and pines which formed a ragged outskirt to the deeper forest behind, and, in a few moments more, reached the dark asylum of its matted boughs and underwood.

Thus far they had walked at the leisurely pace of a pair of idle strollers; but no sooner were they well out of sight, than Max cried, "Come on!" and set out at a run. When he turned, however, and saw the pale face of Morton, already tired with unwonted effort, he took a flask of brandy from his pocket. The fiery draught strung Morton's sinews afresh. They pushed on, over hills and hollows, by cattle paths and brooks, across open glades, and through wooded tracts, dense and breathless as an American forest.

"Look!" said Max, stopping on a rising ground, and pointing back over the woods. Three miles off, the rock of Ehrenberg rose in view, bearing aloft its heavy load of battlements and towers. Morton gave it one look, prayed it might be the last, and motioned his companion forward again.

They came to a lazy brook, stealing out of a marsh. In the mud by its side was the slough where a wild boar had wallowed. The solitude and savageness of the place shot a fresh life through Morton's failing veins. The sense came upon him that his fate was now in his own hands; the resolve that he would never be taken alive. He called Max to stop.

"Have you any weapon besides your bayonet?"

Max produced a pair of pistols, which he had contrived to appropriate; and, keeping one of them, handed the other to Morton.

It was dusk before they stopped, in the depth of the woods, on a grassy spot, shut in by a tall cliff, and a growth of old beeches, oaks, and evergreens. Morton threw himself on the ground. Max made a fire, by plugging up the touch-hole of his flint-lock pistol, and placing in the pan, by way of tinder, a piece of cotton rag, rubbed with a little wet gunpowder. Morton roused himself, and breaking off small branches of the firs and spruces, piled them for beds. The loaf which the jailer had brought for his next day's meal, with some more solid viands which Max produced, served them for supper; and, for drink, they scooped water in their hands from the neighboring brook.

It grew dark, and as they sat together by the fire, the red light flared against the jagged rock, the shaggy fir boughs, and knotty limbs of the oaks. It seemed to Morton as if time and space were done away; as if the prison were a dream; and as if, once more on some college ramble, he were seated by a camp fire in the familiar forests of America. But instead of a vagabond Indian, or the hardy face of a Penobscot lumberman, the flame fell on the frogged uniform and long, waxed moustache of Corporal Max, as he sat cross-legged, like a Turk, on the pile of evergreens.

As Morton looked on his manly face, and thought of the boundless debt he owed him, his heart warmed towards him, and he poured forth his gratitude as well as he could, in the patchwork of languages which Max himself had used as his medium of communication.

The latter soon fell asleep, and lay snoring lustily. With his companion sleep was impossible. He lay watching the stars, and the dull folds of smoke that half hid them, listening to the wind, and the mysterious sounds of the forest, and, as the night drew on, shivering with the damp and cold. His mind was a maze of confused emotions, suspense, and delight, hope, and fear, mingling in a dreamy chaos; till at last fatigue prevailed, and he, too, fell asleep; a sleep haunted by hideous images, yet with its intervals of deep peace and repose.

He woke, shivering; and rising in the twilight, stirred the half-dead embers, and crouched over them for warmth. But, as the fresh odors of the morning reached his senses, they brought so vividly upon him the memory of his youthful health, and hope, and liberty, that his spirits rose almost to defiance of the peril around him. He woke Max, whose slumbers were noisy as ever, and they pushed forward again on a well-beaten cattle path, leading westward.

About sunrise they found a cow, one of the gray, long-horned breed of the country, grazing very peacefully. Max looked about him, and began to move with caution. The cow was wild, and would not let them pass her, but walked before them along the path. In a few minutes, a great number of cattle appeared, grazing on an open glade, with two men watching them. They were of the half-savage herdsmen of this district, little better than banditti. One of them sat on a rock, the other lounged on the grass. Both were dressed in coarse linen shirts and trousers, short, heavy woollen cloaks thrown over their shoulders, a kind of rude sandals, and broad felt hats. For weapons, one carried a club, the other a hatchet, the long handle of which served him for a walking stick.

Max whispered to Morton; and stealing unperceived through the bushes, they suddenly appeared before the two men, much, as it seemed, to their amazement. Max, in a language quite new to his companion, desired them to change clothes with Morton and himself. The voice and air of the applicant, and the butt of a pistol protruding from the breast pocket of each of the strangers, gave warning that the wish could not wisely be slighted. The boors complied, the more willingly as they would be great gainers by the bargain. Max threw off his uniform, and put on the dress of the taller herdsman. Morton satisfied himself with the woollen cloak of the other, in exchange for the jailer's coat.

The exchange made, he signed to the man to give him the hatchet which he carried; but the boor hesitated, scowling very sullenly. Max hastened to interpose, and offered a silver coin in return for the hatchet, which its owner at once surrendered. It was by no means any love of abstract justice which dictated this procedure; but a desire, on Max's part, to leave the men in good humor, lest, being offended, they might set the soldiers on the track of the fugitives.

They parted on the best terms, and Max and Morton betook themselves again to the woods.

CHAPTER XLIII

Like bloodhounds now they search me out;—
Hark to the whistle and the shout!—
The chase is up,—but they shall know,
The stag at bay's a dangerous foe.—*Lady of the Lake.*

Three or four weeks passed. They were deep within the bounds of Tyrol. By avoiding towns and highways, travelling often in the night, making prize of every stray sheep, pig, or fowl, and a diligent robbing of henroosts, they had thus far contrived to elude arrest, and support life.

Morton was greatly changed. Body and mind, he was formed for hardship, and toils which would have broken a weaker frame had nerved and strengthened his. But of late their suffering had increased. They found but poor forage among the poverty-pinched mountaineers, and for two days, had had no better sustenance than the soft inner bark of the pine trees. This, with previous abstinence, had sunk them to the last extremity, and brought Max to the verge of despair.

It was a rainy afternoon; rain drizzling in the valleys, clouds hanging on the mountains, dark vapors steaming up from the chasms, and clinging sullenly to the edge of the pine forests. Max and Morton sat under a dripping rock, on a mountain which overhangs a nameless little valley, not far to the north of the Val di Sole.

"Keep a good heart, Max," said Morton, "it shall go hard but you and I will get out of this scrape yet."

Max shook his head despondingly. His bold spirit was starved out of him. Morton's courage, unlike that of his companion, was the result more of his mental habits than of a native constitutional intrepidity, and was therefore much less subject to the changes of his bodily condition. He had proved Max, and knew him to be brave as he was warm and true-hearted; but the corporal's valor, like that of Homer's heroes, was best displayed on a full stomach.

"There's nothing else for it," said Morton; "we must take the bull by the horns. One of those houses below is an inn, or something that pretends to be one. I can see the bush fastened to the door post. We must go and buy food; or else lie here and die."

"It is better to be shot than starve," said Max.

"Come on, then. You must be spokesman. I am go for nothing in that way; but if there's any trouble, I'll stand by you as well as I can."

Max had had a little money in copper and silver, the greater part of which he had consigned to the keeping of Morton, as the more careful treasurer. With this for their passport, they issued from the cover of the woods, and began to cross the mountain slopes and rough pasture that lay between them and the hamlet.

The latter, as they drew near, seemed by no means so insignificant as at first, a rising ground having hidden a part of it. They came to the inn, a low stone building of a most respectable antiquity, and pushing open the door, were met by a short man who seemed to be the owner. Max produced a handful of kreutzers, and asked for bread and meat. The host looked at the strangers, then at their money; seemed satisfied with both, and showed them up a flight of broken steps to a large room above the half-sunken kitchen. Here, at his call, a girl brought the food and placed it on a table. He next asked if they would not have beer; and Max assenting, went out to bring it.

The fugitives now addressed themselves to their meal with the keenness of starving men; but the prudent Morton took care, at the same time, to secure the more portable of the viands for future need. Having dulled the edge of his appetite, he began to grow uneasy at the landlord's long absence.

"What is that man doing? He might have brewed the beer by this time."

"He *does* take his time," responded Max, also growing anxious.

"This is no place for us. Take the rest of that biscuit, and let's be off."

Max was following this counsel, when—— "Hark!" cried Morton; "what noise is that?"

"Go to the window and look."

Morton did so.

"My God!" he exclaimed, recoiling, his face ghastly with dismay.

Max sprang to the window. Below, at the door, four or five men were standing, and among them two gendarmes, while others were in the act of entering.

The outlandish dress of the two strangers had at once roused the landlord's suspicion. Of Max's character he had not a moment's doubt; for in him no disguise could hide the look and port of the trained soldier. By ill luck, a party of gendarmes were in the village, weather-bound on their way from Latsch. Having secured his guests' money, the landlord thought to make a farther profit from them; and, sure of his reward, reported to the officer in command, that there were in his house two men, the taller of whom was certainly a deserter, while the other could not be a peasant, though he wore the dress of one. The officer mustered his followers, and hastened to beat up the game.

He entered as Max turned from the window, and came up to him, sword in hand.

"I arrest you. Give yourselves up, you and the other."

But before the words were well out of his mouth, the fist of Max fell between his eyes like a battering ram, and dashed him back against the soldier next behind him.

"Come on," cried Max to Morton, and leaped through the open window at the farther end of the room. Morton followed in time to escape two or three bayonet thrusts which were made after him. They both vaulted over a fence, and ran through the narrow passage between an old shed and a huge square stack of the last year's hay. A musket or two were let off at them, but to no effect; and splashing across a shallow brook, they made at headlong speed for the shelter of the mountains.

As they reached the base, Max looked back. Seven or eight gendarmes were after them, and behind, later joining the chase, ran two or three men in a different dress.

"Riflemen!" muttered Max, with an oath.

Breasting the rough heights, clinging to stumps, roots, and bushes, they made their way up with all the speed which desperate need could give them. They were soon among thick trees, hidden from the pursuers, and almost from each other. But the shouts of the soldiers came up from below: they all gave tongue like so many hounds.

"Curse your yelping throats!" gasped Morton. Breathless and half spent, he was clinging to a sapling on the edge of a steep pitch of the hill. One of the soldiers saw him. A musket shot rang from below, the hollow hum of the ball passing high above his head.

Max laughed in fierce derision. They ran forward again across a wide plateau, nearly void of trees; and before they had fairly gained its farther side, the foremost pursuers were at the border of woods they had just left. Their late famine made fatal odds against them. The gendarmes, indeed, gained little in the race; but the more active riflemen were nearer every moment.

Climbing, running, and scrambling among rocks, trees, and bushes, they won their way up till they came to another plateau, which broke the ascent of the mountain a furlong above the former. Across this they dashed at full speed. They were within a rod or two of the woods beyond, Max running on Morton's left, a little in advance of him, when a musket was fired at them from behind. The aim was so bad, that they did not even hear the humming of the bullet. At the next instant, came a dull, plunging report, unlike the former. Max leaped four feet into the air, and fell forward on his face with a force that seemed to shake the earth. Morton kneeled by his side; turned him on his back; lifted him by main strength into a sitting posture. Both his hands were clutched full of grass and earth.

"Max! Max!" cried Morton, in the extremity of anguish; "speak, Max, for God's sake."

But Max said nothing. His hat had fallen off; his eyes rolled wildly under his tangled hair; he gasped; blood flowed from his lips; and a spot of blood was soaking wider and wider upon the breast of his shirt. Then a deathly change came over his dilated eyeballs. Morton had seen the throes of the wounded bison, when the fierce eyes, glaring with angry life, are clouded of a sudden into a dull, cold jelly, fixed unmeaning lumps. It was a change like this that he saw in the eyes of Max. His friend was dead. The fatal rifle of Tyrol had done its work. The ball had pierced him from back to breast, and torn through his heart on its way.

The whole passed in a few moments; but when Morton looked up, nearly all the pursuers were in sight on the open ground, and one of them, the man who had fired the death shot, was almost upon him. He snatched Max's pistol, which had fallen on the grass, and, blind with grief and fury, ran forward, levelled, and pulled the trigger. The pistol, wet with the rain, missed fire. The man was not four paces off. Morton hurled the pistol at his face. The iron barrel clashed against his teeth, and sent him reeling backward, bleeding and half stunned. Griping his hatchet, his best remaining friend, Morton turned for the woods, gained them at three bounds, and tore through the cover like a hunted wolf.

Over rocks, among trees, through thickets and brambles, he struggled and clambered on, seeking safety, like the Rocky Mountain goat, in the rudest and wildest refuge. But in a few minutes, his flight was stopped. Rocks rose before him, and rocks on each side. He was caught in a complete *cul de sac*. He might have climbed the precipices, but, in the act, the shots from below would soon have tumbled him to the earth again. There was no escape; and, grinding his teeth in rage and desperation, he turned savagely at bay.

Three or four of the men were very near him; and almost as he turned, one of them came in sight, pushing through the bushes. As he saw the game, he gave a shout, a sort of view halloo. Then appeared another, and another, all advancing upon him. In a moment, he would have been in their hands, alive or dead; but, without waiting the attack, he sprang on the foremost like a tiger, and plunged his hatchet deep in the soldier's eyes and brain. Then pushing past another, who, with a hesitating movement, was making towards him, he dashed down a sloping mass of rocks, dived into a labyrinth of thickets, and thence into a dark and hollow gorge of the mountain. Along this he ran like one with death's shadow behind him, losing himself deeper and deeper among the chaotic rocks and ragged trees. He stopped, at last, and listened. Far behind, he could hear his pursuers shouting to each other. The pack were at fault, and ranging in vain search after him.

Spent as he was, he pressed on again, following upward for an hour or more the course of a brook, which issued from a narrow glen, reaching far back into the solitude of the mountains. His mind was dim and confused, a cloudland of mixed emotions; deep grief for his murdered friend, deep rage that he had been hunted like a wild beast, a longing for further vengeance, a sense, almost to despair, of his own loneliness and peril. He felt himself outcast from mankind, driven back to find a sanctuary among the dens and fastnesses of Nature. She alone, amid the general frown, seemed propitious; for of a sudden the clouds sundered in the west; a gush of warm light poured across the dripping mountains, and flushed the distant glaciers with their evening rose-tint. In the depths where he stood, all was shadow; but the crags above were basking in the sunshine, and the savage old pines, jewelled with rain drops, seemed stretching their shaggy arms to welcome the kindly radiance. Morton threw himself on the ground, and commended his desperate fortunes to the God of the waste and the mountain.

CHAPTER XLIV

In dread, in danger, and alone,
Famished and chilled, through ways unknown,
Tangled and steep, he journeyed on.—*Lady of the Lake.*

Whoever, journeying southward from Coire, passes through the Via Mala, thence through the village of Andeer, and thence turns to the left, following a mountain path up the torrent of the Aversa, will soon lose himself in the solitudes of the savage valley of Ferrera. Thither Morton made his way; but not by so smooth an access. Ignorant of the country, and guided chiefly by the sun, he had pushed blindly forward by paths best known to the chamois and those who chase them.

His best hope had been to meet some of his travelling countrymen, from whom he could gain help. To this end he had once and again approached the highways, and as often some real or seeming danger had driven him back to the mountains. For a day or more, the food he had taken from the inn served to support him. He had flung away Max's pistol, but still had his own. It served him to kindle a fire; and by loading it with gravel, in place of shot, he contrived to kill thrushes and other small birds. Their nests, too, full at this time of eggs and young, supplied a meagre resource; and once, being hard pressed, he made a Gallic banquet on a party of serenaders who were croaking and trilling their evening concert about the edge of a shallow pool. Frogs have found warm eulogists; but never did the art of Paris or Bologna transmute those delectable reptiles into so savory a repast as did the famine-sharpened appetite of Morton.

Upon fare like this, he wandered on, till he stumbled upon the valley of Ferrera.

He had found at last an asylum wild enough to content the most pious of eremites, or the most desperate of bandits. Below he saw the raging water foaming along the depths of its black ravine; above—the stupendous ramparts that walled the valley in—cliffs, along whose giddy verge the firs were dwindled to feathers. Cascades spouted from their tops, scattering to mist and nothingness long before their measureless leap was done. The tribute drawn from the clouds the lavish mountain flung back to the clouds again. Rocks were piled on rocks, ruin on ruin, and, high over all, the glaciers of the Splugen shone like cliffs of silver.

Take a savage from his woods or his prairies, and, school him as you will, the ingrained savage will still declare itself. Take the most polished of mankind, turn him into the wilderness, and forthwith the dormant savage begins to appear. Hunt him with enemies, gnaw him with hunger, beat him with wind and rain, and observe the result; how the delicate tissues of civilization are blown away, how rude passions start into life, how his bodily cravings grow clamorous and importunate, how he grows reckless of his own blood and the blood of others. "Men are as the times." Young Lovelace of the hussars singing a duet at Lady Belgrave's *soirée*, would hardly know himself, hewing down Russian artillerymen at Balaklava.

Had Meredith met his old comrade as he was making his slow way among the rocks and ravines, in dress no better than the meanest peasant, his face moustached and bearded, and thin and dark with hardship, he would have needed the eyes of a lynx to detect Morton the millionaire. The mind of the latter shared, in some sort, the changes of his outer man. Proscribed and hunted, starved into fierceness, his best friend murdered at his side, his mood was, to say the least, none of the most benign. But, as he toiled on his way, he turned aside to rest in a sunny nook, deep sheltered among rocks. Here, where the fresh grass tempted him, and where, from a jutting crag, the water, trickling from some hidden spring, fell in rapid drops, tinkling into a pool below, and, as they fell, flashing in the sun like a string of diamonds,—here, in this quiet nook, he sat down; and, as he did so, he saw by his side, close nestled in the young grass, a little family of white and purple blossoms. They were blossoms of the crocus, a native of these valleys.

Morton bent over them, and put aside the grass from the delicate petals. A flower will now and then find a voice, and that not a weak one. As he looked, there came in upon him such a surge of recollection, such a memory of New England gardens, such a vision of loved faces, and, chief before them all, the face he best loved, such an awakening of every tender thought that had once possessed him, and all in such overpowering contrast with his present misery, that the famished outlaw burst into a flood of tears.

CHAPTER XLV

The lamentable change is from the best;
The worst returns to laughter. Welcome, then,
Thou unsubstantial air that I embrace. —*Lear.*

The Honorable Charles Augustus Murray, recreating himself with a hunting tour among the Pawnees, killed a buffalo; and being, as he assures us, ravenously hungry, proceeded to regale himself on his game, without asking the aid of the cook. Morton, in his wandering, had the good luck to kill a straggling sheep; and being twice as hungry as the Honorable Charles Augustus Murray, it may be set down largely to his credit, if he did not follow that gentleman's example. At all events, the sheep was a windfall of the first magnitude. Morton had woodcraft enough to turn the fleece into a receptacle for carrying such parts of the flesh as best answered his purposes; and thus he was well provisioned for several days.

After various roamings, by night and by day, he came upon a broad road, clearly one of the great alpine passes. Which of them he could not tell. He would have given the world to learn; for he knew nothing of his whereabouts, and thought himself still in Tyrol, or, at the best, in Bormio. His attempts to gain information from the peasants had always failed, and, in one or two instances, had seemed to threaten serious consequences. Though brave enough in the front of an open danger, the secret toils which had been about him so long had taught him to shrink from the face of man. Moreover, he could not speak the prevalent language of the district, and his Italian, which might sometimes have served him, was none of the best. A little local knowledge could have saved him a world of suffering; but, in the lack of it, he pushed blindly on, resolved to die on the mountains rather than risk another prison.

The sky for some days had been overclouded. He had lost the points of the compass; and when he saw the great highway stretching before him, dim and lonely in the gray of the morning, he thought, or hoped, that it would lead him into the heart of Switzerland. It was the pass of the Splugen, where it leaves the Rheinwald. Turning his back on safety, he began to plod on towards the lion's jaws.

Seeing a small cottage, in a recess of the forest, he reconnoitred it, with the laudable view of robbing a henroost. While thus employed, he saw two men leave the house, and betake themselves to their work in some remote part of the mountain. After a long reconnaissance, he could see no one about the place but a young woman, about six feet high, who, fork in hand, was busying herself in a field with labors much less elegant than useful. Morton watched her for a time, then, taking heart of grace, walked towards her from his lurking-place, holding between his fingers, as a talisman, a piece of silver, part of the scanty trust which Max had left him.

When he beheld her lusty proportions, her white teeth, grinning between perplexity at his appearance and pleasure at sight of the coin, and her broad cheeks, ruddy with health, good-nature, and stupidity, his apprehensions vanished. She seemed not at all afraid of him. In truth, she and her pitchfork might between them have put two common men to flight. He spoke to her in bad Italian, and asked for food, proffering the money in exchange. She answered in a *patois* which was Greek to him, mixed with a few words of Italian, worse than his own. She seemed, however, to catch his meaning very clearly; for, running to the house, she presently emerged with a loaf of barley bread and a formidable piece of bacon. These she gave him, and, taking the silver, tied it up with much care in a corner of her apron.

Thus far successful, Morton next tried to learn something touching the country and the routes; but here his failure was signal. Where food and drink were the topics in hand, and especially when her wits were quickened by the sight of silver, she had contrived to understand him; but with matters more abstruse her faculties had never been trained to grapple. She showed, however, no lack of good-will, nodding, laughing, and answering, "*Si, si!*" to all his questions indiscriminately. With this he had to content himself. He bade her "*addio,*" received a friendly nod and grin in return, and went on his way, much less bitter against mankind than he had been ten minutes before.

CHAPTER XLVI

Auf. Your hand! Most welcome.

1 Serv. Here's a strange alteration!

2 Serv. By my hand, I had thought to have strucken him with a cudgel; and yet my mind gave me his clothes made a false report of him.—*Coriolanus.*

In passing the Splugen, Morton journeyed chiefly in the night, making a wide detour over the crusted snow to avoid the station at the summit. By day, he found some safe retreat where he could rest and sleep in tolerable ease and warmth. His night progress was, for the most part, on a broad, clear road, very different from that rugged path by the Cardinal, where, some forty-seven years before, the avalanches cut through Macdonald's columns, and swept men and horses to bottomless ruin.

The sky was still clouded; but there was a full moon behind the clouds, and the mountains reflected its light, from their vast surfaces of snow. He could hear any approaching foot from a great distance, for there was nothing to break the stillness but the hollow fall of torrents, and the whisper and moan of winds through ravines and gorges.

On the third night, he was descending the defiles that lead from Campo Dolcino to Chiavenna. He passed Chiavenna, and soon a new scene opened upon him. The Alps were behind him, cliff and chasm, torrent and ravine, and the icy sheen of glaciers. Italy received him, robed in her "fatal gift of beauty;" in the midst of her shame, radiant as in her day of honor; breathing still of history, and art, and poetry.

Standing on the heights behind Colico, he saw the Lake of Como stretching southward, its banks studded with villas, its hills green with the chestnut and the laurel, the fig, pomegranate, and vine. But, to the north, the sheer cliffs rose like a battlement, and, higher yet, towered cold white peaks, aloof in stern and lofty desolation.

Reality will now and then make fancy blush for herself. The Easter illumination of St. Peter's may match the wildest dream of the Arabian Nights; and this scene on the Lake of Como, with the sunset upon it, may outvie the highest wrought counterfeit of Claude or Salvator, or both combined. The world, much abused as she is, does her part. She is profuse of beauties; but, in the midst of them, one still drags with him his own workday identity. Go where he will, his old Adam still hangs about him; and the spell-breaking sense that he is himself and no other scatters every charm that Art and Nature would cast over him.

Morton, poor devil, had other matters to think of than scenery. Hunger and danger are a cure for the most rabid love of landscape. His bread and bacon had given out, and the phantom of an Austrian *sbirro* rode him like a nightmare. Mustering his best recollections of geography, he came to the belief that he was either on the Lake of Como, or, as seemed to him much more likely, on the lake farther eastward, that of Garda. One thing was certain: he was on a great route of travel. His best course, as he thought, was to watch for the chance of a meeting with some American or English tourist, to whom he could make his case known; and meanwhile, though a worse actor never appeared on any stage, to pass himself off, if he could, as a beggar.

He passed a night on the hills above Colico, and happily for him, above the malaria; woke half famished from his miserably broken sleep, and wearily walked on his way, wondering if, in support of his character, he could ever find grace to say, "*Datemi qualche cosa.*" There was something in the idea of thus sneaking through a country that grated on him with peculiar discomfort; and to have headed the forlorn hope of a storming party would have been less trying to his nerve.

The thought how to content the cravings of his hunger soon absorbed all other thoughts. Looking about him, he saw a small white house, standing alone on the road by the shore of the lake; and over the door he could read from afar the sign, "*Spaccio di Vino.*" Famine got the better of caution. He approached warily, ensconced himself behind an old wall, and, quite unseen, began his observations. The house was but a few rods off, on the other side of the road. An old wayfarer sat in the porch, busy in breakfasting on curds, pressed hard like a cheese, a slice of very black and solid-looking bread serving him for a plate. In a few moments, the landlord, a freckled-faced Italian, came to the door, and began to chat with his customer. Morton took a coin from his pocket, walked forth from his hiding-place, and was approaching, still unnoticed, when he was startled by the sound of a horse's tread, on the road beyond the house. A single glance at the rider told him that there was no danger, and made his heart beat with sudden hope.

"*Il signor Inglese,*" remarked the host to his friend.—"*Buon' giorno, eccellenza, buon' giorno,*"—lifting his white night cap, and bowing with a great flourish.

The young man touched his hat with a careless smile, and half-turning his horse, asked,—

"Padrone, has my man passed this way?"

He had, to Morton's eye, rather the easy manner of a well-bred American, than the more distant bearing common with an English gentleman.

"*Eccellenza, si,*" replied the padrone,—"he passed a quarter of an hour ago, with the birds your excellency has shot."

The young man rode on, passing Morton, as he stood by the roadside.

"I have seen that face before," said the latter to himself—"in a dream, for what I know, but I have seen it."

It was a frank and open face, manly, yet full of kindliness, not without a tinge of melancholy.

"Come of it what will," thought the fugitive, "I will speak to him."

He walked after the retiring horseman, and when an angle of the road concealed him from the inn, quickened his pace almost to a run. But at that moment the Englishman struck into a sharp trot, and disappeared over the ridge of a hill. Morton soon gained sight of him again, and kept him in view for about a mile, when he saw him enter the gateway belonging to a small villa, between the road and the water. It was a very pretty spot; the grounds terraced to the edge of the lake; with laurels, cypresses, box hedges, a fountain or two, an artificial grotto, and a superb diorama of water and mountains.

Morton stood waiting at the gate. At length he saw a female domestic, evidently Italian, passing through the shrubbery before the house, and disappearing behind it. In a few minutes more, a solemn personage appeared at the door, whom he would have known at a mile's distance for an old English servant. He stood looking with great gravity out upon the grounds. Morton approached, and accosting him in Italian, asked to see his master.

John was not a proficient in the tongue of Ariosto and Dante. Indeed, in his intercourse with the natives, he had seen occasion for one phrase alone, and that a somewhat pithy and repellant one,—*Andate al diavolo.*

He glared with supreme and savage scorn on the tatterdemalion stranger, and uttered his talismanic words,—

"*Andarty al devillio!*"

Morton changed his tactics; and, looking fixedly at the human mastiff, said in English, —

"Go to your master, sir, and tell him that I wish to speak with him."

The Saxon words and the tone of authority coming from one whom he had taken for a vagrant beggar, astonished the old man beyond utterance. He stared for a moment, — turned to obey, — then turned back again, —

"Mr. Wentworth is at breakfast, sir."

The last monosyllable was spoken in a doubtful tone, the speaker being perplexed between respect for the tone and language of the stranger, and contempt for his vagabond attire.

"Then bring me pen, ink, and paper — I will write to him."

And pushing past the servant, he seated himself on a chair in the hall.

John went for the articles required, first glancing around to see what items of plunder might be within the intruder's reach. Morton in his absence opened several books which lay upon a table; and in one of them he saw, pencilled on the fly leaf, the name of the owner, Robert Wentworth.

The pen, ink, and paper arriving, he wrote as follows, John meanwhile keeping a vigilant guard over him: —

> Sir: I am a native of the United States, who, for the past four years, have been a prisoner in the Castle of Ehrenberg, confined for no offence, political or otherwise, but on a groundless suspicion. I escaped by the assistance of a soldier in the garrison, and have made my way thus far in the dress of a peasant. I am anxious to reach Genoa, or some other port beyond the power of Austria, but am embarrassed and endangered by my ignorance of the routes and the state of the country. Information on these points, and the means of communicating with an American consul, are the only aid of which I am in necessity; and I take the liberty of applying to you in the hope of obtaining it. By giving it, you will oblige me in a matter of life and death. The people of the country cannot be trusted; but I may rely securely on the generosity of an English gentleman.
>
> Your obedient servant,
VASSALL MORTON.

He sealed the note, and gave it to the old servant. The latter mounted the stairs, and reappearing in a few moments, said, in his former doubtful tone, "Please to walk up."

Morton followed him to the door of a small room looking upon the lake. Near the window stood the young man whom he had seen at the inn, with the note open in his hand. Morton entered, inclining his head slightly. The other returned his salutation, looked at him for an instant without speaking, and then, coming forward, gave him his hand, and bade him welcome with the utmost frankness.

Astonished, and half overcome, Morton could only stammer his acknowledgments for such a reception of one who came with no passport but his own word.

"O," said Wentworth, smiling, "when I meet an honest man, I know him by instinct, as Falstaff knew the true prince. Sit down; I am glad to see you; and shall be still more glad if I can help you."

The old servant received some whispered directions, and left the room. Morton gave a short outline of his story, to which his host listened with unequivocal signs of interest.

"I wish," said Wentworth, "that you were the only innocent victim of Austrian despotism. It is a monstrous infamy, built on fraud and force, but too refined, too artificial, too complicated to endure."

"Bullets and cold steel are the medicines for it," said Morton.

Here the servant reappeared.

"Here, at all events, you are safe. Stay with me to-day, and I think I can promise you that in a few days more you may stand on the deck of an American frigate. If you will go with John, he will help you to get rid of that villanous disguise."

Morton followed the old man into an adjoining room, where he found a bath, a suit of clothes, and the various appliances of the toilet prepared for him. And here he was left alone to indulge his reflections and revolutionize his outward man.

Meanwhile Wentworth sat musing by the window: "His face haunts me; and yet, for my life, I cannot remember where I have seen him before. I would stake all on his truth and honor. That firm lip and undespairing eye are a history in themselves. Strange—the difference between man and man. How should I have borne such suffering? Why, gone mad, I suppose, or destroyed myself. One sorrow—no, nor a hundred—would never unman *him*, and make him dream away his life, watching the sun rise and set, here by the Lake of Como. I scarcely know why, but my heart warms towards him like an old friend. Cost what it may, I will not leave him till he is out of danger."

He was still musing in this strain, when Morton returned, a changed man in person and in mind. It seemed as if, in casting off his squalid livery of misery and peril, a burden of care had fallen with it; as if the sullen cloud that had brooded over him so long had been pierced at length by a gladdening beam of sunlight, and the sombre landscape were smiling again with pristine light and promise. His buoyant and defiant spirit resumed its native tone; and a strange confidence sprang up within him, as if a desperate crisis of his destiny had been safely passed.

Wentworth saw the change at a glance.

"Why, man, I see freedom in your eye already. But sit down; 'it's ill talking between a full man and a fasting,' and you must be half starved."

Morton was so, in truth. He seated himself at the table, and addressed himself to the repast provided for him with the keenness of a mountain trapper, while his entertainer played with his knife and fork to keep him in countenance.

"Do you know," said Wentworth, at length—"I am sure I have seen you before."

"And I have seen you—I could swear to it; and yet I do not know where."

"Were you ever in England?"

"Only for a few days."

"I was once in America."

"When?"

"In 1839. I was at Boston in March of that year."

Morton shook his head. "I remember that time perfectly. I was in New Orleans in March, and afterwards in Texas."

"From Boston I went westward—up the Missouri and out upon the prairies."

Morton paused a moment in doubt; then sprang to his feet with a joyful exclamation,—

"The prairies! Have you forgotten the Big Horn Branch of the Yellow Stone, and the camp under the old cottonwood trees!"

Wentworth leaped up, and grasped both his guest's hands.

"Forgotten! No; I shall never forget the morning when you came over to us with that tall, half-breed fellow, in a Canadian capote."

"Yes,—Antoine Le Rouge."

"We should have starved if you had not found us, and perhaps lost our scalps into the bargain."

"The Rickarees had made a clean sweep of your horses."

"Not a hoof was left to us. Our four Canadians were scared to death; I was ill; not one of us was fit for service but Ireton; and we had not three days' provision. If you had not given us your spare mules and horses, and seen us safe to Fort Cass, the wolves would have made a supper of some of us."

"And do you remember," said Morton, "after we broke up camp that morning, how the Rickaree devils came galloping at us down the hill, and thought they could ride over us, and how we fought them all the forenoon, lying on our faces behind the pack saddles and baggage?"

"I remember it as if it were yesterday. I can hear the crack of the rifles now, and the yelling of those bloodthirsty vagabonds."

"It is strange," pursued Wentworth, "that I did not recognize you at once. I have thought of you a thousand times; but it is eight years since we met, and you are very much changed. Besides we were together only two days. And yet I can hardly forgive myself."

"Any wandering trapper would have done as much for you as I did; or, if he had not, he would have deserved a cudgelling. What has become of the young man, or boy, rather, who was with you?"

"You mean Ireton. Dead, poor fellow—dead."

"I am very sorry. He was the coolest of us all in the fight. He had a singular face, but a very handsome one. I can recall it distinctly at this moment."

Wentworth took a miniature from a desk, opened it, and placed it before Morton.

"These are his features," said the latter, "but this is the portrait of a lady."

"His sister—his twin sister. Dead too!"

There was a change, as he spoke, in his voice and manner, so marked that Morton forbore to pursue the subject farther. He studied the picture in silence. It was a young and beautiful face, delicate, yet full of fire; and by some subtilty of his craft, the artist had given to the eyes an expression which reminded him of the restless glances which he had seen a caged falcon at the Garden of Plants cast upwards at the sky, into which he was debarred from soaring.

In a few moments, Wentworth spoke in his accustomed tone.

"The point first to be thought of, is to get you out of this predicament. I have a man who took to his bed this morning, and is at present shaking in an ague fit. He is of about your age, height, and complexion; and by wearing his dress, you could travel under his passport. I am not at all a suspected person, and if my friend will pass for a few days as my servant, I do not doubt that we shall reach Genoa without interruption."

Morton warmly expressed his gratitude, but protested against Wentworth's undertaking the journey on his account.

"O, I am going to Genoa for my pleasure, and shall be glad of your company. The steamer for Como touches here this afternoon. 'Dull not device by coldness and delay;' we will go on board, and be in Milan tomorrow."

They conversed for an hour, when Morton withdrew to adjust his new disguise. Wentworth followed him with his eye as he disappeared; then sank into the musing mood which had grown habitual to him.

"When I saw him last,"—so his thoughts shaped themselves,—"my drama was opening; and now it is played out—light and darkness, smiles and tears—and the curtain is dropped forever. When I saw him last, I was gathering the prairie flowers and dedicating them to her,—though she did not suspect it,—and dreaming of her by camp fires and in night watches."

The miniature still lay on the table. He drew it towards him and gazed on it fixedly:—

"Mine for a space, and now—gone—vanished like a dream. You were a meteor between earth and sky, with a light that flickered and blazed and darkened, but a warmth constant and unchanged. Of all who admired the brightness of that erratic star, how few could know what gladness it shed around it, what desolation it has left behind!"

He gazed on the picture till his eyes grew dim; then sat for a few moments, listless and abstracted; then rose, with an effort, and bent his mind to the task before him.

CHAPTER XLVII

O that a man might know
The end of this day's business ere it come. —*Julius Cæsar*.

The diligence rolled into Genoa. Wentworth was in the *coupé*, and on the top sat Morton, as his servant. They had made the journey without interruption.

Morton reported himself to the American consul, and told his story. The wrath and astonishment of that official were great; but they were as nothing to the patriotic fury of three New York dry goods importers, who, mingling pleasure with business, were just arrived from Paris. Nothing was talked of but an immediate bombardment of Trieste, and a probable assault of Vienna.

Escaping as soon as he could from this demonstration, Morton bade his fervid countrymen good morning, and went out with Wentworth, who introduced him to his banker. He learned from the consul that a merchant brig was in port, nearly ready to sail for home, and gladly took passage in her.

And now at last he was safe; and safety should have brought with it a lightening of the spirits, a sense of relief. In fact, however, it brought little or nothing of the kind. The human mind, happily, cannot well hold more than one crowning evil at a time. One black thought, firmly lodged, will commonly keep the rest at bay. The fear of famine and a prison had left him no leisure to plague himself with less imminent mischiefs; but now, this fear being ousted, a new devil leaped into its empty seat. At the first moment when he could find himself alone, he wrote to Edith Leslie, telling her how he had been imprisoned, how, for almost five wretched years, her image had been his constant friend, how he had escaped, and how he was hastening homeward to claim the fulfilment of her word. He hinted nothing of his conviction that Vinal had been instrumental to his detention. He began divided between hope and fear, but as he wrote, a foreboding grew upon him that she was no longer living, or, at least, no longer living for him.

The letter, despatched post haste, would reach home a full fortnight before his own arrival.

Having seen his friend in safety, Wentworth set out on his return; and, as they shook hands at parting, their eyes met with a look that showed how clearly the two men understood each other.

Wentworth smiled as Morton tried to express his gratitude.

"You have cleared that score. I do not mean now the old affair on the Big Horn. I have been dreaming, lately, and you have waked me."

"I should never have imagined that you were dozing."

"Call it what you will. The truth is," added Wentworth, with some hesitation, "an old memory has been hanging about me, and I believe has made a girl of me. But that is past and done. I shall leave the Lake of Como. There is a career for me at home, and a good one, if I will but take it. Come to England, and you will find me there."

Morton went with him past the gates, and, with a heavy heart, watched him on his way northward.

CHAPTER XLVIII

His restless eye
Glanced forward frequently, as if some ill
He dared not meet were there. — *Willis*.

After some days' delay, the brig put to sea, Morton on board. The cliffs behind Gibraltar came in sight at last, and a fresh levanter blew her out like an arrow upon the Atlantic. They were becalmed off the Azores. The sea was like glass; the turtles came up to sleep at the top; the tar melted out of the seams; and as the vessel moved on the long, lazy swells, the masts kept up their weary creaking from morning till night, and from night till morning. Morton walked the deck in a fever of impatience.

At length an east wind sprang up, and with studding sails spread like wings, the brig ran before it, reeling like a drunken sea-gull.

On the forty-first day, the Neversink heights rose on the horizon. Vessels innumerable passed — steamers, merchantmen, war ships. The highlands of Staten Island, with its villages and villas, lay close on their left, and the Bay of New York opened before them, sparkling in the morning sun, and alive with moving sails. On the right lay a forest of masts; in front, the Castle lifted its ugly familiar front; and farther on, the spire of Trinity towered over the wilderness of brick.

Morton called a boat alongside, embarked his luggage, and went on shore. And, in spite of that depression which follows long and deep excitement, in spite of the anxieties that engrossed him, he felt a thrill of delight as his foot pressed American soil.

This pleasure, however, was short. The thought of Edith Leslie had been so long the solace of his confinement, that it seemed to have grown into a part of himself; at all events, now that his doubts were on the verge of decision, for good or evil, it drove every other thought from his mind. Reaching his hotel, he found that he could not set out for Boston till the afternoon; and to get rid of the interval, he turned over the Boston newspapers in the reading room, searching for the mention of any familiar names. Here he was more successful than he cared to be; for he presently discovered the name of Horace Vinal, figuring in the list of directors of a joint stock company.

"The hound!" muttered Morton; "so he is alive yet!"

And leaving the hotel, he walked up the crowded sidewalk of Broadway, in a mood any thing but tranquil.

CHAPTER XLIX

Affliction is enamoured of thy parts,
And thou art wedded to calamity. — *Romeo and Juliet.*

He had not gone far, when he became aware of a footstep closely following him. He was about to look back, when a little man passed before him, glancing furtively in his face with a ludicrous expression of doubt, amazement, and curiosity. Morton at once recognized the features of an odd, simple-minded classmate, named Shingles. "Charley," he exclaimed, "how do you do?"

"It *is* you," cried Shingles, with an ejaculation of profound astonishment; "solid flesh and blood!" — grasping Morton's extended hand — "and not your ghost. Why, we all thought you were dead!"

"Not quite," said Morton.

"Dead and buried," repeated Shingles, "off in Transylvania, or some such place."

"I *was* buried, but they buried me alive."

Shingles, who had a taste for the horrible, took the assertion literally, and dilated his eyes like an owl on the lookout for a mouse.

"But how did you manage to get out?"

"I contrived to break loose, after a few years."

Shingles stared in horror and perplexity.

"Don't be frightened, Charley. I'm all right, — neither ghost nor vampire. But we shall be pushed off the sidewalk, if we stand here."

"Come down into Florence's, then, and let me hear about it. Hang me if I ever expected to see you again. I shouldn't like to have met you alone, at night, any where near a graveyard. At our last class meeting, we were all talking about you, and saying you were a deused good fellow, and what a pity it was. And here you are alive; it was all for nothing!"

"That's very unlucky," said Morton, as they descended into the restaurant.

"By Jove," exclaimed Shingles, whose amazement was still strong upon him, "I was never so much astonished in my life as when I saw you just now. I was coming out of a shop, as you passed along the sidewalk. I felt as if I had seen a spirit. I followed behind you, and wasn't quite sure it was you, till I saw your trick of rapping your cane against the bricks as you walked along. Then I said to myself, it's he, or else old Beelzebub, in his likeness. But come, tell us how it was. How did you get off alive?"

Morton briefly recounted his imprisonment and escape, interrupted by the wondering ejaculations of his auditor.

"Who would have thought," exclaimed Shingles, "when you and I used to go up to Elk Pond, on Saturdays, to catch perch and pickerel, that you would ever have been shut up in the dungeon of an Austrian castle? You remember those old times—don't you?"

"That I do," said Morton.

"Do you remember the old tavern, where we used to lunch, and the pretty girl that waited on the table?"

"The girl that you raved about all the way home? Yes, I remember."

"By Jove, to think you've been shut up in a dungeon! Well, I haven't any very brilliant account to give of *my*self. I began to practise law, but I was never meant for a lawyer; so I gave it up, and have been ever since at my father's old place, just pottering about, you know. I was born in the country, and brought up there, and I mean to live there, only now and then I come down to New York, on a bend,—just for a change."

"I suppose you can tell me the news. How are all the fellows? How is Meredith?"

"Very well, I believe. He is living in Boston."

"Married, or single?"

"Single. We are not much of a marrying class. Wren was the first. Was that before you went away, or after? We voted to send him a cradle; but he did not know how to take it. He thought we were fooling him, and got quite angry. No, we are not at all a marrying class, nor a dying class either, for that matter. There are not more than five or six dead, and twelve or fourteen married; we reckoned them up last class meeting."

"Vinal—what of him?"

"O, he's alive, and married, too."

Morton turned pale. "Married!—to whom?"

"Well, they say he's made a first-rate match. I don't know her myself. I'm not a party-going man; I never was, you know. I haven't been thrown in much with that kind of people. But they tell me he couldn't have done better."

"What's her name?" demanded Morton.

"Miss Leslie—Colonel Leslie's daughter. But what's the matter? Are you ill?"

"It's nothing," gasped Morton; "I had a fever in prison, and have never been quite well since. I grow dizzy, sometimes."

"You *will* grow dizzy, with a vengeance, if you drink wine in that way."

"It's nothing," repeated Morton; "it will be over in a minute. What were you saying?"

"About the fellows that have married,—O, Vinal,—I was saying that he had just got married."

"Well, what about it?"

"Why, nothing particular."

"When was it?"

"Last month."

"Within a month! Are you sure?"

"O, yes. I was in Boston myself at the time, and heard all about it. Her father was ill; so the marriage was private. Vinal is a sort of fellow that somehow I never cottoned to much. I don't think he's very disinterested. I like a fellow that will swear when he is angry, and not keep close shut up, like an oyster."

The tattle of his rustic companion was become intolerable to Morton. He had received his stab, and wished to hear no more. In a few minutes, he rose from the table. "Charley, I am sorry to leave you so suddenly, but I am not well. The fresh air and a hard walk are all that will set me up. I shall see you again."

"But where are you staying?"

"At Blancard's. Good morning, old fellow."

CHAPTER L

Fab. . . . . Elle est——.

Sev. Quoi?

Fab. Mariée!

Sev. . . . . . . Ce coup de foudre est grand!—*Polyeucte.*
   The world's my oyster, which I with
      sword will open.—*Henry IV.*
   Put money in thy purse; follow these wars.—*Othello.*

Morton walked down Broadway at a rapid pace, entered his hotel, mounted to his room, seated himself, rested his forehead on his hand, and, with fixed eyes and compressed lips, remained in this position for some minutes, motionless as if carved out of oak. Then, rising, he paced the room, buried his face in his hands, and groaned with irrepressible anguish. Suddenly the door was burst open, and an Irish servant, apparently in a great hurry, bolted in, and tossed a card on the table, saying at the same time,—"Gen'lman down stairs wants to see you."

Morton broke into a rage, to hide the traces of a different passion.

"Why do you come in without knocking? Learn better manners, or I shall teach them to you."

"I beg pardon, sir," said the servant, reduced at once to the depth of obsequiousness, "there's a gentleman, sir—an officer, sir,—would like to see you, sir."

"An officer!—I don't know any officers. There's some mistake."

"He *said* Mr. Morton, sir. This is his card, sir."

Morton looked at the card, and read the name of his classmate Rosny.

"Very well. Ask the gentleman to come up.—No,—here,"—as the servant was retreating along the passage,—"where is he?"

"In the reading room, sir."

"Tell him I will come down in a moment."

"Yes, sir, I will, sir."

Morton adjusted his dress, strove to banish from his features all traces of the emotion which had just overwhelmed him, went down stairs, and met Rosny with an air of as much cordiality as if there were nothing in his mind but the pleasure of seeing an old friend. Rosny, his first welcome over, surveyed him from head to foot.

"A good deal changed! Thinner,—darker complexioned, decidedly older. And yet you've weathered it well. It's a thing that I could never stand,—to be boxed up in four stone walls. I would throttle the jailer first, and then knock my brains out against the stones."

"Did Shingles tell you of my being here?"

"Yes, I met him just now, with his eyes bigger than ever. When I saw him making a dive at me across the street, among the omnibuses and carriages, I knew that something extraordinary was to pay."

"*You* have changed your outward man, too, since I saw you last," said Morton, looking at his companion's costume, which consisted of a gray volunteer uniform.

"Yes, I'm in Uncle Sam's pay now.—Off for Mexico in a day or two;— revel in the Halls of the Montezumas, you know."

"What rank do you hold in the service, Dick?"

"You'll please to address me as Major Rosny; that is, till good luck and the Mexican bullets make a colonel of me.—I have just dropped in to shake hands with you. I have an appointment to keep in five minutes. You have nothing particular to do to-day—have you?"

"Nothing very particular," said Morton, hesitating.

"Then come and dine with me at Delmonico's at four o'clock. What!— you don't mean to say no, do you?—Is that the way you treat your friends? Come, I shall be here at four, precisely. *Au revoir.*"

And, with his usual celerity of motion, Rosny left the hotel.

Morton slowly remounted to his room, locked the door this time, to keep out intruders, seated himself, and gave himself up to his dark and morbid reveries.

"God! of what is this world made! Villany thrives, and innocent men are racked with the pangs of hell. Poverty starving its victims,—luxury poisoning them;—the passions of tigers and the mean vices of reptiles;— treacherous hatred, faithless love;—deceitful hope, vain struggles, endless suffering,—a hell of misery and darkness. A fair sunrise, to cheat the eye;—then clouds and storms, blackness and desolation! To look back over the last five years! Then I was basking in sunshine; and out of that brightness what a doom is fallen on me! My life—my guiding star quenched in a vile morass—lost forever in the arms of this accursed villain!"

Morton rose abruptly, went to the window, and stood looking out with a fixed gaze, wholly unconscious of what was before him. In a moment he turned again, and there was a wild and deadly light in his eyes. A thought had struck him, shooting an electric life through all his veins, and kindling him into a kind of fierce ecstasy. He would go to Vinal, charge him with his perfidy, challenge him, and put him to death. He paced the room in great disorder. A resistless power seemed to have seized upon him, sweeping him forward with the force of a torrent. He clinched his teeth and breathed deeply. The thought of action and of vengeance lighted up his perturbed and gloomy mind as the baleful glare of a conflagration lights up a stormy midnight. Suddenly he stopped, seated himself again, and remained for some minutes in violent mental conflict. "I thank God," he murmured at length, apostrophizing his enemy, "that you were not just now within my reach. You have ruined me for this life; you shall not ruin me for the next. Live, and work out your own destruction."

He walked the room again, calmly enough, but in great dejection. "It may be," he thought, "that I am not his only victim. Perhaps the same art that snared me, has, by some infernal machination, entrapped her also. I believe it;—at least, I will try to believe it."

He looked from the window upon the keen and busy crowds passing below in unbroken streams, to and from their places of business; and his mind tinged them with its own moody coloring.

"You flight of human vultures! How many of you can show lives governed by any generous purpose or noble thought? Behind how many of those sharp and sallow features, furrowed with early wrinkles, lies the soul of a man? Desperate chasers after wealth, which, when you have won it, you have never been taught to use;—reckless pleasure hunters, beguiling others that your victims may beguile in turn, and both sink to perdition together. What you win with trickery, you throw away in vanity or debauch. The counting room or the broker's board by day;—brandy, billiards, and the rendezvous by night;—so you go,—a short, quick road;—driving to your doom with a high-pressure power of rapacity, vain glory, and lust. Man!—the thistledown of fortune, the shuttlecock of passion;—whirled on to destruction by the wildfire in his veins, unless by struggling and by prayer he can keep the narrow adamantine track laid down for his career!"

In such distempered reflections he passed some time. Even in the darkest passages of his imprisonment, his mind had scarcely been shaken so far from its habitual poise. Growing weary at length of solitude, he went out of the house; and, avoiding the great thoroughfares, where he might perhaps meet an acquaintance, he threaded at a rapid pace those meaner streets and lanes, where even the best balanced mind may find abundant food for gloomy meditation. From time to time, as the image of his enemy rose before him, the desire for vengeance came upon him afresh, like a fever fit. He burned to seize Vinal by the throat, and, at least, force him to unmask his iniquity to the world.

As he was passing down Water Street, he recollected, with some vexation, that Rosny had promised to call for him at four o'clock, and retraced his steps to the hotel, where, true to the minute, that punctual adventurer presently appeared.

"Come," said Rosny; "if you are ready, we will walk down street."

They repaired to Delmonico's, where, in a private room, a sumptuous repast had been made ready. Morton, over his companion's claret, was obliged to recount the circumstances of his imprisonment. Rosny, on his part, gave an outline of his own fortunes since they had last met. He had been once or twice on the point of very considerable success, but his vaulting ambition had always overleaped itself, and by too great eagerness and grasping at too much, he had repeatedly failed of his prize, only, however, to rally after every reverse with undiminished confidence and spirit. Such, at least, were the conclusions which Morton drew from his companion's somewhat inflated account of himself.

After the cloth had been removed, Rosny bit off the end of a cigar, lighted it, puffed at it two or three times, and then, holding it between his fingers, went on with an harangue which the operations of the waiter had interrupted.

"I tell you, these are great times that we live in. The world has seen nothing like them since the days of Columbus and Cortes. These are the times and this is the country for a man of merit to thrive in. Let him identify himself with the progressive movements of the age,—yes, faith, let him be a leader of them,—and there's nothing too large for him to hope for. Why, sir, the day is not far off, when the stars and stripes will be seen from Hudson's Bay to Panama. Cuba will come next; Brazil next. Lord knows where we shall stop. There's a field for a man of ability and pluck!"

Morton smiled. Rosny relighted his cigar, which, in the fervor of his declamation, he had allowed to go out, gave a vigorous whiff or two, and proceeded.

"We have just lost a splendid chance. I *did* flatter myself that there was going to be a row with England, on the Oregon question; but it was a flash in the pan; it all ended in smoke."

"Why do you want to fight with John Bull?" asked Morton.

"For two good reasons. In the first place, I hate him. I hate him in right of my French ancestors, and I hate him as a true American democrat. Then, over and above all that, a war with the English would be the making of me. I should rise then. I would be their Hannibal. But now we have nothing better to do than giving fits to these yellow Mexican vagabonds."

"A shabby employment," said Morton, "and yet I think I should like it."

"You would, ey?—then go with me to Mexico."

"It's a temptation," said Morton, his eyes lighted with a sudden gleam,—"I am in a mood for any thing, I do not care what."

"I knew there was something ailing you," said Rosny; "why, you have had no appetite. You've lost all your spirits. Has any thing happened? Are you ill?"

"Nothing to speak of. I am well enough in health."

"Well, come with me to Mexico. When a man is under a cloud, he always makes the better soldier for it. If you have had bad luck, why, you can fight like a Trojan."

"I could storm Hell Gates to-day," exclaimed Morton, giving a momentary vent to his long pent up emotion.

"Good! I always knew that there was stuff in you, though you *are* worth half a million. It isn't that, though—is it? You haven't lost property—have you?"

"Not that I know. Never mind, Dick; every man has his little vexations, sometimes, and is entitled to the privilege of swearing at them."

"Well, I am not the man to pry into your private affairs. Come with me to Mexico. I can promise you a captain's commission,—perhaps I can get you a major's. I am not a cipher in the democratic party, I'd have you know, though I am not yet what I shall be soon. I helped Polk to his election, and my word will go for something. But, pshaw!—what am I talking about? With your money, and a little management, you can get any thing you want."

"I have more than half a mind," said Morton, hesitating; "but, no,—I won't go."

"Pshaw, man! You don't know what you are saying. You don't know what chances you are throwing away. Look at it. It isn't the military fame,—the glorification in the newspapers,—seeing pictures of yourself in the shop windows, charging full tilt among the Mexicans, and all that. You can take that for what it's worth. Tastes differ in such matters. But, I tell you, the men who distinguish themselves in Mexico are going to carry all before them in the political world. The people will go for them, neck or nothing. I know what our enlightened democracy is made of."—Here a slight grin flickered for an instant about the corners of his mouth; but he grew serious again at once.—"Yes, sir, a new world is going to begin. The old incumbents—Webster, Clay, Calhoun, and the rest—will pass off the stage, before long, and make room for younger men—men who will keep up with the times. Then will be our chance! Put brass in your forehead,—you have money enough in your purse already,—get a halo of Mexican glory round your head,—and you will shoot up like a rocket. First go to the war, then dive into politics, and you and I will be the biggest frogs in the puddle."

"There's a fallacy in your conclusions," said Morton; "the officers of rank, the generals and colonels, will carry off the glory; and we shall have nothing but the blows."

"The Mexican bullets will make that all right. I tell you, they are going to fly like hail. They will dock off the heads above us, and make a clear path for us to mount by."

"Suppose that they should hit the wrong man," suggested Morton.

"Pshaw!" exclaimed Rosny, "we won't look at the matter in that light."

There was a momentary pause.

"Now's your time," urged Rosny. "Come, say the word."

Morton paced the room with knit brows and lips pressed together.

"Glory,"—exclaimed his military friend, summing up the advantages of a Mexican campaign,—"glory,—preferment,—life, of the fastest kind,—what more would you have?"

Morton had a strong native thirst for adventure, and a *penchant* for military exploit. In his present frame of mind, he felt violently impelled to cut loose from all his old ideas and scruples, and launch at once upon a new life, fresh, unshackled, and reckless,—to plunge headlong into the tumult of the active world; fight its battles, run its races, give and take its blows, strain after its prizes,—forget the past and all its associations in the fever of the present. Mexico rose before his thoughts—snowy volcanoes, and tropical forests; the cocoa, the palm, and the cactus; bastioned cities and intrenched heights; the rush and din of battle; war with its fierce excitements and unbounded license. To his disordered mood, the scene had fascinations almost resistless, and he burned to play his part in the fiery drama.

"And why not?"—so his thoughts ran,—"why not obey what fate and nature dictate? Calm, and peace, and happiness,—farewell to them! That stake is played and lost. I am no more fit now for domestic life than a prairie wolf. I should answer better for an Ishmaelite or a Pawnee. *Deus vult.* Why should I fly in the face of Providence?"

Rosny, his uniform coat half unbuttoned for the sake of ease, sat lolling back in his chair, puffing wreaths of cigar smoke from his lips, eying Morton as he paced the room, and throwing out, from time to time, a word of encouragement to stimulate his resolution. He was about to lose all patience at his companion's pertinacious silence, when the latter stopped, and turned towards him with the air of one whose mind is made up.

"Dick," said Morton, "when I was in college, I laid down my plan of life, and adopted one maxim—to which I mean to hold fast."

"Well, what was that?" demanded the impatient Rosny.

"Never to abandon an enterprise once begun; to push on till the point is gained, in spite of pain, delay, danger, disappointment,—any thing."

"Good, so far. What next?"

"Some years ago, I entered upon certain plans, which have not yet been accomplished. I have been interrupted, balked, kicked and cuffed by fortune, till I am more than half disgusted with the world. But I mean still to take up the broken thread where I left it, and carry it forward as before."

"The moral of that is, I suppose, that you won't go to Mexico."

"Precisely."

"Well, I shan't try to debate the matter with you. I know you of old. When your foot is once down, it's useless for me to try to make you lift it up again. But remember what I say,—you will repent not taking my advice."

Rosny finished his cigar, and they left the restaurant together. On their way up the street, they stopped at a recruiting office. "Captain Rumbold, my friend Mr. Morton," said Rosny, who soon after, however, entered into an earnest conversation with the officer upon some affair of business, leaving Morton at leisure to observe six or eight volunteers, who were about to be sent to Governor's Island, in charge of a sergeant.

"What do you think of our boys?" asked Rosny, casting a comical look at Morton, as they went down stairs.

"I never saw such a gang of tobacco-chewing, soap-locked rascals."

"Food for powder," said Rosny, "they'll fill a ditch as well as better. The country needs a little blood-letting. These fellows are not like Falstaff's, though. They will fight. Not a man of them but will whip his weight in wildcats."

CHAPTER LI

A raconter ses maux, souvent on les soulage.—*Polyeucte*.

"Do you remember Buckland?" asked Rosny, as they walked up Broadway.

"The Virginian? Yes, perfectly."

"There he is."

Morton, following the direction of his companion's eye, saw, a little in advance, a tall man, slenderly but gracefully formed, walking slowly, with a listless air, as if but half conscious of what was going on around him. They checked their pace, to avoid overtaking him.

"Poor fellow!" said Rosny; "he's in a bad way."

"I am sorry to hear it. He was a lively, pleasant fellow when I knew him,—very fond of the society of ladies."

"That's all over now. He has been very dissipated for the last two or three years, and is broken down completely, body and mind. It's a great pity. I am very sorry for him," said Rosny, in whom, notwithstanding his restless ambition, there was a vein of warm and kindly feeling.

"Is he living in New York?"

"Yes, he has been here ever since leaving college. He began to practise as a lawyer. It's much he ever did or ever will do at the law! There was never any go-ahead in him—no energy, no decision—and he does nothing now, but read a little, and lounge about, in a moody, abstracted way, with his wits in the clouds. Get him into good company, and wind him up with a glass of brandy, and he is himself again for a while,—tells a story and sings a song as he used to do,—but it is soon over. Do you want to speak to him?"

"Yes."

"Come on, then. How are you, Buckland? Here's an old friend, redivivus."

Hearing himself thus accosted, Buckland turned towards the speaker a face which, though pale and sallow, was still handsome. His dress, contrary to his former habit, was careless and negligent; and, though he could not have been more than thirty, a few gray hairs had begun to mingle with his long, black moustache. Changed as he was, he had that air of quiet and graceful courtesy which can only be acquired by habitual intercourse with polished society in early life; and Morton saw in him the melancholy wreck of a highly-bred gentleman.

When the first surprise of the meeting was over, Rosny related the story of Morton's imprisonment to the wondering ear of Buckland. Having urgent business on his hands, he soon after took leave of his two companions. Morton and Buckland, after strolling for a time up and down Broadway, entered the restaurant attached to Blancard's hotel, and took a table in a remote corner of the room, which was nearly empty.

Buckland was, as Rosny had described him, moody and abstracted, often seeming at a loss to collect his thoughts. He sipped his chocolate in silence, and, even when spoken to, sometimes returned no answer. Morton, in little better spirits than his companion, sat leaning his forehead dejectedly on his hand.

"I am sorry," said Buckland, after one of his silent fits, "to be so wretched a companion; but I am not the man I used to be."

"We are but a melancholy pair," replied Morton.

"I saw from the first that you were very much out of spirits,—not at all what one would expect a man to be who had just escaped from sufferings like yours. There is some trouble on your mind."

Morton was fatigued and sick at heart. He had practised self-control till he was tired of it; and he allowed a shade of emotion to pass across his face.

"There is a woman in it," said Buckland, regarding him with a scrutinizing eye.

"Why do you say that?" demanded Morton, startled and dismayed at this home thrust.

"Are not women the source of nine tenths of our sufferings?" replied Buckland. "The world is a huge, clashing, jangling, disjointed piece of mechanism, and they are the authors of its worst disorder."

"Sometimes," said Morton, "men will blame women for sufferings which they might, with better justice, lay at their own doors."

Buckland raised his head quickly, and looked in his companion's face. "It may be so," he said, after a moment's pause. "Perhaps you are right,— perhaps you are right. But, let that be as it will, there are no miseries in life to match those which spring out of the relation of the sexes."

Morton, for reasons of his own, did not care to pursue the subject, and his companion relapsed into his former silence. After a time, they went into the smoking room, where Buckland lighted a cigar. Morton observed that, as he did so, his fingers trembled in a manner which showed that his whole nervous system was shattered and unstrung.

"I would not advise you to smoke much," said Morton; "you have not the constitution to bear it."

Buckland smiled bitterly. He had grown reckless whether he injured himself or not.

They seated themselves near the window; but Buckland soon grew uneasy, alternately looking at his watch and gazing into the street. At length he rose, and asked Morton to walk out with him. The latter, on the principle that misery loves company, readily complied; and they went down Broadway nearly to the Bowling Green. Here Buckland turned, and they retraced their steps to within a few squares of the Astor House. This they repeated several times, Morton's companion constantly resisting every movement on his part to vary in the least the course of their promenade. While their walk was up the street, Buckland, though evidently restless and uneasy, had the same abstracted air as before; but when they moved in the opposite direction, his whole manner changed, and he seemed anxiously on the watch, as if for some person whom he expected every moment to meet. It was about eight in the evening. The street was brilliant with gas; crowds of people, men and women, were moving along the sidewalk; and upon each group, as it approached, Buckland bent a gaze of eager scrutiny.

They were passing a large bookstore, when Morton felt his companion suddenly press the arm on which he was leaning. Hastily stepping aside, and dragging Morton with him, he ensconced himself behind the board on which the bookseller pasted his advertising placards, which partially concealed him, and, together with the projection over the shop door, screened him from the light of the neighboring gas lamp. Here he stood motionless, his eyes riveted on some approaching object. Following the direction of his gaze, Morton saw a tall man in the uniform of an army officer of rank, and, leaning on his arm, a light and delicate female figure, elegantly, but not showily dressed. They were close at hand when he discovered them, and in a moment they had passed on under the glare of the lamp, and mingled with the throng beyond; but Morton retained a vivid impression of features beautifully moulded, and a pair of restless dark eyes, roving from side to side with piercing, yet furtive glances.

Buckland, stepping from his retreat, made a hesitating, forward movement, as if undecided whether to follow them or not. He stopped with a kind of suppressed groan, and taking Morton's arm again, moved slowly with him down the street. Two or three times, Morton spoke to him, but he seemed not to hear, or, at best, answered in monosyllables, with an absent air. When they reached the hotel, then recently established on the European plan, near the Bowling Green, Buckland entered, called for brandy, and, his companion declining to join him, hastily drank the liquor with the same trembling hand which Morton had before remarked. On leaving the house, they continued their walk downward till they reached the Battery. And as they entered the shaded walks of that promenade, the moon was shining on the trees, and on the quiet waters of the adjacent bay.

"You must think very strangely of me," said Buckland, at length breaking his long silence; "in fact, I scarcely know myself. I am a changed man,—a lost and broken man, body and soul,—a sea-weed drifting helplessly on the water."

"You take too dark a view," said Morton, greatly moved; "there is good hope for you yet, if you will not fling it away."

Buckland shook his head. "I wish I had been born such a man as Rosny. He is a practical man of the world, always in pursuit of something, with nothing to excite or trouble him but the success or failure of his schemes. He cannot understand my feelings. Yes, I wish to Heaven I had been born a practical, hard-headed man,—such, for instance, as your cool, common sense Yankees. What do they know or care for the troubles that are wearing me away by inches?"

"Buckland," said Morton, "your nerves are very much weakened and disordered, and particular troubles weigh upon and engross you, as they could not if you were well. What you most need is a good physician."

"'Could he minister to a mind diseased?' Come, sit down here—on this bench. Perhaps you have never felt—I hope you have never had occasion to feel—impelled to relieve some torment pressing on your mind, by telling it to a friend. Genuine friends are rare. When one meets them, he knows them by instinct. I need not fear you; you will not laugh at me to yourself, and tell me, as some others do, that a man of force and energy would fling off an affair like mine, and not suffer it to weigh upon him like a nightmare."

"When you have recovered your health, perhaps I may tell you so; but not till then."

"I am like the Ancient Mariner," continued Buckland, with a faint smile; "when I find the man who must hear my story, I know him the moment I see his face. Your good sense will tell you that I have been a knave and a fool; but your good heart will prevent your showing me that you think so."

Morton looked with deep compassion on his old comrade, and wondered what follies or misfortunes could have sunk his former gallant spirit so far. In his weakened and depressed condition, Buckland seemed to lean for support on his friend's firmer and better governed nature, and to draw strength from the contact.

"After all," he said in a livelier tone, "what right have I to bore you with this story of mine?"

"Any thing that you are willing to tell," answered Morton, "I shall be glad to hear."

CHAPTER LII

On me laisse tout croire; on fait gloire de tout;
Et cependant mon coeur est encore assez lâche
Pour ne pouvoir briser la chaîne qui l'attache.—*Le Misanthrope.*

"I had an old friend," Buckland began, with some glimmering of his former vivacity,—"De Ruyter,—I don't think you ever knew him. He was the representative of a family great in its day and generation, but broken in fortune, and without means to support its pretensions. This did not at all tend to diminish their pride,—precisely of that kind which goeth before destruction. De Ruyter was a good fellow, however, and, if he had had twenty thousand a year, he would have spent it all. One summer, four years ago, he went with his child—his wife had died the year before—and his two sisters to spend a few weeks at a quiet little watering-place on the Jersey shore, frequented by people of good standing, but not fashionably inclined. De Ruyter praised the sporting in the neighborhood, and persuaded me to go with him.

"His sisters were very agreeable women,—cultivated and lively, but proud as Lucifer, and desperately exclusive. A *nouveau riche* was, in their eyes, equivalent to every thing that is odious and detestable; and to call a man a *parvenu* was to steep him in infamy forever. The men at the house were, for the most part, of no great account—chiefly old bachelors, or sober family men run to seed, with a number of awkward young boobies not yet in bloom. The two ladies liked the company of a lazy fellow like me, a butterfly of society, with the poets, at least the sentimental ones, on my tongue's end, and the latest advices from the fashionable world. I staid there a week, and when that was over they persuaded me to stay another.

"On the day after, there was a fresh arrival,—a gentleman from Philadelphia, with his sister and his daughter. He only remained for the night, and went away in the morning, leaving the ladies behind. The sister was a starched old person,—a sort of purblind duenna, with grizzled hair, gold spectacles, and cap. The daughter I need not describe, for you saw her half an hour ago.

"Her family was good enough; her father a lawyer in Philadelphia. She was well educated—played admirably, and spoke excellent French and Italian. How much or how little she had frequented cultivated society, I do not know,—her own assertions went for nothing; but she had the utmost ease and grace of manner, and an invincible self-possession. Her ruling passion was a compound of vanity and pride, an insatiable craving for admiration and power. Whatever associates she happened to be among, nothing satisfied her but to be the cynosure of all eyes, the centre of all influence. I have known women enough,—women of all kinds, good, bad, and indifferent; but such a one as she I never met but once. I shall not soon forget the evening when I first saw her, seated opposite me at the tea table. She was a small, light figure,—as you saw her just now,—the features, perhaps, a trifle too large. I never recall her, as she appeared at that time, without thinking of Byron's description of one of his mischief-making heroines:—

"'Her form had all the softness of her sex,
Her features all the sweetness of the devil,
When he put on the cherub to perplex
Eve, and paved—God knows how—the road to evil.'

"She was utterly unscrupulous. The depth of her artifice was unfathomable. She soon became the moving spirit of that little cockney watering-place—some admiring her, some hating her, some desperately smitten with her. I can see through her manoeuvres now, but then I was blind as a mole. She understood every body about her, and held out to each the kind of bait which was most likely to attract him. There was a sort of *dilettante* there whose heart she won by talking to him of the Italian poets, which, by the way, she really loved, for there was a dash of genius in her. She aimed to impress each one with the idea that in her heart she liked him better than any one else; and it was her game to appear on all occasions perfectly impulsive and spontaneous, while, in fact, every look, word, or act of hers had an object in it. In short, she was an accomplished actress; and, had her figure been more commanding, she might have rivalled Rachel on the stage. No two people were exactly agreed in opinion concerning her; but all—I mean all the men—thought her excessively interesting; and I remember that two young collegians had nearly fought a duel about her, each thinking that she was in love with him. Nothing delighted her more than to become the occasion of the jealousy of married women towards their husbands,—nothing, that is, except the still greater delight of fascinating a certain young New Yorker who had come to the house on a visit to his betrothed.

"For some time every one supposed her to be unmarried. She did her best, indeed, to encourage the idea, since she thus gained to herself more notice and more marked attentions. At length, to the astonishment of every body, it came out that she had been, for more than a year, married to a cousin of her own, a weak and imbecile youngster, as I afterwards learned, who was then absent on an East India voyage, and who, happily for himself, has since died.

"I said that all the men in the house were interested in her; but you should have seen the commotion she raised among the women! There were three or four simple girls about her who admired her, and were her devoted instruments; but with the rest she was at sword's point. There were a thousand ways in which they and she could come into collision; and, of course, they soon found her out, while the men remained in the dark. If they were handsome and attractive, she hated them; and if they would not conform to her will, she could never forgive it. The disputes, the jars, the jealousies, the backbitings, the tricks and stratagems of female warfare that I have seen in that house, and all of her raising! She was a dangerous enemy. Her tongue could sting like a wasp; and all the while she would smile on her victim as if she were reporting some agreeable compliment. She had a satanic dexterity in dealing out her stabs, always choosing the time, place, and company, where they would tell with the sharpest effect.

"With all her insincerity, there was still a tincture of reality in her. Her passions and emotions were strong; and she was so addicted to falsehood, that I am confident she did not always know whether the feeling she expressed were real or pretended.

"The grace and apparent *abandon* of her manner, her beauty, her wit, her singular power of influencing the will of others, and the dash of poetry, which, strange as you may think it, still pervaded her, made her altogether a very perilous acquaintance. I, certainly, have cause to say so. I lingered a week, a fortnight, a month, and still could not find resolution to go. I had an air, a name in society, and the reputation of being dangerous. She thought me worth angling for, put forth all her arts, and caught me.

"I have read an Indian legend of a fisherman who catches a fish and drags him to the surface, but in the midst of his triumph, the fish swallows him, canoe and all. The angler, however, kills him by striking at his heart with his flinty war club, and then makes his escape by tearing a way through his vitals. The case of the fish is precisely analogous to mine. She caught me, as I said before; but I caught her in turn. She fell in love with me, wildly and desperately. Her passions were as fierce and as transient as a tropical hurricane. She had no scruples; and I had not as many as I should have had. One evening we were gone, and two days after we were out of sight of land on board one of the Cunard steamers.

"For the next two months, I was in paradise. Then came a purgatory, or something worse. Her passion for me subsided as quickly as it had arisen. She was herself again. Her vanity and artifice, her insatiable love of intrigue and adventure, returned with double force. I wore myself out with watching, vexation, and anxiety. She tried every means to attract attention and draw admirers, and every where she succeeded. I remember that one night at Naples she insisted on going with me to the theatre of San Carlo, in the dress of a young man, and wearing a moustache. The disguise was detected, as she meant it should be, and eyes centred upon her from all the boxes. I tried to travel with her through remote and unfrequented countries, such as the interior of Sicily; but it was all in vain. There was no resisting her fiery will, and I was compelled to go wherever she wished.

"One afternoon, at Messina, at the *table d'hôte*, we met a lively young Spanish nobleman. She caught his eye; I saw them exchange glances. In spite of all my precautions, messages, billets, and momentary interviews passed between them. I challenged the Spaniard, gave him a severe flesh wound, and thought I had taught him a lesson. Not at all. On the next day, coming to my lodgings, I found her gone, no one could tell whither. I was desperate, and could have done any thing; but there was nothing to be done. I could not find her, and if I had it would have availed me nothing.

"I returned to America, wrought up to the verge of a nervous fever; and, by mingling in amusements of every kind, tried to forget her. In six or eight months I had partially succeeded. My health was not good, and I had made a journey of a few weeks to the west; when, on returning,—it was a sultry July afternoon,—I remember it as if it were yesterday,—sitting in the reading room window of the New York Hotel, I saw her passing down Broadway in an open carriage; and, with the sight, my passion awoke again at fever heat. She had left the Spaniard, and come to America with a New York gentleman, who had lived for some time in Paris. I had an interview with her, and she promised to join me again; but she broke her word. She saw at once what a power she still held over me; and she has used it most mercilessly ever since. She practises all her arts on me, as if I were a new lover, whom she wished to insnare. Sometimes she flatters me; sometimes she repels me; now and then she allows me stolen interviews, or long walks or rides with her. She plays me as an angler plays a salmon that he has hooked, till he brings him gasping to his death. I have plunged into dissipations of all kinds, to drown the memory of her. It is all useless. She knows the torments I am suffering, and she rejoices in them. Perhaps she remembers that it was I who made her what she is, and takes this for her revenge. But, pshaw!—if I had not eloped with her, some one else would have done so soon; and that she perfectly well knows. It is her vanity—nothing but her vanity: she delights to hold me in bondage; she knows that I am her slave, and she glories in it."

"But why, in Heaven's name," demanded Morton, "do you not break away from this miserable fascination?"

"There it is!" Buckland answered; "I only wish that I had the power. I have resolved twenty times to leave New York, and my resolution has failed me as often."

"Who takes charge of her now?"

"Colonel — —. He seems as crazy after her as I was."

"I can hardly comprehend," pursued Morton, "how, understanding her character as you do, you can still remain so infatuated with her."

"Neither can I comprehend it. I can only feel it. Strange—is it not?—that I, who used to be regarded as a mere flirt; who, as a lady acquaintance once told me, had a great deal too much sentiment, but no heart at all; I, who, in my time, have written love verses to twenty different ladies,—should be so enchained at last by this black-eyed witch!"

"Very strange."

"And now what would you recommend? what advice do you give me? You see in what a predicament I stand. What ought I to do?"

"With your broken health and weakened nerves," said Morton, "it is useless for you to attempt contending against this fancy that has taken possession of you. You must run away from it. Take a long voyage; the longer the better. I will go with you to engage your passage to-morrow."

Buckland hesitated at first, slowly shaking his head; but in a moment he said, with some animation, "Yes, I will go, on one condition; you must promise to go with me."

The will, the motive power,—never very strong in him,—was now completely relaxed. He was unfitted for action of any kind, and was, as he himself said, no better than a sea weed drifting on the water. Morton walked the streets with him for some hours. He seemed to cling to his companion, like an ivy to the supporting trunk, and was evidently reluctant to resign his company. At length, Morton, who was exhausted with the excitements of the day, pleaded fatigue, and bade him good night. He turned again, however, and, by the blaze of the gas lamps, followed with his eye Buckland's slowly receding figure.

"A few hours ago," he said to himself, "I thought myself unhappy; but what is my suffering compared to his? I am not, thank God, the builder of my own misfortunes, nor pursued with the reflection that they are a just retribution for my own misdeeds. With health, liberty, self-respect, and a good conscience, what man has a right to call himself miserable?"

CHAPTER LIII

The paths of glory lead but to the grave.—*Gray's Elegy.*

Mr. Shingles had an acquaintance among the gentlemen of the press; and, chancing to meet his quill-driving friend, he told him Morton's story. It appeared, accordingly, beautifully embellished, in one of the evening papers, and was copied, the next morning, into several others. Consequently, Morton had scarcely risen from breakfast, when he was visited by half a dozen persons, editors and others, eager to hear his adventures, for the gratification of their own curiosity, or that of the public. As he detested such visitations, and as several of his callers, from their countenances alone, inspired him with an earnest longing to kick them down stairs, he hastened to avoid the nuisance by escaping into the street. Since the tidings he had heard from Shingles, his native town had lost all attraction for him; in fact he shrank from going thither, and willingly lingered another day in New York.

Going to Buckland's lodgings, he renewed his persuasions of the evening before, and strongly urged him to leave New York. Buckland assented to every thing he said; and, hearing of a ship about to sail for the East Indies, Morton went with his friend to the merchant to whom she belonged, and induced him to engage a passage in her.

Returning to his hotel at about two o'clock, a waiter brought him a card, telling him that a boy had just left it for him. It was Rosny's; and on it were scrawled with a pencil the following concise and characteristic words:—

> Dear M.: Uncle Sam in a deuse of a hurry. Ordered to the island this afternoon. Off for Mexico to-morrow. Sorry not to see you, but haven't a minute to spare. Good luck.—*Au revoir.*
>
> Yours till doomsday,
> ROSNY.

Morton went to the recruiting office where he had been with Rosny on the day before, learned the time and place of the embarkation, was on the spot at the hour named, and in a few minutes saw Rosny striding down the wharf in most unmilitary haste, his hair fluttering in the wind. He was so engrossed in making certain arrangements, and issuing his mandates to the soldiers who were to row him and some other officers to Governor's Island, that he did not observe Morton, who stood quietly leaning against a post.

"Hallo, Dick," said the latter at length. "Haven't you eyes to see your friends?"

Rosny turned, in great surprise, and greeted him most emphatically.

"Come, Morton," he said, as he was stepping into the boat, "you'll change your mind after all,—won't you?—and meet me at Vera Cruz."

"I'll sit at home, and read your exploits in the papers," replied Morton.

"Well; a wilful man must have his way. Adieu."

"Good by. May you live to be a general, or any thing else you like, short of the presidency."

"Why, shouldn't I make a good president?"

"No."

"What? too progressive,—too wide awake,—too enlightened, ey?"

"Yes, and too pugnacious."

"There you are again, Boston all over. I'll be president yet, if only to spite the Bostonites. You shall write my life, and I'll give you an office for it. Farewell."

Morton watched the receding boat till it was almost out of sight, waved his hat to Rosny, who waved his own in return, and walked back to the hotel, wondering what would be the issue of his old classmate's ambitious schemes.

How, among a throng of brave men, Rosny gained a name for determined daring;—how, on every occasion that offered, he displayed the fire of the Frenchman, and the stubborn mettle of the Saxon, whose blood mingled in his veins;—how, though sick and wounded, he dragged himself from the hospital at Puebla, and, mounting his horse, pushed forward with the advancing columns;—how gallantly, under the murdering storm of musketry and grape, he led his intrepid blackguards up the rocks of Chapultepec;—how, while shouting among the foremost, he climbed the hostile rampart, a bullet plunged into his brain, and dashed him, quivering and dead, to the foot of the scaling ladders;—all this, and more likewise, is it not written in the New York Herald?

About a year after Rosny's departure, Morton chanced to be again in New York, when, in going out one morning, he beheld all the symptoms of some impending solemnity. Flags, festooned with crape, were strung across Broadway from building to building. The shops were half closed, and the streets were fast filling with people. Patriot citizens, exchanging the yardstick for the sword, strode the sidewalk in gorgeous panoply; and now and then a mounted warrior cantered along the pavement, struggling to keep his balance on his fiery coach horse. In an hour or two more, the pageant was in full operation. Looking from his hotel window Morton beheld a radiant river of shining bayonets, many colored plumes, and martial millinery, solemnly flowing down the middle of Broadway, to strange and lugubrious music, between melancholy shores of black broadcloth and beaver hats. At length a train of hearses appeared slowly advancing to the wailing music of the bands, encircled by the harmless sabres of the civic warriors, playing soldier, around the remains of those who had borne the part in tragic earnest. Over every hearse the national flag was drooping, and upon each was inscribed the name of its unconscious tenant. They were officers slain in battle during the last Mexican campaign. Four of the hearses passed. Morton read the names. They were all unknown to him; but as the fifth approached, he looked, started, and looked again; for wrought in white upon the sable drapery he saw, distinct and clear, the name of Rosny. Descending to the street, he joined the procession; he even underwent the funeral oration at the City Hall; and when it was over, shouldering through the crowd, he stood by the side of all that remained of his old classmate. Rosny's cap, and the sword he had used so well, lay on the lid of the coffin; and Morton turned away, with eyes not quite dry, as he recalled his many genial traits and his undaunted spirit.

To resume. On returning to his hotel after taking leave of Rosny, Morton found a note awaiting him, directed in a female hand. He opened it, and read the signature,—Ellen Ashland,—the name of a lady whom he had well known in Boston, and who, just before he had sailed for Europe, had been married to an eminent lawyer of his acquaintance. She wrote that she had seen an account of his escape from prison, and arrival in New York, in the morning paper,—expressed an earnest wish to see him, and invited him to visit her at the New York Hotel, where she was spending a few days with her husband.

As the time named was almost come, Morton called a coach, and drove up town. His friend received him with a peculiar warmth and earnestness of manner. Morton had known her as a person of marked character and strong but strictly governed emotions, not always permitting the expression of a feeling to keep pace with the feeling itself. He greatly liked and esteemed her, and her presence disarmed him, in a great degree, of his usual reserve.

Her husband had been absent all day in Brooklyn, and would not return till late in the evening.

"It is five years since I have spoken to a lady," said Morton, as he seated himself at the tea table.

As he was not scrupulous to wear a mask before her, she quickly discovered the depressed condition of his mind; and on her charging him with being very much out of spirits, he admitted that he was so.

"One would think," she observed, "that after the sufferings that you have passed, you would have come home in a different mood of mind."

"And so I did," said Morton.

"You seem in no great haste to see your friends and relations in Boston."

"I have no near relations there."

"But you have friends."

"Yes; I have heard from them. I met an acquaintance yesterday."

"You have heard, then ——" And she bent her eyes upon his face, with a look searching but full of kindness, as if studying his thoughts.

"Five years," she continued, "is a long time. Great changes may have taken place."

"Changes *have* taken place," said Morton.

"You have lost none of your intimate friends, as far as I know them; but some have left Boston, and some are married."

Morton did not look up; but an undefined expression passed across his face, like the shadow of a black cloud. When, a moment after, he raised his eyes, he saw those of Mrs. Ashland fixed upon him with the same earnest gaze as before. Such scrutiny from another would have been intolerable to him; but in her it gave him no uneasiness.

A servant entering changed for a time the character of their conversation. A quarter of an hour afterwards they were again alone, and Morton was seated near the window, when his friend approached him, her features kindling with a look of ill-suppressed feeling, laid her hand on his shoulder, and said, "Vassall,"—she had always before addressed him as Mr. Morton,—"my heart bleeds for you—for you and for Edith Leslie."

Morton looked up till he met her eyes. The surprise, the sudden consciousness that she was privy to his grief, the warm and heartfelt woman's sympathy that he read in every line of her face, were too much for his manhood, and he burst into tears.

CHAPTER LIV

Elle n'est point parjure, elle n'est point légère;
Son devoir m'a trahi, mon malheur, et son père. —*Polyeucte.*

Morton's evening with Mrs. Ashland, and the story which she told him, removed at least one pain from his breast. He learned that Edith Leslie was not in fault; and that, great as his misfortune might be, his idol was not turned to clay.

His friend's narrative, however, was very defective. She could give results merely, not knowing, or suspecting, the hidden springs which produced them; and Morton was left to form his own conclusions. The following is a more explicit statement.

Morton embarked for Europe, and the return steamer brought, in due course, a letter to Edith Leslie. With the next steamer came another; with the next, a third; all as absurd epistles as the most exacting mistress could desire. The succeeding mail was silent. She wondered and hoped; but when the next arrived, and brought no tidings, her heart began to fail. The winter wore away, and still no letter came. She was living, at that time, with her father, at his country seat. Leslie's health was declining, and when Vinal returned from his short European tour, he consigned to his hands the care of his affairs, and spent the greater part of his time at Matherton; for he had a strong love for the home of his boyhood.

Spring returned, and blossomed into summer; but nothing was heard of Morton. The season ripened; the fringed gentian sprang in the meadow, and the aster by the roadside; but no word came. In the forests, the October frosts began their gorgeous work. The ash put on its purple; the oak its varied coloring; the sumach its blood-red glare; and at evening, the sun went down in cold, stern splendors behind the painted mountains. Dry leaves whirled upon the ground; chill clouds mustered in the sky; and flakes of snow, the harbingers of storm, were blown along the frozen road. Then winter sank upon the landscape, and deeper winter on the heart of the unhappy girl.

Time passed on, and the hope of Morton's return grew fainter. Leslie, seeing his daughter's deep distress, made a journey to Europe; but his search was fruitless. Meredith, who spent a year on the continent, pursued the same inquiries, but could trace his friend no farther than the town of Neuburg, in Bavaria. Morton, before his departure, had made his will, and in the ardor of his attachment, had left the bulk of his property to his betrothed, distributing a comparatively small residue among a number of poor relations, none of whom had either the means or the worldly knowledge to take measures for ascertaining his fate.

Meanwhile, Leslie had fallen into a decline; and there was no hope that his life could be protracted beyond a year or two. He became more than ever dependent upon Vinal, who now assumed nearly the whole charge of his affairs, acquitting himself with great ability, and, in this instance, with entire faithfulness. A rickety manufacturing concern, which for years had been a drain upon Leslie's purse, began, under Vinal's control, to yield a good profit; and the former saw all his resources quickened and replenished, as if by an infusion of new life.

Vinal was mounting very high in the general esteem. His polished address,—a little too precise, however,—his acknowledged scholarship, his character for honor and integrity, and his energy and capacity for business, commended him to all classes. He passed current alike in ball rooms and on change. Men of the world never doubted him; and, after all, this confidence was not quite groundless, for Vinal, who had a sage eye to his own interest, had embraced the maxim that, in matters of business, a course of absolute integrity is, under all ordinary circumstances, the only wise policy.

As, in process of time, the conviction of Morton's death was confirmed, Leslie's old wish for a union between his daughter and Vinal began again to grow strong within him. Some two years after her lover's disappearance, he ventured to speak to her of this favorite plan; but it was long before he dared allude to it again. Meanwhile, Vinal's attentions had been assiduous and constant, yet so tempered as to convey the idea that he despaired of any other reward than the continuance of her friendship. At length, however, certain of her father's countenance, and assuming Morton's death as now beyond a doubt, he began, with all possible delicacy and caution, to renew his former addresses. He was not long in discovering that his cause was quite hopeless, unless he could produce some positive proof that Morton was no longer alive.

During the third summer of the latter's absence, Vinal went, for two or three months, to Europe, the state of his health being the alleged motive. While in Paris, he tried to find his former confederate, Speyer, but could only learn that he was no longer in that city. On returning to America, he told Leslie that he had inquired after Morton, on all sides, without the least success, but had taken measures which, he thought it not impossible, might in time lead to some discovery. In various parts of Germany, there was, as he affirmed, a class of travelling merchants and commercial agents, who, from the nature of their avocations, had every facility for making inquiries within the districts which they frequented. He had taken pains, he said, to become acquainted with a large number of these men, to whom he had stated the case of Morton's disappearance, and promised a reward for any information concerning him.

Some time after this, he told Leslie that he had had word from one of these correspondents. The latter, he affirmed, had heard that a young man, said to be an Englishman, had died very suddenly three or four years before, in an unfrequented part of Bohemia. The German declared himself ready, if desired, to go to the district in question, and inquire into the matter. Leslie was anxious that the inquiry should be made; upon which Vinal, though seeming not at all sanguine as to any result, gave him the name of his imaginary correspondent, and advised that he should write to him. Leslie, however, as Vinal had foreseen, desired that the latter should carry on the correspondence. He accordingly wrote a letter, directed to Jacob Hatz. This he showed to Leslie, and mailed it in his presence, consigning it to a long repose in some continental dead letter office. At the same time, he secretly despatched another letter, directed to Henry Speyer; for he had meanwhile discovered the address of this serviceable person. This letter was as follows:—

> Dear Sir: You cannot have forgotten some interviews and correspondence which formerly passed between us concerning a person who soon after was unfortunate enough to fall under the notice of the Austrian police. Nothing has since been heard of him, and it is commonly believed here that he is dead. It is my desire to have this opinion confirmed; and having found you honorable and efficient on another occasion, I cannot doubt that I shall find you so in this. May I beg your services in the following particulars?
>
> 1st. To take an imaginary journey into Bohemia, Moravia, or parts adjacent.
>
> 2d. To discover that, three years or more ago, a young man, an American, named — — — —, travelling alone on horseback in an unfrequented part of the country, (this was his habit,) was attacked by cholera, or any other violent

disease prevalent thereabouts, which carried him off in less than three days.

3d. That he died at a small village inn; that a Lutheran clergyman took charge of his effects, and wrote to his friends; but that the letter may have miscarried, or the clergyman may have played false, and kept the windfall that had come to him.

4th. That two years ago, the clergyman removed into Hungary, but that the innkeeper, a stupid, beetle-headed fellow, showed you a headstone in the Protestant burial ground, with ——'s name upon it. The innkeeper may describe him as a young man of twenty-four, or less, but must not remember too much, as this might attract further inquiry.

This is the outline, and will serve to indicate the kind of thing required. Vary it, in respect to details, as your judgment and your knowledge of the customs of the country may suggest. Names are omitted. Please observe the ciphers which stand in their places. You will soon receive, through another channel, means to supply the deficiency, if, indeed, your memory will not do so unaided.

Sign your letter *Jacob Hatz*. There is another point, which I beg you to observe particularly. Mention that on the gravestone, besides the name, was carved a figure, like an urn or cup, with a large ball above it. Date of death, also;— December 7, 1841.

I herewith enclose five hundred francs. On receiving your reply, *with this letter enclosed*, I shall immediately send you five hundred more. If I were not a poor man, and expecting always to be so, I could remunerate your services better.

With the fullest reliance on your honor and discretion, I remain,

        Yours, truly, —— ——.

P. S. For your better direction, I subjoin a formula to be followed in the beginning of your letter. You can word the rest in your own way. Write in French.

 Vinal, if he had dared, would gladly have forged such a letter as he required, instead of trusting to another person; but art or nature had not gifted him with the needful skill; and he was anxious, moreover, to have the foreign postmarks stamped upon it in form.

In due time, Speyer's answer came. He had neglected to return Vinal's letter, as desired; but in other respects, his performance gave his employer ample satisfaction. The latter showed it to Leslie, who seemed convinced by it; while his daughter, on reading it, abandoned at once the hope to which she had hitherto clung, that Morton might still be living.

"I remember this Hatz very well," said Vinal; "he seemed to be a plain, honest sort of man,—an agent, I believe, of a merchant in Strasburg. And yet the reward I promised might have been too great a temptation."

"Then," said Leslie, "you would not receive this as a proof of Mr. Morton's death?"

"No, I would not: that is, I should not but for one thing;—it is so very much like Vassall Morton to be travelling alone, on horseback, in an out-of-the-way part of the country."

"Did you observe," pursued Leslie, "what he says of figures of an urn and ball cut on the gravestone?"

"I saw it, but did not observe it particularly."

Leslie gave him the letter, and Vinal read the part referred to.

"What can it mean?" asked Leslie.

"I can't conceive," replied Vinal.

"It is the vase and sun," said Edith Leslie; "the device of his mother's family, the Vassalls."

"Ah," exclaimed Vinal, looking up with a face of mournful interest, "you must be right; the same figures are carved on the tomb of the Vassalls, in the old churchyard at Cambridge."

"They were cut," pursued Miss Leslie, "on a garnet ring, which he always used as a seal."

"I remember his showing me that ring," said her father, "and telling me that it was older than the voyage of the Mayflower. It was a kind of heirloom, which his mother had left him."

"Yes," suggested the sympathizing Vinal, who had long known that Morton used no other seal than this ring; "and the device on it was supposed to be his armorial bearing, and so cut on the gravestone, as it is on the Vassall tomb at Cambridge."

All doubt of Morton's death was now dispelled. His betrothed stored his image in her thoughts, as that of one lost for this world; and Vinal saw the field clear before him. Leslie was failing fast; and, as his life ebbed, his wish for his daughter's marriage with Vinal grew and strengthened. He urged her, daily, to listen to his suit; extolling his favorite's talents, energy, acquirements, and unimpeachable character—praises which she believed to be wholly just. Vinal, on his part, seconded these parental efforts with most earnest, beseeching, not to say abject importunities. The compassion which he contrived to excite, an idea of duty, and an urgent wish to gratify her dying father, at length prevailed with her; and laying before Vinal the true state of her feelings, she consented, on such terms, to accept his suit.

Vinal had gained his point; but he had scarcely done so, when his spirits were dashed by an untoward incident, the nature of which may be guessed hereafter. And, as it never rains but it pours, this reverse of luck was soon followed by a second, of another kind.

One afternoon, returning from his customary constitutional ride, he was in the act of turning the upper corner of a street which slopes downward somewhat steeply till it meets a main thoroughfare of the town. A small ragamuffin boy was standing on the curbstone, with a blade of grass between his thumbs, through which he blew with might and main, evidently to startle Vinal's horse, whose head was within a yard of him. He succeeded to his complete satisfaction. Vinal switched at the youngster with his whip; but this only made matters worse. The horse galloped down the street at a rate which his rider's weak arm could not check; and, at the corner of the main street, wheeling suddenly to the left, he slipped on the wet pavement, and fell with a crash on his side. Horse and man lay motionless, till a city teamster, running up, raised the former by the bridle. Two or three passers by came to Vinal's aid; but as they lifted him, he set his teeth with pain. The horse had fallen on his left leg, breaking it above the knee.

Vinal was timid to excess in time of danger; but he could bear pain with the firmness of a stoic. While he felt himself run away with, and at the moment of his fall, he had been greatly confused. He no sooner saw that the worst was over, than he rallied his faculties, and asserted his usual self-mastery. His face was fast growing pale with violence of pain; but he was quite himself again.

A crowd gathered about him, as he lay leaning on the steps of the neighboring church.

"Shall we carry you to the —— Hotel?" asked a gentleman.

"Yes, if you please. But first be kind enough to bring a shutter. They will give you one at the school round the corner. When a man is killed, drunk, or maimed, there is nothing like a shutter. How do you do, Edwards?"—to a man whom he recognized in the crowd.

"I hope you are not badly hurt."

"My leg is broken."

"Are you in great pain?"

"Yes; a bad business, I think. Will you oblige me by seeing that my horse is led to the stable in — — Street?"

The shutter was soon brought.

"Thank you. Lift me very gently."

As they moved him he clinched his teeth again in silent torture.

"All right. Now one take the shutter at the head, and one at the feet. You'll find me a light weight."

And thus, between two men, escorted by a procession of schoolboys just let loose, Vinal was carried to the hotel.

The event justified his presage. He was forced to lie motionless for weeks, suffering greatly from bodily pain, and no less from certain anxieties which of late had harassed him. Leslie, on his part, was in great distress at the disaster. He felt, or fancied himself, near his end; and the wish next his heart was to see the marriage accomplished before he died. It was therefore determined that, notwithstanding the inauspicious plight of the bridegroom, it should take place at the time before fixed upon, four months after the beginning of the engagement.

The ceremony was very private. None were present but two or three friends of Miss Leslie, the dying father, borne thither in a chair, the disabled bridegroom, and the pale and agitated bride; for that morning, standing before Morton's picture, a strange misgiving and a dark foreboding had fallen upon her, and the sun never shone on a bride more wretched. Her nearest friend, Mrs. Ashland, was at her side. She was the only person, besides her father and Vinal, who knew of her engagement to Morton, and, indeed, had been her confidante from first to last. Soon after Morton's disappearance, an accident had brought them together, reviving an old school intimacy; and Edith Leslie, in her suspense and misery, was but too glad to find a friend in whom she could trust without reserve.

The rite was ended, and Edith Leslie was Edith Vinal. Days and weeks passed; Leslie slowly declined, and Vinal slowly recovered. She divided her time between them, passing the greater part of the day with the latter, and returning at evening to watch by her father's bed or rest within sound of his voice. At length, three weeks after her marriage, on a morning the horror of which remained scarred always in her memory, Morton's letter from Genoa was put into her hands; and the long-disciplined patience with which she had armed herself, the religion which she had called to her aid, all the guards and defences of her mind, were borne down, for a time, by the resistless flood of passion, which, like a river bursting its barriers, swept all before it.

CHAPTER LV

> We twain have met like ships upon the sea,
> Who hold an hour's converse, * * *
> One little hour! and then away they speed
> On lonely paths, through mist, and cloud, and foam,
> To meet no more. —*Alexander Smith.*

"Good morning, Ned," said Morton to his friend Meredith. He had come to Boston the day before, and had already seen Meredith more than once.

"Going already? Sit down, man. Why are you in such a hurry?"

"I shall look in again before night."

"You are not well. I never thought you could look so worn and haggard."

"Try the prison of Ehrenberg for four or five years, and see how you will look when you get out. It's nothing, though. A little rest will make all right again."

"You are not very likely to get it. You are a lion now, and people will not leave you alone."

"They shall. I am not in the humor for balls and dinner parties."

He went to the house of Mrs. Ashland, whom he had accompanied homeward from New York.

"Have you the letter for me?"

The letter was that which had come from Europe with the story of his death. On hearing Mrs. Ashland's account, he had at once conjectured that this was but another stroke of Vinal's diplomacy; but he had been careful not to intimate to his friend the least suspicion against the latter.

The commission of obtaining from Edith the letter in question was far from an agreeable one; but Mrs. Ashland had accomplished it, and now placed the paper in Morton's hands.

The signature was not that of Speyer; but at the first glance, Morton was sure that the small, neat handwriting was the same with that of the treacherous notes of introduction given him by Vinal at Paris. As he studied the letter, reading and re-reading it, his companion, who remembered him chiefly as a frank, good-humored young man, was startled at the stern and almost fierce expression which once or twice came over his features, and seemed to be banished by an effort. A vague suspicion of some mystery rose in her mind, but Morton hastened to divert her.

"I hope that Edith will not refuse a visit from me."

Here, again, Mrs. Ashland promised to mediate for him, and in the afternoon he received a note from her, saying that Vinal's wife would see him on the next morning.

At the hour named, he rang at the door, forced his lips to inquire for "Mrs. Vinal," gave his name to the servant, and was shown into the drawing room.

It was nearly five years since he had last seen that well-remembered room. Nothing was changed. It remained precisely as he had known it when he stood prosperously on the farther verge of that dreary chasm of time; and as each familiar object met his eye, such a flood of bitter recollection came upon him, that for a moment he bent his head upon his breast.

He raised it, and started as he did so. Reflected in the mirror at the end of the room, as if the art of some new Cornelius had evoked it, stood, pale as marble, the form that had so long attended his sleeping and waking dreams. Morton turned quickly, and saw Edith standing motionless in the doorway.

He advanced towards her, and took her hand in both his own. She raised her eyes to his face in silence. He tried to speak, but tried in vain. At length he found utterance.

"I know it all. Ellen Ashland has told me every thing. I do not blame you;—no one can blame you."

"Thank God that you think so."

"Yes, thank God; for when I thought that you had forgotten me——"

"Then you *did* think so?"

"For a time; and it seemed to me as if no more constancy were left on earth; as if it had been sapped and undermined in its very citadel."

"Do not believe that I forgot you for a single hour; or that I can ever forget you. You and I have been joined at least in an equal sorrow and suspense. We have walked through depths together, and drank the same gall and bitterness."

"That one month—four miserable weeks—should have worked all this! One month sooner, and this black picture of our lives would have been bright again as the sunshine. I could believe that some infernal power had taken the reins of our fate."

"Do not say so, nor think so. You have fronted death; you have braved despair; and now bear this blow victoriously as you have borne the rest."

"The crowning blow is the heaviest of all."

"Look into my heart,—if you could look into it,—and see on which of us it has fallen with the more sickening and withering force."

Morton looked into her face. It was like a deep lake becalmed, into which strong springs are boiling up from rocks at the bottom. The surface is still; but looking more closely, one may discern faint gliding undulations and trembling lines, which betray the turmoil below. Morton saw them, and felt their purport.

"I would to God," he said, "I could bear your burden for you."

Edith buried her face, and burst into a flood of weeping.

Grief, mixed with more ardent emotion, wrought with such violence in Morton's breast, that he scarcely restrained his impulse to throw himself at her feet. In a few moments, she raised her head.

"Do not think from this, that I am not resigned to what has fallen on us. It is best. Incomprehensible as it is, it is best for us both."

A passionate denial rose to Morton's lips; but he did not utter it.

"I overrated my strength. I am weaker than I hoped to have found myself. You wish to bear my burden! You have had enough to bear of your own, Vassall; but with you, endurance is not the whole. You still have youth, health, vigor. To one of your instincts, the world has noble tasks enough. With a heart steeled by dangers, refined by sufferings, tempered in fires of anguish, what path need you fear to tread? Forget the past;—no, do not forget it; only forget all in it that may damp your courage or weaken your hand. When I knew you first, you were full of zeal in a worthy and generous enterprise. Cling to it still. Let me see the tree which I knew in its blossoming bear a full fruit at maturity. Let me see the ardent and earnest spirit which I knew in the beginning, not quelled or flagging by the way, but holding on its course to the end. The pure chivalry of your heart which constrained me to love you, the instinct which turned towards honor and nobleness as a tree turns its branches to the sun,—do not part from it; keep it unstained for my sake, and let it brighten and strengthen all your life."

"If preachers could speak with your tongue," exclaimed Morton, "the world would forget itself and grow virtuous. The love that I have lost on earth I will set among the stars. It shall be my beacon till the day I die."

"We are too delicate and timorous to bear a part in the active struggles of life; but it is a woman's office to raise and purify the thoughts of those who do. You, whose strong natures are formed for warfare, cannot be so sensitive as we are to every spot that dims the brightness of your armor. It is easy for me, before one whom I have loved as I have loved you, to hold this tone, and be borne up for a time above the thought of grief and renouncement. But it is a different task to still, through all a lifetime, the longings of a woman's heart, and the impatient surgings of a woman's temperament. This is the task assigned me, and I accept it. Life—action—are before you. Patience is my medicine; the slow talisman which must open in the end my door of promise."

Morton pressed her hand to his lips.

"'There is some soul of goodness in things evil.' A sorrow under which, feebly borne, the mind would wither to the earth, borne well will lift it above the clouds. Do not believe that I have deceived any one. He knows on what terms he takes me. I feel respect, esteem, confidence, warm friendship for him."

"May you never be undeceived," thought Morton to himself.

"But for any more ardent love,—that, I told him, was buried in the grave with you."

She was silent for a moment, and then went on.

"It will not be wise, or right, for us to see each other often. In time, you will meet some one with whom you can forget the pain of this separation."

Morton shook his head.

"Yes—at least I trust you will. But we can never forget what we have been to each other. Our reality is melted into a dream, but we must not allow it to remain a dream. Let it be to us a fountain of high thoughts, whose streams may water all our lives."

"You are an alchemist, Edith," said Morton; "you have found the secret to change lead and iron into pure gold. And yet you make me feel, more than ever, if that can be, what a crown I have lost."

When Morton left the house, after a half hour's interview, the agitation with which he had entered it had sunk into quiet; for an influence had fallen upon him as soothing and elevating as if he had been listening to the paschal music in the chapel of the choir at St. Peter's. And as an aeronaut, tossed among tempestuous clouds, is borne of a sudden above the turmoil, and floats serene in a calmer sky, so the troubled mind of Morton felt itself buoyed up for a space above the tumult of passionate and bitter thought.

CHAPTER LVI

For close designs and crooked counsels fit,
Sagacious, bold, and turbulent of wit.—*Dryden.*

On the next morning he was walking near the Court House, when a man accosted him, touching his hat with one hand, and holding out the other in the way of friendly salutation. Morton, however, was at a loss to recognize him. He had an air which may most conveniently be described as *raffish*, a hat set on one side of his head, and a good-natured, easy, devil-may-care face.

"Richards is my name," said the stranger. "I met you at Paris, just before you went into Austria."

This was quite enough. Morton, who had repeatedly revolved all the circumstances connected with his arrest, at once recalled the accident by which he had discovered Richards and Vinal, on their way together to visit Speyer. Morton determined to cultivate this new acquaintance; which, however, seemed likely to grow without much tillage.

"I went on two or three excursions about the city with you, Mr. Vinal, and the rest. Perhaps you have not forgotten it."

"Not in the least; but you are changed since then."

"Yes," said Richards, touching the place where his moustaches had once grown, "I cut them off when I went into practice here in Boston. I found they were ruining my character as a professional man."

"How long were you in Paris after I saw you?"

"Two years, off and on. I wish I were there now." And taking Morton's arm, he proceeded to catechize him touching his imprisonment and escape, of which he said he had first read in the New York Herald. Morton satisfied his curiosity, taking care to give him no suspicion of Speyer's connection with the affair, and allowing him to infer that the arrest was caused by an accidental concurrence of suspicious circumstances. Richards, at the end, broke out into a savage, red republican tirade against Metternich and the Austrian government.

"By the way," said Morton, when his companion's heat had subsided, "do you happen to remember a man called Speyer, or something like it,—a republican propagandist, at Paris? I believe you knew him."

"I never knew any body else," replied Richards, adopting a cis-Atlantic figure of speech for which rhetoricians have as yet found no name.

"Do you know where he is now?"

"What, have you lent money to Speyer, too?"

"He is heavily in my debt," said Morton, evasively.

"That's odd. He seems to have been borrowing money all round. I remember, about a year or more ago, I met Mr. Vinal, and he began to talk about Paris. 'By the way,' said he to me, 'do you happen to remember a man named Spires, or Speyers, or some such thing? I lent him five hundred francs.' 'I wish you may get it,' said I. 'Well,' said Vinal, 'I have a friend going to Paris, who will try what can be done for me.' So I set him on the track. I don't know whether he got his money or not, but I saw him talking with Speyer in the street, one evening last spring, and Vinal looked as sour as if he had swallowed a bottle of vitriol."

"Talking with Speyer last spring!" repeated Morton; "has he been to Paris?"

"Speyer has come out to America. There is not a country in Europe but has grown too hot for him. He was under surveillance in Paris, all the time I knew him."

"When did he come?"

"Six or eight months ago."

"Where is he to be found?"

"In New York, chiefly. If you could have caught him when he was here in Boston, in the spring, you might have got something out of him; for he seemed flush of money."

"What, after you saw him with Vinal?"

"Yes."

"Have you seen him more than once in Boston?"

"Yes, two or three times."

"Is he in New York now?"

"I suppose so; but I would not advise your trying to do any thing with him. You had better pocket your loss, and let him go. However, if you want to try, I can refer you to a man who can probably help you to find his whereabouts."

"Thank you; there's no harm in making the attempt. I don't know Speyer well. What kind of man is he?"

"Well, I will draw his portrait for you. He is sly as a fox; always contriving, plotting, and working under ground. Intrigue is his native element. He takes to it like a chameleon to air, or a salamander to fire."

"An artful, managing fellow, not bold enough to make a direct attack?"

"Bold! There is nothing on the earth, or under it, that he fears. He will not make a direct attack, if he can help it, because it is against his instinct; but press upon him—crowd him a little—and he will show his teeth like a Bengal tiger. He is always in hot water; for he never could be happy out of it. He has his weaknesses, though. A woman whom he takes a fancy to can turn him round her finger. I never knew a man so desperate in that way, or such a devil incarnate when a fit of jealousy seizes him."

"You draw a flattering likeness of your friend," said Morton."

"O," said Richards, laughing, "I cut half my foreign acquaintance, now that I am at home."

Before leaving his new companion, Morton obtained from him the name and direction of the person of whom he had spoken as likely to know where Speyer was to be found. Left alone at length, he pondered on what he had heard:—

"So Vinal applied to Richards, to learn Speyer's address, when he wrote to him to report me dead. Speyer in America!—having interviews with Vinal!—and flush of money! Can it be possible that this agent of his villany has become the instrument of his punishment?—that the Furies are already on his track? If Speyer kept Vinal's letter, as, under the circumstances, such a calculating knave would be apt to do, he has that in his hands which would make my friend open his purse strings; yes, make him coin his life blood, to satisfy him. It is past doubting; Vinal has it now; this cormorant is preying upon him."

That afternoon Morton took the night train to New York, in search of Speyer.

CHAPTER LVII

Though those that are betrayed
Do feel the treason sharply, yet the traitor
Stands in worse case of woe.—*Cymbeline*.

Vinal sat alone, propped and cushioned in an arm chair, when a clerk from his office came to bring him his morning letters. He looked over the superscriptions till he saw one in a foreign hand. Vinal compressed his pale lips. When the clerk had left the room, he glanced about him nervously, tore open the letter, and read it in haste.

"The bloodsucker! Money; more money! He soaks it up like a sponge; or, rather, I am the sponge, and he means to wring me dry. In jail! Well, he has found his place, for once. Six hundred dollars! That, I suppose, is to pay his fine; to uncage the wild beast, and set him loose. I wish he were sentenced for ten years; then he might lie there, and rot. I must send him something—enough to keep him in play. No, I will send him nothing. He is in trouble; and I may turn it to account. I will write to him that, if he will return me my letters, I will give him a thousand dollars now, and an annuity of five hundred for six years to come. I shall do well if I can draw the viper's teeth at that price. Then I can breathe again; unless Morton should have suspected the trick I played him, or—what if he should meet with Speyer! But that is not likely, for he never knew him, nor saw him, and Speyer will shun him as he would the plague. I wish they had shot him in the prison, as I am told they meant to do. There would have been one stumbling block away; one lion out of my path. But now the sword hangs over me by a hair; I am racked and torn like a toad under a harrow; no rest, no peace! What if Speyer should do as he threatens, print my letters, and placard them about the streets! I will buy them out of his hands if it cost all I have. And even then I shall not be safe, as long as this ruffian is above ground. With him and Morton to haunt me, my life is a slow death, a purgatory, a hell."

He tore Speyer's letter into small fragments, rolled and crushed them together, and scattered them under the grate.

CHAPTER LVIII

> When rich villains have need of poor ones, poor ones may make what price they will.—*Much Ado about Nothing.*

Morton reached New York, and found the person to whom he had been referred by Richards. He proved to be a German, of respectable appearance enough; but Morton could learn nothing from him. He admitted that he had once known Speyer; but stubbornly denied all present knowledge concerning him; and after various inquiry elsewhere, which brought him into contact with much vile company, without helping him towards his end, Morton gave over the search, and returned to Boston.

A day or two after, he met Richards in the street.

"Well, Mr. Richards, I was in New York the other day, and saw your man; but he knew nothing about Speyer."

Richards laughed.

"I dare say not; just let me write to him; he will tell me a different story. I used to be hand and glove with all these refugees; and I will lay you any bet I find Speyer's whereabouts within a week."

Accordingly, three or four days after, Richards called at Morton's lodgings, with an air of great self-satisfaction.

"I have spotted your game for you, sir, and he won't run away in a hurry, either. He'll be sure to wait till you come. He's in jail."

"What, for debt?"

"No, for an assault on a Frenchman. It was about a woman, a friend of Speyer's. You know I told you what a jealous fellow he is." And he proceeded to recount what further information he had gained.

"Odd," pondered Richards, after parting from Morton, "that a millionnaire like him, and not at all a mean man either, should trouble himself so much about any picayune debt that Speyer can owe him. There is something in this business more than I can make out."

While Richards occupied himself with these reflections, Morton repaired to his lodgings and made his preparations. On the next morning, he was in New York again.

He went to the jail where Speyer was confined, and readily gained leave to see him. A somewhat loquacious officer, who was to conduct him to the prisoner's room, confirmed what Richards had told him, and gave him some new particulars. Speyer, he said, had never before, to his knowledge, come under the notice of the police. He had been living in good lodgings, and in a somewhat showy style. The person who had occasioned the quarrel was an Italian girl. "She comes every day to see him," said the policeman—"she's a wild one, I tell you; and he frets himself to death because he is shut up here, and can't be round to look after her."

"So much the better," thought Morton, who hoped that this impatience would aid him in his intended negotiation.

"For how long a time is he sentenced?" he asked.

"For three weeks; unless he can find somebody to pay his fine for him."

On entering the prisoner's room, Morton saw a man of about forty, well dressed, though in a jail, but whose sallow features, deep-set eyes, and square, massive lower jaw, well covered with a black beard, indicated a character likely to be any thing but tractable. If he had been either a gentleman on the one hand, or a common ruffian on the other, his visitor might have better known how to deal with him; but he had the look of one to whom, whatever he might be at heart, a various contact with mankind had armed with an invincible self-possession, and guarded at all points against surprise.

Morton was a wretched diplomatist, and had sense enough to know it. He knew that if he tried to manoeuvre with his antagonist, the latter would outflank him in a moment, and he had therefore resolved on a sudden and direct attack. But when he saw Speyer, he could not repress a lingering doubt whether he were in fact the person of whom he was in search. His chief object was to gain from him, if possible, any letters of Vinal which might be in his hands. There was no direct evidence that he had any such letters; yet Morton thought that the only hope of success lay in assuming his having them as a certainty, and pretending a positive knowledge, where, in truth, he had no other ground of action than conjecture. So he smothered his doubts, and as soon as the policeman was gone, made a crashing onset on the enemy.

"My name is Vassall Morton. I escaped four months ago from the Castle of Ehrenberg. I have known something of you through Mr. Vinal."

If Morton were in doubt before, all his doubts were now scattered, for a look of irrepressible surprise passed across Speyer's features, mingled with as much dismay as his nature was capable of feeling. At the next instant, every trace of it had disappeared; and slowly shaking his head, to indicate unconsciousness, he looked at Morton inquiringly, with an eye perfectly self-possessed and impenetrable. His visitor, however, was not to be so deceived.

"I have no enmity against you, nor any wish to injure you. On the contrary, I will pay your fine, and set you free, if you will have it so. You have letters concerning me, written to you by Vinal. Give them to me, and I will do as I say. No harm shall come to you, and I will give you money to carry you to any part of the world you wish."

"What letters?" asked Speyer.

"We will have no bush-beating. You wish to get out of jail, and have good reason for wishing to get out at once. If you will give me those letters, you shall be free in three hours, and safe. If you will not, I may give you some trouble."

Speyer was silent for a moment.

"I know the letters are of use to you. You can play a profitable game with them; but I can stop your game at any moment I please."

"I can get four thousand dollars for them to-morrow," said Speyer.

"Then why are you here in jail?"

"Vinal offers it; here it is." And taking a note from his pocket, Speyer read Vinal's proposal to buy the letters.

"Let me see it," said Morton, taking the note from Speyer's hand. "This, of itself, is evidence against him. With your leave, I will keep it. Now hear my offer. Give me the letters, and I will pay your fine. Then go with me to Boston, and I will make Vinal pay you on the spot every dollar that he has offered, on condition that you promise to leave the United States, and never return."

Speyer reflected. He came to the conclusion that Morton did not mean to expose Vinal; but only, like himself, to extort money from him; and wished that he, Speyer, should leave the country in order to get rid of a competitor. Morton's object was quite different. He could not foresee to what extremities Speyer's extortion might drive its victim; and he aimed to check it, by no means out of any tenderness for Vinal, but lest his wife might suffer from its consequences.

Speyer, on his part, fevered with jealousy, was chafing to be at large again.

"When will you pay my fine?"

"Now."

"Then I accept your proposal."

"Can I rely on your promise to leave the country, and make no further drafts on Vinal?"

Speyer cast a glance at him, as if he had read his mind.

"I will promise."

"Will you swear?"

Speyer readily took the oath, insisting that Morton should swear in turn to keep his part of the condition.

"Now let me see the letters."

"I must send to my lodgings for them. If you will come back in two hours, you shall have them."

"I should have thought you would keep them by you."

"No; but they are safe. Come back at twelve with the money for my fine, and they shall be here for you."

Morton had no sooner left the room, than Speyer despatched an underling of the jail to buy for him a few sheets of the thin, half-transparent paper in common use for European correspondence. This being brought, he opened his trunk, and delving to the bottom, drew up a leather case, from which he took the letters in question. Laying the thin paper over them, he proceeded to trace with a pen an exact facsimile. He was well practised at such work, and after one or two failures, succeeded perfectly. Folding his counterfeits after the manner of the originals, he placed them in the envelopes belonging to the latter; and within a half hour after his task was finished, Morton reappeared.

Speyer gave him one of the facsimiles. He read it attentively, without seeing the imposture. The handwriting, though disguised, was evidently Vinal's; but it had neither the signature of the writer, nor Morton's name. The place of each was supplied by a cipher.

"Reference is made here to another letter. Where is it?"

Speyer gave him the second counterfeit. The envelope bore a postmark of a few days later than the first. The note contained merely the names of Morton and Vinal, with ciphers affixed, referring to those in the first letter.

"Have you no more of Vinal's papers?"

Speyer shook his head. Indeed, the letters, if genuine, would have been amply sufficient to place their writer in Morton's power. The latter at once took the necessary measures to gain the prisoner's release. Speyer no sooner found himself at liberty than he hastened to search out the fair object of his anxieties, promising to meet Morton on the steamboat for Boston in the afternoon. His doubts were strong whether the other would keep faith with him; but he amply consoled himself with the thought that, at the worst, he still had means to bring Vinal to terms.

CHAPTER LIX

> What spectre can the charnel send
> So dreadful as an injured friend? —*Rokeby.*

"Strange," thought Vinal, "that I hear nothing from him."

It was three days since he had written to Speyer; and his chief anxiety was, lest his note should have miscarried. Pain and long confinement had wrought heavily upon him. Every emotion, every care, thrilled with a morbid keenness upon his brain and nerves; but hitherto he had ruled his sensitive organism with an iron self-control, and calmed its perturbations with a fortitude which in a better man would have been heroic.

His wife was in the room, and, as his eye rested on her, it kindled with a kind of troubled delight, for he loved her strongly, after his fashion. He had remarked of late a singular assiduity and tenderness in her devotion to him. Her position, in fact, was not unlike that of one who, broken and overborne by some irreparable sorrow, had renounced the world and its happiness, to embrace a new life, and build up for herself a new hope in the calm sanctuary of a convent. In the same spirit, Edith Leslie, bidding farewell to her girlish dream of life, its morning rose tint, and cloud draperies of gold and purple, gave herself to the practical duties before her, and sought, in their devoted fulfilment, to strengthen herself against the flood which for a time had overwhelmed her.

Vinal, who, acute as he was, could not understand the state of mind from which her peculiar kindness of manner towards him rose, pleased himself with the idea that his rival's return was not so great a shock to her as he had at first feared, and that, after all, she was more fond of him than of Morton. This notion consoled his disturbed thoughts not a little. Still he was abundantly anxious and harassed.

"If Morton should suspect! He has not come to see me; but that is natural enough, under the circumstances. And if he does suspect, he can have no proof. No one here suspects me. They say it was strange that my European correspondent should have made such a mistake; but that is all. No one dreams that I had a hand in it; and why should they? No one knew of Edith's engagement to him, except herself, her father, and her confidantes. I suppose she has confidantes—all girls have them. I wish their epitaphs were written, whoever they are. Well,

> 'Come what come may,
> Time and the hour run through the roughest day.'

But this is a dangerous business—a cursed business. Why does not Speyer write?"

As his thoughts ran in this strain, he looked up, and his eye caught that of his wife. She was struck with his troubled expression.

"You look anxious and care-worn. Are you ill?"

"Come to me, Edith," said Vinal, with a faint smile.

She came to the side of his chair, and he took her hand.

"Edith, I am not well to-day. My head swims. This long confinement is eating away my life by inches."

"In a week more, I trust, you will be able to move again. The country air will give you new life. But why do you look so troubled?"

"Dreams, Edith,—bad dreams, like Hamlet's, I suppose. It is very strange,—I cannot imagine why it is,—but to-day I have felt oppressed, weighed down, shadowed as if a cloud hung over me. I am not myself. A man is a mere slave to his nervous system, and when that is overthrown, his whole soul is shaken with it. The country is my hope, Edith. We will go there together, soon, and begin life anew."

A knock at the door interrupted him.

"Come in," cried Vinal, in his usual quick, decisive tone.

A servant entered.

"Well, what is it?"

"A gentleman wishes to see you, sir."

"Did he give his name?"

"Mr. Edwards, sir."

"Ask him to come up."

"A man whom I expected this morning on business," he said, in explanation to his wife, as the servant closed the door. "I wish he were any where but here. And so you are going away."—She was dressed to go out.—"He will be here only a moment; do not be gone long."

"No, I will be with you again in an hour."

"Do not forget," said Vinal, pressing her hand, "for when you leave the room, Edith, it is as if a sunbeam were shut out."

As Vinal, sick in body and mind, thus leaned in his distress on the victim of his villany, he cast into her face a look that was almost piteous. She, seeing nothing but his love for her, warmed towards him with compassion; the more so since, till that moment, she had known him as a calm, firm man, a model, to her eyes, of masculine self-government. A mind tortured with suspense, acting upon a weak and morbidly sensitive body, had betrayed him into this unwonted imbecility.

The step of the visitor sounded in the passage; and returning the pressure of his hand, his wife went out at the door of a small adjoining room, opening upon the side passage by which she commonly entered and left the hotel.

After a few minutes' interview, Edwards took his leave, and Vinal, left alone, fell into his former train of thought. In a moment, he was again interrupted by a knock at the door, quite unlike the hasty rap of the hotel servant.

"Come in," cried Vinal.

The door opened, and Vassall Morton entered. He had learned from the retiring visitor that Vinal was alone.

"My dear fellow!" exclaimed Vinal, his face beaming with a transport of welcome. "My dear fellow!"

But Morton stood without taking his proffered hand. The smile remained frozen on Vinal's face, and cold drops of doubt and fear began to gather on his forehead.

"There is another friend of yours in the passage," said Morton.—"Come in, Speyer."

Speyer entered, bowing with his usual composure. Vinal sank back in his chair, collapsing like a man withered with a palsy stroke.

"Vinal," said Morton, after a silence of some moments, "you have a cool way of receiving your acquaintances."

He made no answer, but still sat, or rather crouched, in the depths of his easy chair, where the thick bounding of his heart almost choked him. Morton stood for some time longer, looking at him. He had not reached such a point of Christian forgiveness as not to find pleasure in his enemy's tortures, and he saw that his silence tortured him more than words.

"Vinal," he said at length, "I used to know you in college for a liar and a coward; and since then you have grown well in both ways. You have hatched into a full-fledged villain; and now that I have found you out, you crouch like a whipped cur."

No answer was returned, and Morton's anger began to yield to a different feeling. If he could have seen the condition of Vinal's mind and body, he might, between pity and contempt, have spared him.

"I came to upbraid you with your knaveries; but I find you hardly worth the trouble. Do you see this letter? It is the same that you wrote to this man at Marseilles, instructing him to forge a story that I was dead, and that he had seen my gravestone, with my mother's family device upon it. Will you dare deny that you wrote it? You will not! I thought as much. I have unravelled you from first to last. Five years ago, you bribed Speyer, here, to compromise me with the Austrian police. Pretending to be my friend, you gave me letters which betrayed me into a prison, where you hoped that I would end my days; and, next, you contrived this trickery to prove me dead. Is there any name in the English tongue too vile to mark you?"

Vinal sat as if stricken dumb.

"I know your reputation," pursued Morton. "You are in high feather here. You pass for a man of virtue, integrity, and honor. You make speeches at public meetings; Fourth of July orations; Phi Beta orations; charity harangues—any thing that smacks of philanthropy and goodness; any thing that will varnish you in the public eye. Why am I not bound to lay bare this whitewashed lie? What withholds me from grinding you like a scorpion under my boot-heel, or flinging you on the pavement to be stared at like a scotched viper? A word from me, and you are ruined. You need not fear it. Stay, and enjoy your honors as you can; but my foot shall be on your neck. This letter of yours is the spell by which I will rule you, body and soul."

Here he paused again; but Vinal's tongue was powerless.

"I tell you again, for I would not have you desperate, that I do not mean to ruin you. Bear yourself wisely, and you are safe, at least from me. Have you lost your speech? Are you turned dumb?"

Vinal muttered inarticulately.

"There is another danger which I have done my best to ward off from you. This man, who had you at his mercy, has sworn to leave the country, and never to return; on which score you will please to pay him the money you offered him for the purchase of your letters."

Vinal seemed confused and stupefied, and Morton was forced to be more explicit in his demands. At length, the former signed a note for the amount, though not without stammering objections to his name appearing on it in connection with Speyer's. Morton, however, turned a deaf ear to these remonstrances.

"Here is your pay," he said to Speyer. "Any bank will discount this for you. Now, to what place do you mean to go?"

"To Venezuela. I have a friend there in the army. He will get a commission for me."

"Very well. See that you stay there; or, at all events, do not come back to the United States. If you do, you will perjure yourself. Now, go; I have done with you. Vinal, I will leave you to your reflections; and when you can sleep in peace, free from Speyer's persecutions, remember to whom you owe it."

Vinal sat like a withered plant, his head sinking between his shoulders, while his hand, still unconsciously holding the pen, rested on the arm of his chair. There was something in his appearance at once so abject and so piteous, that a changed feeling came over Morton as he looked on him. By a sudden impulse, akin to pity, he stepped towards him, and took his wrist. The pen dropped from his pale fingers, which quivered like an aspen bough; and as Morton stood gazing on him, Vinal's upturned eyes met his, as if riveted there by a helpless fascination.

"You unhappy wretch! You are burning already with the pains of the damned. Flint and iron could not see you without softening. I have saved you,—not out of mercy, nor forgiveness,—not for *your* sake;—but I have saved you. I have pushed away the sword that hung over you by a hair. You are free now to be happy."

But as he spoke this last word, so fierce a pang shot into his heart, remembering what he had lost, and what Vinal had won, that his pity was scattered like mist before a thunder squall. He flung back the passive hand against the breast of its terrified owner, turned abruptly, and left the room.

No sooner had the door closed behind him, than the door of the anteroom opposite was flung open, and Edith Leslie, rushing in, stood before Vinal with the wild look of one who gasps for breath. She attempted to speak, but broken words and inarticulate sounds were all her lips would utter. Strength failed her in the effort, and pressing her hands to her forehead, she sank fainting to the floor.

CHAPTER LX

> I will not go with thee;
> I will instruct my sorrows to be proud.—*King John.*

On the next morning, Vinal learned that his wife was ill, and confined to her room in her father's house. On the day following, he was told that she was no better; but on the third morning, a letter, in her handwriting, was given him. He opened it, and read as follows:—

> I heard all. I have learned, at last, to know you. These were your bad dreams! This was the cloud that overshadowed you! No wonder that your eye was anxious, your forehead wrinkled, and your cheek pale. To have led that brave and loyal heart through months and years of anguish!—to have buried him from the light of day!—to have buried him in darkness and despair, if despair could ever touch a soul like his! And there he would have been lost forever, if you had had your will,—if a higher hand had not been outstretched to save him. One whom you dared not meet face to face; one as far above your sphere as the eagle is above the serpent to which he likened you! You have taught me how sin can cringe and cower under the anger of a true and deeply outraged man. That I should have lived to hear my husband called a villain!—and still live to tell him that the word was just! My husband! You are *not* my husband. It was not a criminal, a traitorous wretch, whom I pledged myself to love and honor. You have insnared me; you have me, for a time, safely entangled in your meshes. The same cause which led me to this yoke must withhold me from casting it off. I cannot imbitter my father's dying moments. I cannot bring distress and horror to his tranquil death bed. For his sake, I will play the hypocrite, and stoop to pass in the world's eye as your wife. For the few weeks he has to live, I will lodge, if I must, under your roof; I will sit, if I must, at your table; but when my father is gone, let

the world impute to me what blame it will, I will leave you forever. You need not fear that I shall expose your crimes. If *he* could spare you, it does not become me to speak. Live on, and make what atonement you may; but meanwhile there is a gulf between us wider than death.

EDITH LESLIE.

An accident, arising out of her very devotion to Vinal, had made known his secret to her. In the anteroom which led from the side passage of the hotel to his apartment, and through which, on the morning of his interview with Morton, she had intended to pass on her way out, was a table, covered with books and engravings, with which the invalid had been amusing his leisure. The sight of them reminded her that she had promised to get for him a series of German etchings, which he had expressed a wish to see. She seated herself, to write a request to the friend who had them, that he would send them to the hotel. Her hand was on the bell, to call the servant, when the peculiarly emphatic and earnest manner with which Vinal greeted some new visitor caught her attention. The door had sprung ajar on the lock; the speakers were very near it, and Morton's tone was none of the softest. She remained as if charmed to her seat; and every word fell on her ear as clearly as if she had stood in the same room.

CHAPTER LXI

> I hold the world but as the world, Gratiano,
> A stage where every man must play a part,
> And mine a sad one.—*Merchant of Venice.*
>
> The past is past. I see the future stretch
> All dark and barren as a rainy sea.—*Alexander Smith.*

Morton took possession again of his house in the country, which still remained in the keeping of one of his humble relatives, into whose charge he had given it. He turned the key of his long-deserted library. A loving influence had presided here in his absence, and, even when he was given up for lost, every thing had been scrupulously kept as he had left it.

Here he immured himself; avoided all society but that of a few personal friends; and by plunging into the studies which had formerly engrossed him, tried to escape the persecution of his own thoughts. It was a forced and painful task. The marks in his books, the pencil notes on their margins, his voluminous piles of memoranda, were all so many sharp memorials of the past, to remind him that he was resuming in darkness and despondency the work that he had left in sunshine.

In process of time, however, his ancient interest in his favorite pursuit began to rekindle. He began to feel that the years of his imprisonment had not been the dead and barren blank which he had inclined to think them. His mind had ripened in its solitude, and the studies which he had before followed with the zeal of a boy, more eager than able to deal with the broad questions which they involved, he could now grasp with the matured intellect of a man.

But while Morton was thus laboring on, Edith Leslie was passing through an ordeal incomparably more severe. Month after month dragged on, and her father still lingered, sinking again and again to the very edge of the grave, and then rallying, as if with a fresh life. Vinal, meanwhile, was in a good measure recovered from the effects of his accident. His home and hers, if it could be called a home, was now a house in town, which her father had fitted up for her in view of her marriage. She had a painful and delicate part to act—at her father's bedside, to appear as the happy and contented wife; at home, to endure the presence of the man whose treachery filled her with horror, and whose love for her, though she had never spoken a word of reproof, had changed into fear and hatred. Of his actual presence, however, she had to endure little; for he shunned her studiously; and her house was to her a solitude, where she passed hours of a suffering more intense than Morton had ever known in the dungeons of Ehrenberg.

Meanwhile, the servants, those domestic spies, did not fail to rumor abroad the singular mode of life of the bride and bridegroom; that Vinal avoided the house; that they seldom met, even at meals; and that no word or look of sympathy or confidence seemed ever to pass between them. Such rumors found their currency among the busier gossips of the town; but Morton, secluded among his books, remained wholly ignorant of them.

CHAPTER LXII

Old friends, like old swords, still are trusted best.—*Webster.*

It was nearly a year since he had landed at New York, and Morton still remained a literary hermit. Society was stale and distasteful to him. He passed three fourths of his day in his library, and the rest on horseback. At length, however, it happened that a cousin of his mother, one of his few relatives in the city, was to give a ball on occasion of her daughter's *début;* and lest his refusal should be thought unkind, Morton promised to come. He drove to town in the afternoon; and walking through a somewhat obscure street, suddenly, on turning a corner, saw, some four or five rods before him, a well-remembered face. It was the face of Henry Speyer. The discovery was mutual. Speyer instantly turned down a by-lane. Morton quickened his pace, and reached the head of the lane in time to see the broad shoulders of the patriot in full retreat. He soon lost sight of him among a wilderness of back yards and squalid houses. The incident greatly disturbed and exasperated him. "A broken oath is nothing to him," he thought to himself; "he is at Vinal again, dragging at his veins like a vampire."

The evening drew on, and he entered the ball room in a gloomy and dejected frame of mind. After a few words to his relatives, he took his stand among a group who were watching the dancers; and had scarcely done so, when he saw a young lady, simply, but very richly dressed, whose fine figure and powerfully expressive beauty arrested his eye at once. The indifference and listlessness with which he had entered vanished. He soon observed that she was not an object of attention to him alone; for near him stood a certain old beau, well known about town, and a young collegian, both following her with their eyes. The music ceased, and her partner led her to a seat at the farther side of the room. Glancing at his two neighbors, Morton saw that they were in the act of moving towards her; but he, being nearer, had the advantage. Gliding through the dissolving fragments of the dance, he stood by her side.

"Miss Fanny Euston, I see two persons coming to ask you to dance. May I hope that you will reject them for an old friend's sake, and let me be your partner?"

She raised her eyes with a perplexed look, which instantly changed to a bright gleam of recognition, and cordially took his proffered hand.

"So," said Morton, "you have not forgotten me. And yet, as I see you, I hardly dare to take up again the broken thread of our old intimacy. I used to call you Fanny."

"Call me Fanny still," she said, "if only for the memory of auld lang syne."

"I hoped to have seen you before, but you have been away."

"Yes, with my relations, and yours, at Baltimore. I have heard a great deal about you. Your story is the talk of the town. You might be the lion of the season; but I have not seen you at parties."

"No, I have outlived my liking for such matters."

"I cannot wonder at it. What horrors you have suffered! what dangers you have passed!"

"I have weathered them, though."

"You were more than four years in a dungeon."

"Yes, but I gave them the slip."

"You were led out to be shot by the soldiers."

"They thought better of it, and saved their ammunition."

"And yet I see," said Miss Euston, smiling, "that you still remain your former self. I remember telling you that, if you were sentenced to the rack, you would go to it with a gibe on your tongue, and speak of it afterwards as a pleasant diversion. But," she added, with a changed look, "you have not come off unscathed. Your face is darker and thinner than it used to be, and there are lines in it that were not there before."

"Fortune fondled me till she grew tired of me; then turned at me, tooth and nail."

"You banter with your lips, but your look belies your words. You have suffered greatly; you have suffered intensely."

Morton looked grave in spite of himself.

"Perhaps you are right. I have very little heart left for jesting."

The eyes of his companion, as they met his, assumed a peculiar softness.

"You must have suffered beyond all power of words to speak it. The world to you was fresh and full of interest. You were ambitious; full of ardor and energy; loving hardship for its own sake, and obstacles for the sake of conquering them. You were formed for action. It was your element—your breath; and without it you did not care to live. You were high in confidence, and believed that whatever you had once resolved on must, sooner or later, come to pass."

"Why are you saying this?" demanded Morton, in great surprise.

"Out of this life you were suddenly snatched and buried in a dungeon; shut off from all intercourse with men; your energies stifled; your restless mind left to prey upon itself, or sustain a weary siege against despair. Pain or danger you could have faced like a man; but this passive misery must to you have been a daily death."

"Who," interrupted Morton, "taught you, a woman, to penetrate the nature of a man, and describe sufferings that you never felt?"

"Your mind was like a spring of steel, springing up the more strongly the harder it was pressed down. The suffering must have been deep indeed from which you could not rebound. To have escaped, to have reached home, and to have found any thing but relief and delight——"

"Home!" ejaculated Morton, bitterly, as a sharp memory of the anguish which had met him on the threshold came over him. "A prison may be borne with patience. Those are fortunate who have felt no keener stabs."

The words, equivocal as they were, were scarcely spoken, when he had repented them. Fanny Euston was silent for a moment. "Can it be possible," she thought, "that the stories whispered about, that before he went away he was engaged to Edith Leslie, are something more than an idle rumor?"

"Why do you look at me so searchingly?" thought Morton, on his part, as, raising his eyes, he saw those of his friend fixed on him in a gaze in which a woman's curiosity was mingled with a fully equal share of a woman's kindliness and sympathy. He hastened to escape from the critical ground which he had approached.

"I can retort upon you," he said. "You have had your ordeal, too."

"What, do you see its traces? Do you find me scorched and withered?"

"I see," said Morton, "such traces as on gold that has passed through the furnace."

"Truly, I have cause to rejoice, then; for I remember that, among other compliments, you once intimated your opinion that I was possessed with a devil."

"I am afraid that I pushed to its farthest limit my privilege of cousinship."

"And yet, when I look back to that time, I cannot help thinking that you had some reason for believing that an influence from the nether world had some share in me."

"Now pardon me, if I am rude again. Looking at you, I can see the same devil still."

"Indeed, and you will console me now, as you did then, by telling me that a dash of viciousness is necessary to make a character interesting."

"I should prune and explain my speech. By a devil, I did not mean a malicious imp of darkness, wholly bent on evil. I meant nothing more than certain impulses and emotions,—passions, if I may call them so,—very turbulent tenants, yet of admirable use when well dealt with. These were the devil whom I used to see in you, and whom I see still."

"I shall tremble at myself."

"Then you are not so brave as you were when you leaped the fallen tree at New Baden. Your demon has ceased to have an alarming look. I think you have turned him to good account. Shall I illustrate from the legends of the saints?"

"In any way you please; but I should never have expected you to resort to so pious a source."

"St. Bernard, crossing the Alps on some holy errand, was met by Satan, who, being anxious to prevent his journey, broke one of his carriage wheels. But St. Bernard caught him, sprinkled him with holy water, doubled him into a wheel, and put him upon the carriage in place of the broken one. The legend says that he answered the purpose admirably, and bore the saint safely to the end of his journey."

"Your legend is absurd enough; but I think I catch your meaning, and wish I could think you wholly in the right. It is singular that you and I have never met without our conversation becoming personal to ourselves. We are always studying each other—always trying to penetrate each other's thoughts."

"On one side, at least, the success has been complete. As you look at me, I feel that you are reading me like a book, from title page to finis."

"You greatly overrate my penetration. I am conscious, at this moment, of movements in your mind which I do not understand."

"And would you have me confess them to you?"

"You might repent it afterwards; and that would make a breach between us."

"You are a miraculous woman, to postpone your curiosity to a scruple like that. No, I would not have spoken of confession, if I should ever repent it. Do you know, I would rather open my mind to you than to any one else I am now acquainted with."

"But you have male friends; very old and intimate ones."

"Excellent in their way; but I would as soon confess to my horse. Find me a woman of sense, with a brain to discern, a heart to feel, passion to feel vehemently, and principle to feel rightly, and I will show her my mind; or, if not, I will show it to no one. Now, after this preamble, you have a right to think that I should begin to confess something at once. But first, I will ask you a question."

"What is it?"

"Tell me what effect you think any long and severe suffering ought to have on a man—something, I mean, that would bring him to the brink of despair, and keep him there for months and years."

"What kind of man do you mean?"

"Suppose one given over to pleasure, ambition, or any other engrossing pursuit not too disinterested."

"It would depend on how the suffering was taken."

"Suppose him resolved to make the best of a bad bargain."

"Why, the effect ought to be good, I suppose,—so the preachers say."

"I do not wish to know what the preachers say. I wish your own opinion."

"Are you quite in earnest?"

"Quite."

"Such suffering, rightly taken, would strip life of its disguises, and show it in its naked truth. It would teach the man to know himself and to know others. It would awaken his sympathies, enlarge his mind, and greatly expand his sphere of vision; teach him to hold present pleasure and present pain in small account, and to look beyond them into a future of boundless hopes and fears."

"Now," said Morton, "you have betrayed yourself."

"How have I betrayed myself?" asked his friend, in some discomposure.

"You have shown me the secrets of your own mind. You have given me a glimpse of your own history, since we last met."

"And so, under pretence of confessing to me, you have been plotting to make me confess to you!"

"No, you shall hear my confession. I have it now, such as it is, at my tongue's end."

"I have no faith in you."

"Perhaps you will have still less when you have heard this great secret. You remember me before I went away. I was a very exemplary young gentleman,—quiet, orderly, well behaved,—of a studious turn,—soberly and virtuously given."

"You give yourself an excellent character."

"And what should be the results of the discipline of a dungeon on such a person?"

"Discipline would be a superfluity, considering your perfections."

"So I thought myself. Nevertheless, for four years, or so, I was shut up, with nothing to look at but stone walls, under circumstances most favorable for the culture of patience, resignation, forgiveness, and all the Christian virtues; and yet the devil has never been half so busy with me as since I came out; never whispered half so many villanous suggestions into my ears, nor baited me with such scandalous temptations."

"That is very strange," said Fanny Euston, who was looking at him intently.

"For example," pursued Morton, "a little more than a year ago, in New York, he said to me, 'Renounce all your old plans, and habits, and antiquated scruples—reclaim your natural freedom—fling yourself headlong into the turmoil of the world—chase whatever fate or fortune throws in your way—enjoy the zest of lawless pleasures—launch into mad adventure—embark on schemes of ambition—care nothing for the past or the future—think only of the present—fear neither God nor man, and follow your vagrant star wherever it leads you.'"

Morton knew that, restrained and governed as it might be, there was quicksilver enough in his companion's veins to enable her to understand what he had said, and prevent her being startled at it. But he was by no means prepared for the close attack she proceeded to make on him.

"Such a state of mind is foreign to your nature. You have prudence and forecast. You used to make plans for the future, and study the final results of every thing you did. There is something upon your mind. It is not imprisonment only that has caused that compression of your lips, and marked those lines on your face. You have met with some deep disaster, some overwhelming disappointment. Nothing else could have wrought such a convulsion in you."

Morton was taken by surprise; and, as he struggled to frame an answer, his features betrayed an emotion which he could not hide. Fanny Euston hastened to relieve his embarrassment, and assuage, as far as she could, the tumult she had called up.

"With whatever fate you may have had to battle, your wounds are in the front,—all honorable scars. Your desperation is past;—it was only for the hour;—and for the other extreme, it is not in you to suffer that."

"What other extreme?"

"Idle dreaming;—melancholy;—weak pining at disappointment."

"No, thank God, it is not in me to lie and whine like a sick child."

"You are the firmer for what you have passed. Manhood, the proudest of all possession to a man, is strengthened and deepened in you."

"What do you call this manhood, which you seem to hold in such high account?"

"That unflinching quality which, strong in generous thought and high purpose, bears onward towards its goal, knowing no fear but the fear of God; wise, prudent, calm, yet daring and hoping all things; not dismayed by reverses, nor elated by success; never bending nor receding; wearying out ill fortune by undespairing constancy; unconquered by pain or sorrow, or deferred hope; fiery in attack, steadfast in resistance, unshaken in the front of death; and when courage is vain, and hope seems folly, when crushing calamity presses it to the earth, and the exhausted body will no longer obey the still undaunted mind, then putting forth its hardest, saddest heroism, the unlaurelled heroism of endurance, patiently biding its time."

"And how if its time never come?"

"Then dying at its post, like the Roman sentinel at Pompeii."

Her words struck a chord in Morton's nature, and roused his early enthusiasm, dormant for years.

"Fanny," he said, "I thank you. You give me back my youth. An hour ago, the world was as dull to me as a November day; but you have brought June back again. You would make a coward valiant, and breathe life into a dead man."

Miss Euston seemed, for a moment, in embarrassment what to reply; indeed, she showed some signs of discomposure, contrasting with her former frankness. They were still in the recess of the window. She was visible to those in the room; while he, standing opposite, was hidden by a curtain. At this moment, a gentleman, with a slight limp in his gait, approaching quickly, accosted Miss Euston, smiling with an air of the most earnest affability. She looked up to reply, but, as she did so, her eyes were arrested by a sudden change in the features of her companion, who was bending on the new comer a look so fierce and threatening, that she scarcely repressed an ejaculation of surprise. Mr. Horace Vinal followed the direction of her gaze, and saw himself face to face with the victim of his villany. He started as if he had found a grizzly bear behind the curtain. The smile vanished from his lips, the color from his cheeks, and he hastily drew back, and mingled with the crowd.

This sudden apparition, breaking in upon the brightening mood of the moment, incensed Morton almost to fury; and his anger, absurdly enough, was a little tinged with a feeling not wholly unlike jealousy. He made an involuntary movement to follow his enemy, but recollecting himself, smoothed his brow and calmed his ruffled spirit as he best might.

"You seem to know that man very well," he said to Miss Euston.

"Yes, I know him."

"He seems to think himself on excellent terms with you."

"He has charge of my mother's property."

"You are good at reading faces. I hope you liked the expression on his, as he slunk away just now."

"It was fear—abject fear. Why are you so angry? Why is he so frightened?"

"His nerves, you may have observed, are something of the weakest. He is my attendant genius, my familiar. A word from me, and he will run my errand like a spaniel."

"How could you gain such power over him?" she asked, in great astonishment.

"Magnetism, Fanny, magnetism. The effects of the mesmeric fluid are wonderful. See, the polking is over; they are forming a quadrille. Shall we take our places in the set?"

During the dance, Morton looked for his enemy, but could not discover him till it was over, and he had led his partner to a seat.

"Look," he said, "there is our friend again; in the next room, just beyond the folding doors, talking with Mrs. — — and Mrs. — —. He seems to have got the better of the shock to his nerves; at least, he stands up manfully against it. Mr. Horace Vinal has a stout heart, and needs nothing but valor, and one other quality, to make a hero. But his face is flushed. I fear he suffers in his health. See, he makes himself very agreeable. Vinal was always famous for his wit. Pardon me a moment; I have a word for my friend's ear."

Fanny Euston looked at him doubtingly.

"Pray, don't be discomposed. There's no gunpowder impending. Vinal is not a fighting man; nor am I. What I have to say is altogether pacific, loving, and scriptural."

And passing into the adjoining room, he approached Vinal, who no sooner saw the movement, than he showed a manifest uneasiness. His forced animation ceased, his manner became constrained, and while Morton stood near, waiting an opportunity to speak to him, he withdrew to another part of the room. Morton followed, and pronounced his name. Vinal, with pretended unconsciousness, mingled with the crowd. Morton again tried to accost him, and again Vinal moved away. Impatient and exasperated, Morton stepped behind him, touched his shoulder, and whispered in his ear,—

"You fool, do you know your danger? Speyer is looking for you. I saw him this afternoon. He looks as if he needed your charity. You had better be generous with him. He is a tiger, and will be upon you before you know it."

Anger and terror, of which the latter vastly predominated, gave a ghastly look to Vinal's face, as he turned it towards Morton. But he drew back without a word, and soon left the room.

"Where is Mr. Vinal?" asked the wondering Fanny Euston, as her companion returned to her side. The momentary interview had been invisible from where she sat.

"Obeyed the magic word, and vanished. Never doubt again the power of magnetism. Now you may see that the claptrap of the charlatans about the mutual influence of congenial spheres is not quite such trash as one might think. Vinal and I, being congenial spheres, put each other, the one into a passion, the other into a fright. But I have a request to you. Whoever knows you, knows, in spite of the libellers, a woman who can keep counsel; and as I am modest in respect to my magnetic gifts, I shall beg it of you, that you will not mention these experiments to any one. Good evening. I have revived to-night an old and valued friendship. If I can help it, it shall not die again."

He took leave of his hostess, wrapped his cloak about him, and walked out into the drizzling night.

CHAPTER LXIII

> Nought's had, all's spent,
> Where our desire is got without content.
> 'Tis safer to be that which we destroy,
> Than by destruction dwell in doubtful joy.—*Macbeth*.

Morton walked the street, on the next day, in a mood less grave than had lately been his wont, but in one of any thing but self-approval.

"It is singular," he thought, "I could never meet her without forgetting myself,—without being betrayed into some absurdity or other. I thought by this time that I had grown wiser, or, at least, was well fenced against that kind of risk. But it is the same now as ever. I was a fool at New Baden, and I was a fool again last night, though after a different fashion. After all, when a fresh breeze comes, why should I not breathe it? when a ray of sun comes, why should I not bask in it? But what impelled me to insult that wretch, who I knew dared not and could not answer me?"

He pondered for a moment, then turned and walked slowly towards Vinal's place of business.

"Is Mr. Vinal here?" he asked of one of the clerks.

"Yes, sir, he is in that inner room."

"Is any one with him?"

"No, sir." And Morton opened the door and entered.

Vinal sat before a table, on which letters and papers were lying; but he was leaning backward in his chair, with a painfully knit brow, and a face of ghastly paleness. It flushed of a sudden as Morton appeared, and his whole look and mien showed an irrepressible agitation.

Morton closed the door. "Vinal," he said, "you need not fear that I have come with any hostile purpose. On the contrary, I will serve you, if I can. Last night I used words to you which I have since regretted. I beg you to accept my apology."

Vinal made no reply.

"I saw Speyer in the street last evening, and tried to speak with him, but could not stop him. He can hardly have any other purpose in breaking his oath and coming here again, than to get more money from you. Has he been to you?"

Still Vinal was silent.

"I think," continued Morton, "that you cannot fail to see my motive. I wish to keep him from you, not on your account, but on your wife's. If you let him, he will torment you to your death. Have you seen him since last evening?"

Vinal inclined his head.

"Where is he now?"

"I don't know."

"Has he left the city?"

"I don't know. I suppose so."

"And you gave him money?"

Vinal was silent again. Morton took his silence for assent.

"When he comes again, tell me of it, and let me speak to him. Possibly I may find means to rid you of him. Meantime remember this. He has given your letter up to me. He has no proofs to show against you, unless he has other letters of yours;—is that the case?"

Vinal shook his head.

"Then, if he proclaims you, his word will not be taken, unless I sustain it; and I shall keep silent unless you give me some new cause to speak. I do not see that he can harm you much without my help; so give him no more money, and set him at defiance."

Morton left the room; but his words had brought no relief to the wretched Vinal. Speyer had shown him his letter, and told him the artifice by which he had kept it, and palmed off a counterfeit on Morton. He felt himself at the mercy of a miscreant as rapacious, fierce, and pitiless, as a wolverene dropping on its prey.

CHAPTER LXIV

> Ah, would my friendship with thee
> Might drown the memory of all patterns past! — *Suckling*.

Some few days after, riding, as usual, in the afternoon, Morton saw on the road before him a lady on horseback, riding in the same direction. At a glance, he recognized the air and figure of Fanny Euston. This remnant, at least, of her former spirit remained to her, — she did not hesitate to ride unattended. Morton checked his horse, reflected for a little, then touched him with the spur, and in a moment was at her side. After they had conversed for a while, she said, —

"I have heard a great deal of your imprisonment from others, but nothing from yourself. Will you not let me hear your story from your own lips?"

"It was a long and dull history to live through, and will be a short and dull one to tell."

"I have never been able to hear clearly why you were arrested at all."

"It was a simple matter. The Austrian government is like a tyrant and a coward, frightened at shadows. I had one or two acquaintances at Vienna who had been implicated, though I did not know it, in plots against the government. I, being an American, was imagined to be, as a matter of course, a democrat, and in league with them. It needed very little more; and they shut me up, as they have done many an innocent man before me."

"Looking back at your imprisonment, it must seem to you a broad, dark chasm in your life."

"Broad and black enough; but not quite so void as I once thought."

"No; in struggling through it, I can see that you have not come out empty handed."

"Not I; I should be glad to rid myself of the larger part of the load. One is sometimes punished with the fulfilment of his own whims. I remember wishing — and that not so many years back — that I might sound all the strings of human joys and sufferings, — try life in all its phases, — in peace and war, a dungeon, if I remember right, inclusive. I have had my fill of it, and do not care to repeat the experiment."

"Some of the damp and darkness of your dungeon still clings about you, and out of the midst of it, you look back over the gulf to a shore of light and sunshine, where you were once standing."

"You read me like a sibyl, as you always do. None but a child or a fool will seriously regret any shape of experience out of which he has come with mind and senses still sound, though it may have changed the prismatic colors of life into a neutral tint, a universal gray, a Scotch mist, with light enough to delve by, and nothing more."

"One's life is a series of compromises, at best. One must capitulate with Fate, gain from her as much good as may be, and as little evil."

"And then set his teeth and endure. As for myself, though, if gifts were portioned out among mankind in equal allotments, I should count myself, even now, as having more than my share."

"That idea of equalized happiness is a great fallacy."

"Every idea of mortal equality is a great fallacy; and all the systems built on it are built on a quicksand. There is no equality in nature. There are mountains and valleys, deserts and meadows, the fertile and the barren. There is no equality in human minds or human character. Who shall measure the distance from the noblest to the meanest of men, or the yet vaster distance from the noblest to the meanest of women? The differences among mankind are broader than any but the greatest of men can grasp. With pains enough, one may comprehend, in a measure, the minds on a level with his own or below it; but, above, he sees nothing clearly. To follow the movements of a great man's mind, he must raise himself almost to an equal greatness."

"A hopeless attempt with most. Every one has a limit."

"But men make more limits for themselves than Nature makes for them."

"You seem to me a person with a singular capacity of growth. You push forth fibres into every soil, and draw nutriment from sources most foreign to you."

"An indifferent stock needs all the aliment it can find. I am fortunate in my planting. Companionship is that which shapes us; and I have found men, and what is more to the purpose, women, who have met my best requirement. One's friends have all their special influence with which they affect him. Yours, to me, was always a rousing and wakening influence, an electric life. You have shot a ray of sun down into my shadow, and I am bound at least to thank you for it."

"I hope, for old friendship's sake, that your shadow may soon cease to need such farthing-candle illumination.—Here is my mother's house. She will be glad to see you."

"I thank you: I will come soon, but not to-day."

And, taking leave of his companion, he turned his horse homeward.

"A vain attempt! I thought a light might kindle again; but it is all dust and ashes, with only a sparkle or two. No more flame; the fuel is burnt out. Shall I go on? Shall I offer what is left of my heart? A poor tribute for her. She should command a better; and there is something in her manner, warm and cordial as she is, that tells me that I should offer it in vain."

CHAPTER LXV

> Art thou so blind
> To fling away the gem whose untold worth,
> Hid 'neath the roughness of its native mine,
> Tempts not the eye? Touched by the artist's wheel,
> The hardest stone flashes the diamond's light.—*Anon.*

A few days later, Morton was seated with his friend Meredith.

"Ned, this is a slow life. Do you know, I have made up my mind to change it."

"You have been so busy this year past, that I thought you would be content to stay where you are."

"On the contrary, my vocation takes me abroad."

"Where will you go?"

"To Egypt, Arabia, India, the East Indies, the South Sea Islands."

"All in the cause of science?"

"At any rate, the thing is necessary to my plans."

"The old Adam sticks to you still. Are you sure that no Pequot blood ever got into your veins?"

"I don't know as to that. My ancestors were Puritans to the backbone, witch-burners, Quaker-killers, and Indian-haters. I only know that when I am bored, my first instinct is to cut loose, and take to the woods. It comes over me like an ague-fit. There are two places where a man finds sea room enough; one is a great metropolis, the other is a wilderness. There is no freedom in a place like this. One can only be independent here by living out of the world as I have been doing."

"Here in America, we have political freedom *ad nauseam;* and we pay for it with a loss of social freedom."

"You remember an agreement of ours, years ago, that you and I should travel together. Now, will you stand to it, and go with me?"

"Other considerations apart, I should like nothing better; but, as matters stand with me now, it's quite out of the question."

Morton was silent for a moment. "Ned," he said, at length, "I heard a rumor yesterday. It is no part of mine to obtrude myself into your private affairs, and I should not speak if I had not a reason, the better half of which is, that I think I can serve you. I heard that you were paying your addresses to Miss Euston."

"One cannot look twice at a lady without having it noted down in black and white, and turned into tea-table talk."

"I met Miss Euston a few evenings ago. I used to know her before I went to Europe, but had not seen her since. If what I heard is true, I think you have shown something more than good taste."

"You remember her," said Meredith, after a pause, "as she was the summer when you and I went to New Baden."

"Yes, I knew her then very well."

"I liked her better at that time than you ever supposed. She was very young; just out of school, in fact. She had lived all her life in the suburbs, and had grown up like an unpruned rose bush,—a fine stock in a strong soil, but throwing out its shoots quite wildly and at random."

"I know it; but all that is changed, I can't conceive how."

"I can tell you. The one person whom she loved and stood in awe of was her father. He was a man, and a strong one. He died suddenly about the time you went away. It was the first blow she had ever felt; and his death was only the beginning of greater troubles. You remember her brother Henry."

"I remember him when he was at school—a good-natured, high-spirited little fellow, whom every body liked."

"With wild blood enough for a regiment, and as careless, thoughtless, and easy-tempered as a child, such as he was, in fact. His father, being out of the country on his affairs, sent him to New York, where he fell in with a bad set, and grew very dissipated. Then, to get him out of harm's way, they shipped him off to Canton, where he soon began to ruin himself, hand over hand. At last, a few months after his father's death, his mother and sister heard that he was on his way home, with his health completely broken. The next news was, that he was at Alexandria, dangerously ill of a slow fever. His mother, who, with all respect, is the weakest of mortals, broke down at once into a state of helplessness, and could do nothing but weep and lament. The whole burden fell upon his sister. She went with her mother and a man servant to Alexandria, and took charge of her brother, whose fever left him in such an exhausted state that he fell into a decline. She brought him as far as Naples, but he could go no farther; and here she attended him for five months, till he died; her mother sinking, meanwhile, into a kind of moping imbecility. By that time, her uncle had found grace to come and join them. Then her turn came; her strength failed her, and she fell violently ill. For a week, her life was despaired of; but she rallied, against all hope. I was in Naples soon after, and used to meet her every morning, as she drove in an open carriage to Baiæ. I never saw such a transformation. She was pale as death, but very beautiful; and her whole expression was changed. She had always been very fond of her brother. There were some points of likeness between them. He had her wildness, and her kindliness of disposition, but none of her vigorous good sense, and was altogether inferior to her in intellect. Now you can have some idea why you find her so different from what you once knew her to be."

"I knew," said Morton, "that she had passed through the fire in some way; but how I could not tell. I think, now, still better of your judgment, Ned."

"Then you see why I will not go with you. I must bring this matter to an issue. For good or evil, I must know how it goes with me. It is not a new thing. It is of longer date than you imagined, or she either. What the end of it may be, Heaven only knows; but one thing is certain,—you will not see me in the South Seas before this point is cleared."

"Then I shall never see you there."

"Why do you say that?"

"Your travelling days are over. At least I think so."

"Do you mean——?"

"That you are playing at a game where I think you will win."

"What reason have you to think so?" demanded Meredith, nervously.

"Take the opinion, and let the reason go. On such an argument a good reason will sometimes dwindle into nothing when one tries to explain it."

His hand was on the door as he spoke, and bidding his friend good morning, he left him to his meditations.

CHAPTER LXVI

*Why waste thy joyous hours in needless pain, Seeking
for danger and adventure vain?—Fairy Queen.*

Morton mounted his horse, and rode to the house of Mrs. Euston. He found her daughter alone.

"I have come to take leave of you. I am on my travels again."

"Again! You are always on the wing. I supposed that you must have learned, by this time, to value home, or, at least, be reconciled to staying there in peace."

"My home is a little lonely, and none of the liveliest. Movement is my best repose."

"You are wholly made up of restlessness."

"That is Nature's failing, not mine; or if Nature declines to bear the burden of my shortcomings, I will put them upon Destiny, and with much better cause. But this is not restlessness; or, if it is, it has method in it. This journey is a plan of eight years' standing. I concocted it when I was a junior, half fledged, at college, and never lost sight of it but once, and then for a cause that does not exist now."

"Where are you going?"

Morton gave the outline of his journey.

"But is not that very difficult and dangerous?"

"Not very."

"You will not be alone, surely."

"I provided for a companion years ago. My friend Meredith and I struck an agreement, that when I went on this journey he should go with me."

An instant shadow passed across the face of Fanny Euston.

"So you will have a companion," she replied, with a nonchalance too distinct to be genuine.

"Not at all. He breaks his word. He won't hear of going."

The cloud vanished.

"I take it ill of him; for I had relied on having him with me. He and I are old fellow-travellers. I have tried him in sunshine and rain, and know his metal." And he launched into an emphatic eulogy of his friend, to which Fanny Euston listened with a pleasure which she could not wholly hide.

"He best knows why he fails me. It is some cogent and prevailing reason; no light cause, or sudden fancy. Some powerful motive, mining deep and moving strongly, has shaken him from his purpose; so I forgive him for his falling off."

As Morton spoke, he was studying his companion's features, and she, conscious of his scrutiny, visibly changed color.

"Dear cousin," he said, with a changed tone, "if I must lose my friend, let me find, when I return, that my loss has been overbalanced by his gain. I will reconcile myself to it, if it may help to win for him the bounty that he aspires to."

The blush deepened to crimson on Fanny Euston's cheek; and without waiting for more words, Morton bade her farewell.

CHAPTER LXVII

Mais ai-je sur son ame encor quelque pouvoir,
Quelque reste d'amour s'y fait il encor voir.—*Polyeucte.*

With a slow step and a sinking heart, Morton entered Mrs. Ashland's drawing room. He told her of his proposed journey; told her that he should leave the country within a few days, to be absent for a year or two at least, and asked her mediation to gain for him a parting interview with Edith Leslie.

Mrs. Ashland, and she only, knew the whole misery of her friend's position, and feared lest, exhausted as she was by mental pain and long watching, and divided between her unextinguished love for Morton, and her abhorrence of the criminal who by name and the letter of the law was her husband, the meeting might put her self-mastery to too painful a proof. She therefore, though with a very evident reluctance, dissuaded Morton from it.

"Edith has been taxed already to the farthest limit of her strength. She is not ill, but quite worn and spent. She is almost constantly with her father, who, now, can hardly be said to live, and needs constant care. To see you at this time would agitate her too much."

"Can the sight of me still have so much power to move her?"

"You know what she is. A feeling once rooted in her mind does not loosen its hold. There are very few who comprehend her. Her character is so balanced and so harmonious, so quiet and noiseless in its movement, that no one suspects the force, and faith, and energy that are in it. It is not in words or in looks that she shows herself. It is in action, in emergencies, that she declares her power over herself and over others."

Morton's passion glowed upon him with all its early fervor.

"I will tell her what you wish. But her cup is full already, and you can hardly be willing to shake it to overflowing. It is impossible that her father should linger many days more; and when that is over, it will bring her a relief, though she may not think it so, in more ways than one."

Morton assented to his friend's reasons, and leaving his farewell for Edith Leslie, mournfully took his leave.

CHAPTER LXVIII

Grief and patience, rooted in her both,
Mingle their spurs together.—*Cymbeline*.

Leslie was dead; beyond the reach of wounds and sorrow; and the only tie which held his daughter to Vinal was at last broken. She left him, as she had promised, and made her abode with Mrs. Ashland, in her cottage by the sea shore.

She sat alone at an open window, looking out upon the sea, an illimitable dreariness, waveless and dull as tarnished lead; clouded with sullen mists, but still rocking in long, dead swells with the motion of a past storm.

Her thoughts followed on the track of the absent Morton.

"It is best for you to have gone; to have made for yourself a relief in your man's element of action and struggle. Such a change is happiness, after the misery you have known. It was a bitter schooling; a long siege, and a dreary one; but you have triumphed, and you wear its trophy,—the heroic calm, the mind tranquil with consciousness of power. You have wrung a proud tribute out of sorrow; but has it yielded you all its treasure? Could you but have rested less loftily on your own firm resolve and unbending pride of manhood! Could you but have learned that gentler, deeper, higher philosophy which builds for itself a temple out of ruin, and makes weakness invincible with binding its tendrils to the rock!

"Your fate and mine have not been a bed of roses; but the fierceness of yours is past, and I must still wait the issues of mine. I have renounced this fraud and mockery of empty words which was to have bound me to a life-long horror. The world will think very strangely of me. That must be borne, too; and such a load is light, to the burden I have borne already."

A few days later, tidings came that Vinal was ill. Edith Leslie rejoined him; but, finding that her presence was any thing but soothing to him, she left him in the care of others, and returned to her friend's house. It was but a sudden and short attack, from which he recovered in a week or two.

CHAPTER LXIX

Fal.—Reason, you rogue, reason; thinkest thou I'll endanger my soul gratis?—*Merry Wives of Windsor.*

Pistol.—Base is the slave that pays.—*Henry V.*

Time had been when, his youth considered, Vinal was a beaming star in the commercial heaven. On 'change,

"His name was great,
In mouths of wisest censure."

The astutest broker pronounced him good; the sagest money lender took his paper without a question. But of late, his signature had lost a little of its efficacy. It was whispered that he was not as sound as his repute gave out; that his operations were no longer marked by his former clear-headed forecast; that he was deep in doubtful and dangerous speculation. In short, his credit stood by no means where it had stood a twelvemonth earlier.

Possibly these rumors took their first impulse, not on 'change, but at tea tables, and in drawing rooms. His wife's separation from him had given ample food to speculation; and gossip had for once been just, asserting, with few dissenting voices, that there must needs be some fault, and a grave one, on the part of Vinal. The event had ceased to be a very recent one; but surmise was still rife concerning its mysterious cause.

Meanwhile, Vinal was being goaded into recklessness, frightened out of his propriety, haunted, devil-driven, maddened into desperate courses. Late one night, he was pacing his library, with a quick, disordered step. His servants were in their beds, excepting a man, nodding his drowsy vigil over the kitchen fire. Vinal's affairs were fast drawing to a crisis. A few weeks must determine the success or failure of a broad scheme of fraud, on which he had staked his fortunes and himself, and whose issues would sink him to disgrace and ruin, or lift him for a time to the pinnacle of a knave's prosperity. But, meanwhile, how to keep his head above water! Claims thickened upon him; he was meshed in a network of perplexities; and, with him, bankruptcy would involve far more than a loss of fortune.

There was a ring at the door bell. Vinal stopped short in his feverish walk, raised his head with a startled motion, and listened like a fox who hears the hounds. His instinct foreboded the worst. His cheek flushed, and his eye brightened, not with spirit, but with desperation.

The bell rang again. This time, the sleepy servant roused himself. Vinal heard his step along the hall; heard the opening of the street door, and a man's voice pronouncing his name. The moment after, his evil spirit stood before him, in the shape of Henry Speyer.

Vinal gave him no time to speak, but shutting the door in the servant's face, turned upon his visitor with such courage as a cat will show when a bulldog has driven her into a corner.

"Again! Are you here again? It is hardly a month since you were here last. What have you done with what I gave you then? Do you think I am made of gold? Do you take me for a bank that you can draw on at will?"

"I am sorry to trouble you so soon, but I am very hard pressed."

"Hard pressed! So am I hard pressed. Here for a year and more I have been supporting you in your extravagance—you and your mistresses; you have been living on me like princes,—dress, drinking, feasting, horses, gambling!—among you, you make my money spin away like water. Every well has a bottom to it, and you have got to the bottom of mine."

Speyer laughed with savage incredulity.

"Any thing in reason I am ready to do for you; but it's of no use. More! more! is always the word. You think you have found a gold mine. You mistake. Here I have a note due to-morrow; and another on Monday—that was for money I borrowed to give you. Heaven knows how I shall pay them. Go back, and come again a month from this."

"It won't do. I must have it now."

"I tell you, I have none to give you."

"Do you see this?" said Speyer, producing a roll of printed papers, and giving one to Vinal.

It was Vinal's letter, in the form of a placard, with a statement of the whole affair prefixed. Speyer had had it printed secretly in New York, the names of Morton and Vinal being left blank, and ingeniously filled in by himself with a pen.

"Give me the money, or show me how to get it, or I will have you posted up at every street corner in town. I have your letter here. I shall send it to your friend, the editor of the Sink."

The Sink was a scurrilous newspaper, which the virtuous Vinal, always anxious for the morals of the city, had once caused to be prosecuted as a nuisance, for which the editor bore him a special grudge.

But Vinal at last was brought to bay. Threats, which Speyer thought irresistible, had lost their power. He threw back the paper, and said desperately, "Do what you will."

Speyer made a step forward, and faced his prey.

"Will you give me the money?"

"By G—, no!"

"By G—, you shall!"

And Speyer seized him by the breast of his waistcoat.

Vinal had been trained in the habits of a gentleman. He had never known personal outrage before. He grew purple with rage. The veins of his forehead swelled like whipcord, and his eyes glittered like a rattlesnake's.

"Take off your hand!"

The words were less articulated than hissed between his teeth.

"Take off your hand."

Speyer clutched him with a harder gripe, and shook him to and fro. Quick as lightning, Vinal struck him in the face. Speyer glared and grinned on his victim like an enraged tiger. For a moment, he shook him as a terrier shakes a rat; then flung him backward against the farther side of the room. Here, striking the wall, he fell helpless, among the window curtains and overturned chairs. Speyer would probably have followed up his attack; but at the instant, the servant, who, by a happy accident, was at the side door, in the near neighborhood of the keyhole, ran in in time to save Vinal from more serious discomfiture.

Speyer hesitated; turned from one to the other with murder in his look; then, slowly moving backwards, left the room, whence the servant's valor did not mount to the point of following him.

CHAPTER LXX

He is composed and framed of treachery,
And fled he is upon this villany.—*Much Ado about Nothing.*

Edward Meredith, the affianced bridegroom of Miss Fanny Euston, sailing on a smooth sea, under full canvas, towards the pleasing but perilous bounds of matrimony, was walking in the morning towards the post office, in the frame of mind proper to his condition. He passed that place of unrest where the Law hangs her blazons from every window, and approached the heart and brain of the city, the precinct sacred to commerce and finance. Here, gathered about a corner, he saw a crowd, elbowing each other with unusual vehemence. Meredith, with all despatch, crossed over to the opposite side. But here, again, his attention was caught by a singular clamor among the rabble of newsboys, as noisy and intrusive as a flight of dorr-bugs on a June evening. And, not far off, another crowd was gathered at the office of the Weekly Sink. Curiosity became too strong for his native antipathy. He saw an acquaintance, with a crushed hat, and a face of bewildered amazement, just struggling out of the press.

"What's the row?" demanded Meredith.

"Go and read that paper," returned the other, with an astonished ejaculation, of more emphasis than unction.

Meredith shouldered into the crowd, looked over the hats of some, between the hats of others, and saw, pasted to the stone door post, a placard large as the handbill of a theatre. Over it was displayed a sheet of paper, on which was daubed, in ink, the words, *Astounding Disclosures!!! Crime in High Life!!!!* And on the placard he beheld the names of his classmate Horace Vinal, and his friend Vassall Morton.

Meredith pushed and shouldered with the boldest, gained a favorable position, braced himself there, and ran his eye through the whole. Then, with a convulsive effort, he regained his liberty, beckoned a newsboy, and purchased the extra sheet of the Weekly Sink. Here, however, he learned very little. The editor, taught wisdom by experience, had tempered malice with caution. He spoke of the duty he owed to the public, his position as guardian and censor of the public morals, and affirmed that, in this capacity, he had that morning received through the post office the original of the letter of which a copy was printed on the placards posted in various parts of the city. With the letter had come also an anonymous note, highly complimentary to himself in his official capacity, a copy of which he subjoined. As for the letter, he did not think himself called upon to give it immediate publicity in his columns; but he would submit it for inspection to any persons anxious to see it, after which he should place it in the hands of the police.

Though the editor of the Sink was thus discreet, the letter, in the course of the day, found its way into several of the penny papers, to which copies of the placard containing it had been mailed. From the dram shop to the drawing room, the commotion was unspeakable. The mass of readers floundered in a sea of crude conjecture; but those who knew the parties, recalling a faint and exploded rumor of Morton's engagement to Miss Leslie, and connecting it with her separation from Vinal, gained a glimpse of something like the truth.

The only new light thrown upon the matter came from the servant, who told all that he knew, and much more, of the nocturnal scene between Speyer and Vinal, affirming, with much complacency, that he had saved his master's life. Miss Leslie and Mrs. Ashland studiously kept silent. Morton was at the antipodes; while the unknown divulger of the mystery eluded all attempts to trace him. Speyer, in fact, having sprung his mine, had fled from his danger and his debts, and taking passage for New Orleans, sailed thence to Vera Cruz.

Meredith, perplexed and astounded, wrote a letter to Morton, directing it to Calcutta, whither the latter was to repair, after voyaging among the East India Islands.

Meanwhile, great search was made for Vinal; but Vinal was nowhere to be found.

CHAPTER LXXI

Now would I give a thousand furlongs of sea for an acre of barren ground.—*Tempest*.

    Let the great gods,
That keep this dreadful pother o'er our heads,
Find out their enemies now. Tremble, thou wretch,
That hast within thee undivulged crimes
Unwhipped of justice! Hide, thou bloody hand;
Thou perjured and thou simular man of virtue,
That art incestuous! Caitiff, to pieces shake,
That under covert and convenient seeming,
Hast practised on man's life!—*Lear*.

    At one o'clock at night, in the midst of the Atlantic, a hundred leagues west of the Azores, the bark Swallow, freighted with salt cod for the Levant, was scudding furiously, under a close-reefed foresail, before a fierce gale. On board were her captain, two mates, seven men, a black steward, a cabin boy, and Mr. John White, a passenger.

    The captain and his mates were all on deck. John White, otherwise Horace Vinal, occupied a kind of store room, opening out of the cabin. Here a temporary berth had been nailed up for him, while on the opposite side were stowed a trunk belonging to him, and three barrels of onions belonging to the vessel's owners, all well lashed in their places.

    The dead lights were in, but the seas, striking like mallets against the stern, pierced in fine mist through invisible crevices, bedrizzling every thing with salt dew. The lantern, hanging from the cabin roof, swung angrily with the reckless plungings of the vessel.

    Vinal was a good sailor; that is to say, he was not very liable to that ocean scourge, seasickness, and the few qualms he had suffered were by this time effectually frightened out of him. As darkness closed, he had lain down in his clothes; and flung from side to side till his bones ached with the incessant rolling of the bark, he listened sleeplessly to the hideous booming of the storm. Suddenly there came a roar so appalling, that he leaped out of his berth with terror. It seemed to him as if a Niagara had broken above the vessel, and was crushing her down to the nethermost abyss. The rush of waters died away. Then came the bellow of the speaking trumpet, the trampling of feet, the shouts of men, the hoarse fluttering of canvas. In a few moments he felt a change in the vessel's motion. She no longer rocked with a constant reel from side to side, but seemed flung about at random, hither and thither, at the mercy of the storm.

She had been, in fact, within a hair's breadth of foundering. A huge wave, chasing on her wake, swelling huger and huger, towering higher and higher, had curled, at last, its black crest above her stern, and, breaking, fallen on her in a deluge. The captain, a Barnstable man of the go-ahead stamp, was brought at last to furl his foresail and lie to.

Vinal, restless with his fear, climbed the narrow stairway which led up to the deck, and pushed open the door at the top; but a blast of wind and salt spray clapped it in his face, and would have knocked him to the foot of the steps, if he had not clung to the handrail. He groped his way as he could back to his berth. Here he lay for a quarter of an hour, when the captain came down, enveloped in oilcloths, and dripping like a Newfoundland dog just out of the water. Vinal emerged from his den, and presenting himself with his haggard face, and hair bristling in disorder, questioned the bedrenched commander touching the state of things on deck. But the latter was in a crusty and savage mood.

"Hey! what is it?"—surveying the apparition by the light of the swinging lantern,—"well, you *be* a beauty, I'll be damned if you ain't."

"I did not ask you how I looked; I asked you about the weather."

"Well, it ain't the sweetest night I ever see; but I guess you won't drown this time."

"My friend," said Vinal, "learn to mend your way of speaking, and use a civil tongue."

The captain stared at him, muttered an oath or two, and then turned away.

Day broke, and Vinal went on deck. It was a wild dawning. The storm was at its height. One rag of a topsail was set to steady the vessel; all the rest was bare poles and black dripping cordage, through which the gale yelled like a forest in a tornado. The sky was dull gray; the ocean was dull gray. There was no horizon. The vessel struggled among tossing mountains, while tons of water washed her decks, and the men, half drowned, clung to the rigging. Vast misshapen ridges of water bore down from the windward, breaking into foam along their crests, struck the vessel with a sullen shock, burst over her bulwarks, deluged her from stem to stern, heaved her aloft as they rolled on, and then left her to sink again into the deep trough of the sea.

Vinal was in great fear; but nothing in his look betrayed it. He soon went below to escape the drenching seas; but towards noon, Hansen, the second mate, a good-natured old sea dog, came down with the welcome news that the gale had suddenly abated. Vinal went on deck again, and saw a singular spectacle. The wind had strangely lulled; but the waves were huge and furious as ever; and the bark rose and pitched, and was flung to and fro with great violence, but in a silence almost perfect. Water, in great quantities, still washed the deck, but found ready escape through a large port in the after part of the vessel, the lid of which, hanging vertically, had been left unfastened.

The lull was of short space. A hoarse, low sound began to growl in the distance like muffled thunder. It grew louder,—nearer,—and the gale was on them again. This time it blew from the north-west, and less fiercely than before. The venturous captain made sail. The yards were braced round; and leaning from the wind till her lee gunwale scooped the water, the vessel plunged on her way like a racehorse. The clouds were rent; blue sky appeared. Strong winds tore them apart, and the sun blazed out over the watery convulsion, changing its blackness to a rich blue, almost as dark, where the whirling streaks of foam seemed like snow wreaths on the mountains. Jets of foam, too, spouted from under the vessel's bows, as she dashed them against the opposing seas; and the prickling spray flew as high as the main top. The ocean was like a viking in his robust carousals,—terror and mirth, laughter and fierceness, all in one.

But the mind of Vinal was blackness and unmixed gall. His game was played and lost. The worst that he feared had befallen him. Suspense was over, and he was freed from the incubus that had ridden him so long. A something like relief mixed itself with his bitter and vindictive musings. He had not fled empty handed. He and Morton's friend Sharpe had been joint trustees of a large estate, a part of which, in a form that made it readily available, happened to be in Vinal's hands at the time of his crisis. Dread of his quick-sighted and vigilant colleague had hitherto prevented him from applying it to his own uses. But this fear had now lost its force. He took it with him on his flight, and converted it into money in New York, where he had embarked.

At night the descent of Hansen to supper was a welcome diversion to his lonely thoughts. The old sailor seated himself at the table:—

"I've lost all my appetite, and got a horse's. Here, steward, you nigger, where be yer? Fetch along that beefsteak. What do you call this here? Well, never mind what you call it, here goes into it, any how."

A silent and destructive onslaught upon the dish before him followed. Then, laying down his knife and fork for a moment,—

"I've knowed the time when I could have ate up the doctor there,"— pointing to the steward,—"bones and all, and couldn't get a mouthful, no way you could fix it." Then, resuming his labors, "Tell you what, squire, this here agrees with me. Come out of that berth now, and sit down here alongside o' me. Just walk into that beefsteak, like I do. That 'ere beats physicking all holler."

Thus discoursing, partly to himself and partly to Vinal, and, by turns, berating the grinning steward in a jocular strain, Mr. Hansen continued his repast. When, at last, he left the cabin, Vinal found the solitude too dreary for endurance; and, to break its monotony, he also went on deck.

The vessel still scoured wildly along; and as she plunged through the angry seas, so the moon was sailing among stormy clouds, now eclipsed and lost, now shining brightly out, silvering the seething foam, and casting the shadows of spars and rigging on the glistening deck. Vinal bent over the bulwark and looked down on the bubbles, as they fled past, flashing in the moon.

His thoughts flew backward with them, and dwelt on the hated home from which he was escaping.

"What an outcry! what gapes of wonder, and eyes turned up to heaven! Gulled, befooled, hoodwinked! and now, at last, you have found it out, and make earth and heaven ring with your virtuous spite. I knew you all, and played you as I would play the pieces on a chess board. The game was a good one in the main, but with some blunders, and for those I pay the price. If I had had that villain's brute strength, and the brute nerve that goes with it, there would have been a different story to tell. Before this, I would have found a way to grind him to the earth, and set my foot on his neck. They think him virtuous. He thinks himself so. The shallow-witted idiots! Their eyes can only see skin-deep. They love to be cheated. They swallow fallacies as a child swallows sweetmeats. The tinsel dazzles them, and they take it for gold. Virtue! a delusion of self-interest—self-interest, the spring, lever, and fulcrum of the world. It is for my interest, for every body's interest, that his neighbors should be honest, candid, open, forgiving, charitable, continent, sober, and what not. Therefore, by the general consent of mankind,—the inevitable instinct of self-interest,—such qualities are exalted into sanctity; christened with the name of virtues; draped in white, and crowned with halos; rewarded with praises here and paradise hereafter. Drape the skeleton as you will, the bare skeleton is still there. Paint as thick as you will, the bare skull grins under it,—to all who have the eyes to see, and the hardihood to use them. How many among mankind have courage to face the naked truth? Not one in a thousand. Cannot the fools draw reason out of the analogy of things? Can they not see that, as their bodies will be melted and merged into the bodily substance of the world, so their minds will be merged in the great universal mind,—the *animus mundi*,—out of which they sprang, like bubbles on the water, and into which they will sink again, like bubbles when they burst? Immortality! They may please themselves with the name; but of what worth is an immortality where individuality is lost, and each conscious atom drowned in the vast immensity? What a howling and screeching the wind makes in the rigging! If I were given to superstition, I could fancy that a legion from the nether world were bestriding the ropes, yelping in grand jubilation at the sight of— —"

Here his thoughts were abruptly cut short. A combing wave struck the vessel. She lurched with violence, and a shower of foam flew over her side. Vinal lost his balance. His feet slipped from under him. He fell, and slid quickly across the wet and tossing deck. Instinctively he braced his feet to stop himself against the bulwark on the lee side. But at the point where they touched it was the large port before mentioned. Though closed to all appearance, the bolt was still unfastened. It flew open at his touch. Vinal clutched to save himself. His fingers slipped on the wet timbers, and with a cry of horror, he was shot into the bubbling surges. There was a blinding in his eyes, a ringing in his ears; then, for an instant, he saw the light, and the black hulk of the vessel fled past like a shadow. Then a wave swept over him: all was darkness and convulsion, and a maddened sense of being flung high aloft, as the wave rolled him towards its crest like a drift sea weed. Here again light broke upon him; and flying above the merciless chaos, he saw something like the white wing of a huge bird. It was the reefed maintopsail of the receding vessel. He shrieked wildly. A torrent of brine dashed back the cry, and foaming over his head, plunged him down into darkness again. Again he rose, gasping and half senseless; and again the ravenous breakers beat him down. A moment of struggle and of agony; then a long nightmare of dreamy horror, while, slowly settling downward, he sank below the turmoil of the storm; slowly and more slowly still, till the denser water sustained his weight. Then with limbs outstretched, he hovered in mid ocean, lonely, void, and vast, like a hawk poised in mid-air, while his felon spirit, bubbling to the surface, winged its dreary flight through the whistling storm.

CHAPTER LXXII

> Adventure and endurance and emprise
> Exalted his mind's faculties, and strung
> His body's sinews.—*Bryant*.

On a rock, at the end of the promontory which forms the harbor of Beyrout, stood Vassall Morton; and at his side his friend Buckland, whom he had met in New York just after his return from Austria. They had encountered again in the East Indies, and had made together a long and varied journey, not without hardship and danger, among the tribes of Upper India and Central Asia. Buckland was greatly changed. His look and bearing betokened recovered health and spirit; while his companion, in the fulness of masculine vigor, was swarthy as an Arab with the long burning of the Eastern sun.

"Our travels are over, Buckland. We have nothing to do, now, but to get on board ship, and lie still for a few weeks, and we shall be at home again. I hardly know why it is that I wish so much to shorten the space, unless from a cat-like propensity to haunt old places."

"And to see your friends again."

"Yes, that is something—a good deal. I have friends enough, unless they have died since I last heard from them. But for household gods, I have none; or, rather, my ancestral Lares have no better abode than an old clapboarded parsonage in an up-country Yankee village. You are much more fortunate in that respect. You go home again, besides, a new man, rejuvenated in mind and body."

"Thanks to you for that. I was a wreck till you set me afloat and refitted me."

"I gave you a shove off shore; but the refitting came afterwards, and was no doing of mine. I should hardly know you for the same man."

"That infatuation seems to me like a dream, as I remember you prophesied on the evening when we sat together on the Battery."

"Half of a woman's weakness springs from the sensitiveness of her bodily organization; and three fourths of your infatuation may be laid to the same account. One may say that, without any tendency to flounder into materialism. You are a man again now; and even if you had not heard of your sorceress's death, you might go back, I think, without the least fear of her spells."

"I hope so; but I wish that, like you, I had some engrossing object to return to."

"I wish that, like you, I had a family, and a fixed home to return to. My travels are finished, though. I have roamed the world enough. My objects are accomplished, as well as I could ever accomplish them. I have not wandered for nothing; and now I shall bend myself to make my journeyings bear what fruit I can. By the sun, and by my watch, it is time for the consul to have returned. Did not his servant say that he would come ashore from the frigate at about six?"

"Yes."

"If he does not, I will get a boat and go to find him. He must have letters for one or the other of us."

"I will ride to the town, and see if he has come."

"Very well; I will wait for you here."

Their horses were near at hand, in the keeping of an Arab servant. Buckland mounted his own, and rode off.

Morton seated himself on a jutting edge of the rock overhanging the bay, and gave himself up to his thoughts.

"Two years of wandering! Two years more, and I should grow like the man in Anastasius, never happy at rest, never content in motion. I have had my fill of adventure. I must learn repose before it is too late. Why is it that I look so longingly towards America? Except half a dozen near friends, I have no ties there that are worth the name. America is the paradise of the laboring class, the purgatory of those of educated tastes. What career is open to me there, that I could not better follow elsewhere? I have chosen my path. I have an object which fills and engrosses me, and would fill the lifetime of twenty men abler than I. America is not my best field of labor; but where else should I plant myself? I could not live in England. I am of English race, but of an altered type; too like, and too unlike, to find harmony there. The continent is more cosmopolitan; but it would be a dreary life. I should grow homesick, thinking of the old woods and rocks. I will go home, buckle to my work, and end my days where I began them.

"My life has been, in its small way, a varied one; very hard, at times, but perhaps none too much so. Blows are good for most men, and suffering, to the farthest limit of their endurance, what they most need. It is a child's part to complain under any fate; and what color of complaint have I, or any man sound in mind and body, and with the world free before him? And yet I turn girl-hearted when I think of that summer evening by the lake at Matherton. What is my fate to Edith Leslie's? How will a few years of suffering, with one deadening memory in their wake, compare with her life-long endurance? A woman's nature, it is said, will mould itself into conformity with her husband's. I will rather believe that Vinal's presence, instead of drawing her to itself, has repelled her upward into a higher atmosphere, and made her life as lofty as it must be sad. I wish to go back, and yet I shrink from this voyage. I have some cause, remembering my last welcome home. Heaven knows what I may learn of her this time. It was her marriage then; perhaps it will be her death now. And which of the two will have been the worse either for me to hear or for her to undergo? Perhaps these letters may bring some word of her; though that is not likely, for none of my friends, but one, know that I should have any special interest in hearing it. If they write of her, it will be some news of disaster."

These dismal forebodings weighed upon him, and his desire to have them resolved soon grew so importunate, that mounting his horse, he followed Buckland's track towards the town. Threading the busy streets, he stopped before a door adorned with the effigy of a spread eagle wearing a striped shield about his neck, and clutching thunderbolts and olive boughs in his claws. He threw the rein to his servant, mounted the consular stair, and at the head met Buckland emerging.

"Is the consul come?"

"Yes; and letters for you. I am sorry for you, if you mean to answer them all."

And he gave Morton a formidable packet. Morton cut the string.

"These are all six or eight months old. They are postmarked from Calcutta."

"Yes, they came after we had gone up the country, and were sent back to this place to meet you. Wait a moment; here are more. These two have just come from England."

Morton took them; recognized on one the handwriting of Meredith; on the other, that of his friend Mrs. Ashland. His heart leaped to his throat; he tore open the seal, and glanced down the page.

Buckland saw his agitation.

"No bad news, I trust."

"I had an enemy, and he is dead. You shall know more of it to-morrow."

And hastening from the house, he mounted again, and through the midst of mules, donkeys, dromedaries, men, children, and old women, rode at an unlawful speed towards his lodging.

Here, with a beating heart, he explored his profuse correspondence from beginning to end. By the Calcutta packet, he learned how his native town had been thrown into commotion by the exposure and flight of Vinal, and how his friends were eager and impatient to hear his explanation of the affair. The more recent letters bore tidings still more startling. The bark Swallow had touched at Gibraltar, and a letter from her captain to her owners, forwarded by the Oriental steamer on her return voyage, told how his passenger, John White, had been lost overboard during a gale, two of the crew having seen the accident; how, arriving at Gibraltar, his trunks had been opened in the consul's presence, to learn his address; and how, along with a large amount of money in gold, letters and papers had been found, showing that he was not John White, but Horace Vinal, of Boston.

On the next morning, Morton despatched a letter to Meredith. In it, he told his friend the whole course of his story; and these were the closing words:—

"One thing you may well believe—that, before you will have had this letter many days, I shall follow it. There will be no rest for me till I touch American soil. An old passion, only half stifled under a load of hopelessness, springs into fresh life again, and burns, less brightly, perhaps, but I can almost believe, more deeply and fervently than ever. I was consoling myself yesterday with trying to think that blows were my mind's best medicine; but I feel now, that after being broken with the plough and harrow, it will yield the better for the summer sunshine. Yet I am afraid to flatter myself with too bright a prospect. Miss Leslie loved me, and the planets in their course are not more constant and unswerving; but I cannot tell what may have been the effect of so much suffering, or what determination, fatal to my hope, it may not have impelled her to embrace. She will soon know my mind. I have written to her, and begged her to send her reply to New York, where, if my reckoning does not fail, I shall arrive about the middle of June. By it I shall be able to judge to what fortune I am to look forward.

"You have so lately passed your own anxieties, that you will easily appreciate mine. I can wish for them nothing more than that they may find as happy an issue; and I will take it as an earnest of the intentions of destiny towards me that it has just brought together my two best friends."

CHAPTER LXXIII

> Joy never feasts so high
> As when his first course is of misery. — *Suckling.*

Again the Jersey heights rose on the eye of Morton, and the woods and villas of Staten Island. Again the broad breast of New York harbor opened before him, sparkling in the June sun; the rugged front of the Castle, and the tapering spire of Trinity. He bethought him of his last return, and its unforgotten blackness threw its shadow across his mind. He turned, doubting and tremulous, towards the future; but here his horizon brightened as with the sunrise, shooting to the zenith its shafts of tranquil light.

Meanwhile, the telegraph had darted to Boston a notice that the approaching steamer had been signalled off the coast. Meredith took the night train to meet his friend; but, arriving, he learned that Morton was already on shore. Driving from one hotel to another, he found, at length, the latter's resting-place.

"Shall I take up your name, sir?"

"No, show me his room; I will go myself."

He knocked at the door. There was no answer. He knocked again, and a voice replied suddenly, like that of a man roused from a revery.

He entered; and at the next moment, Morton grasped his hand.

"You have found yourself again," said Meredith; "you have grown back again to your old look."

Morton's eye glistened.

"I think I know the handwriting of that letter. Miss Leslie's, — I will call her so still — it is hers, is it not?"

"Yes."

"She writes, I trust, what you hoped to hear."

"All that I hoped, and much more."

"I am glad of it from my heart. Fortune has been hard enough upon you. She was bound to pay you her score."

"She has done so with usury."

"Are you going to Boston this afternoon?"

"Yes."

"Then you have just two hours to spare. If you have any leisure for such sublunary matters, we had better get dinner at once. Romeo himself, at his worst case, asks his friend when they shall dine."

Three hours later, the eastward-bound steamer was ploughing the Sound, and Morton and Meredith paced her deck.

"I have told you now the whole history, from first to last. I need not ask you to forgive my having kept it secret from you so long."

"Why should you ask me? Every man has a right to his own secrets, and I like him the better for keeping them. Vinal, at all events, had good cause to thank you."

"He is dead; and his memory, if it will, had better die with him."

"You said in your letter that his agent was called Henry Speyer. I thought, at the time, that I had seen the name before; and a day or two since, I found it accidentally again. The newspapers, two months or more ago, mention a foreigner called Henry Speyer as an officer in this last piratical forray into Cuba. His party lost their way, fell into an ambuscade of government soldiers, and Speyer was shot through the head."

"He found a better end than his principal."

"And deserved a better one. A professed rascal is better than a pharisee."

CHAPTER LXXIV

The rainbow to the storms of life;
The evening beam that smiles the clouds away.—*Bride of Abydos*.

Morton rode along the edge of the lake at Matherton. He passed under the shadowy verdure of the pines, and approached the old family mansion of the Leslies. It was years since he had seen it. His imprisonment, his escape, his dreary greeting home, all lay between. He was the same man, yet different;—with a mind calmed by experience, and strong by action and endurance; an ardor which had lost all of its intoxication, but none of its force; and which, as the past and the present rose upon his thoughts, was tempered with a melancholy which had in it nothing of pain.

The hall door stood open, as if to welcome him. The roses and the laurels were in bloom; the grass, ripe for the scythe, was waving in the meadow; and, by glimpses between the elm and maple boughs, the lake, crisped in the June wind, was sparkling with the sunlight.

Morton dismounted; his foot was on the porch; but he had no time for thought; for a step sounded in the hall, and Edith met him on the threshold.

That evening, at sunset, Miss Leslie and Morton stood on the brink of the lake, at the foot of the garden. It was the spot which had been most sweet and most bitter in the latter's recollections.

"Do you remember, Edith, when we last stood here?"

"How could I ever forget?"

"The years that have passed since are like a nightmare. I could believe them so, but that I feel their marks."

"And I, as well; we were boy and girl then."

"At least, I was a boy; and, do you know, I find you different from what I had pictured you."

"Should I be sorry for it, or glad?"

"I had pictured you as I saw you last, very calm, very resolute, very sad; but you are like the breaking of a long, dull storm. The sun shines again, and the world glows the brighter for past rain and darkness."

"Could I have welcomed you home with a sad face? Could I be calm and cold, now that I have found what I thought was lost forever?—when the ashes of my life have kindled into flame again? Because I, and others, have known sorrow, should I turn my face into a homily, and be your lifelong *memento mori?*"

"It is a brave heart that can hide a deep thought under a smile."

"And a weak one that is always crouching among the shadows."

"There is an abounding spirit of faith in you; the essence which makes heroes, from Joan of Arc to Jeanie Deans."

"I know no one with faith like yours, which could hold to you through all your years of living burial."

"Mine! it was wrenched to its uttermost roots. I thought the world was given over to the devil."

"But that was only for the moment."

"I consoled myself with imagining that I had come to the worst, and that any change must needs be for the better; but now I am lifted of a sudden to such a pitch of fortune, that I tremble at it. Many a man, my equal or superior, no weaker in heart or meaner in aim than I, has been fettered through his days by cramping poverty, while I stand mailed and weaponed at all points. Many a man of noble instincts and high requirements has found in life nothing but a mockery of his imaginings,—a bright dream, matched with a base reality. Who can blame him if he turn cynic? I have dreamed a dream, too; wakened, and found it a living truth."